SOME
OF
HER
FRIENDS
THAT
YEAR

Some of Her Friends That Year

NEW + SELECTED STORIES

by

Maxine Chernoff

COFFEE HOUSE PRESS

2002

COFFEE HOUSE PRESS is an independent nonprofit literary pub-
lisher supported in part by a grant provided by the Minnesota
State Arts Board, through an appropriation by the Minnesota
State Legislature, and in part by a grant from the National
Endowment for the Arts. Significant support was received for
this project through a grant from the National Endowment for
the Arts, a federal agency, and the Jerome Foundation. Support
has also been provided by Athwin Foundation; the Bush
Foundation; Buuck Family Foundation; Elmer L. & Eleanor J.
Andersen Foundation; Lerner Family Foundation; McKnight
Foundation; Patrick and Aimee Butler Family Foundation; The
St. Paul Companies Foundation, Inc.; the law firm of
Schwegman, Lundberg, Woessner & Kluth, P.A.; Star Tribune
Foundation; Marshall Field's Project Imagine with support from
the Target Foundation; Wells Fargo Foundation Minnesota;
West Group; Woessner-Freeman Family Foundation; and many
individual donors. To you and our many readers across the coun-
try, we send our thanks for your continuing support.

COFFEE HOUSE PRESS books are available to the trade through
our primary distributor, Consortium Book Sales & Distribution,
1045 Westgate Drive, Saint Paul, MN 55114. For personal orders,
catalogs, or other information, write to: Coffee House Press, 27
North Fourth Street, Suite 400, Minneapolis, MN 55401.

LIBRARY OF CONGRESS CIP INFORMATION

Chernoff, Maxine, 1952–
    Some of her friends that year : new & selected stories / by
Maxine Chernoff.
        p. cm
    ISBN 1-56689-127-2 (alk. paper)
        I. Title.

PS3553.H356 S66 2002
813'.54—DC21

2001052946

In memory of my father

For Julian, Philip, Koren,
Marsha, Idell,
and always for Paul

Stories in the new section of **Some of Her Friends That Year** have appeared in the following magazines: *Agrippina:* "Onto the Past," *First Intensity:* "You Suck," *Zyzzyva:* "Coming Apart and Together," *Bridge:* "Rent-a-Pet," *American Letters and Commentary:* "Jeopardy," *Salon (Editor's Choice):* "The Nobel Prize for Shoes," *Thus Spake the Corpse, v.2; Exquisite Corpse, Fish Stories:* "Jewish Urban White Trash Story," *Slope:* "Snowflake, Come Home," *ACM:* "Acts of Nature."

Stories in **Signs of Devotion** appeared in *The Marriage Bed* (Harper-Collins), *West Side Stories* and *Chicago Stories* (City Stoop Press), *Ploughshares, Mississippi Review, Story, Formations, North American Review, Santa Monica Review, ACM, St. Mark's Papers, Women's Glib* (Crossing Press), *The Country of Ourselves* (Third Side Press), *The Unmade Bed* (HarperCollins), *Caprice, New American Writing, Painted Bride Quarterly, What!* and *Emergence. Signs of Devotion* was originally published by Simon and Schuster in 1993.

Stories in **Bop** appeared in *Triquarterly, City, Playgirl, Oyez Review, North American Review, ACM, Uncle, Iowa Review, Women Fiction Writers of America* (New Delhi: East-West Press), and *A Contemporary Introduction to Literature* (Macmillan). *Bop* was originally published by Coffee House Press in 1986; reprinted in the Vintage Contemporary Fiction Series in 1987.

The author wishes to thank the editors.

NEW STORIES

FROM *SIGNS OF DEVOTION*

FROM *BOP*

SOME
OF
HER
FRIENDS
THAT
YEAR

New
Stories

Some of Her Friends That Year

I.

ONE WROTE A BESTSELLER. She had no husband—no lover—until the book did so well that hundreds of men wrote her love letters with offers of marriage. She met one man in Paris, one in Costa Rica. Neither was that engaging, but she felt such confidence that it seemed she might be able to transform one with less work than it had taken to write the book.

II.

One went to her mother's sixtieth high school reunion in lieu of her mother, who was too ill to attend. There were few survivors, but a couple nearing one hundred, who'd been her mother's teachers, were in attendance. They still took walks together and traveled when they could. The woman wore braids wrapped around her head—to keep her looking young, she said.

III.

One friend's children all moved back: one married with a husband, and one single. Her father-in-law moved in after his wife passed away. Every room in the house became a bedroom. The bathtub in front contained her daughter's turtles. The cleaning service left a note. "Should we clean them too?" Raccoons lived under the floor of her wine cellar. They brought their babies to her glass dining room door every night at 9 P.M. Having no more available bedrooms, she was slow to respond when her own mother got sick that summer. There's always the hammock on the patio, the son-in-law suggested.

IV.

One took classes in Chinese cooking, in wild plants of the West, and in fiction. She called with questions like, "Who does good epiphanies?" She suggested her friend read Joyce. "Someone not quite so good," her friend replied. "I'm new to this, you know."

V.

One of her friends got nominated for an Oscar in short subjects. She got to choose from a fleet of dresses reserved for Oscar nominees. "I'll need two to fit me," she said, until a designer, hearing of her trouble, called to give her a long velvet gown. Everyone waited and wondered if they'd be thanked in her acceptance speech, but she didn't win.

VI.

One of her friends canceled her vacation to give her cat, now sixteen, two shots of insulin a day, and chemotherapy when he slept. She found a baby bird and wrapped him in a winter watch cap and fed him with a dropper, but he died a few days later.

VII.

One left her husband of many years after finding him snorting cocaine with a junior partner in his firm. She had known about his habit for a long time but somehow seeing him engaged in the process created a vividness she couldn't endure.

VIII.

One took her partner on a train ride to Vancouver as soon as the school year let out. Before getting her degrees and becoming a professor, she'd been a truck driver and driven big rigs in the Pacific Northwest. It was the first good vacation they'd taken in twenty years. Before finding this woman, she'd been married to a "small man with a large head." The train was filled with geriatric travelers, who wouldn't let the other passengers open a window. It felt like the train from Kosovo.

IX.

One took in her niece after her husband's sister was murdered in Greece by a famous lawyer who didn't want to pay child support. Her sons fought about having to share a bedroom but soon made peace with each other.

X.

One's daughter finished college and went to Ecuador, where her friend's friend got kidnapped by revolutionaries. Her parents went to Ecuador to bring her home but she refused to leave.

XI.

One friend's cancer came back, and though she was still fighting, things didn't look good. "I hoped to get thin from this," her friend told her when they went to a sale at a Flax outlet. She bought a pretty patterned scarf. They spent the afternoon experimenting with turban designs. "We need an architect," her friend said, "or a Sufi."

XII.

One had her first baby at forty-nine, a beautiful round-faced creature named Nellie. "I got in just under the wire," her friend said as she hummed and nursed her miracle baby.

XIII.

Her teenage daughter stayed depressed that year, and she thought of ways to help her. She got her a flute, new watercolors, a kitten, a telescope.

"Will I ever feel better?" her daughter asked, repeating the question throughout the day like someone tossing out crumbs to mark a trail.

"Look at the sky," the mother said, pointing to the cloudless blue.

"We've lost the ozone layer."

"Look at those leaves," the mother said of the Japanese maple shaking in the wind.

"They look like blood."

"How can I cheer you up?"

"Why do you think *you* can make me happy?"

"Why do I write if not to make people happy?" the mother asked.

"I don't read your stories."

"Maybe if you did, you'd be happier."

"You write about old people with pathetic lives. How could that help me?"

"I need to think I can make her happy," she told her friends. She wanted to tell her daughter that she knew how everyone felt, that their lives were somehow hers, her daughter's life even more, that she wasn't happy as long as someone else was suffering. But then she sounded like Jesus or some martyr. Her daughter wouldn't fall for it, but that was how the mother felt.

Coming Apart and Together

LL THE BUDDHISTS were getting divorced that spring: first her son's favorite teacher, then her cousin's cousin, and now her neighbor. Maybe that's why Diane hated California. It was a land of temporary commitment, future disappointment, human frailty. People's lives fell apart. Endings were too frequent. No wonder she kept hearing the word "closure" bandied about. That day on the news a tough-looking police detective had announced "We want closure on this episode" over an anonymous human corpse. Was everyone here philosophical, ministerial, even the cops?

Or maybe it was the personal gray cloud that had hung over the family since it settled here. First there was the price of houses. Their new ranch home, made of wood and glass, had cost twice as much as their sturdy Cape Cod back home, as much, Diane liked to add, as an estate in Maine she'd seen advertised in the Sunday *New York Times*. Yet another problem: the local newspapers seemed quaint. Often the front page contained the California version of scandals: unleashed dogs at beaches, money missing from a "Save the Redwoods" fund. Did she miss the murder and mayhem of Chicago, the steadfast cold, the glaring sun?

Maybe, as her children themselves lamented, she missed a simpler life. Her sons' childhoods had been prematurely shortened by the move. After a year of grade school here, her twins were middle-schoolers with teenage anxieties and tales to tell.

"Giselle says she'll kiss my penis in the bathroom," Jeremy reported one day after school.

This news came shortly after Diane had come back from the mailbox, where she'd encountered her neighbor weeping. "What's wrong?" she had whispered to the woman she barely knew.

"First he left."

He was her "partner," a word which made Diane think of her father's business associate, chinless Larry. Their partnership had lasted forty years. *Mother lode, partner ship:* odd words for human ties. Had her neighbors been married or not? What did it matter when the tears were real? Still, it made Diane's brain work harder to process relationship information when no one was clearly attached, except the same-sex couples whom the mayor dutifully married each year on some day that maybe had an official name. Couples Day? Partners Day?

Her neighbor had been speaking to her all along. Occasionally Diane had caught a word like "dating" or "package" or "retreat."

"But this is too much."

"Too much?" she questioned.

"Now my dog too."

"Your dog left?" She imagined a Border collie carrying his own leash. Leashes were also de rigueur. The dog would be holding a map of hiking trails in Marin. Or nude beaches. Or kill-free shelters.

"He died. After the operation."

"Oh no," Diane commiserated. It made her truly sad that dogs died, that children grew up, that husbands seemed happier elsewhere. And in a land which flowered so abundantly, where spring came on with the gusto of an Italian opera and the growing season lasted nine months, not to flourish seemed a sin. "Failure to thrive," she pictured as a sash on her own chest.

"I'm sorry," Diane lamely offered as her neighbor hurried back to her cottage with the mail.

She'd been so impressed when she and Dan had been invited for a drink at the neighbors' elegantly simple, child-free, perfectly nestled "cottage" shortly after they'd moved in. How could their house have such a view and her and Dan's have none? Luck was a matter of inches in this land where the geography was as unsteady as people's lives. As their road curved on endlessly, houses perched closer or farther from the fronts of their property affording some a view of trees and fence and others a vista beyond. In Chicago, east had meant the lake, and everything else could be located from that fact. Which way did their house face now? Diane couldn't decide.

Whatever their location on the planet, the penis issue, as they now called it, was a subject of commentary between her and Dan in bed that night.

"Imagine an eleven-year-old girl saying that. Did you even know that was a possibility at eleven?" Dan asked, shaking his head wearily.

So many commiserating nods, so little time. So many regrets they juggled in their bedtime conversations until sleep erased their uneasiness.

"No way," she added.

"Isn't it sexual harassment?"

"Probably."

"What are you going to do about it?"

That was the other problem. Moral dilemmas were among Diane's duties. "I'll call the school," she vowed into her pillow.

The principal, a thick, serious woman who didn't seem indigenous to the state, wasn't available the first time Diane called.

"Did she harass you too?" Diane asked Alex the next day.

"No, she doesn't like me," Alex said matter-of-factly. He was the child with glasses. Maybe perfect eyesight or contact lenses caused troubles in life. Glasses kept a person more serious, a viewer of life's developments rather than a participant. It had cheered Diane to read that Orson Welles had been awkward and friendless in grade school. Her son with glasses was maybe a genius, the world would realize later.

"How do you know she doesn't like you?"

"She knows me too, but she just asked Jeremy."

What was Diane to say? Should she tell him that the girl who didn't like him secretly wanted to kiss his penis too, just to keep things even? "Oh," she muttered.

So many moments ended this way. Maybe "oh" could replace the period or semicolon, she thought.

When the principal called back several days later, Diane had been at the grocery store. Dan was home editing the material that gave him a convenient and portable life. Her job offer and his portability had led them here. They'd given up friends and comfortable lives for moments like these.

"Your wife left a message about a problem your son's having with another child," Ms. Brockport stated.

"Well, it's more like the other child's giving my son a problem," Dan explained.

"Could you elaborate?" the principal asked innocently enough.

"A girl is telling my son she'll kiss . . . Well, another child is offering my child sexual favors," Dan said shyly.

That night in bed, Dan had made a joke about it: "I wanted to tell her that this kid is offering Jeremy a 'Lewinsky.'" Both of them laughed nervously. Half the time, it was a moral abomination; the other half a joke. Either way, it seemed to fit their new uneasiness.

In Chicago, kids took lunch money, acted wild on the playground, or chased each other relentlessly. Suddenly Diane recalled a girl there too. "Remember Sheila?" she asked Dan.

"How many stores do we own?" Jeremy had asked Diane one night during a phone call.

"Not any. Why?"

"Sheila's asking." Sheila was famous for her ardent games of chase. She was an East Indian whose father owned a chain of doughnut stores.

"Tell her we don't own stores."

"We don't have stores," Jeremy reported sadly, not making the connection between the information and the playground-chase activity. Sheila, after all, was a tradition-bound suitor. Her interest in Jeremy waned soon after the call.

Maybe it wasn't California but some change in their frontal lobes, Diane imagined, recalling the Sheila episode. As a group, they had been generally happy, at least before California, easy to please and amuse. "You all laugh so easily," her neighbor once told her. Now the family subscribed to the Discomfort Channel. Every moment contained new anxieties and questions about their adjustment. Maybe they should have moved to Denmark, land of melancholy, Diane sometimes thought.

"You're so Rubensesque," Dan whispered when she entered the kitchen that morning.

"Reuben sandwich?" Alex asked. Maybe he was the unmelancholy one, the one not chased by girls. Maybe contact with the other sex brought on melancholy. Maybe the only happy Californians were the newlyweds with the hers and hers towels and the two big mama chairs in front of the TV. But no. A colleague at work had reported to Diane that a lesbian student of hers had been battered by her partner. Was Diane aware of any more problems of this nature among the students? Should the department hold a meeting about this problem?

Why should Diane be aware of *any* problem? What was the probability of having such a problem? Was it greater than, lesser than, or equal to living in California for as long as humans have existed on Earth? None of her acquaintances were statisticians, so Diane would never get a reliable answer.

"Dan," she asked toward the end of the week. "Did the principal ever call?"

"A few days ago."

"You never told me."

"I'm sorry."

"And you told her?"

"Sure," I did. Dan had gone tight-lipped on her. She'd have to wait until bedtime to receive more clues.

"Jeremy, did anything happen at school about Giselle?"

"Jeremy had to stay in at lunch," dependable Alex explained.

"Why was that?" Diane felt alarmed.

"We had to go to a mediator," Jeremy said calmly.

"Who's we?"

"Me and Giselle."

"What did the mediator say?"

"She told us to work it out."

"Work what out?"

"She told us to figure out what boundaries we want in our relationship."

Diane and Dan exchanged troubled glances. Of course nothing would be simple in California.

"Was that okay with you?" Dan probed. Diane was relieved at Dan's concern. Maybe he could take over as the moral compass for the family's difficult journey through their sons' adolescence. Dan was making his serious trouble face, the oddly crunched-up eyes and pursed lips of concentration.

"Sure," Jeremy shrugged.

"So what did you decide with her?" Diane asked.

"We decided not to talk for a while."

"Is that all right with you?"

"Sure."

Later that evening, she asked Alex for more details.

"I don't hear everything, Mom. That part was private."

Tucking Jeremy in, she asked later that evening, "Are you satisfied with how this turned out, honey, because if . . ." How would she finish that sentence, she wondered, staring at her son's pajamaed back, his fragile neck.

"Sure," he answered sleepily. "It's fine."

"Do you think you'll ever want to talk to her again?"

"Maybe when I'm older."

Diane went outside and stood on the deck that she still preferred to call a porch, though porches didn't exist here. The deck, like their whole house, was in need of repair. Seen by day it looked as if it might just be swallowed up by its environment if they ignored it much longer. Some windows lacked sills. Here and there shingles hung loosely. The roof was rotting near a dining room skylight. When it rained hard, they put buckets on the rug. She imagined the place returning to pulp, trees concealing its former existence from the world, as if it were a plane lost in the jungle. Her realtor had put it right when they'd bought the place. "Better to have the worst house in the neighborhood than the best one in a bad neighborhood."

Diane looked away from the place and up into the sky, clearer on this side of the Mississippi, she'd read once. She tried to find some familiar stars, but so many things were moving overhead, clouds and airplanes she *could* see and telecommunication satellites she *couldn't*, that she got distracted. Somewhere in space, some Russians and Americans were trying to get a telescope to work properly. "A Billion-Dollar Repair," the paper had announced, was taking place right over her head.

So much up in the sky had no meaning to the casual gazer. And besides, the stars weren't needed for charting the galaxy anymore. At her own university, a perfectly ordinary-looking fellow younger than Diane herself was finding new planets and now even a new solar system without the usual props. Computers and formulae, methods Diane couldn't begin to conceive of, had been invented while she was doing what? Having children and trying to raise them? Moving to a ridiculous new location? There were new methods for everything. No wonder people wanted to seal things off before their own eyes calculated all the possible terrors of the moment. Maybe that's why their new life seemed so . . . what? So full of misgivings. But she knew that wasn't what she wanted to call it, that the word she wanted needed to contain so much that it couldn't possibly bear the pressure. Maybe there would be new words soon to describe these feelings. Maybe her boys would be alive when all the old fears turned into knowledge. Maybe Dan would know what to call their new lives already. He was so good with words. Or that soulful detective she'd seen on TV, eager to give death a new name, maybe he'd come up with something she'd hear about soon on the news.

The Middle Ages

O N A SUNNY, WARM DAY in March, the Northern California hills are as fresh and green as a new crayon. This is the time of year Peg loves when she could as easily be living on the coast of Ireland. The landscape would need sheep, of course, and some stone shacks. She thinks of a trip she and Les took to Scotland and Ireland when Esther was just an infant. In a small coastal town with its broken-down castle, a Labrador retriever had adopted them. Standing on a hill overlooking the sea, they had been a happy, new family. Twenty-five years later, Esther is driving the car. The family has lived through three dog generations. Their latest dog, Ivy, has failing kidneys and bad eyesight. She rests comfortably in the backseat of the car. No longer very interested in the world, she will sleep for most of the trip.

"We need to find Dad a brother," Peg tells Esther as they speed toward Stinson Beach in her daughter's newly leased black Honda Accord, sleek as a panther. Her previous two cars had been killed in tragic accidents, neither of which Esther had caused, though her car woes are legendary, the stuff of mock epic.

"Dad's an only child. How can we do that?" Esther asks, searching the radio for a good song. It has to be a woman's voice and a complaint about love to qualify. In this way Esther is like most girls her age, fixated on what she does not have. Love is her current negation, her unscalable wall. She's dated maybe twelve men in the last year, all of them coming up short in significant categories.

"Maybe there are organizations like Fresh Air programs or Boys Clubs that find brothers for only children."

"Why does Dad need a brother now?"

"Because it would be good for him. They could hang around together. Go to football games and rodeos and play golf."

"Dad doesn't even play golf."

"He could learn. His brother could teach him."

"Why don't you learn to play golf?"

"I can't be Dad's brother. He needs an older brother to box his ears and give him a little whatfor and be there when he needs someone who isn't me."

"But he's already grown," Esther says, smoothing back her glorious red hair. "What's the problem anyway?"

"Human relations. Sometimes Dad seems lonely."

"Maybe he needs therapy," Esther adds sensibly. But then her attention wavers. She gazes over the cliff into the sparkling distant sea. Were those islands or clouds on the horizon? As always, when the conversation veers from her, her latest coursework, or triumphs at her terrible administrative job, she becomes bored. How is Peg going to keep her interested in this scheme to save Les? "Why are you thinking about this anyway?" Esther asks as they head down the first straight leg of road for miles, just outside of Stinson Beach.

"Because Dad needs help, and I don't know how to help him."

"And you think some stranger could do better?"

"Not a stranger. A brother."

"How's he going to change now?" Esther shakes her head with impatience, gets out of the car, and clicks something on her keys that makes the abandoned car hoot twice like an owl.

Technology passed up Peg long ago. She's happy she can turn on her computer, happy to change a CD. She marvels at Esther's dominance in this arena. When she wants to tape a show on PBS or HBO or reprogram her sprinkler system, she asks Les or calls her capable daughter.

At the Stinson Beach parking lot, the shark sign is now a permanent fixture. People are warned calmly but explicitly that sharks have been sighted as close as fifty yards from shore. Since Esther and Peg are only going to eat lunch, sharks are of no concern. As long as the restaurant is open, nothing can interfere with their simple plans. Imagine, though, Peg thinks, what Les would say of the sign. Even though he hasn't been swimming at Stinson since Esther was maybe twelve, he'd note the danger. "Sharks," he'd say pointing, voice lowered in the elegiac mood so frequent these days. "Even the ocean is unsafe these days."

As if it hadn't always been. Peg imagines what an adequate sign would include: *Beware of sewage, discarded needles, global warming, arsenic, mercury, PCBs, agricultural runoff, war in the Gulf, jellyfish, sea snakes off of Costa Rica, oil spills, red algae, tidal waves, modern-day pirates, etc.* Why limit the warning to local issues? Maybe she'll manufacture a new bumper sticker, *Worry Globally*, Peg thinks, as she seats herself at a corner table under a nattily striped umbrella. A white spider makes its way across the round plastic table.

"We're out of chicken, scallops, mussels, and corn of any variety," the slim young waitress says as she leaves menus with them. "Our specials today are grilled ahi, mahimahi, tilapia, and calimari fried or grilled. Need a minute?"

"Please," Peg says, and looks at Esther, whose attention is fixed beyond their table.

Across the terrace, a small gray-haired woman with sunglasses is sitting across from her two huge sons. They resemble her enough for the relationship to be clear and each other enough for it to be comical. One wears glasses and one doesn't. Aside from that, the brothers are a matching pair: middle-aged, jowly, losing their hair in the same haphazard pattern of recession. Even their hands, which are small for the size of their torsos, are folded identically.

"Maybe we could clone Dad a brother," Esther suddenly smiles.

"How could that help?" Peg asks.

"And besides, then Dad would have to help us raise himself."

Her laugh makes Peg bold. "That's what marriage is, honey. You raise them, and if they turn out all right, they think they've done it themselves and leave you, and if they don't turn out all right, they blame you and leave you anyway."

"Is Dad leaving you? Is that why you want him to have a brother?"

"What do you mean?"

"Someone like Dad but not quite Dad to stay with you?"

"He's not leaving me, honey."

"I didn't really think so." A look of relief crosses Esther's features. "Hey," she continues. "Maybe he needs a guru like those men who sit naked on hills, waiting."

"Waiting for beseechers."

"Maybe Dad could become a beseecher."

The waitress returns to announce that they are out of calimari, fried or grilled.

"I'll have a burger and fries."

"Regular or garlic fries?"

"Garlic."

"If you're not out of garlic, I'll have the same," Peg adds. "And two glasses of chardonnay."

When Les comes home at dinnertime, he's inordinately cheerful. His eyes look sparkly and full of playfulness. He whistles at dinner and compliments Peg's capered chicken breasts and noodles, then busies himself with his car trunk.

"What are you doing?" Peg calls through the open back door. It's a beautiful night. The jasmine is blooming, its fragrance so overwhelming that she wonders if the yard needs a "Beware of Jasmine" sign.

"I'm looking at my new golf clubs."

"You're taking up golf?"

"Me and a friend."

"Do I know him?"

"Nope."

"Esther and I went to lunch today. They were out of everything, but the beach has a new resident shark. That's what a sign said," Peg offers with import.

Les looks up to catch Peg's eye. His face is full of benevolence. "I wouldn't worry about it, honey," he answers reassuringly. "You can't let everything bother you." Then he adds, "I need to get going. I'm meeting Bill to hit some balls at the driving range up in Terra Linda."

"Who's this Bill?"

"A new guy at work who's half my age. A program analyst. I told him I'd been thinking of taking up golf, and he said he could lend me this set of clubs until I get the hang of it."

"He has several sets?"

"Apparently so."

"Maybe I can come along and watch."

"Wait till I know what I'm doing," Les smiles.

An empty nester, Peg thinks. No pets, no Esther, no Les, no golf. Just jasmine and "Beware of Jasmine."

She's reading in bed when Les comes home from the range. The word makes her picture a flat tract of land populated by deer and antelope, "Home on the Range."

"How did it go?" Les's sport shirt is streaked in the front with sweat. From the aspect of exertion, it looks as if it's gone very well.

"I hit one a mile," he smiles with satisfaction. "Way past the yardage markers. Bill says I'm a natural."

"And just think. You've waited all these years to start. By now you could have been a regular Sam Snead if only you'd known your talent."

"Peg, when's the last time you watched golf?"

"With my father in the Middle Ages."

"We're in our Middle Ages now," Les says undressing. "Look," he points, holding a pair of black and white Oxfords towards Peg's face. "Golf shoes."

The next morning Peg calls Esther at work.

"All the machines are broken and my boss is having a hissy fit, so make it quick," she insists. "He's even lost his palm pilot, and I just programmed the damn thing for him yesterday."

"Dad's found a brother all by himself."

"What do you mean?"

"Someone from work is teaching him golf."

"Why would he want to learn that?"

"It's what men do. If they can't fulfill their golf wish, they go mad or suffer apoplexy."

"Please, Mom. People aren't as generic as you think."

"Well, Dad is and I am. Maybe you're not."

"How do you figure you're generic?"

"My worries typify my age group, my social status, my demographic niche, honey." Peg can hear her daughter snickering. Why are young people so quick to dismiss trends and portents? Do they make life seem too limited? "No, I mean it," she continues. "If I lived in Mozambique, I'd be worried you'd be having a baby in a tree to escape a flood. That would be my preoccupation instead of Dad and golf."

"Please, Mom. I'm not even married. Don't pressure me about kids all the time."

Les asks Peg if Bill and his wife can come for dinner a week from Friday. Requests like these are rare. Mostly they see a few old friends, those whose marriages have somehow endured like theirs, a shrinking, unpredictable list. Some whose relationships seemed like a cinch have vanished like the passenger pigeon. Others perilously hold on, dangling by their knuckles for years, then gain a grip at a crucial moment. Other times dinners include Esther and her roommate Nan, despite Nan's limited palate.

"Still a vegan?" Peg confirms on the phone before each attempt, always hoping for better news.

"I'm doing macrobiotic now. I can eat rice and most vegetables except mushrooms and onions." Whenever Peg cooks for Esther and Nan, she feels like a mad scientist, missing essential parts of a formula.

For Bill and his wife, she'll make salmon Sicilian style, risotto, and a salad combining arugula, fava beans, and pecorino cheese. She'll buy a dessert at the new French bakery, a mocha rum torte, and have it readied on a plate with mint leaves from her garden that somehow endure despite their bossy jasmine neighbors.

But to tell of the dinner party. To introduce complication just when Peg is satisfied that maybe life will go on, that she and Les will survive their dangerous middle years, that golf will be a talisman of renewed hope and energy for them both. Not that Peg is having energy problems. She has her twenty hours a week of work at the bookstore and all the reading she does when she's off. She has her yoga class and her mother up the road a few suburbs away requiring sugarless cough drops or Kleenex or other expendable resources. She has her thoughts about Esther and Les, her garden, her bum knee, her stiff back, her fibroids, her perfect vision, her empathetic smile. She has her worries about the Middle East and Macedonia and the homeless and the hungry. She has her fears that she'll die before Les or have to face her own death utterly alone. She has a lot.

But now she needs to have a difficult dinner party for important new guests, one Bill and his wife, whose name neither she nor Les knows.

"Maybe it's coo," she jokes as she mixes the salad.

"What's coo?"

"Bill and coo. You know. A joke."

Les is polishing the wineglasses, which he has found too streaky for Bill and Coo. Peg tries to remember the last time they had new guests to dinner, how many years ago.

"I think the last new guests we had were Noah and his wife."

"It wasn't in Biblical times, Peg."

"Noah Franzen and Susan what's-her-name."

They both laugh, remembering how the dinner had been a disaster. Noah, a friend of theirs from college, had come with his new young wife on a business trip. Susan had replaced Grace, a woman they'd known as long as Noah. Watching Noah and Susan was disorienting at best and distressing at times. At one point it seemed as if Noah was explaining to Susan, as if she were a child, why they had to be there. "Old friends," Peg heard in passing as she cleared the table. Susan had looked miserably bored when they talked of the past but had seemed equally sullen about the present. She told them her job involved venture capital, which Peg hadn't understood. And when Peg told them that she used to teach Latin, Susan had either snorted or snickered or choked on her wine. Dinner was an early affair, ending before dessert had been on the table for seven minutes. She and Les had analyzed the moment many times after that evening.

"What happened to Noah?" Peg asks.

"They had babies. He's probably pushing a stroller down Fifth Avenue right now."

"And Grace, I hope, is on the Riviera."

"She wasn't the Riviera type."

"You're right. Grace, I hope, is at an artists' colony in New Mexico throwing pots and braiding her hair and having many lovers."

When the bell rings, Peg hurries to the door. There is something deliciously strange about meeting new people and serving them dinner. "Beware of Dinner?" Beware of guests bearing gifts, she thinks, as a handsome dark man and his darker wife stand at their threshold with a bottle of wine.

"For you, Mrs. Porter."

Mrs. Porter is Les's mother. She is Peg Lewin and always has been. "Just call me Peg," she tells the smiling couple, who are greeted by Les, who's still holding the dishrag from his earlier glass polishing.

"This is Bill," Les adds, "and you're . . ."

"I am Naria," the lovely woman says. "And he is only Bill for the purposes of living in America," she explains. "At home he is Evanesh."

The name sounds like "Evening" to Peg, Evening in Paris, a terrible cologne of her teens. She remembers dousing it on herself like barbecue igniter before a school dance. Originally from Kenya, Bill and Naria were both children of East Indians who had been merchants in Mombasa. Their families fled the country, but Bill and Naria had met at Berkeley where they were both studying computer programming. It was their hope to stay in California and eventually have a family. All this is settled before Peg shows them into the living room and points them toward the sofa.

"Your house is so lovely," Naria says to Peg, who suddenly worries whether her guests can eat the dinner she planned.

"I made salmon," Peg smiles. "I hope you like fish."

"Bill is especially fond of salmon," Naria says. "We eat fish regularly. Bill has told me you have a child."

"Our daughter is twenty-five. She lives in Oakland."

"I hope to have a large family, maybe four children. But Bill wishes to wait, so we do."

"I wanted more too," Peg replies, "but this is how it happened."

"We are lucky to have whatever we're given," Naria says softly. Peg can't take her eyes off this young woman whose long hair glistens and whose teeth are whiter than she remembered teeth can be.

At the other end of the room, Les shows Bill the garden just outside the sliding glass doors.

"The jasmine is very powerful this time of year," Peg adds from across the room.

"Jasmine reminds me of home," Naria states, her huge eyes suddenly ready to flow over.

"It's all right," Peg tells her. "You can come here any time you want to see the jasmine."

Naria looks grateful, so Peg continues.

"Maybe when the men are golfing, we could have tea and sit in the garden."

"I would like that very much. We live in a condominium. I see other neighbors and envy their balconies with flowers."

"You could plant what you like here if there's something you miss," Peg offered. "I could clear a little place next to Les's part of the garden." She pointed toward a mossy birdbath, where no bird has bathed in years.

"You are very kind," Naria says.

The following Saturday, Bill and Les are trying eighteen holes. Les isn't sure of the wisdom of spending the whole day golfing, but on the other hand, a "trial by fire," as he calls it, will give him a good sense of how seriously he wants to play the game. Peg rolls over in bed and pulls the sheets tightly around her. Les showers and dresses quietly in the early morning sun and kisses Peg good-bye.

"Where are your golf shoes?" Peg asks sleepily.

"You put them on there, honey," Les explains. "Listen, have fun with Naria, and be careful of your back if you dig. Let her do the work."

Peg smiles to think of how old and rickety she has gotten, falling apart like their trellis, where wisteria explodes every March. The rest of the year it's ugly with tangly vines and huge bean-shaped pods. A stranger unfamiliar with wisteria might wonder what Les and Peg had in mind were they to visit between late May and February. The pods make Peg think of "Jack and the Beanstalk," the foolish boy who traded a cow for nothing and had to tell his mother. In real life, he would have remained a disappointment, Peg is afraid, but that is the power of stories, to glide past the difficulties on to the prize. Straw for gold, kisses waking sleeping princesses, a kindly woodsman sparing the life of a child. If only the news were full of such goodness—and some critics say fairy tales are cruel. Not compared to school shootings, beached whales, and beautiful girls without balconies or children.

The green Toyota enters their driveway at ten sharp, and Peg is in the carport to greet it. "Shall we go to the garden shop right away, or would you like to have some tea?"

"Maybe some tea," Naria says cheerfully. "I am slow to wake today."

Peg has been excited enough to get several new blends just for her guest. Aside from her usual Earl Grey, she has green tea and jasmine and chamomile. A coffee fan herself, she remembers now that chamomile is good for upset stomachs. She has also bought some Chai-flavored cookies and two raspberry tarts topped with dollops of whipped cream.

"We have quite a selection," she says as the girl follows her into the kitchen. Instead of the beautiful sari she'd worn to dinner, she's dressed in a white T-shirt and beige shorts. She is a tiny thing, Peg thinks, much smaller than Peg or even Esther, whose body is ample like her mother's but more elongated like her father's. Naria's like a pretty bird at the feeder, Peg thinks, a type of finch, as Naria absentmindedly stirs her cup of green tea and pokes at the crumbs of a cookie. Peg has always had too good of an appetite. Although she is sturdy rather than fat, she can match Les bite for bite.

"I am very grateful," Naria says softly, "to have an American friend. At work people are polite to me, but they treat me differently. Even the women who gossip do not ask me personal questions."

"And yet we're all so alike. Don't you think? The more Les and I travel, the more I think how everyone's the same."

"I am not so sure," Naria says. A distant look overtakes her features, as if she's looking past Peg, past her life here, past Bill or Evanesh or whomever her husband is. How long have the two been together, Peg wonders, and what is their story? Surely if they met at Berkeley, they have chosen each other. But nothing is guaranteed. Peg knows that too.

"I am beginning to take some medications," Naria continues, "to perhaps lighten my mood. I am sorry that your jasmine made me cry, but I miss my home so much at times. And the odd thing is that I miss it more here than I did when I lived as an undergraduate in Massachusetts. Here it is almost like home. The resemblance makes it worse, I'm afraid."

"Does Bill know how you feel?"

"Bill is very busy trying to get along at work. He makes many plans and tells me to put on a smiling face. What else can I do?"

Peg doesn't know what to say. They sit quietly for maybe three minutes while Peg thinks of herself and Les, the island of relative comfort and familiarity they've built over the years, how each shrub and vine and flagstone is a part of the story of their lives, of their house and yard, which also houses the graves of three cats and two dogs. Without a word, Peg motions for Naria to come into the garden. She takes her by her narrow, skinny hand. It's like leading a child to a present. "Now close your eyes," Peg says as she walks Naria toward the jasmine, "and keep them closed. Stand here with me and just inhale. You're in a beautiful garden," Peg says softly, lovingly. "It's morning, and you're home."

We Kill What We Love

His

THE PRENUPTIAL AGREEMENT had made everything his: the clocks that ticked on the walls, the pictures of her family, the children, the pool, the weeping fig in its Chinese bowl, the house, the windowsills, his. And she was his too. Her blondeness his. Her voice his. The cleft of her breast, his. When she playfully called him asshole, it came out of his mouth. When she said, "I love you," for she loved him deeply, it was like a mirror: her mouth was his saying "I love you."

She lived inside him. There was no world with her in it. She was part of him.

Even after she left him, she was there, maybe hidden but inside him nonetheless. When he stood outside on the sidewalk and watched her take another man in her mouth, candles lit, music playing, as they had done in the years of their marriage, it was his mouth committing the treason. They were his lips. It was his crime.

There were no borders to this love. The world didn't exist to hold her. He held her inside him like a bright jewel in a box.

Wrestling

Once he said he was only trying to get her to leave his bedroom, that they were wrestling.

Another time he threw her desk out on the driveway.

Once when the room was dark, he threw the nanny out the door thinking it was her.

Once he locked her out of their hotel room nearly naked.

Once, when he felt rage, he struck her over and over with a wine bottle that cracked several ribs.

But the pain was his. He felt it more, he knew.

David Bowie

She was eighteen and just out of high school. She had left her teenage bedroom, where David Bowie papered the walls, where the turquoise phone was always ringing, where socks and Levi's and beauty magazines and old school yearbooks accumulated on wicker chairs, and moved in with a friend in Los Angeles. The apartment was so small, they had to share a bed. But it was chaste. He was like a brother to her, and her parents approved.

At the Daisy Restaurant where she waited tables, people went out of their way to be nice to her. Maybe it was her golden skin or hair, maybe the strength of her body, taut and tan in the way California makes girls look healthy as fresh produce. Boys had always liked her, but now men, some old enough to be her father, some just slightly older by two or seven or twelve years, looked at her all the time. Just telling people her name felt thrilling.

The one who wanted to take her out was famous, but she really didn't know who he was. People kept telling her how everyone knew him. When they went out for the first time and he ripped her jeans in his eagerness to have her, what she mainly liked was the low voice, the perfect smile, the strong arms and big chest. He put the boys she used to know to shame. And his eagerness too was what she loved, how he needed her from the start.

Almost as famous as David Bowie, she laughed to her sister.

Life was big and about to open like a gift.

History

From the start she was necessary as air.

He'd call her at night. If she didn't answer—and sometimes she didn't just for the fun of it, for the teenage joy of playing games with him—he could feel his head emptying out and his chest getting hot and sick inside. How could someone he'd just met make him feel so much?

He had a wife for whom he felt nothing. His children were history too despite how small and perfect they once had been.

No one had ever affected him the way she did.

She's like an angel, he told people. They returned his goofy smile with a consoling one and wondered what had gotten into him.

Reading

Neither of them had read *Othello* or studied psychology. Neither thought of history, how we're condemned to relive it if we don't learn from it.

How many older men had whispered undying love to golden girls still really children, girls who watched *Brady Bunch* reruns and bought Scottie dog clips for their hair? The restaurant was her first real job other than babysitting. She missed her family, especially her mother, who'd give her warm milk with honey at night. Sometimes she woke up at night with her thumb in her mouth.

With uncharacteristic boldness, one friend told him to think of his wife, sick and huge as a cow, pregnant with his third child. But that was no argument against the powerful attraction he felt. He hated how women looked when pregnant, their ankles swollen, their walks slow and grandmotherly. He made a deep sound in his throat and shrugged off the advice.

Get a grip, his friend told him, watching how he observed her that afternoon as she flitted from table to table. It was as if he were watching flowers blooming.

I'm in love with her, he said, having never read Shakespeare.

Actions

She hid in the bushes. She called the police. She told them he was going to kill her. She changed her phone number. She wrote a letter and put it in a safe deposit box. *He's going to kill me,* it said.

Definitions

Is this a murder story or a love story?
Where can it hang its hat?

The romantic version: a voice saying, as teenagers do every night before they fall asleep, *I'm lonely, I'm afraid, Does anyone love me?* She was reported as saying these things, as going back to him time and again for these reasons, forgiveness like a magnet, need its dumb force.

The id: that reptilian resident of our deeply embarrassing prehuman brains. The place in us that shouts commands in the voice of a 1930s dictator: fuck, eat, drink, sleep, pee, shit, kill if you must.

The heart: where good intentions dwell like robins' eggs.

Forgiveness: giving up on our wish for a perfect past.

Still

It was someone he didn't recognize, not the man that people greeted like a friend at restaurants, bars, wherever he went. Not the man who made stadiums cheer and eyes glaze with expectation. He could never do such a thing. He had a place in the community, a mother, children, friends he protected. He sent other people's children to college. He attended graduations and weddings and funerals.

Once, his son saw him following the babysitter, who had her car, and said, "Look! It's Daddy."

He showed up at restaurants and stared at her.

No words could express how it wasn't him. He loved her more than he should. He flashed the victory sign to the cameras. He worked things through. It wasn't him any more than a dolphin is a shark.

Endings

They couldn't end it. She'd call him and ask him over. He'd try not to respond, but as soon as they were together again all the passion and rage spilled over. After she told him again that their relationship was hopeless, he bought the disguise, theatrical glue and a beard. He planned out a time. She'd be home alone after the big outing, after the dinner to which he hadn't been invited. She'd never touch another man's lips or ride around town with one of her golden boys. She'd never take another man in her mouth or be taken like that.

He had learned how to slit a throat in a TV role where he was playing a Navy Seal. He sneaked up on her, on the two of them talking. It happened with blinding speed. He used all the power he ever had, all the love. He would clean this up with swiftness. He was an avenging angel. Each stroke was justice.

Aftermath

Senator Arlen Specter has revealed a second witness with a sexual harrassment complaint against Clarence Thomas. Because of time considerations, she was never called.

"This is a lynching," Thomas said, to cover the scent of his wrongdoings.

"Furhman's a racist," Johnny Cochran told the jury, citing the history of lynchings in America, a truth witnessed strongly in Billie Holiday's haunting rendition of "Strange Fruit," written by a Jewish high school English teacher from New York.

❖

At the store a father is searching for orange juice.

"Where's the O.J.?" he asks his son, a boy of perhaps four.

"O.J. Simpson?"

"How do you know about O.J. Simpson?"

"I see him on TV."

❖

I loved her too much, he was reported to have told his ex-mother-in-law.

You Suck

I.

SUSAN TAUGHT ENGLISH as a Second Language, neither art nor science, to people from all corners of the world. In the highest level ESL classes, Susan easily conversed with her students, who made jokes at her expense and devised clever and not-so-clever methods of cheating. A Russian man of seventy had the conjugation of the verb *to be* written on his wrinkled palm. A Nigerian student told her that he had written "The Tyger" when the assignment was to turn in an original poem. At the lower levels, students weren't capable of cheating. Just getting them to understand was almost a miracle. In those classes, she felt more like a cross between a baseball coach and a mime. One class of fourteen was comprised of three Russians, three Poles, two Ethiopians, two Salvadorans, a Colombian, two Vietnamese, and one Laotian.

The goal of the evening was to get through a two-page story about Niagara Falls, heavily illustrated with line drawings of dangerous activities. Barrels went over the falls. People carrying parasols walked above it on tightropes. It was Susan's job to explain that some people took risks while others actually committed suicide via the falls. Like Anna Karenina, like Madame Bovary, like all the famous suicides of great literature that maybe a few of the Russians had maybe read. Like Ernest Hemingway, she could tell them, America's most famous writer after Jack London in former communist countries.

Susan didn't know why the concept of suicide was essential to beginning-level English students. Who would come all this way, then give up in such ultimate fashion? But there she was, desperately miming different methods of dying. She wrung her own neck. She took poison. She held her finger to her temple, closed her eyes, and shot. The Salvadorans looked concerned.

Selbsttod, she heard one of the Russians whisper to a Pole. She knew German from college. Suddenly she was in business. She could teach the students English via German, the language they had in common. She didn't want to think of the political circumstances that had introduced this language to the elderly Russians and young Poles but felt happy she could communicate with a minority of the class.

The only younger Russian of the group, Vlad, an awkward, homely young man, had begun waiting for her after class. He too was as new to the language but had a deep commitment to plumbing its depths.

"Please," he asked, as the classroom emptied and she packed her bags to drive home, "What means 'suck?'"

"That's a difficult one," she smiled. "It literally means to use one's lips to receive nourishment as a baby does with a bottle." She did a polite version of the action, and he looked confused.

"How can it be," he wondered, "I see 'School sucks.' What means 'suck,' please, Teacher?" He spoke to her as one impatient with a person who won't reveal a necessary truth.

"In this case," she continued, "it expresses an attitude. It is a metaphor." She said the word louder than she normally would. "'School is very bad,' the person is saying."

"I see!" he smiled, finger waving in the air, and walked off happily into the night. It saddened her to think how little it took to please some people, how they were used to having so little that even tiny crumbs of knowledge were a prize.

Back at her car, she turned on the radio. It was an NPR show about paint-by-number art, a genre practiced by Herbert Hoover, Ethel Merman, and Dwight David Eisenhower. She learned that a show recently in New York sold paint-by-numbers by anonymous artists for as much as $500 a canvas. She couldn't wait to tell Dino when she got back to their apartment. He appreciated such madness. He would look up from whatever he was reading and smile the crooked little smile that lifted his mustache so poignantly. No one would call Dino handsome—prematurely bald and small, but his intelligent eyes and winsome face had convinced Susan long ago.

Dino had felt trapped in a good marriage for two years now. Before he really knew Susan, knew her stories and habits and penchants for garlicky food and tendency to get a little cross-eyed when she was sleepy and habit of losing essential items when she was alert and rushing around doing too much as she always was, everything was fine. It was year four and five on which he was basing his decision.

And Janice.

Janice was new. She was wild. Dino couldn't anticipate what she'd do next. Once she had stayed late with him at work. She had brought him some shrimp chow mein while he finished looking at proofs for an art book he was helping her edit. She laid everything out on her desk and offered him chopsticks. When he came around to her side of the desk to pick up his pair, she grabbed his crotch and began softly massaging.

Susan never surprised him. Sex was a weekly function, as was foreign movie night, and even those were categorical. They'd watch everything Indian, then move on to Nepal. They'd try one position for months, then discard it in favor of another Susan had seen in some woman's magazine. "*Elle* says that if I bend my legs like this, I can feel my orgasm more profoundly," she'd explain. Movies happened on Saturday and sex on Thursdays, Susan's last day of classes for the week. It was maybe the four-day work week that was killing their marriage. Fridays were the worst day for Dino. He couldn't relax until five, when his miserable week ended, but there Susan always was on Thursdays, a little sleepy, a little happy, waiting for him, naked under the covers.

Mostly things were all right, but maybe it was just too much. After all, he was only thirty-six, a youngster these days. When his dad was thirty-six, he already had three little kids underfoot, Buzzy and Dino and Tony, born with a hole in his heart. In those days men settled down early. His father was manager of a rug installation shop, Dino's childhood supported by orange and brown shag carpeting. His mother, a third-grade teacher, didn't even work until Dino went to high school. But Susan and Dino didn't have a baby or a cat or even a Christmas cactus to tie them down. They were traveling light.

He'd tell her tonight when she came home from work, before she undressed or even tried to. He couldn't leave someone who was naked. That would be like killing the king in prayer, which had stopped

Hamlet in his tracks for pages on end. He owed at least as much to Susan, the gift of a decent departure. He had Janice's phone number and would call her when the mission was completed. He began loading a few essential objects into the backpack that Susan had bought him at Crate & Barrel last Christmas. Every Christmas she bought him a new valise of some kind. Sometime soon it needed to end.

3.

Instead of feeling abject after the first miserable weeks alone, Susan was feeling triumphant. Her mother consoled her and her brother vowed revenge. "I'll get that Persian," her brother said.

"Dino's Italian," Susan replied.

"Iranian, Italian, it's all 'A' words to me."

"The words begin with I, Ronnie. Didn't you ever learn to read?"

Anyway, it didn't bother her much after the first few nights alone in bed. She was surprised at how modest and controlled her feelings were. When her class said, "Good evening, Teacher," a tear never fell though at first her throat felt like it was closing forever, and when her officemate, Don Teller, directed his vague smile in her direction, she assured him that everything was fine. Since no one knew much about her life as a part-time teacher, there was very little explaining to do. She remembered when Beverly Vance, a part-timer of long standing had passed away. Only then had the faculty learned of a former husband, a new husband, two sons in the city, and one in Stuttgart, Germany. Only then had they found out that Beverly had taught in Norman, Oklahoma, when her first husband was in the military. Only then did it come out that she was an avid painter of mountain landscapes and traveler to twenty-nine countries, seven in Africa. Until then she had been the small gray-haired woman whose class let out early and noisily at times. So much for knowledge.

It was only when Vlad asked a fateful question one night that Susan felt something doughy and sweaty swelling inside her, as if someone bigger and softer and sadder might burst out of her nicely smooth skin.

"Please, Teacher, what means heartbreak?" Vlad asked her in front of the class.

"A person is sad," Susan said, and the frown and heart-clutching chosen to illustrate the proposition were every bit as true as the gray sky and gassy green lights outside the classroom window.

4.

Diego had soft eyes and a limited vocabulary, and Susan knew that every moment in the car and riding home and letting him sleep where Dino had once slept jeopardized her lousy job. But there were many lousy jobs to be had out there. She could always work for her brother's florist shop, which specialized in funerals, or her aunt's Turkish import business. She could always get a factory job bottling dill pickles or putting potato chips into shiny foil bags. There were many opportunities for a twenty-nine-year-old woman with a master's degree in English, no husband, and a student named Diego regarding her with a daffy, hopeful smile.

She closed her eyes and waited. When nothing happened within seconds and then minutes, she opened them up and saw that Diego had fallen asleep. His two jobs and the night class were probably too much for him already. This opportunity had probably pushed him over the brink. Susan listened discretely to the heartbeat in his thick, hairy chest. He was nothing like Dino, who had been short and streamlined, greyhound-thin. Diego was barrel-chested and hairy as an animal. She took a few sleeping pills, easily acquired along with Xanax and sympathy, when she told her nurse-practitioner that her husband had left her, and fell asleep quickly.

Sometime in the middle of the night, she heard some commotion in the room. "Diego?" she asked the shadow dressing in the corner.

"Please, Teacher, I must go to work now." He smiled sweetly, bent over her side of the bed, and gave her a small tidy kiss on her cheek. "I will see you tonight, Teacher."

"Please call me Susan," she said softly and drifted back to sleep.

5.

The first time she tried to call Dino, Janice answered. Susan knew her name was Janice but that was all she knew.

"Please tell him we need to get divorced," she told Janice, who was speechless. "Have him call me soon," she added.

She didn't spend too much time thinking about him. She could go to movies alone, sitting up close and even buying butter for her popcorn, and take the trip to Egypt that her college sponsored every Christmas. Her mother offered her a loan, which would easily cover the airfare and lodging. The tour, which lasted three weeks, included all the major sights. So what if her companions would be widows and she would have to bunk with a stranger. So what if she'd pose alone in front of the pyramids and at Luxor and on the Nile—Susan and all that water, Susan and all that sand. Susan Vincent, formerly Bussatori, would use her own last name come spring. She'd make slides of all the sights and show her classes. She'd become as well traveled as Beverly Vance, a visitor to twenty-nine countries in all, a citizen of the world.

Jewish Urban White Trash Story

NOT ONLY IN TOWNS named Lead Bottom and Shirley do bad things happen to good people. Not just to Billie Jean or Roy, Jr. It can be Detroit or Queens or Los Angeles. It can be Chicago, a middle-class neighborhood of optometrists, steelworkers, leather salesmen, and minor insurance agents, where disaster may strike. Its cousin, fate, already led you here when your father, anonymous victim of the world economic crisis, quit school. He had hoped to become a doctor and control the destinies of those he loved. Failing at that, he became a man with numbers stuck in his head. Like the wizened men you see on Crete in cafés doing math problems for pleasure, your father loved the cold logic of sums. His numbers arrived without life, and it was up to you to resuscitate them. "I have so little to work with!" you complained to no end, for this is what you were given, this is what you made of it, and what it made of you.

On your block itself, there were countless dangers beyond the vague threats of polio and nuclear emergencies. The boy next door, Stevie, whose mother was Glamorina of the recent divorce, was left in the yard in his underwear in bone-chilling weather. There Stevie is, trembling near the gate, where he must stay until she has finished entertaining the man she's brought home from a date. Through the fence you feed Stevie crackers. Like a dog, he crunches on them gratefully. You offer him an old sweater. Instead of thanking you, he aims his penis at you. A wet stream shoots through the mesh that separates you as you jump back and stare.

"Aren't penises as long as hoses?" you ask your sister later.

"You're thinking of elephant trunks, crazy person," she says before she tells your mother on you.

You stop asking questions, which is dangerous, because sometimes you could use more information. Mr. Moore next door is a foreman at the steel mill. What does it mean that he is also a moneylender and immigrant importer, that the labor his plant needs is shipped straight to his basement on Constance Avenue? One of the men has steady eyes and shows no fear. He walks down the street in daylight. "Sweet, sweet, little Mama," he whispers to you as you pass him. Having not yet discovered shame, you have no modesty. It doesn't occur to you to close your Venetian blinds or ask your mother why that man watched you undress at night. It becomes as much a part of your weekly routine as Saturday night baths and Sunday school. When you move away many years later, Mr. Moore plants an open-mouthed kiss on your surprised lips.

"I'll never see you again," he blinks sadly.

"I should have closed my blinds," you lament, eight years after the fact.

The Moore family is your substitute for asking questions. You learn so much from them. Freddie, the eldest son, drinks heavily. He shoots a gun in the alley on New Year's Eve. "Don't take rides from him ever!" your mother has warned. After a fight about the rent, Freddie threatens to send the severed head of his family dog home in a box. You watch the mail for weeks. What shape will the box be? What color? Will the mailman shake the box wondering what it holds? It never arrives, and the dog returns. Freddie too. Bearing a knife, he chases his mother, who is trying to collect his rent. She shows up breathless at your door. You have been watching *American Bandstand* and practicing the vaguely obscene gestures of the dance called The Jerk. "He's trying to kill me," she says quietly. You show her to a chair. "I shouldn't sit. I've peed my pants."

"Don't worry," you reassure her. "We have plastic covers."

It isn't a neighbor but a stranger who touches you first. You are on a trip with the Girl Scouts to the Wisconsin Dells. A fat theme park Indian, authentic but in bad faith about his work, grabs your nub of a breast. You don't register it until your sister sees the photo and makes a remark. So much that happens is only given a name later, you note after your Wisconsin experience. You are learning. When Bobbie L., a demented boy with tight curls and a three-year stint in eighth grade, knocks you off your bike and grabs you in the same place, you know something is wrong, but you don't say anything. Your sister would laugh. Your father would calculate the probability of such an event occurring, which is high in a city. "I'm not surprised," he would say with the glint of sad circumspection that makes you anxious for his health.

One Halloween at Missy's house down the street, her mother prepares dinner. But you see that her hands tremble as she slices the London broil. When she finally sits down with you, she bursts into tears. She's been frightened by a boy who reached into her car and grabbed her purse off the passenger seat. "I've learned my lesson!" she announces, wiping her eyes and sniffling bravely. The doorbell rings. It's Ronnie Roberts, the cutest boy in eighth grade, who is dressed as a bum. He reaches his hand out to grab you there again, but you're ready. Your knee shoots up into the extra-long crotch of his hobo pants. There are so many stars in the October sky, you think as he writhes on the porch. You are learning to protect yourself. You aren't like Missy's mother's purse, sitting there for the taking.

Once when your mother got off the Jeffrey Express at your corner, a tall black kid snatched her shopping bag. Against the advice of experts, including your father, who lectures the family on miscellaneous dangers, she held on and wrestled it back. "You son of a bitch!" she called him, your mother who never swore. In telling the story, she made a point of her race neutrality. "You son of a bitch!" could be aimed at anyone. Her open-mindedness was a point of pride. This event has some vague correlation with the invention of refrigerator art in your household. The collage shows the Montgomery bus boycott and newspaper photos of Cheney, Schwerner, and Goodman. You'd think someone had an ideology looking at it, but your mother never speaks about the cause of civil rights. A few months later, she tapes up pictures of astronauts. The white wall of your refrigerator commemorates seasons, minor holidays, and family victories. When your father bowls a 700 series and his photo makes the local paper, your mother creates a three-dimensional bowling display. The street thief has brought out your mother's artistic side. You want to find him and thank him. But your father is driven to another conclusion. He buys a handgun and does target practice in the basement. Your family closes its ears and turns up the TV as bullets ricochet off the washer and utility sink.

Down the street, Sharon Silverberg dies of cystic fibrosis on the night that Teddy Kennedy's plane crashes in a storm. You were supposed to babysit for her that night, but first she was hospitalized and then she was gone. She couldn't eat ice cream. You would serve her marshmallow whip with colored sprinkles if she managed to swallow at least half of her bird-sized meal. Her skin was as white as paper. She slept in an oxygen tent and was the bossiest kid you knew. Two doors down, tiny, stooped Mr. Bernstein has a massive stroke. His son who sells furniture fashions a crank bed for him that is placed in the center of the picture window. As often as not, his father is asleep in that bed. But sometimes, when you ride by on your red Schwinn singing songs from *West Side Story,* you see his passive face in the window. His eyes appear to cry without volition. Ancient Mr. Bernstein reminds you of saints that your friend Kathy Kaszmarek has in her big saint encyclopedia. You'd like to own that book, but you know your parents would say no. Across the alley from you, Martin Morley's father gets killed in a car crash. The policeman comes to your house first, thinking it is the Morleys'. You know before Martin or his mother that his father is dead. When Darlene holds her breath to scare her mother, she isn't dead. She is just making a point about power to her mother Irene, who had replaced Glamorina as your next-door neighbor. Three doors down, Ellen, who is a devout Catholic, tries to smother the fourth child she and Frank have had in six years. She is sent to a rest home and given a prescription for contraceptives. The doctor is Jewish, she tells your mother upon her return to the block. You notice that the baby she tried to kill is prettier and more alert than the three she has tolerated. You question her intelligence. Across from you, Mrs. Neilson's husband falls off the roof he is shingling and breaks his neck. "He drank too much" is part of the story your family hears upon their return from Niagara Falls. You wish sometimes that your parents drank. It would be sophisticated for them to hold a martini or a highball like the classy adults you watch in movies. You've since read that Jewish men suffer from a higher rate of depression than their Christian brothers, who rely more on liquor to fix their moods. Maybe a Tom

Collins or two could have helped your father through his dark middle years.

When your grandmother tries to commit suicide on a bench facing the lake, the police come again. "We're off to the hospital," your parents whisper. "Don't go anywhere." Where are you supposed to go at one in the morning? You turn on the television and watch *The Best Years of Our Lives*. One nice man in it has a hook for a hand. Maybe your grandmother has chopped off her hand, you think. Two weeks later she comes home with a big bandaged fist, where the i.v. incision has gotten infected. By now you know she had taken pills. You stare at her vials of medications when you visit her apartment. There are blue satellites and long yellow rockets. You glue some to a barette and hide it in your drawer, the way your father hides things in his. Between the handkerchiefs and old wallets, you've seen rubbers, World War II shrapnel, and photos of the South Pacific. When your sister can't find a clip for her long hair, you offer her the barette. "You're sick!" she shouts. The year you start college, you pry a few pills off the barette and try them. The blue ones make you sleepy. Your grandmother never misses them.

"I don't believe in God," you tell the rabbi after your grandmother tries to kill herself. He doesn't seem surprised, which distresses you greatly.

"Then I'll give you a different part," he shrugs in response to the context, the recitation of a Sabbath prayer in a play your class is performing. "You can be a prophet. They were all crazy."

When your family moves away, when they take their lives to the socially engineered suburbs, when your father's attitude improves and the refrigerator door is once again bare, you think the story will end. But that is another story. It will wait in the wings like a patient, hopeful understudy until someone gives it a name.

Rent-a-Pet

IF JULIA OPENS A BUSINESS for the new millennium, it will be a Rent-a-Pet, a concept that's caught on big in Japan. Here's the idea: People love pets, but Japanese homes are too small for them, so pet stores lend their pets to people to enjoy for a day. It costs about $100 to rent a parrot and $600 to rent a sheepdog. Men rent big dogs to take on dates to impress women. There are also pet theme parks, where people pay for the privilege of walking a dog for an hour or throwing a frisbee to its waiting jaws.

This is what Julia reads in the doctor's waiting room while Bill has his biweekly appointment. The doctor will probably be pleased at Bill's progress, but they aren't home free yet. He'll have to endure two more rounds of chemotherapy before doctors can be sure that the insurgent cells in his blood won't return. But things seem better. Julia no longer sits there in tears fearing what terrible secrets the doctor is revealing to Bill. Nor does she resort to mathematics, doing tables of nines or elevens, her favorite for some reason, to keep herself occupied. She feels it is all right to pick up a magazine and just browse through, fairly certain that nothing dire will ambush her.

When Bill was really sick that winter, every article seemed to be about cancer or widowhood. But can she become a widow if they aren't even married? That's what's so unfair. Here she is, still in her twenties, thinking about a life ending, wondering where she'll be if this damn thing doesn't go away, wondering what moment its presence will invade.

Maybe she'll be in the hospital giving birth to twins. When the noise and celebration die down, Bill will check out his nagging dizziness and find—what? That he has six or twelve or twenty-four months to live. No wonder Julia never does three or six tables in her mind. And what if they have only twenty-five more years together, a good parcel by some standards, but not enough to do all they have planned, to get married and travel and settle into good jobs and buy a little house and have children and raise them and become comfortable in old age.

When she imagines life without Bill, she pictures herself alone forever, unbearably and unalterably alone for the rest of her life. She'll be someone's aunt or godmother, but that's all the human connection she'll know. Someone else will get her life. Maybe the lady sitting opposite her, dressed in khaki from head to toe. She'll get what Julia and Bill were supposed to have. What will Julia be given instead? A polite note telling her that things don't always work out, a black-edged funereal thing.

Which brings her back to the article and to the first thing she says when Bill comes out of the oncologist's office and matter-of-factly presses her hand and tells her to come on. He's so calm about it now, so pedestrian about his illness—her fate—that it needles her.

"So?" she says in the hallway, which smells oddly of swimming pools.

"So I'm fine."

"That's what you always say. And then later there's more. Something alarming."

"Not this time. There's no problem at all. Only . . ."

She hangs on the word. "Only what?"

"Since my blood count is better, we can resume the chemo any time."

"Why don't we get married right now?"

"You mean *right* now?"

"Not like this second but soon. Before more chemo takes the summer away from us."

"Wasn't there a show, *December Bride?*"

"How do you know shows that are a hundred years old? How old are you, really?"

"You found me out, Julia. I'm a hundred twenty-nine."

By the time they get to Julia's car, they've dropped the subject of marriage. That Julia drives is a ritual they follow on doctor's visit days. It's a remnant from the past when Bill felt too sick to drive on Fridays after the chemo had drained him all week.

They take off into the sunlight, but when Julia approaches their usual route home, she doesn't turn left.

"Where are we going?"

"I have a plan today."

"You have a plan every day. Don't you ever work anymore?"

"Very funny." He knows that her attentiveness to his illness has cost her two jobs. Employers don't really care when you say your boyfriend is sick and you can't come to work. They tend to think it's some excuse, especially when you have a degree in art history and you're miserably underemployed as an office temp. Thank God Bill's equally horrible job in a graphic design firm provides good benefits. If it weren't liberal San Francisco and its AIDS-inspired medical benefits, Bill would be a charity patient. Julia tries to push it out of her mind. If Bill loses his job, and so far through all this he hasn't, he'll lose his insurance too, and no one will hire him again. Life is so unfair, her tears say as she sweeps them away with her forearm. Twice they've cried together, but mainly it's been Julia's tears accompanying every doctor's visit.

"Did I tell you about my friend Yoshi?" Julia asks bravely. She imagines Katherine Hepburn cheering up a serious, glowering Spencer Tracy in her clipped, New England brogue.

"I didn't know you had a friend named Yoshi." Bill is suddenly interested. His look contains rare energy.

"Yoshi lives in Japan in a very small apartment. Unless he wants a goldfish or an ant farm, he can't have a pet."

"I once had an ant farm," Bill offers, "only it didn't turn out so well."

"What happened?"

"I added some ants from my yard to the ants that came with the set. They had a big war and started eating each other."

"Why didn't you take the invaders out?"

"They all looked alike. That's why I put them together in the first place. It wasn't like I mixed red ants with termites or anything."

"Are termites ants?"

"How would I know?"

By this point, Julia has forgotten why she was talking about Yoshi in the first place. Oh yes. She was going to time it just perfectly. They'd be in front of the pet store just as she finished her story. She'd have to tell the rest of the story quickly.

"So Yoshi wanted a pet but he didn't want a goldfish."

"Isn't it poi?"

"Isn't what poi?"

"Those Japanese goldfish you kind of look like the ones with the big bulging eyes and cute lips?"

"Aren't those koi?"

"Right. So Yoshi probably didn't want koi."

"What is it with you? Will you just please listen?"

"Okay," Bill says and nods his head in exaggerated reverence.

"Yoshi went to the pet store. And do you know what?"

"What?"

"He rented a pet."

"Why would he do that?"

"Because space is limited and people in Japan can't own pets, so they rent them for a day."

"That's dumb."

"Not if you long for a pet, for a dog or a cat or a rabbit, for instance."

"I once had a rabbit," Bill says, "that died a slow, sickening death. Its name was Candy."

"I'd ask you why, but all I really want is for you to shut up and get out of the car."

"Why?"

"Because we're in front of a pet store and we're about to choose a pet."

"Why do we need a pet?"

"Because we can't get married." There, she said it. The truth makes her energy dissolve. She doesn't know if she can gather the strength to get out of the car and land her feet on the sidewalk and walk the twelve steps from the curb to the awning that reads "Critterland."

"And why do we need a critter right now?" Bill asks lovingly, quietly, as if he understands that Julia is maybe a little mad, maybe a little dangerous, and needs humoring.

"Because we do," she insists, pulling her legs out of the car and taking Bill's arm. Feeble is what she feels, like an invalid or a cancer patient herself. She hadn't expected that even without the vow, so much of his sickness would become her own.

Inside the shop a nice man offers Julia a chair. It's crammed between a cage holding a white cockatoo that keeps saying "Birdie Birdie" and a gigantic dog, a mastiff, inside a pale blue plastic doghouse shaped like an igloo.

"I'm all right now," she smiles at Bill. "I'm all right," she repeats, as if the customers and proprietor and animals all needed to know.

"We haven't eaten lunch," Bill explains to the man who's provided the chair.

"Well, this isn't a restaurant," he smiles.

"We're here for a pet," Julia replies. Pointing as if into the sun, she squints. "We'll take that one."

The hamster named Blackie lives seven months. When he dies, they bury him in the park across the road because they don't have a house yet or a patch of green to call their own. Bill says a few words about the hamster generations, and Julia cries openly for their sweet first pet. By the time Blackie is buried, Bill has been ill from the treatments and then much better again, so they begin to plan their wedding. When Bill asks Julia if she is going to invite Yoshi, she doesn't take the opportunity to explain her lie. She says that she lost touch with him after high school.

"I wonder if he thinks about you," Bill says.

"Why should he?"

"Because he can't have a pet."

"And?"

"You're like a pet. You're always loyal and happy to see me, and you like to lick me sometimes."

Julia doesn't understand why his joking is making her feel angry. Maybe because things are always a joke to him, even his cancer is a cosmic joke.

"Maybe I'll call Yoshi," Julia says.

"How will you do that if you've lost touch?"

"Maybe someone from high school knows how to find him."

"That'll be easy. He'll be at the Rent-a-Pet concession in Tokyo."

"Let's call right now and ask if he's there."

"Do you know how much it costs to call Japan?"

"More than a hamster?"

"More than a bushel of hamsters."

"That's a terrible thought."

"A bushel of dead hamsters."

"Maybe we shouldn't get married."

"You're sick of me?"

"How did you know?"

"You grind your teeth when we sleep."

"So?"

"That's a sign of frustration."

"Stop listening."

"All right."

"And I don't want to invite Yoshi."

"I know."

"How do you know?"

"Yoshi's some equivalent of Elijah, right?"

"What do you mean?"

"How at a Seder there's a place set for Elijah, who never shows up. Yoshi's the same."

"I still don't get it."

"You talk about Yoshi whenever there's a space between us. When a dangerous little chasm opens up, you Yoshi it together for our sakes."

"I guess so."

"So Yoshi's your imaginary friend."

"I guess so."

Julia feels her face heating up. She doesn't understand why being found out feels so much worse than lying. "Maybe Yoshi's not the equivalent of Elijah. Maybe he's more like your cancer. He's something I have that you can't share."

"But you've just shared him by giving him up."

"So now I'm cancer-free."

They couldn't have predicted the problem with the cottage they rented that spring. What turns out to be mulberries grow on a bushy thing. Whether it's a bush or a tree, Julia can't decide. The mulberries attract a flock of crows that cry out to each other all day and fly in dramatic swooping circles over their little yard.

Bill is thinner now that the cancer has taken permanent residence. He's slower to stand or eat or come to bed. Some days he seems all right, but other ones, Julia has to help him with practically everything. The nurse who stays with him while she goes to work shows her how to fix his IV and what to inject to ease the pain. Things are being managed, the doctor says. Julia doesn't tell the doctor or the nice lady from the hospice that when Bill lies on the front room couch, shadows of crows pass over him as they circle over the eaves of the house. It's terrible for him, Julia imagines, to have his last June on earth full of crows.

After Julia gets home from work each night, she runs out to the garden and attaches more pie tins and tinsel and foil to the scarecrow she's fashioned from an old sundress, her mother's hat, and a yardstick. She doesn't bake, so she has to buy the pie tins at the grocery. Seeing the larger foil pans, the ones for turkey, makes her wince with regret. She's added spatulas and carving forks and a windchime, but so far her design isn't impressing the crows. Her thoughts as she labors to enhance it are the same ones she harbors at work: I'm wasting time I could be spending with Bill. Any day now I will come home and find him gone.

But that isn't really the case. It's more like a long, slow cruise the disease is taking with them. People get married and divorced, have children, change careers, move away, and come back while she and Bill endure whatever comes next. Sometimes at night he whispers things she doesn't want to hear. "It's good we didn't get married," he once whispered. Julia was glad she'd pretended to be sleeping when she saw his breathing chest next to hers and felt grateful they'd been given another day.

Until the crows. "Why have they come?" Bill asks in a plaintive tone that frightens her. Often things she would have found funny—a grown man worrying about crows—are the worst to translate.

"They're here for the mulberries," she reassures.

"They're here for me," he replies.

She tries to reason him out of his mood. "It's an owl that comes. Remember that movie?"

"Or crows," he whispers.

When his mother arrives for her fourth or fifth last visit—they've stopped counting—she agrees that it's terrible to have one's last months invaded by crows. "If they were robins, it would be different," she adds.

"It would be too weird if a hundred robins descended in the yard. Then I'd really be afraid."

Julia and Bill laugh too loudly as they sometimes do when their imaginations manage to transcend their fears.

"Mom's a fan of David Lynch," Bill explains.

"David who?" his mother asks, distracted as she always is when she visits.

But it's his mother's concern with the crows that finally cures Bill. "Everybody eats," Bill tells her reassuringly. "What we have here is a crow buffet."

When no one seems to mind them anymore, as suddenly as they had appeared, the crows are gone.

"I miss the crows," Bill says.

"Me too," Julia adds.

"Time to tear down the scarecrow."

"I'll go do that," Julia smiles.

"You two live in your own little world," Bill's mother says the morning she's to leave for the airport. "You don't even die like normal people," she whispers to Julia. After kissing her son on both cheeks, she makes a beeline for the door where a bored and disheveled cab-driver waits to take her bags.

"We live in our own little world," Bill repeats after his mother has gone.

"Just you and me and it."

"We've known it for how long?"

"Five years and two months."

The night it finally happens, what they talk about less and less, Bill asks Julia to tell him about Yoshi. At first Julia is startled to hear the request. They haven't spoken of Yoshi in months. But the soft, dire whistle of his voice makes Julia want to tell him the best Yoshi story ever.

"Just as Yoshi was getting tired of rent-a-pets," Julia begins, "a one-eyed cat with a bitten ear appears at his door. Now, stray cats are about as rare as unicorns in Tokyo, so Yoshi felt it was a sign. He let in the cat and fed it a bowl of milk and took a long nap with it.

"And the cat became his pet. He kept it inside and flushed its waste down the toilet, so no one ever knew that Yoshi was keeping a pet. Just to be safe he never gave it a name. He imagined the cat wouldn't mind much if instead of one name Yoshi called it all kinds of endearments all the time. 'Come here, little flower,' he'd say, or 'Want some milk, big guy?' Because it had no name, he could always say it was something that had found him for better or worse despite his best efforts not to seek it out."

Even though Bill stops listening at some point in the story, Julia feels that finishing it is important.

"All alone in his room, Yoshi felt complete. Nothing could come between him and his wishes, not even a name."

Satchmo

1.

SYLVIE WAS NEITHER old nor young. She was neither fat nor thin. She lived in the Southwest but missed the Northeast, where she'd spent much of her happy, formerly uncomplicated life. *Where there's snow, there's truth*, she said whenever she needed to fill her buzzing mind with a soothing tune. She loved her husband but wondered why he needed to still call his lover, whom Sylvie referred to simply as Stupid. *Stupid*, Sylvie repeated with love in her voice. After all, he had stayed with Sylvie despite his attachment to her.

He explained that she needed his friendship because she was leaving her husband.

People leave their husbands all the time, Sylvie told him. A majority of women leave their husbands without dragging you in. She can't just stop being a wife. She wants to be *your* wife, Sylvie told him, her voice rising a register above love.

I'll never leave you, he repeated, and Sylvie believed him, despite her fears.

2.

Suppose we play a game, Sylvie said.

What game?

Suppose we pretend I'm Stupid, and you talk to me instead.

What will that prove?

Nothing.

Then why do it?

Because I'm asking you to.

Okay. You start.

Hi, Sylvie said in a meek, zealous voice.

Is that all you're going to say?

What should I say instead?

I quit.

Why do you quit?

Because this isn't fun.

But it's fun to talk to her.

He was silent.

Why can't you just talk to me?

This is how their conversations went.

This is what Sylvie said and thought about too much. If she could just get on with her life. But that didn't seem possible for now.

Once he said she was obsessed. Once he said she was disabled. That made her sad, then angry. She marshalled her forces. She began to get back to work. She smiled again. Had conversations. This made her husband happy. She considered going off the antidepressants she had begun to take after she'd learned of the affair.

I've been good to you all of our life, she said, thinking of the many services she had provided. She was about to list them for him but reminded herself of a commercial and stopped.

I don't want to sound like a commercial, she said.

He smiled vaguely and kissed her. And I hope I've been good to you.

Mostly he had. Mostly Sylvie was satisfied.

If I died today, I'd remember the good things.

Do you have to be so dramatic? he asked.

I didn't cause the drama. I didn't bring danger into our house, she continued. I didn't cast our lives into a cyclone to see where they'd blow. Since she didn't say any of this aloud, he didn't reply. *Where there's snow, there's truth,* she whistled, a five-syllable tune.

3.

I love you as much as your mother, she told him at breakfast.

He put down the grapefruit spoon in midscoop. How can you know that? he asked.

Because I love you like a mother.

What do you mean?

What do mothers always do?

Forgive anything?

4.

How can you fuck a Republican? Sylvie asked.

How do you know she's a Republican?

Don't you know?

I've never asked.

But what about our lives?

What do you mean?

The authenticity of our lives. Do you really hate George Bush or do you just pretend for my sake?

I hate him simply and fully.

And Nixon and Ford and Reagan and Bush's dad too?

Of course.

Don't you cheer Geraldo Rivera for being a liberal despite his distasteful personality?

Sure.

Then how can't you know?

We don't talk about politics.

What do you talk about then?

Once she said she was sorry she couldn't talk intellectually with me like you do.

Humph! Sylvie said aloud.

Humph! she repeated during the day, time and again, half mantra, half snort. She began to wonder if people were noticing. Maybe Esther the checkout clerk, who always wore purple accessories at the grocery, or her mother, whom she called once a week on Tuesdays.

Maybe the sound was more like a cloak. A cloak of reason, a richly embroidered word that said in a comforting way that all life was a lie, a complex deep lie, as deep and complex as her love for him.

5.

I'm thinking of becoming a children's writer, Sylvie said.

He raised his eyes from the *Times*.

I have four ideas for books.

What are they? he asked.

The first is *Ethnic Cleansing for Children*.

That's not very funny.

The second is the O.J. Simpson murder story from Kato's point of view.

Kato Kaelin?

Kato the dog. All he'll say is *arf* but we'll get a good illustrator.

I think they renamed him.

Kato Kaelin?

I think they renamed Kato the dog.

Who's they?

O.J.'s older son.

What's his new name?

Satchmo.

Maybe the book can have music like *Really Rosie*. Remember when that was Wayne's favorite book?

He didn't remember, he said.

People are fickle, Sylvie added. Poor dog. They shared a commiserating glance.

So do you want to know the third?

Sure.

Charlotte the Harlot based on *Charlotte's Web*. The fourth is a story Wayne told me. He said he saw a news show about a whole family with flippers instead of hands. So I thought about a narrative poem for kids. How's this? She picked up the journal with the paisley cover she had recently acquired:

Judy wanted to be a stripper / but her hand was a long skinny flipper.

It scans.

Her father tried being a plumber / but his hands were named Dumb and Dumber.

Can we have supper now?

There's more. Her mother tried fashioning braids / but her hands were weak and afraid.

I smell something cooking. What are we having?

Scrod. Remember that joke?

No.

Where in this town can a girl get scrod?

The answer is Boston.

What answer?

A girl can get Boston scrod.

There's a new song Wayne listens to, "Californication." Wayne asked me what it meant.

What did you tell him?

I told him it was a neologism.

What did Wayne say?

He rolled his eyes at me. So I said it meant copulation.

And then what?

And then Wayne asked what that meant.

And what did you say?

I said *fucking*.

So Wayne's learning a lot of good words.

That's because I'm a good mother. I bet Stupid doesn't teach her kids the useful Anglo-Saxon words. I bet they say *pantaloons* and *neckerchiefs* because of her, and other kids laugh and point and think they have the cooties.

C'mon, Sylvie. Try to be a little normal.

Humph! Sylvie said. This time the word felt like a purr or a tickle in her throat.

6.

The man who asked Sylvie to sleep with him wasn't unappealing, except for his crepey neck, his little gray ponytail, and his silly European-style sandals, but Sylvie was against revenge. She thanked him for the nice offer and went back to the school book sale, where she was buying lots of children's books, none as inspired as the ones she was inventing by the minute: *The Plague Visits Johnny, A Month of Menstruation, Roald Dahl Must Die.*

I'm not going to sleep with him, Sylvie said that night in bed.

Who is that?

You don't know him. He's an urban planner. Or maybe you do.

So do I or don't I? I have a better idea. Don't tell me.

Okay, I won't, Sylvie smiled, and turned her back to him. She remembered another strange moment when she'd been surprised by a come-on. Back in Massachusetts, his old boss, the one whose eyebrows looked like vulture wings, had been in an empty hallway with her. She was three months pregnant with Wayne and feeling a little dowdy when he said, You have a luscious waist.

It's not to eat, Sylvie had said quietly, and he had subsided.

Maybe I'm too literal, she said to his back.

What do you mean? he asked sleepily.

She could tell by his voice that she'd startled him awake.

Maybe I take things at a level of interpretation different than others.

Like what?

Like our marriage vow.

Please don't start up.

Well, let's talk about fishing then.

We never have gone fishing.

Then I guess it's a bad topic.

He reached his hand under her nightgown. Sylvie, I love you. Just leave it at that.

And you love her?

I love you.

And someone else?

For a second he looked at her with anger, like maybe he would strangle her.

I'm trying to be patient and objective, Sylvie offered, but this is pretty personal.

When he remained silent, she got out of bed and sat on the toilet. She wasn't going to cry again. It wasn't useful to waste your tears. She pictured them as a depletable resource like fossil fuels. *Humph!* Sylvie shouted.

What did you say?

Something like *humph*.

Please come back to bed.

What's the use?

I want to tell you about a children's book I'm going to write.

Good night, Sylvie said, before she quietly got back under the covers and closed her eyes with malice.

7.

This is the Republican party taking a survey, Sylvie said into the phone. She kept her hand cupped over her mouth, so her voice wouldn't be in any way familiar. Are you available for a survey?

I'm afraid not, the other voice said. I'm quite busy.

What are you currently doing?

The other voice hesitated, then hung up the phone.

Ultimate proof: not only was she a Republican, she lacked a sense of fair play.

8.

Would you say our humor's offbeat? she asked him.

Whose humor?

Ours, of course.

Sure, why?

I'm just taking a survey.

She looked in his face for a recognition of these words. Had the Republican-in-camouflage told him of the call?

Of course our humor's offbeat, but Sylvie, you've got to relax.

Okay. I have a joke.

You never tell jokes.

I never do anything. I just sit here while you do incomprehensible things. Maybe that's the joke.

Seizing on a feeling of panic that began in her chest and ascended her neck to her chin to her nose to her forehead like a rock climber, she picked up a local phone book and threw it in his direction.

It's decided. We'll buy a new mattress, he said, pointing to the page it had fallen open to.

9.

Wayne told her another story. There was a village in Guatemala where people had hair covering their whole faces. He said it was wavy, dark hair when she asked further details.

Where do you see these things?

On the news, Wayne replied.

Bizarro news?

Regular news, Mom.

Probably there's every kind of person in the world. Smart people, dumb people, nice people, awkward people.

Mom, what's the point? Wayne asked.

What am I?

You're my mom, Wayne smiled. His smile was still a little goofy, the hybrid smile of a baby and a man.

What, Wayne asked, are you looking at?

I've always liked your smile.

Thanks.

You're welcome.

Does Dad still see that whack lady?
I don't know.
Do you have a boyfriend?
No way.
They both laughed.

10.

That winter she knew his affair was over though she didn't know why it had ended or exactly when. She could tell by the way he sighed and looked at her bashfully, almost with mortification, that he had come to his senses. She knew from his sad downcast eyes at dinner and the tenderness in his hands when he touched her in bed. Maybe the Republican had cast him aside for a banker or a mortician or an official party member. Maybe he had simply looked up one day and asked himself what he was doing.

Sylvie decided not to ask. Someday, maybe with tears in his eyes, he'd tell her all the gory details. The many books on affairs, which she'd taken to reading in bookstores but never buying, said this was a necessary part of the healing process, but Sylvie wasn't sure. All she knew was that this was life with its *humphs* and sighs and its resilient moments of forgiveness and love, which, unlike tears, were as vast as Siberia.

Onto the Past

HEN *SONG OF A BEDWETTER* hit the stores, Bryce Conway was already in the embryonic stages of a second and third memoir, *Win One for Myself,* about the false accusations of sexual harassment he had faced at work, and *Onto the Past,* about his stepfather's cross-dressing. He was about to begin the twenty-nine city reading tour that would take him to Texarkana, Rancho Cucamonga, Chilocothe, and Industry, West Virginia, among other places, when he got the call.

"It's Oprah!" Tammy shouted. She was planning on leaving Bryce in the next few months but would wait for this tally to register before speaking further to her divorce lawyer.

Bryce had never imagined when he enrolled in the writing therapy class at the Clear Lake Community Center that his silenced self would be able to produce so many lucrative words so quickly.

"You're a pro," Holly Levis told him after they finished celebrating by doing it doggie-style at The Rushes, the new motel on the side of town only tourists and lovers had come to know. Bryce uncorked the Cook's and let it flow onto Holly's small breasts. He took one in his mouth and licked its delicate nipple. He had never poured champagne on Tammy in twenty-two years. That was proof enough that Holly was different. Now that he was going to be famous, he probably needed a new wife anyway, one who understood his heart and its desperate language.

But he wasn't going to commit to Holly just yet. This reading tour would be fertile ground, he was sure, for women like Holly, who recognized his talent. He remembered the first time he read from *Song of a Bedwetter* at Waldenbooks. A pretty, bucktoothed woman in the back of the store had approached him after the reading and asked him out for a drink. What was he thinking that night when he said, like a schoolboy, that he was expected home? Of course, Tammy was already prepared to shoot him for what had happened at his former job. He was in the process of not messing things up further, he told himself, though all the way home he regretted not having taken the opportunity to kiss the woman's dishevelled mouth and to go on from there.

What had happened at work was a familiar story all around the United States today. In every city, town, and suburban office complex, men were losing their jobs for a simple caress in the copy room or a compliment at the water cooler. In his case, they said, it was a pattern of harassment directed at one woman in particular, his former boss Xenia Custor, who, after demotion, was back near his cubicle selling car insurance over the phone. First he tossed a few notes over the partition. "You're beautiful when you're angry, and you're always angry." "For a mature gal, you have great legs," no more potent or harmful than Valentine's hearts or the pithy messages of encouragement one finds inside fortune cookies. One night after working late on a marketing project, he drove Xenia to the park-and-ride and touched her in the car, claiming she had wanted it for years. The result was a rapid hearing and dismissal. After the initial shock, he thought of bringing suit until in his unemployment he found the writing group and realized there was a better and more direct way to exact revenge.

Tammy wept angry tears when Bryce was let go, his pension lost, his reputation sullied, but finally had said, "I'm not named Tammy for nothing. I stand by you, honey." When it turned out there were other women ready to come forth with stories of their own, when the company sent agreements for him to sign that promised he wouldn't take legal action if they wouldn't press formal charges, Tammy grew unsettled. She stopped looking at Bryce and even talking much except for the necessary exchange of messages about whether Heather, their only child away at college, could have a Discover card, or whether Bryce had washed their limping German shepherd Hank as Tammy had asked before going off to work.

She was the breadwinner now and had succeeded in getting two promotions since he'd lost his job. They called her a go-getter in the Home Equity Department. "Someone has to keep our tract house in green paint," she joked with coworkers in the Wells Fargo housing loan department, where she worked a six-day week. Fueled by the growth of the untrendy town that was becoming an outlying suburb during the economic boom, her department was swamped with applications for loans. If the week had nine days, she could work all of them, she told Bryce when she came home weary but happy at the end of the day and put her feet up on the redwood burl table they had bought the first year of their marriage. It had been over a year, and sometimes she felt herself forgiving him. She remembered the Bryce of old, the shortstop on her co-ed softball team, the man who could sing great imitations of Hank Williams's "Hey, Good-Lookin'" and love her like no one she had ever met.

But the new Bryce had become a danger to herself and others, first with his behavior and then with his word processor. Who wants to be known as the wife of a bedwetting, woman-harassing, son of a cross-dresser? This was the information that Bryce stayed home to leak to the world? This was his excuse for not getting a day job? Tammy had imagined that Bryce would be producing pirate adventures or cowboy novels set in the high golden hills above their town. Maybe he could write a book like *The Bridges of Madison County*, a love song to their enduring marriage, bathtub scene and all. Who needed to know these dark swarming secrets about Bryce? It was like opening a lingerie door and finding it crawling with ants. Maybe Bryce should see a therapist, but who could afford therapy with only one job and an expensive daughter in college, who had her hopes set on seven more years including veterinary school?

Maybe this Holly person was out to humiliate her students, Tammy thought, as she steered her shopping cart to the Martha Stewart collection of bedding at K-Mart. Whenever she was upset, she bought new sheets. These had muted blue tulips on a dull yellow background, how tulips might look in France. Tammy had never been to France, but this Holly probably had. Teaching the writing group was her only job, this class of screw-ups and Peter Pans at the rec center. Probably Holly had a rich husband in the wine trade or a dead husband with a trust fund. Maybe this Holly, like so many wealthy women who had attended fancy Eastern schools—Bryce told Tammy she'd gone to Vassar—was a member of a feminist coven whose mission was to shame and expose ordinary people. Devil's work directed at the middle class, devious class warfare by aristocratic missionaries of ill-will. All

those dance and art and rebirth therapists set to make fools of ele-
phantine women who could neither paint nor lift a leg rhythmically if
their lives depended on it. All those men crawling on the floor without
shoes, wailing as they remembered birth traumas. Tammy had seen a
show about it and thought it not the least bit funny. Until a while back
Bryce had been her companion in wry laughter. He made jokes about
everything, even signers for the deaf at football games, until he joined
the writing group and the victim brigade like everyone else. And here
was a national heroine, a billionaire, in fact, agreeing that Bryce's writing was fine, honest, brave, and wanting the American people to know.
Who could argue with Oprah?

Wobbling under the weight of Oprah's judgment, Tammy set out
to educate herself before making any more decisions about Bryce. She
told the lawyer, a handsome young man named Mark Gomez-Parilla,
who'd been calling her weekly since their first meeting, that she hadn't
made any decisions. Because she didn't want the local library or bookstore to think she was some kind of deviant, she went online and
ordered memoirs by women who had been raped, badly burned, born
without noses, abused by their brothers, husbands, lovers, and attacked
by wolves and pit bulls. She bought books by men who had had disap-
proving mothers, psychotic wives, overbearing coaches, exploitative
teachers, and sadistic fathers. One man in Idaho had been born with a
sexually ambiguous organ and changed into a girl. One girl in
Scranton, New Jersey, had been born with what looked like a penis and
raised as a man. One Nebraska college dean well into his seventies was
a recovering sexual predator. One Long Island priest had fucked every
woman member of his church under fifty in his three-year tenure. One
bearded rabbi had had an affair with the only female rabbi in his district of Northern Ohio. One Tennessee man who had grown up to be
a fine husband and father had killed seven cats and three dogs before
he was eleven. One New York psychiatrist had forced her adopted son
to perform oral sex on her every night for seven years. One young
Latino in South Central L.A. had killed someone with a screwdriver
before finding Jesus. One Filipino nurse in Utah had put four elderly
patients to death after finding Jesus and was awaiting execution herself.
Tammy suddenly felt sick at heart. The number of loans she was writing plummeted, and she was advised to go on Prozac by a sympathetic

young HMO doctor, who appeared to be quietly weeping behind his shaded glasses as he wrote her a prescription.

She had never known how much chaos was in the world until Oprah discovered Bryce and set Tammy on her path of self-education. Given what the other various confessors were up to and had perpetrated, Bryce was hardly in contention. He was mild and innocent as springtime. She thought of the analogies on Heather's SATs. Bryce Conway is to vice as a pond is to an ocean. If the analogies had been that easy, Heather might be attending Harvard. Maybe with the Oprah deal, she could transfer to an Ivy League school from Chico State. Maybe Tammy would keep Bryce after all. Judging from the present dangers presented in these books, he was a safe harbor with a slightly rickety pier.

Did any women in Ohio wear underwear? The first two nights of bookstore appearances made Bryce think that the undergarment dress code for girls under twenty had definitely changed, at least in Chilicothe. He tried not to remind himself that Heather was just a tad younger than Diana and Tiffany, but as Diana, a former bedwetter herself said, his book had really spoken to her. That was how conversations with women began. Usually they or their sons or their brothers had been bedwetters, and his memoir, the story of his suffering, his mother's patience, and his stepfather's cruelty, had been illuminating. Then usually several drinks, over which they'd linger. Diana liked something called a Cosmopolitan. Tiffany was a fan of Long Island iced tea. Didn't anyone have Scotch and soda anymore except him and Tammy?

Sometimes he missed her soft predictable presence, her long-term love for him despite the nuisance he'd become. There was no nonsense about her, and there never had been. She could cuss a blue streak. There was no coyness about sex either. These girls with their lack of underwear don't have inhibitions or the need to play games until he sometimes grew sleepy, then bored. Soon he realized that going to their places worked better than inviting them back to the hotel. That way he could leave before committing himself to spending the night. Back at the hotel, he'd press his eyes under the pillow and call home and hear Tammy sweetly say that she missed him. He even thought of inviting her to join him on the trip, especially after Holly Levis told him not to call her at home again, that there were some limits to her interest in him as a teacher and special friend. "I miss you," he told Tammy, just hours after Tiffany had held him between her legs and said she never got orgasms. "I miss you too," her sleepy voice replied, and he knew she meant it.

The televised segment with Oprah was over in a flash and barely remembered by the country, which was fixed on another of Oprah's guests that day. The *TV Guide* said "Reading Programs with First Lady Laura Bush and a bedwetter's debut book." "A bedwetter's debut book," Bryce half-snorted in the limo that took him to her studio. He'd never been to Chicago before, was impressed by its chill wind and lakefront and great architecture. Maybe he and Tammy should start a new life in this City of Big Shoulders, this city of immigrants from war, pestilence, famine, segregation, and midlife crises. Maybe in a high-rise facing the lake built by some architect whose German-sounding name kept slipping from his mind, she'd forgive him forever. He'd tell her once and for all that he was sorry for being such a fool for so long. Maybe that was the meaning of Holly's message and this trip to Harpo Studios and his meeting with the First Lady, who asked him and his wife to come to dinner at the White House.

"You'll never believe this," he told Tammy on the phone. "Laura Bush wants us over for dinner."

"Better pull the plug on your Xenia harassment project," Tammy said, "before they decide you're a security risk."

"You're right about that," Bryce smiled through the phone, a desperate toothy grin. Instead of feeling ravenous as he had for several years now for women and sex and drinks and food and recognition, he suddenly felt a little queasy. But it was a pleasant sickness that gripped him equally all over his body like a terrible hug. It was the universe telling him to shape up. It was the whole world telling him to cancel the rest of the tour and go home and on his knees if necessary tell Tammy that she was his prescription for healing, his only hope at rescue, his Twelve Step Program and his road to forgiveness. He wouldn't write a word about it forever—that would be his promise and his salvation.

Jeopardy

"CORTEZ STREET, MA," I shout into the phone. "Didn't you grow up on Cortez?"

"Yes," my mother says quietly, suspiciously, as if I've called to finger her in some crime.

"Well, guess what? I read that Saul Bellow grew up on Cortez Street too."

Silence and breath. I can see her reclining on her striped couch, glazed with medication, trying to watch *Jeopardy*. How do I always manage to call during her favorite half hour of the day?

"And so I was wondering, since you're about the same age, did you know him?"

"How should I know?"

"Wouldn't you remember if you knew Saul Bellow?"

"That was seventy-five years ago."

"But wouldn't you . . . ?"

"What, I'm six or seven, that's when I lived there, and maybe I played with some little boy . . ."

". . . named Saul?" I coax.

"Why not? Half the boys I knew had names like that."

"Ma, do you know who Saul Bellow is?"

"Maggie, for heaven's sakes . . ."

"Well, wouldn't you remember? The guy got a Nobel Prize."

"There was a little Italian, Sal something, with eyes like green olives and a smile . . ."

"So you do remember . . ."

"But no Saul," she says decisively. "Wait a minute, there was also a Sol something. His father was a third-rate gangster. He didn't even have bodyguards he was so unimportant."

"A midlist gangster," I joke to myself. "Not enough sales. Dropped by his publisher."

"Maggie, what are you yakking about? Did you call to wish me happy birthday? I'm in the middle of double jeopardy."

"Who's winning?"

"Not me, I can tell you that."

"And didn't Dad live on LeMoyne?" I add. "Bellow lived there too."

"Dad lived everywhere because his folks couldn't pay the rent. They'd move out in the middle of the night like gypsies. From week to week when we were dating, I didn't know where your father lived."

"Why did you move away from Cortez?"

"My grandmother got the building from Harry's fruit store earnings. Fruit was big then. But somehow she lost it, and we moved away too."

"But no time during your years on Cortez did you ever know a kid named Saul? He was probably kind of slight and I'd imagine extremely intelligent." *Ma'am,* I almost say, as homage to Jack Webb in *Dragnet.*

"Half my neighborhood was Jews and Italians, and if they're anything, they're small and intelligent. There was this Sal Magnani, like the actress. Such a mouth on that kid."

"What do you mean?"

"The things he said to me, Maggie, all about love when we're what? Eight years old? I wonder about him now and then."

"But no Saul Bellow?"

"Will you leave me alone? Forty years old, you still pester me like a kid in a car—'Are we there yet? Are we there yet?'—What did he write anyway?"

"Lots of things."

"Did he write *Exodus?*"

"That's Leon Uris."

"How about *A Tree Grows in Brooklyn?*"

"Ma, he grew up on your street in Chicago. Why would he write about Brooklyn?"

"Why do you write about all kinds of places, Miss Smarty Pants? He won a Nobel Prize. Can't he write about wherever he pleases?"

"It's a free country, but he didn't write those things, Ma. *Mr. Sammler's Planet, Herzog,* he wrote lots of other things."

"There's an actor named Herzog."

"Maybe."

"Which reminds me of Ben someone . . . Ben Gazzara. Do you think he's Jewish?"

"Why?"

"I don't know. Maybe he is."

"So how are you celebrating your birthday?"

"I'm going out with some of the girls."

"Those eighty-year-old girls?"

"Some are, some aren't. And I'm looking in my old yearbook."

"You have a yearbook from then?"

"Cameron School. I made up the class song. Want to hear it? *The Cameron School loves springtime / when children dance and sing / etc. etc. / and now here comes our Molly / at recess in the ring,* etc. etc."

"Nice song, Ma. Who was Molly?"

"Some little brat with big curls. Everyone liked her, but I didn't really."

"So why did you put her in your song?"

"Later in the song she rhymes, but I don't remember with what."

"And in that yearbook, is there a Saul Bellow?"

"How should I know?"

"Is there an index, Ma? Are there names?"

"If you discovered I sat next to Saul Bellow and watched his nose run, so what?"

"Then you could say . . ."

"Maggie, I don't care."

"Then *I* could say . . ."

"So tell your friends whatever."

"What do you mean, Ma?"

"Think of all the people I've known. Think of the people I must have forgotten. Make up some story about me and Saul Bellow. How in the hell will anyone know the difference?"

"But I'll know, Ma."

"You mean everything you say is true all the time? All that stuff in your novel about me and your father, how we fell in love, how he got that camera . . ."

"That wasn't you and Dad."

"That lady Ivy, she's my age. She has my same hair. She makes my same jokes, Maggie, the one about the golfer, and she's not me?"

"Not really."

"And Stan? Short and sweet, quiet, with a radio all the time. That's not Dad?"

"Maybe it's a little of Dad."

"So take Cameron School and change the song. Molly can be Solly, easy enough."

"Ma!"

"You have no courage, Maggie."

"You have no shame."

"Where can shame get me? I'm eighty years old."

"Ma, will you do me one favor?"

"Only one?"

"Ask your friends." My mother's group of friends has stayed together. It's one of the benefits of living in the city of your birth. "Maybe one of them remembers Saul Bellow."

"And if she does, though I doubt it, what should she do?"

"She shouldn't do anything. You just tell me next time we talk."

"And when will that be?"

"Same as usual." Our weekly routine for the decades that a continent has separated us, that and Christmas visits.

"And if she doesn't?"

"Then she doesn't, Ma."

"Seems to me, Maggie, that you're putting too many eggs in one basket. Why don't I ask around? I bet everyone knows someone famous. It's a small world."

"That's true. But I'm interested . . ."

"You're making me crazy, Maggie. I know. You're looking for the whereabouts of this Bellow on Cortez."

"I know where he lives. He lives in Boston. I just want to find out if anyone remembers him."

"Does this Bellow have children?"

"Yes."

"Well, I hope they remember him on his birthday. It's lonelier for men, I think, after a wife passes."

"But his wife didn't pass. He's had tons of wives."

"Like Elizabeth Taylor?"

"She's had tons of husbands."

"What I mean is, this Bellow guy, he just sleeps around?"

"He marries them, Ma. It doesn't work out. He tries again."

"Like you and Sam."

"Sam and I have been together for fourteen years. What are you saying?" I know what she's saying. She still misses my first husband Arthur, the pathological liar. If I called Arthur now, he'd tell me he knew Saul Bellow, no problem.

"Well, I'm glad your Mr. Bellow never laid eyes on me. A man like that is no good. You tell Sam to be good to you, Maggie."

"He is good to me."

"If he's so good, why are you trying to find out about this mamser, Bellow?"

"Curiosity, Ma. Forget it."

"It's forgotten."

"Then we'll talk next week?"

"If I'm alive. Only one thing, Maggie."

"What Ma?"

"Forget about Bellow. He's a gonif. He steals hearts. I saw a nice writer on Larry King. The guy who wrote *Kovacic Park.*"

"Michael Crichton wrote *Jurassic Park.* The Kovacics lived near us on Euclid. They had a construction company and a Croatian *oompah* band. All their wives were always pregnant."

"Well, this writer on Larry King, he's rich and handsome too, better looking than your Sam. Why not find out about him?"

"I read about Bellow and Cortez Street. They take him back to the street and show him his old house."

"What's there to see?"

"Ma, thanks for your time."

"I have lots of time, Maggie. But you could do better to think about something important, maybe."

"It was important to me whether you knew him, that you both lived on Cortez. I was excited about it."

"Okay, he was my best friend. We sat in the big elm together. The city's probably chopped it down by now. We sang songs. One summer I taught him how to read. Boy, was he a smart cookie. About the time his mother died, he took comfort in my arms."

"How did you know his mother died?"

"I'm making it up, Maggie, like you do. It isn't so hard. When his mother died, I helped him a lot. I really did."

"This is pretty good, Ma."

"Maybe I should write stories?"

"Why not?"

"I'll send you one, and you can tell me what you think."

"You will, Ma? That's great."

"I can tell you anything, Maggie, my empty little head. What won't you believe?"

"I believe my mother. Mothers don't lie."

"Boy, you are something."

"I'd better let you go. Final jeopardy must be looming."

"I wasn't going to say a word, but I already missed it, Sweetie. Know why?"

"Why?"

"Because I'm a good mother."

"You are."

"A better mother than that Saul Bellow. A better family, I bet I have."

"Who's to know?"

"I'll ask around. Maybe Florence knows this heartbreaker Bellow. She's been with lots of men."

"Little Florence with the enormous nose?"

"Maggie, she was a beauty. You wouldn't believe it. Men lined up for her. You know how I really met Dad?"

"How?"

"He was standing in line for Florence, but I stole him away. Like that Bellow fellow, I just took off with him. For years he was my slave of love. Put that in one of your books, Maggie. Tell it like it is."

Cloris

T NINETY-TWO most people don't begin new careers or new anything. Most stare into space holding baby dolls while people at the retirement home call them Grandpa or Ida or Sweetie. But Cloris is different. At eighty-nine she got two new knees, and today we're here, me and my sister Tess, to watch her debut. Our stepmother is part of a fashion show. What the organizers make on this event will raise money for more varied entertainment for the seniors. Cloris is on the entertainment committee too. She says she signed up for it because she got sick of bingo. Getting sick of bingo was her inspiration. Her knees were her courage.

"Frankly," Tess says to me under her breath, "some of these models need masks." Tess's chestnut hair is in long curls that frame her face. She has looked essentially the same since we were girls. "I was thinking that old folks homes could buy baby seal masks and make the inmates wear them on visiting days," she continues.

I smile at my older, irrepressible sister. Oblivious to Tess, Cloris smiles too. She's in her small, cluttered room dressing for the event. "I'm into everything now," she explains. "I made a picture frame from macaroni the other day and painted it silver. Imagine what your father would say to that." Her wide stockinged foot enters a large satin flat.

I can remember when Cloris was our new stepmother and that smile which we've known now for more than three decades had seemed sinister.

After our mother died, Dad was beside himself. They had been close even though the closeness wasn't always sweet. Sometimes at night we heard them shouting and throwing objects. Tess and I would jump into her bed and pull the quilt over us and put our heads together and begin to purr as loudly as we could. We were two noisy cats, and our purring and licking and general cat behavior got us through many nights of strife. But they loved each other, that was clear, and they were close as a couple could be. Mom finished Dad's thoughts, and he didn't object. Dad knew exactly how to make Mom laugh. Whether it was the witty things he said about art (they were both trained as art historians) or the awkward pantomimes he did to please her as he went about daily tasks—John Wayne with a lawnmower, Quasimodo of the woodpile, Charlie Chaplin of the art gallery—there was only one time when Mom was animated, and that was in his presence. She was otherwise shy and a little morose. Maybe because she had never had a real mother herself and hardly a father, only a series of indifferent aunts. "I was an add-on," Mom once explained, "Like a rec room or finished basement. I'm very lucky I met your father," she told us, "and you're very lucky to have two parents who wanted you so much." Then she'd kiss us with too much feeling and get back to her work.

My parents were best when they kept busy and my mother's fierce energy had an outlet. They ran a small art gallery together, and they were never happier than when they put up shows or had openings or expanded the business. They were perfect partners until Mom got sick.

We think Dad met Cloris after Mom died, not before. She wasn't anything like Mom. First, she didn't have the brainpower of our mother, who had escaped her miserable foster childhood by going to college very young and staying there a long time. Mom had lived in New York and had had a few serious romances before she ever met Dad. She was a brilliant student before she moved with him to Chicago to open the gallery. Cloris had been to college later in life. In fact, Dad met her when she was looking for an internship for a class she was taking at the Art Institute and called his gallery. Sure, he'd be glad to help a student. Maybe Dad pictured someone almost the age of his daughters. Then Cloris showed up at the door, newly divorced, an ingenue at most everything, ready to learn whatever Dad could teach her. Wide-eyed and a little slow-witted, she exuded the pleasing calm and immutability of a still life.

We were only sixteen and seventeen then and still recovering from Mom's quick and tragic death, a disease of the blood, so the details of my Dad's courtship, furtive and shy anyway, are sketchy. I can imagine late Chicago afternoons, long shadows, a chill wind, Cloris answering the phone at the cozy gallery in her sweet somewhat foreign-sounding voice, and Dad suddenly feeling that maybe he could finally go on after months of staggering through life. Soon he was buying us TV dinners and calling to say he'd be home late, which was all right with us. High school became one extended party at our house. By the time Dad got home, we'd have cleared out our friends, vacuumed the front room, washed the glasses, poured more water into the vodka and gin bottles, and begun our homework.

"I had work to do," he'd say at first. Then he slowly started introducing the subject of Cloris as if she were a destination on the globe. "Cloris and I had dinner" sounded like "Bermuda is best in spring" to our unaccustomed ears. We had never really traveled though Mom and Dad had sometimes taken buying trips all over the globe. We saved their postcards to play a game about the places they'd seen, wondering whether we'd ever get to Florence or Paris or even New York as our wordly parents had.

Once Cloris came into our lives, we traveled too. Apparently running the business without us became more difficult after Mom's death. Suddenly Dad wanted our opinions, so we went to art fairs and auctions all over the place in late springs and early summers. "I think that's nice," Cloris would say about almost anything framed, and her taste in sculpture was downright perverse. If something was dowdy or misshapen, she'd encourage Dad to buy it as if she were trying to adopt misfits. So Dad came to depend on us, especially Tess, who called a spade a spade. I remember a bronze that captured Cloris's attention. It was of a woman getting ready for a bath, only her hands were misshapen and she rose from a great clot of something liquidy and incomprehensible.

"What do you think?" Cloris asked as she led us to her treasure.

"I think it's too bad the artist died before he finished this one," Tess said with great seriousness.

"I didn't know that," Cloris responded. "You girls do know your art," she added brightly.

"Want to go to Paris next spring?" Dad asked the summer before Tess's senior year. The question, which left us hysterical with anticipation, was followed by a long pause. While we cheered and chattered about what we'd need and what the other kids would say about our glamorous destination, Dad quickly added the following: "Cloris at work would like to have us over for dinner."

Tess and I looked at each other, bewildered. Paris disappeared as unexpectedly as it had arrived in the conversation. We were wild, motherless girls without a father for months now. What was this thing called dinner? What was this thing called Cloris?

"Who's that?" Tess asked pointedly.

"That nice lady who's come to work for me."

"That strumpet?" she asked. Tess was a great reader, and strumpet must have been a new vocabulary word.

"What's a strumpet?" I asked.

"Never mind. Cloris is a nice lady who helps me a lot. She just wants to give you kids a warm meal."

"We can cook for ourselves if you haven't noticed," Tess replied.

"Sounds good to me," my hungry mouth said, and Dad smiled as widely as I'd seen in years.

Cloris lived in a little apartment near Lincoln Park Zoo. She appeared to be a refugee from some country with lots of plastic and not much else. There were no antiques or paintings, which covered our house richly. Her walls were largely bare except for a little Matisse print in the kitchen, framed in paper and thumbtacked to the wall, and a glossy plaque in the bathroom that said something Swedish. There were no family photos except for several of a rather homely girl at various stages of development.

"Who's this?" Tess asked, carrying the photo across the room to Cloris's small galley kitchen. "She sure has big ears."

"My daughter," Cloris said a little sadly.

"Where is she?" Tess continued. I had guessed maybe dead from the weight of Cloris's response.

"In Minnesota with my husband."

"Must take after the husband," Tess added casually.

Minnesota explained a lot of things: Cloris's loneliness here, her desire to meet new people, her light blue eyes and attractive blonde hair, which was beginning to turn white. We had been a dark family. My parents had looked more like brother and sister: small, wiry, large-eyed, quick, and intelligent. Cloris looked big and calm, like a statue of a saint or a ship's masthead.

Dinner with the masthead was a quiet affair. The food was ample and much better than TV dinners but Tess did her best to even some scores.

"My mother was very intelligent and beautiful," Tess told Cloris for no apparent reason.

"Robert's been telling me that," Cloris said softly.

"His name is Bob. Everyone calls him Bob," Tess added with impatience.

"I always liked Robert," I added, feeling a little traitorous.

Robert or Bob stared at his plate, waiting for the endless moment to pass. Dinner was like the painting "Nude Descending a Staircase," a series of awkward poses framed by Tess's interruptions.

Probably Dad's usual dinners with Cloris were passionate affairs. From what I remember of my youth, having to eat in those first heady days of love is more a burden than a need. Probably she and Robert frequently skipped the appetizer, entree, and dessert in favor of her bedroom, which I had quickly surveyed when I left my coat on the bed. She had a white chenille bedspread. There were definitely two pillows. In the bathroom, I saw an extra toothbrush even though my father had never stayed the night. Maybe it was her hope or the promise he'd left her with one night when he made yet another excuse for getting home to his girls.

I thought of my mother, victim of the Depression and her own parents' tragedies, shifting from house to house like an unloved curio, a lamp, say, with an ugly base. We should count our blessings that our father came home at all, I thought while Tess provoked and prodded and generally ran amok. Feeling urgently grateful, I smiled wide at Dad and Cloris. My sister gave me a chilling look. I would hear about this later, I was sure. I was the dog and Tess the cat. I would pant loyally at Dad's feet no matter who he took up with. With one year to go before college, Tess was about to make her cat-like exit.

The summer after that, Cloris and Dad were married. Her own daughter Leala was allowed to come to the wedding but could stay only three days. The Friday before the wedding she arrived at O'Hare and Robert, as he was now called by everyone but Tess, took Cloris to meet her.

Leala was two years older than Tess, three years older than me. Cloris had left her husband the year Leala began college, where she was now a junior majoring in something called "information engineering." Even though she was older than us, she seemed younger, as if losing a mother to choice rather than necessity delays one's maturity. It was the opposite with us. While Mom was dying, we were making leaps and bounds in our maturation process. The world wasn't going to play any more tricks on either of us. I was going to learn to take care of myself by force of will and my general good nature. Wagging my tail, I would be friendly and get through life. I would hide my flaws, making myself as likeable as a mutt from a shelter, more enthusiastic than accomplished at dog tricks.

It was harder for Tess, whose scrappy insolence was a banner of her independence and her need. She clawed too much and sometimes actually bit, I saw it the weekend of Dad's wedding. She presented Leala with a sheaf of memories, a cheery retrospective of all the less than cheery dinners we'd endured since our mother had died. What Cloris cooked, what she said, what she gave us for Christmas were registered with the exactitude my parents saved for gallery catalogues. Leala, already a girl who showed little emotion, seemed to grow smaller and smaller as Tess continued. Finally, out of discomfort for the angular blonde from the North country, I interrupted with the story of our mother's unfortunate death. We have sadness to share, I tried to tell her, diverting Tess's belated onslaught of false good cheer.

The wedding passed quietly and tastefully in our front room with only a handful of friends and relatives and a bewildered minister who, out of respect for the mixed marriage of Lutheran and Jew, kept Jesus and even God out of the ceremony. My father and stepmother promised very little to each other, exchanged simple rings, and kissed with trepidation.

The following summer when Leala came to visit, things were more normal. I was a senior in high school. Tess was majoring in protests at the University of Wisconsin. Her personal edge had been recruited to serve a larger political cause. She was therefore able to be kinder to Cloris and Leala. Mainly her kindness consisted of ignoring both of them, but sometimes at night the three of us girls would whisper like we had known each other for centuries. We would laugh so hard at something stupid, usually some dirt Tess was dishing over a girl who'd gone too far with an unlikely boy, that I could actually see the happy girl Leala must have been before her mother left her large-boned Nordic family and headed for the big city, where she encountered the exotic Robert and his swarthy daughters.

With Leala still up in Minnesota and Dad gone for seven years, Tess and I make it a point to visit Cloris at least once a month now. This is a big day for her, a coming out party of sorts. She was never a confident mother to us. She took it upon herself to leave us lots of room, which was Tess's requirement more than mine. We sometimes goaded and tested her patience and acted downright cruel to see if we could get her to budge. Once when I came home roaringly drunk and had a strange boy sleep in my bedroom, she said nothing. Once in Hawaii, I bought marijuana with her in the car, and I was supposed to be the *good* step-daughter. Tess had a different strategy involving few words and lots of absence. She never gave Cloris a gift until she was married and had unkind children of her own. But like those saints who can endure scalding water as well as ice, Cloris was above it all. I think she lived in a small world where only two things mattered, the love of Robert and the loss of Leala. Other troubles meant so little they were hardly noticed.

When Robert died, she had a very bad period. We wondered if she'd make it through, but then her native patience, two new knees, and a rebirth followed. "So many wonderful years," she said as we drove her past the storefront that once had housed the gallery. It was a brokerage firm now. A tickertape ran through the window that used to display Tiffany lamps, period furniture, and Fairfield Porter paintings.

"To more good years," Tess adds gallantly, toasting Cloris with an invisible glass. This is something Tess has learned over the years, to be more thankful, to take her starving self and subdue it before it hungrily gnaws at others. Cloris smiles warmly and is ready to emerge.

As we watch our stepmother approach the runway in a shiny beaded evening dress with small capped sleeves, I think of how proud Mom would be that we've hung on all these years, that we took someone in and made her feel like a valued piece of furniture. We've done a good job raising this one, I want to tell my sister, but she's looking so sweetly at Cloris that I don't think I'll spoil their moment of glory.

The Nobel Prize for Shoes

I.

THEY LOVE MOVIES and see many of them, but one night after a very long, dull Slovakian movie in which every character eventually dies, they figure that they have probably made love more times than they've seen movies. Lots of times they begin sex in this way: she strokes and rubs and kisses his penis. It is quick and easy for him, but it has become harder for her to reach orgasm, maybe because she is older, maybe because she is depressed. He had seemed for a while not to like to touch her, especially last year during his affair. This year, after the affair, she is interested in one thing only: his happiness. If he had been happy, the last terrible year wouldn't have happened. Maybe, she worries at night, and sometimes in the car when she plays loud music and cries, it isn't in her power to make him happy. Maybe she's never made him happy, or maybe she's lost the power since he met someone else. But here he is with her, where he wants to be, he assures her. So it is her mission to think of ways to please him.

She knows she isn't as smooth as he'd like, as calm. She thinks of ways to be smoother. She listens to a message on his ex-lover's phone and hears her delicious, smooth voice. She considers lowering hers, breathing differently. She practices talking more slowly. Once she had read that before we speak, we should think through what it is we want to say. That way it won't come out rushed or forced or out of control. She practices slowness and grace.

But there are certain things she can't change. She can't, for instance, get taller or shrink her breasts which she knows some men love—she can tell by how they glance at her. She can't be someone he's just met and chosen by himself. She can't be new and surprising.

He told her that the other woman hadn't understood his art, and that pleased her. But maybe it meant that he didn't want her to understand it either. Maybe all these years of listening to him and helping him with his work hadn't pleased him. Maybe she needs to be less smart. Maybe he wants someone who understands nothing, someone whose understanding amounts to opening her legs. But she knows it isn't that simple. They had been close, he said. It wasn't ending when she learned of it; it might have continued for who knows how long if she hadn't.

So she tries to please him in all the small ways she always has. She brings him Bing cherries as soon as the season begins and takes his shirts to the laundry and requests light starch and presses the small of his back when it hurts. When he can't find a book he needs, she looks for it. When it seems he might require chocolate milk, she brings it from the store. When his father dies, she comforts him for weeks. Is that enough, she wonders? Or does he want a happiness she doesn't know how to provide? All she can do is be herself with some notable changes, some rounded edges, more sweetness.

But is it working? If only he would hold her in his arms and tell her how much he loves her body. She wants to hear that her imperfect self is the one he wants. Although it isn't new or capable of everything, it is the only one she has for him. If he will accept that from her, she knows she'll feel happy again. She doesn't know if he'll be happy, but she knows that she will.

II.

Maybe he doesn't want happiness. He wants to crash and burn, to tumble over a cliff, to end it all in a glorious, flaming moment of destruction. Maybe he'll take hostages or commandeer a tank and run over bicycles, compact cars, and old ladies. Maybe he wants a lonesome recklessness, a reckless loneliness that has nothing to do with what holds them together. Maybe she is of no consequence to him. Their kids have become old enough not to need her. Maybe he has too. Maybe she's useless, like a bustle, or an old photo of people no one recognizes anymore. Maybe she should ignore how he feels, his sudden fits of anger, his sighs, his sad, dark eyes that she loves more than anything. Marcello Mastrionni's eyes remind her of his. She will drive away and disappear so he can decide on his own what he wants. If it isn't her, if it's a rendezvous with death, who is she to stop him?

III.

Maybe it isn't her and it isn't death or even the woman who'd seduced him and doesn't understand his art. Maybe he wants random wild sex, Thailand, massage parlors, lap dancers. So let him. What does it have to do with her? She is about listening and sleeping at his side and doing what people do for each other. When his father died she said, "You have me, Sweetie." But maybe what he wants is a tall heroin addict with lots of tattoos and a penchant for violence, a sweet schoolgirl with knee-length socks and a mouthful of chewing gum, a female police sergeant, nightstick and all. Sometimes they joke about these things, as couples do, but maybe it isn't a joke. Maybe she should buy some outrageous shoes—red with spangles and ankle straps, or a whip, or the Bad Wives Video that *Redbook* suggested along with its lowfat recipes, adoption stories, and bondage gear. It seems that this is maybe a national crisis judging from women's magazines with articles on blow jobs, S & M, and the right kind of dildo. Maybe one of the major parties will take up the sex toy issue as part of its platform. What do Bill and Hillary, Al and Tipper, George and Laura use? Maybe they need cocaine or crack or a little introductory dose of heroin to patch things up.

IV.

Her dreams are always about responsibilities to others. Sometimes people, sometimes animals. The worst is her recurring dream of an aquarium (she's a Pisces) that she forgets to look after. There are skeletons of fish and a few miraculous survivors, which she guiltily feeds. Since his father died, she's had a recurring dream of him. She is in a bathtub being fondled by two young boys while his father looks on. His father hadn't been unkind but he had been unaffectionate. She never knew whether she was supposed to kiss him or shake his hand, but the last time they saw him, a week before he died, she had kissed him on his skull as they left the room.

Maybe happiness is circumspect. Maybe it is furtive, sidelong, a slant of light as the sun travels elsewhere. Thinking this somehow calms her. It is reassuring to know how small and deliberate a thing it might be.

Jealousy

DAN AND I had just put some money into our meager collection of stocks, something we just began this year as a promise to our future. All three of our children were away at college, and we were spending much of our time alone together for the first time in twenty years. The first few months of this experiment had left us rather testy and battered. It was as if each of us had been abandoned by the world but were not ready yet to tell the other how alone we felt. In that way we were the same, but neither of us could stretch out our arms to hold anything more than ourselves. I wondered what Dan was thinking as we slept together, his arms wrapped tightly around themselves, his back facing away from me. We had finished our stock transaction and were sitting down with our foccacia and lemonades when we noticed a sobbing girl in a wheelchair pulling up next to our outdoor table. Her electronic speaking board, which she was pressing with great urgency, emitted a difficult, quaking voice which asked, "May I join you?"

"Why are you crying?" I asked her.

She pressed the board again, but the sentence she formed wasn't coherent to Dan or me, who worked with great effort, in collaboration, to get it right.

Finally she said in her own voice, far more clear than her contraption's, "My aide didn't meet me for lunch."

"Would you like to join us with lunch?" Dan offered.

"Are you angry?" she sobbed anew, her tears big and wet on a sweet plain face contorted by pain and effort. She was in her late twenties and had been meticulously dressed by someone.

"We're not angry," Dan assured her.

"Am I bothering you?" she sobbed.

"Not at all," I added. "We're eating lunch too, so it's no trouble for you to join us."

I only then realized what we had committed ourselves to. She had a large coffee mug with a special cap and twisty straw, which she seemed able to access by simply moving her head, but the rest of her lunch was sealed as a crypt. She would be unable to unwrap her sandwich or eat a single chip without our help.

I opened what turned out to be a tuna sandwich and began to offer her small bites of tuna, which I took from the bread with a fork. Her smile was sweet and childlike. How many times had I lifted a spoon to the mouths of our children and how quickly had they wanted their independence, grabbing the spoon away, sabotaging my efforts with glee? I remember their looks of delight as they used their hands to shove Cheerios into their greedy mouths. As Jennifer ate, she continued to express her fear that she was bothering us, that we were angry with her, that we would tell her father.

"Why would we do that?" Dan asked sincerely.

"Is your aide very late?" I added, wiping her mouth with a napkin. How many times had I performed this same courtesy for our own children?

"She hasn't been meeting me for a month," she explained with labor and torment.

Dan and I looked at each other, taking in this last puzzling piece of news.

"Does your father know?"

"I don't want him to know," she continued. "He'll be mad at me."

"Why should he be mad at you?" I asked. "It's not your fault."

"My aide is greedy. I gave her my TV and VCR, but she still isn't reliable."

"Is that your aide?" I asked her of a woman who seemed to be approaching our table.

"My aide is from Fiji."

"Maybe she went back," Dan suggested.

"Maybe," Jennifer smiled.

We were on to the lettuce now, which I tore into small pieces and placed in her mouth as gently as I could. I remembered feeding a turtle of mine lettuce like this once and how he had stopped eating entirely a few months before he died.

"No more rabbit food," Jennifer laughed.

Taking my hand, she smiled into my eyes.

"Were you in an accident?" I asked her.

"No, I had a tumor when I was a baby and got paralyzed when they operated. You can't catch it, and I don't have AIDS."

Now it was time for me to talk. The pressure of the moment, the girl's helplessness, my maternal instinct, my pity for myself, a feeling that had lately been my primary one, all welled up. Trying to control my voice, I normalized the moment by asking her about her earrings.

"They're Swedish," she labored to explain. Swedish took three tries.

"I thought they were from Guatemala. My daughter has a pair almost like those."

"My mother is Swedish," Jennifer explained. "When she went there, she left me with my brother. He likes getting high and didn't take care of me. I had to go to the bathroom, and there was no one there. He used to be in rehab, but it didn't help." More tears as I balanced the fork in midair with the last bite of tuna.

"Are you angry at me?" she repeated, her continuing refrain. Taking my husband's hand, she held it for a moment and smiled shyly. "Are you jealous that I'm holding his hand?"

"No," I smiled. "As long as you don't run away with him."

We all laughed and finished lunch. Jennifer assured us that she would be all right until her father came for her in half an hour.

That night Dan and I held each other for a long time. I felt the tension leave my body after many months of holding myself together by sheer will. I had everything I needed for life. I could take care of myself, just like Jennifer, who must find a troubled couple every day and come to them as an emissary. Maybe helplessness is all we need for a life we can bear. Maybe all we have to do is ask to share it.

Snowflake, Come Home

HE POSTER SHOWS a lost white and gray cockatiel, who "loves to sing and talk" and is "missed very much." I wish I could report having seen him, but then it wouldn't be fiction. It would be a phone call to Todd and Ashley.

"Todd or Ashley," I'd say. "I've found your beloved bird. Yes, he's alive. He's sitting right here on my shoulder, and he's singing *Indian Rhapsody*. Yes, the male part. No, I didn't know that he can sing both. Shall I put him on?"

In real life, the bird in your cat's mouth is limp as a rag. He has stopped speaking altogether.

In real life, you're happy when your children come home alive from high school. You're happy when your daughter visits after a weekend of heartbreak. You're happy when your husband doesn't leave you.

"She's nothing compared to me," you tell your friend.

"They never are," he says sadly. A large gay man, his lovers have never been faithful.

You have learned to live with imperfection, even to embrace it. Mostly, everything is funny for you now except the disappearance of Snowflake, whose existence seems like a center of reason in a world gone mad.

On television the Dalai Lama is interviewed. The irreverent interviewer asks him why a godlike man has to wear glasses.

"Even the Buddha dies," the Dalai Lama smiles. Somehow this wisdom pertains to Snowflake for whom there is a large reward.

On the peninsula there is a California-style ranch house full of the Lost Boys of the Sudan, children who grew up as homeless orphans, a result of the bitter religious war in their homeland. At the age of twenty-one, they have been allowed to come to the United States, where Catholic Charities looks after them. They are extremely tall and have wispy carvings on their foreheads, tribal markings, the helpful reporter explains. Within the course of the report, you also learn that Manute Bol, the seven-foot-six basketball powerhouse, is a member of this tribe.

The Lost Boys are learning to use a rice cooker purchased from Williams-Sonoma. They are learning to cross on the red light. A cheery nun with an Irish accent has accompanied them to Target and provided them with a new wardrobe of preppy-style clothes. One is drinking a Dr Pepper next to someone's Honda Accord. The camera follows one into the house.

"This is the first bed I've had since I was a boy," he tells the reporter in slow, perfect English. His skin is very dark. He has accepted hunger and loss and probably death.

"I think I'll go to heaven when I die," you tell your husband, who looks amused. "Am I that unworthy?" you ask.

"I just want to understand your reasons."

"If anyone's ever loved you, you get to go to heaven," you say conclusively, making it up as you go along. Later you decide the criterion is too broad. Love must be defined by its value, and yes, some love is more valuable than others. Without quoting from Erich Fromm, you forge on. "Some love doesn't have value. Only if someone of value has loved you," you tell your husband, later in the day.

"You'll go to heaven too," you assure him, as he watches basketball on ESPN.

"Todd or Ashley," you say into their machine. "My friends' thirteen-year-old son died last month even though they fed him a macrobiotic diet and wrapped him in poultices. The beautiful pasture where the California live oaks are growing is infested by a fungus that will kill them, and the Dalai Lama must wear glasses."

But just then you see a white and gray cockatiel sitting in the juniper tree outside your kitchen window next to a Stellar's jay. The Stellar's jay is yapping its head off at Snowflake. You don't believe it could happen, but here it has, and you're grateful.

Acts of Nature

ADMIT IT, Meg's silently lecturing voice continues, sons keep us alive. Where would she be without Peter? Married to someone, her irrepressible dialectic winds on, maybe not so solitary? But raising a son alone for ten years has been good for her, she argues with herself. Think of all the things she knows that her more privileged sisters and friends never mastered: she can coax out a stubborn lug nut, whip a fastball over the plate, scale her roof to remove pine needles from the gutter, and Indian wrestle Peter to the floor. She can find her way all over Mount Tamalpais in hiking boots, she thinks, as the gentle green mountain which some say looks like a reclining girl comes into view. When Fred died, she had thrown like a girl. At twenty-seven, she had been a girl.

How could a marriage, sworn to last a life, have survived only two years, three months, and six days? How could Fred have died before Peter was born, Peter of the gorgeous gray eyes and quick wit, her debonair ten-year-old son, who would be pitching the final game of the minor league season in just twenty-two minutes? Greg, the ponytailed coach with the laid-back smile, has assured Meg that Peter is a natural. She wears his validation like a medal for bravery. Her good work has kept Peter sane, unlike so many fatherless kids, so aggressive they get placed in special classes for disruptive boys (why is it always boys?) or so placid they are classified as slow learners. Greg can't imagine the cautions she's exerted not to be overly cautious, how many times she has sealed her eyes to the danger, snorted the fear out of her system, eaten her concern.

As tragic as it was to lose Fred, she didn't really grow up until that terrible night when her worst fears materialized. Though it is almost as improbable to get eaten by a tiger in India as to get killed in a plane crash in America, it had happened. So much for blind fate. When she heard a plane had crashed, a San Francisco to Pittsburgh flight, it hadn't been Fred's until a small man she barely knew was pressing his perfumy hands around hers and calling her Mrs. Pastore. "I'm Ruben," she vaguely remarked. "I kept my last name." Five months pregnant, Meg Ruben was a convex-bellied widow at a funeral for a man she had known for fewer years than she had attended college or been a Girl Scout.

What could Fred have accomplished in twenty-eight years? Still, Meg had vowed to keep him alive for Peter. It was easy when Peter asked if his dad had liked baseball or if he would have taken them to Hawaii for Christmas. After a while, Peter's questions had gotten too particular to sustain the general myth. He had started to confound his mother with sophisticated, almost perverse demands for information: "Did Dad have a good change-up?" "What did he think of the designated hitter rule?" "What weight bat did he use?" "What kind of glove did he own when he was ten?" She envied her divorced friends their glib rudeness: "Ask the man himself!" "How in the hell do I know, kiddo?" All her ingenuity was siphoned on Fred's behalf, all her energy needed to keep Fred's torch glowing in Peter's posthumous life.

For months, she had cried and cried. In the demanding noises of infancy, Peter's own solo was accompanied by a chorus of sobs. "Really, your mother isn't supposed to cry more than you!" she had told the baby who couldn't support his head, couldn't get her nipple in his mouth without help, certainly couldn't comfort her. She had never re-echoed the terrible words that had crept into her mouth as she tried to doze off in her solitary bed with too much space and fine bridal shower linen, her breasts leaking milk: that she'd have been better off, well, never mind, that life would have been less of a trial if . . . she was not going to say it.

Like a star imploding on itself, Meg's world has gradually shrunk. Outside of her job and an occasional date, Peter is everything. She dwells on his stories like gospel, quotes them to tactful colleagues at work, provides him with enough video games to open an arcade, listens so acutely to his friends that she makes them nervous, keeps her home open to boys so late that parents grow anxious and testy. In the company of Peter, she forgets all her essential problems. Will her area (she sells small personal computer systems to fledgling businesses) be rendered irrelevant by new technologies? Will her floating mortgage ride up again? Will her mother contribute to the latest cause, the new flame-resistant shingled roof which her house so badly needs?

What she has learned from losing a husband and having a son is to give herself up like a Catholic does meat at Lent, to lose her reflection like a Jew who covers mirrors after a death in the house, to throw her best self on Fred's pyre like the women along the Ganges. Her college major in anthropology has informed her choice, providing metaphors for her lost self, placing her strategy of denial in a cultural context which smooths it over, sealing it like a vow. Meg, the only parent on the baseball team to be widowed, not divorced, is Peter's mother. Peter, his mother's significant other.

Yet she can't help remarking as she occasionally takes to the jogging path along sunny Richardson Bay, which the next earthquake might subsume at any moment, what fine calves men have: even the bald ones with the thick middles who sweat through their shirts, not to mention the showy ones whose spandex grips their tight buttocks. What more can she want than this landscape, which provides her such a lusty, impersonal view? Plenty, Meg laughs caustically, as she walks to the stands where the regular cast of parents gather for every game. So many nice men and women she has come to know this season. It was right to have moved from the city, where Peter was bused across town for no good reason, where his friends lived miles away and spoke forty languages, to this village where she feels part of a community. In her current setting, the word "microcosm" takes on new meaning. Nine divorces and one death on a team of eleven boys and one girl: an easy group to join for its broad demographics of single parenthood. Still, her special category kept her at bay when a certain divorced father with pleasant brown eyes and a clever malevolent wit took an interest in her earlier in the season.

Peter is almost as tall as Meg. His gangly arms lifted over his head, he pretends to hurl a pitch in his mother's direction, then waves nonchalantly as she takes a place in the grandstand next to Gloria and Hettie. Gloria is a dance and yoga instructor who has her son on weekends but has made every game. Hettie is a rarity among single women: in two weeks she will fly home to Ann Arbor to remarry. The other women regard her with wonder, Hettie who flashes a diamond the size of a grape, Hettie of the immense good fortune.

According to Hettie, whose status confers special wisdom upon her, this is the seventh game of the season threatened by rain. It has been the rainiest spring in one hundred years. Coming to the game, in fact, Meg saw lightning fracture the sky over Mount Tam. Lightning is so unusual here—unlike the Midwest where she had grown up—that cars pull over to watch the display.

"Let's hope they can play at least four innings," everyone agrees. One more victory is all the team needs to get into the playoffs. If they make it that far, no doubt Peter will be named to the all-star team and get the special cap that Meg had seen some older boys tossing to each other in the stands. "Let's hope," she repeats as the umpire puts on his mask and their team takes to the field.

In the Midwest when it rained, the storm approached with novelistic slowness. First, there'd be a change in the smell of the air, then a subtle wind stirring the trees, then a few small drops announcing the theme before the torrent. Lightning and thunder occurred later in the narrative. Living in San Francisco with Fred, she'd observed a different progression: first lightning, then gale-force winds, then more water than she'd ever seen falling from the sky. Probably the proximity to the ocean makes storm patterns different, more abrupt and dangerous. By the time Peter strikes out the first batter, bushes are flattening toward the ground, trees bending, and the sky growing pitch-black.

Meg stifles her fear of lightning striking the field. "Aluminum bats don't conduct electricity," Hettie is heard saying. "We can't call this one off." "Playoffs are in two days." "Kids can't pitch two days in a row," the stands of parents pipe in. Looking with big eyes toward Mitch, who has memorized the Little League rule book, and is short, bald, and reliable, Meg hears the reasonable words that make her stop thinking of Peter as a potential electrical storm victim and help her concentrate on his pitching. "The umpire will call the game if it gets too bad," Mitch smiles benignly. It's that simple.

Now in the field a hit squeezes through at third base, where Ronnie, a nasty kid with slow hands, ineptly guards the line. Two batters are down, but Peter's inning continues with a boy on second. Meg is thinking of how much she dislikes Ronnie for causing Peter trouble when she hears an enormous remote clap and a sizzle.

She locates Peter first, untouched on the mound but wide-eyed as everyone with the latest blow of fate: the scoreboard in center field, the new $29,000 scoreboard that the local newspaper has recently head-lined with such pride, has been hit. A small coiffure of flames leaps across its straight hairline.

"Call 9-1-1!" people shout. "Get the kids off the field!"

Without further instruction, the children scatter to dugouts, to the snack booth, to the comforting, wet laps of their parents. It's touching how quickly five-foot tall sons become children under duress.

"Mom, I'm going to sit in Andy's car," Peter shouts. "Did you see it? Wasn't it cool?" he asks, regarding the scoreboard. Meg is ready to include Fred in her reply. "Once when Dad and I were driving west . . ." she begins, but Peter is already off, striding with Andy toward his father's blue van.

Meg sees Mitch, purveyor of information, short and sturdy, allayer of fears. "Want to sit in my car during the storm?" she asks quietly. "I have a CD player."

She is glad he didn't hear her, occupied by his eagerness to join the others in the field waiting for the fire department to save the smolder-ing scoreboard. The men, surrounding it like doctors in a surgical the-ater, call information back to the women, who huddle near the refreshment stand. When a space clears, Meg notices that already, doused by the rain, the board has stopped blazing. She begins to con-coct a version of the experience that will include Fred, who had never said anything about lightning that she can remember. Short of form-ing her sentence, she runs across the field to stand next to Mitch in the circle of men observing the act of nature.

From

Signs of
Devotion

Jury Duty

HAD SPENT the first part of the summer distraught, writing a story about a woman I know, a lesbian, who had a baby. I wanted to do the story justice, nothing preachy or high-toned, just honest observation and discussion.

The story was boring. It was boring to me when I was writing it, and I assumed it would be boring to anyone who might read it. Brenda and Mary were portrayed as loving, concerned future parents, the problems of pregnancy discussed with sympathy. Integrity was my byword. In my story Brenda was fertilized at a medical center by a doctor she called The Inseminator. The best scene involved the couple sitting at the breakfast table, sharing a cranberry muffin, telling insemination jokes. They weren't male stand-up comic jokes that someone like Tom Dreesen might tell, but a scenario involving a series of movies called *The Inseminator*. Arnold Schwarzenegger would fertilize whole cities, metropoli, continents. This was the comic relief.

In art, as in life, accidents happen, and Brenda lost her baby. I kept hoping as I wrote the story that I wasn't punishing her by resolving the plot in that way. I went through the list of all my friends who'd miscarried and felt reassured that at least in real life justice plays no role.

Then two things happened. First, my good friend Lois told me that the woman on whom I'd based Brenda had fallen in love with the man who'd gotten her pregnant. In real life Brenda hadn't gone to a doctor at all. She'd gone to the Drake Hotel, and when her basal temperature was perfectly adjusted, had made love to her friend's friend Mark, a book designer. She's the kind of person who cuts corners. Her night of heterosexual passion led to Kyle, who's now almost two, and is said to resemble Mark more strongly than Brenda.

Meanwhile, Mark had begun to call. It was only natural that he'd be interested in his son. They had dinner a few times and one thing led to another. Now Brenda's wearing makeup again, seeing Mark regularly, and having very little to do with Mary, the woman with whom she was supposed to be raising Kyle.

Lois spared no details. The makeup she can accept. After all, who doesn't want to look nice? Why should women deny themselves what's best from the past to make a statement about the present that's finally puritanical? "No, the makeup is great," Lois said. "Besides, even men wear makeup these days. My butcher wears something that keeps his skin looking tight and young. It's the damned shoes."

"The shoes?"

"She buys shoes to match all her outfits now. She's a regular Imelda. And the hair. It's sleek. It's contemporary. It could co-anchor the news without a face to hold it up."

"Good for her," I said, thinking that my story was probably too weighty and moralistic. "As long as she's happy."

"Good for Kyle that the father's interested. Old Brenda's too ditzy to raise that child herself."

"So it's a happy ending?"

"Not really. It's a crying shame. Why is it love that always changes women? Even in the highest art. Even in Jane Austen. Why can't it be nautical adventure or politics or ideas?"

I was thinking this over Monday morning when I arrived for jury duty. It was the Criminal Court, where I hoped I might get involved in a short, interesting case that would yield a story. Twelve weeks on Claus Von Bulow didn't appeal to my immediate sense of my future self. I had stories to write, dinners to cook, a tennis backhand to improve. Give me a small murder, an unambiguous kidnapping. Give me a purse thief with musical abilities or a man who'd pruned his neighbor's tree while high on angel dust. Let me be out of here by rush hour.

I spent nearly the entire week of jury duty sitting on the bench. Twice I was asked not to read. Many potential jurors snored blissfully around me. None were asked not to sleep. The third time I began reading nobody bothered me. I was set in my ways. Besides, the book was nonfiction. I was a serious person. The book's cover was navy blue. The title was engraved.

While sitting on the bench waiting to be called, I spent part of each day staring at a pregnant woman. She was small and dark, maybe Indian or Pakistani, and sweated profusely. I wondered if she really had to endure the week or could have used her pregnancy as an excuse. I wondered if she would have liked my story about Brenda.

I began thinking of pregnancy itself as a form of jury duty. I remembered when I had my first child. The nurse held her up to my face, but because I wasn't wearing glasses and was groggy from labor, I thought the nurse's elbow was part of my daughter's back, a protrusion.

"She's beautiful," they assured me, but I was overcome by fear and unable to ask about what I suspected until a second viewing.

At the time of my jury duty, I was on medication for my nerves. I'd been having panic attacks in unlikely places. One, for instance, had been in a women's locker room at a YMCA. Its origin remained a mystery. The others—before lecturing to my class on deconstruction, while driving to work, during rush hour, while visiting my mother at the hospital—I could explain. Not understanding my latest one sent me straight to my physician.

"Can you help me?" was all I wanted to know.

Before he answered, he made his eyes small and meaningful and told me all about his own panic, panic while giving a medical paper on liver disease, panic at his father's funeral.

"Did your father have liver disease?"

"A boating accident," he replied, and wrote me a prescription for a new drug that nips panic in the bud. No more adrenaline coursing through my system like a commuter train to Tokyo. It was his simile, and I thanked him.

The trial on which I actually served as an alternate involved a gang shooting in February. I mention the month because crimes of passion seem barely plausible in winter. A bloodless killer, I concluded, a sociopath. Even before the gun with his fingerprints had been introduced and the witnesses had given their testimony, my mind was made up.

I'd rewrite the story. Mary would kill Brenda for having betrayed her. It was plausible. It was justice. It would happen in August.

Baudelaire's Drainpipe

O N THE LAST DAY of our vacation in Paris, I was thinking that it's better to be content at Our Lady of Perpetual Aluminum Siding than to feel disappointment at Notre Dame Cathedral. John, sitting beside me during the Spanish-language service, held my hand and stared down at the floor. He looked morose because the day had already failed to contribute the poignancy he demanded of our travels. I whispered to him that missing a tour of Baudelaire's house was nothing to pout about, but John was inconsolable.

I wondered if some people are naturally drawn to beauty, others to necessity. My sister has a son who pointed his baby hand, declaring objects beautiful as soon as he could speak. My aesthetic ledger contains many blank pages and is opened only under special circumstances. Its entries are for what I imagine beauty might be at a distance. On my bedroom wall as a child, I had a travel poster of Portofino. My mother had placed it there because the glistening water and sandy winding path blended with my draperies. Her decorating concept was my touchstone for beauty. Finding myself in Portofino twenty years later, I was more aware of the shooting pain in my Achilles tendon and the tingle of my skin as the sun pierced the back of my polo shirt. As hymns were sung and the collection plate was passed, I reduced my philosophy to a slogan: It's better to have seen Baudelaire's drainpipe than to have missed the house altogether.

Besides, some aesthetic notions can be dangerous. I read in the paper back home that a neighborhood teenager wanted to change his image by giving himself a mohawk. He asked his grandmother for an electric razor. When she was unable to find it, he stalked her around the house with a baseball bat, a Raskolnikov of New Wave. The story was printed in the local crime blotter, but it seems a cautionary tale about ardor. Until I read that story, I hadn't thought much about a line in a poem that said, "Too much beauty could detonate us." Looking at John moping next to me, I wondered if too little beauty could produce the same effect.

John had a profound reaction to Baudelaire's house being around the corner from our hotel yet inaccessible. He stormed around the bird market banging into cages, swearing under his breath. I suggested we visit Notre Dame again, hoping its grimacing angels might offer commiseration. As we walked there, he recounted all the places we hadn't seen in our travels. It was a list of startling variety, with nuances of hope, resolve, and despair. It contained a Buddhist temple we were unable to locate on a remote mountain in Japan; the shrine at Delos, unapproachable by boat in rough water; London's Highgate Cemetery, padlocked to visitors; Freud's house in Vienna, closed for remodeling. Later at a cafe he actually wrote out the list after ordering a second espresso.

Before I could remind him that we had been successful on other occasions, a goat had climbed a ladder set up on the sidewalk and his trainer was extending a red metal coin box in our direction. The goat wore a green Alpine hat and made me recall an out-of-context camel we'd chosen not to mount for a photo years ago on Crete.

I reminded John that we'd seen many sights. My list ranged from Apollinaire's grave to locks of Keats's hair to the birth of our own daughter. I thought I might jostle him into better cheer by adding that final intimate detail, but John was unwilling to be consoled. His list continued. It included the Pope at Yankee Stadium and Simon and Garfunkel in Central Park. When I told him that he didn't even like Simon and Garfunkel, he said that was beside the point. I looked at his troubled eyes and wondered why he took these disappointments personally. Someday, I worried, he might read a news story about trash dumped in space, say, "Look what they've done to my galaxy!" and jump out a window.

Then the street performer tied the goat to the ladder and took a little dog dressed like a clown out of a carrying case. The man was dressed in black tights that made his legs seem spindly. The dog looked perilously mortal. It was an aged Chihuahua, categorically uninterested in the commands that the man delivered in increasingly loud, vehement French. I suggested to John that right then we were witnessing something memorable, France's most inept dog trainer.

Usually he would have laughed at that, but instead he described Baudelaire's drainpipe in detail, as if he were fixing it in his mind.

"Bronze," he said. "A fish whose head points downward and whose tail is soldered to the drainpipe itself."

"I'm not sure," I answered, "that the fish is turned upside down. Maybe the fish's mouth is open, and the drainpipe emerges from it. I think I remember the tail curled in one direction or another at the bottom."

He turned his face away from me and watched the man throw small embroidery hoops over the dog's neck. Then the man picked up the dog and tossed him onto the goat's back. The dog's hind legs quivered with tension.

"We'll have to go and look at it again." John slugged down his espresso and started off in the direction of Baudelaire's corner. I followed him silently down the narrow lanes of L'île St. Louis. When we approached the entrance to our hotel, I told him I was going to take a nap. He looked at me wearily and said he'd take a picture of the drainpipe, since I wasn't interested enough to join him.

I must have slept for a long time. I woke up in darkness and thought about a museum in Montreal, where we'd seen an exhibit of Rodchenko's Futurist furniture, an aesthetic based on perceptual miscues. Chairs that resembled greyhounds seemed too fragile to sit on. I remembered a museum for children with a room that distorted perspective and how happily my nephew, the one who loved beauty, had sashayed up and down the slanting floor.

When John finally returned, he didn't say a word. He'd brought a sack filled with dinner items that he noisily unwrapped. He placed a tin of sardines next to a ball of cheese. Then he unwrapped a pentagon-shaped slab of bread. Next to it he placed two orange-yellow pears, a bottle of Bordeaux with a swan on the label, and some chocolates with hazelnuts from Italy. Someone should have painted it all before I bit into a slightly unripe pear.

"Did you see Baudelaire's drainpipe?" I asked him.

"Remember that bus ride in the Philippines?" he asked.

That called me back to our days in the Peace Corps before Glenna was born. I wasn't sure which bus ride he had in mind, though most were of the same character and duration: stifling, acrid, and endless. "Which exact one?" I finally asked, tearing a corner of crusty bread.

"The one with the chickens and pigs and the man who bumped his head on the roof of the bus when we went over a rut in the road."

"Not really," I said.

"The man's head bled, and the people on the bus pointed and laughed. You were irate. You don't remember that?"

"It all sounds familiar, but I can't say that I actually remember."

"Then my afternoon's been a waste," he said, shrugging his shoulders. He speared a sardine with surprising ferocity. "Why do I need to take photos when I can tell you anything, and you'll believe me?"

When we got back to New York a week later, the photos we'd taken in Paris were developed. There was Père Lachaise Cemetery with Apollinaire's flower-strewn grave. There was our tour guide, whose radiant copper-colored eyes shone like new pennies. There I was, smiling in the bird market on that ill-fated Sunday. Among the photos I saw no evidence of Baudelaire's drainpipe, but I decided not to reopen the case.

A few weeks later we were dining with Glenna and Ramon. It's hard to believe that my daughter's a married woman with a baby of her own. John was holding little Aaron and playing with his fingers when Glenna asked him how we'd liked Paris. John said I'd been satisfied enough, having lower standards than he does. Glenna wondered whether the hotel wasn't up to par.

Preparing to respond, he handed back the baby, and I said, "Dad means Baudelaire's home. We missed the weekly tour by fifteen minutes. We did see his drainpipe, though, and it was lovely."

John snorted with disdain. I wondered how I could love this man.

To make matters worse, Glenna started laughing. "Remember Melville's toolshed and Emily Dickinson's parking meter? Didn't we drive two hundred miles to see them?"

"Quiet, you'll wake the baby," John told Glenna.

"The baby's awake," Glenna said, coaxing Aaron's head under her blouse to nurse him.

John turned away from Glenna and me, adjusted his glasses and spoke. "Women don't understand the purpose of traveling," John told Ramon in a confidential whisper.

"Who was Baudelaire?" Ramon asked.

I was just brushing my teeth before bed when John flashed a photo in front of my eyes. He moved it into and out of my field of vision so quickly that I wasn't sure what I'd seen. "What was that?" I asked him.

"Baudelaire's drainpipe," he answered, voice registering triumph.

"Then you were right about the fish?" I asked him.

"No," he said smugly, "but at least I cared enough to do the necessary research."

The next morning John told me that he was sick of traveling. "I thought it would be better for us to stay home in the future," he said pointing to an island-shaped place on the kitchen ceiling where the plaster needed repair. He gestured outside to our crumbling staircase veined with weeds and fledgling trees.

I looked up from the garden catalog I'd been reading. "Look," I said pointing. "Green tulips. Don't they remind you of something?" John kissed me on my shoulder and said no. I was thinking of the color of old bronze, the color the drainpipe fish had become over a century of weather and change.

The Untouchables

JANE KNEW THAT her father, a leather-goods salesman, was of the merchant class. She had been studying the caste system in school and worried that his job might put him in jeopardy, since Untouchables dealt with animal skins. As long as her father only sold the stuff, he'd be safe. Salespeople were never Untouchables. She would have liked her father to have been a Brahmin, but after all, her family lived next to a gas station and showed no particular interest in learning or religion. Usually this pleased her. While her Catholic friends were tortured in Sunday clothes, Jane could ride around the block on her old Schwinn bike singing "Some Enchanted Evening," her favorite song from *South Pacific*. Every time she passed the Shell station, she'd ride over the hose that made the bell ring. Sometimes it punctuated the song mid-chorus. Other times it accompanied her as she reached for a high note. When she got bored, she'd park her bike, walk back to the gas station, put her quarter in for a Coke, and swig the bottle down, leaning against the red metal housing of the machine. No one noticed her. She could stare at anyone she pleased. Mostly she looked at the m'woman, which was what her father called the person who pumped gas on weekends.

Jane had concluded that she was definitely a woman because the badge on her shirt didn't lie flat over her breast pocket. It puckered, as her own pockets had begun to. But no woman in her right mind would have her hair way above the ear or that short on the neck or let grease accumulate all over her face and hands without trying to clean herself up. Once Jane asked her mother about the m'woman but was told to be quiet. If she'd followed with "Why?" one of her parents would have said, *"Why* is a Chinaman's name," which had never made any sense to her. Victoria Pranz's mother had told Jane that the m'woman was probably a lesbian. Victoria's mother was definitely a Brahmin, an art professor at the University of Chicago, though her status was questionable, considering her recent divorce.

Dr. Pranz would be a Brahmin too, Jane calculated, by virtue of his classical music training. Even though he'd given up the flute to practice dentistry, he might have played in a symphony. Once Victoria had told Jane that dentists have the highest suicide rates. From then on Jane had stared at Dr. Pranz, trying to detect a sudden sadness behind his jocular manner and jaunty little Vandyke. When he left Mrs. Pranz, Jane wondered if he'd take to wandering aimlessly along Lake Michigan until a surge of emotions vaulted him into the water. But when he came to pick up Victoria on Saturdays, he never looked anything but animated. Sometimes he'd include Jane in a special outing. En route he'd hum to the classical music on the car radio. One morning they'd gone to Calumet Harbor to tour a merchant-marine ship from Denmark. Someone depressed couldn't have thought of such pastimes. Jane's own father, absorbed in the Cubs' problems with left-handed hitting, or bills or edging the lawn, looked far sadder than Dr. Pranz. Perhaps Brahmins were naturally more content than the merchant class.

On Sundays Victoria and Jane rode their bikes together. On the particular Sunday it happened, Jane was in the lead, Victoria well behind. That was a difference between them. Victoria dallied, taking in details, reserving judgment. Maybe she'd inherited her mother's preoccupation with seeing. Jane remembered a horrible Columbus Day spent at the Art Institute with Victoria and her mother, who paused for one, sometimes two minutes, at every painting before moving on. Even worse, Mrs. Pranz asked Jane what she thought of several Cézannes, as if Jane could tell her something she didn't already know. "You're the artist," Jane had finally said when Mrs. Pranz seemed dissatisfied with her replying, "I think they're okay."

When Jane went over the gas hose this time, her tire skidded in some grease and she went flying over the handlebars, landing on both palms and knees. Before Victoria caught up with her, the m'woman had rushed out of the gas station and was helping Jane up. She made a greasy fist around Jane's forearm. Pulling Jane to her feet, she surveyed the damage.

"Guess you'll be all right," she said and offered Jane a clean flannel cloth.

Jane stared at her palms, which were red and smarting under the grease, and at her poor knees, which had taken the brunt of the fall. One was bloodier than the other. Jane dabbed at them with the rag. Before Victoria arrived on the scene, the m'woman had walked back into the garage.

"She talked to me!" Jane told Victoria as they walked their bikes home.

"Who?" Victoria asked, cocking her head like her mother while waiting for the reply.

"The m'woman came out when I fell. She has a lady's voice. She gave me this cloth." Jane held it out.

"Yuck," Victoria said.

By then they'd reached Jane's house. As Jane expected, her mother asked Victoria to go home. Whenever Jane got hurt, her mother used the occasion to lecture not only about safety but whatever had been on her mind since the last injury.

"Let's go to Woolworth's," her mother said, wiping the last grease off Jane's legs. "I need some yarn, and I'll buy you a vanilla Coke."

Bandages on both palms and knees, Jane limped to the Fairlane. She made a halfhearted effort to comb her hair and wet her lips shiny as her mother started the car and headed off.

"Jane, I was wondering, honey, whether I've told you enough."

"About what?" Jane asked, alert to a very different line of questioning.

"About growing up," her mother said.

"I guess it's just happening anyway," Jane said, looking down at her hands, which, with the extra bandages and the stiffness they caused, appeared huge.

"I mean something else," her mother mumbled. Why wasn't Mrs. Pranz her mother? She had brought home a gynecological text and taken Victoria to a health seminar on her eleventh birthday. Whenever Jane's mother wanted to talk about sex, she got all self-conscious and stuttery and even drove funny.

"Mom, you're going twelve miles an hour. I think the speed's at least twenty-five."

"Do you know about babies?" Jane's mother blurted out as she parallel-parked the car in front of Woolworth's. Parking had taken three tries.

"They're those little things with diapers, right, Mom?"

Before her mother could reply, their attention was caught by the couple standing in front of Woolworth's. The thin young man had his arms around the girl, who was younger still, perhaps sixteen. Her hands were tucked demurely in her pockets. What fascinated Jane was how their bodies connected at the tongue, and how they twisted against each other for what seemed like forever.

"They're Frenching," Jane explained to her mother, who looked either confused or stricken. "Hey, that's Nina Treesom!" she added. Nina lived across the alley and had been dating a college boy.

"Hi, Nina," Jane said, as her mother whisked her past them into the store.

"Yarn?" her mother asked, a tired monosyllable. The woman pointed them toward the back of the store, Jane's favorite area, where she could watch the parakeets crowding together, chirping on their perches.

Her mother bought pink and blue and yellow mohair, promising Jane she'd make her a sweater. Every so often she took on such projects, but most ended in failure. There was a whole box of half-made sweaters and scarves in the bottom of the linen closet. Jane said that would be nice but spent her time over the vanilla Coke thinking about the m'woman. After the flannel cloth was clean, Jane would return it to her. Maybe the m'woman would explain to her why she dressed that way. Maybe she was from another country, but Jane hadn't detected an accent.

"The couple you saw outside Woolworth's," her mother began once she was back behind the wheel, "had better be careful." She was shaking a manicured index finger toward Jane's nose.

"Mom, that was Nina. Remember, she used to walk me to school when I was in kindergarten?"

"Nina or not, one thing leads to another." Squinting to look serious, she added, "Remember Tammy Swartz?"

"Yes," Jane said, recalling Mrs. Swartz's hefty daughter who'd gone away one summer to work at a resort in the Wisconsin Dells.

"She didn't go to college after that summer, Jane, like Mrs. Swartz told everyone. She had a baby."

"But she wasn't married."

"I'm telling you, Jane, it's dangerous to be a woman." She was looking crazed again. They took a sharp left. The tires squealed around their corner, engraving the afternoon on Jane's eardrums, and they were home.

Jane lay on her bed and wondered whether the m'woman worried about such matters. It would be nice to worry about nothing at all or just dumb things like her father did. Jane wondered what the m'woman's status would be in India. Then she remembered that unmarried women were always a disgrace to their families.

When Jane walked into the gas-station garage, the m'woman was reading the Sunday paper and smoking a cigarette. She had stretched out her legs so that her work boots rested against the edge of the counter.

"Excuse me," Jane said.

The m'woman looked up and smiled at her.

"I have your cloth." Jane held it toward her.

"Thanks," the m'woman said. "Are you all healed?"

"I'm fine," Jane said. She noticed that the insignia over the m'woman's pocket read "Ike." She smiled to think that the m'woman and the President shared the same name.

"I'm Jane."

"I'm Sheila."

"Your pocket says 'Ike.'"

"I'm Sheila Ikenberry. People call me Ike."

"I'm twelve."

"I'm thirty-two."

Then the gas-bell rang, and a blue Chevy was waiting at a pump.

"Right back," Ike said.

Jane picked up the paper Ike had been reading. It was folded at the classified car ads.

"I'm looking for a car," Ike continued upon her return.

"My dad buys Fords."

"Right now I have a Studebaker." She pointed outside to a two-toned sedan colored like toast with jelly. "It's getting kind of old, and I live way out in the sticks. I need a more dependable car for winter."

"My mom drives my dad's car. Someday I'll probably have my own car. I wouldn't mind a Thunderbird."

"Right now your bike is fine, I'd guess."

"Sure it is. I'm talking about the future."

"What do you want to be in the future?" Ike asked.

This is leading somewhere, Jane thought. If she just said the right thing, Ike would explain herself. "Maybe a truck driver," Jane said, hoping to prod her along.

"When I was little, I wanted to be a nurse."

A Plymouth pulled up. The man got out of the car and walked into the gas station.

"Got some change for the Coke machine?" he asked. Ike gave him quarters, nickles, and dimes.

"Your hair's pretty short," Jane said while the man was opening his Coke.

"Yeah, it's convenient for me that way." Ike picked up her paper and started looking down the column again. "I used to wear it longer when I was your age." She drew red circles around two car ads in a row.

"Do you have any pictures?" Jane asked.

"Of what?"

"Your family, or how you looked before you cut your hair."

"Not on me," Ike said. "Why don't you come by next Sunday? I'll bring a photo of me when I was your age."

"I'll try," said Jane. "Mostly I'm free on Sundays."

"Want a Coke?"

"I don't have any money."

"I'll treat you to one," Ike said, "and then I have to close up for the day."

All the time Jane drank the Coke, she watched Ike reading the ads. Ike never looked up or seemed to notice that Jane was staring. If she did notice, she ignored it, just as she did Jane's riding over the gas-station hose again and again.

That Tuesday Mrs. Pranz took Jane and Victoria back to the Art Institute. In one gallery right near *American Gothic,* which Jane remembered from her previous visit, she saw a painting she hadn't noticed before. It was a gas station painted at night by someone named Edward Hopper. The station itself was lit up, and the majestic red pumps were topped off with white globes. There was a lone attendant standing at one edge of the painting and a road that went off into darkness. Jane liked how the painting admitted that gas stations mattered. She hoped Mrs. Pranz would ask her about it. For once she'd have had something to say.

On the way out Mrs. Pranz asked the girls what they'd like in the gift shop. Victoria picked out some stationery with Degas dancers. Jane chose a few postcards. Between a Renoir mother and child and Van Gogh's bedroom, Jane slipped the Hopper painting.

Because it was raining that Sunday, it was harder for Jane to get out of the house. She knew she couldn't just say she was going to the gas station or mention Ike's name, even as Sheila Ikenberry. She was glad for one thing. Her mother had gotten all involved in the sweater and forgotten about Jane's education in being a woman.

"I'm taking a bike ride," Jane said. Her father, who was reading *National Geographic*, didn't look up.

"In the rain?" her mother asked, peering over her glasses.

"I need a few things at Woolworth's," Jane said, "and I want to look at the parakeets."

"Don't look too long," her father said, "or they'll charge you."

Ike was sitting exactly where she'd been last week. She was wearing a rubber raincoat over her slacks and shirt.

"Lousy weather to pump gas," she said when Jane walked in. "On days like this I wish I *had* been a nurse."

"I guess you still could be," Jane said but regretted it immediately. It was the kind of thing her mother would have said to cheer someone up.

Ike smiled and opened the drawer under the cash register. "Voilà!" She produced a picture of herself as a little girl. "That's me at six. I couldn't find me at twelve. Pretty cute, huh?"

She was sitting on a stuffed bear at a zoo. Her hair was short and the little skirt she wore revealed thick, sturdy legs. Because she was smiling into the sun, her face was wrinkled up.

"Where was it taken?" Jane asked.

"The Bronx Zoo. That's where I grew up. Not in the zoo. In the Bronx," she laughed.

"Why did you come to Chicago?"

"Just to follow a friend. The friend was going to move here, so I did too."

"Where's your friend now?"

"That's a long story." Ike looked out the window.

"I brought you something," Jane said, reaching under her rain slicker and pulling out the postcard. She placed it on the counter next to the cash register.

"A postcard of a gas station," Ike said. "Now when I'm at home, I'll be able to remember where I work on weekends." She laughed. "It's really very nice, especially those old-fashioned pumps."

"It's of a painting at the Art Institute."

"Right. A pretty nice painting."

"I go there all the time with Victoria and her mom. Her mom's an art professor."

"I saw you yesterday with your mom. Pardon me for saying this, but your mom's driving leaves something to be desired."

"She just learned two years ago. Believe me, she's gotten better. Did your mom drive?"

"My mom didn't drive and neither did my dad. My older brother drove, though. He taught me one summer."

"Why didn't they drive?" Jane asked.

"You ask a lot of questions," Ike said. "How about a little break? Can I buy you another Coke?"

They were at the machine when Jane saw her father approaching. He was wearing a rubber raincoat identical to Ike's.

"Jane, I saw your bike. You're wanted at home," he said.

"Dad, this is Sheila Ikenberry."

"Pleased to meet you," he said, turning to hold the door for Jane.

"Do you spend a lot of time there?" he asked when they were out of the rain under the overhanging porch of their house.

"Not really," Jane said. "Ike saw when I fell off my bike. She came out and asked if I was all right. I guess that got us talking."

"You know, Jane, there's something strange about that woman."

"Daddy, you call her 'the m'woman.' Anyone can see there's something strange about her."

"You probably shouldn't hang around there. Let's not tell Mom for now. She's off in all directions with worries."

"Yeah, what's her problem?"

"Well, we didn't tell you, but for a while we thought that she might be having another baby. Then we found out that she wasn't."

"Is that why she needed yarn?" Jane asked.

"No, she needed yarn later. After she found out she wasn't going to have another baby."

"Why would you want another baby," Jane asked, "when you have me?" For a reason she didn't understand, she felt tears forming in her eyes. She knew her eyes turned greener when she cried. She didn't know if she was crying because she wanted her parents all to herself or didn't want them at all.

They were standing in the foyer when her mother asked where Jane had been. Her father held his finger up to his lips, looked Jane in the eye, and said, "Oh, just around the neighborhood. I treated her to a Coke at the Shell."

The next Sunday Jane looked up Martinegro's Shell Station in the phone book. When Sheila Ikenberry answered, Jane said she thought she'd just say hello. Then she told Ike that her mother had been pregnant but that things hadn't worked out.

"I mailed that postcard to my friend," Ike said. "You know, the one of the gas station? I thought she'd get a kick out of seeing what I've made of myself."

Death Swap

"Is Lou Reed Jewish?" Frank asks Della.

"How do I know? Do you think we're all acquainted with each other?" Della wipes sweat off her eyebrows, which are heavy and slightly curly. No one else is at the pool, which looks like a blue lima bean. She peers toward the dining-room door, hoping that someone will step through it. Not that she's seen anyone interesting or young at the Napa Glen Lodge. The rest of the guests resemble her grandparents. She wonders if young people go on vacation these days.

"I'm just reading this article, and Lou Reed says he admires Bob Dylan and Paul Simon." Frank swats a place on his back where a fly has landed, then cries out in pain. He shouldn't have gotten so much sun. Looking at his legs, which are striped pink, he imagines them as landing strips in a jungle.

"My mother called," Della says.

"If a man bites a dog, that's news," Frank answers, letting the magazine fall over his forehead. He turns on his side, extending his knees toward Della. He performs this act slowly, since his back is so tender. Lying this way, he can admire Della as something composed of tan flesh, muscular shoulders, firm breasts, and long legs. For a minute he feels content again, as if their vacation isn't an acknowledged mistake they have to endure for three more days.

"Mom hasn't called since we were back home. I don't know why it pisses you off that she calls."

Frank watches Della wait for his response. Her upper lip is squeezed together like a piece of soft candy.

"Why did she name you Della? It's old-fashioned."

"That's the point. After Della Reese."

"What?"

"The woman on the *Perry Mason Show.* Oh, I forgot. You only watch

Madonna videos on MTV. You wouldn't know who Perry Mason is."

"He's the guy in the wheelchair who solves crimes even though he's grossly overweight."

"Fact check. That's Ironsides, a later incarnation of Raymond Burr. At least you have the right actor." Della closes her eyes and hums something to herself.

Frank thinks of Della singing "Like a Virgin." In his mental video, her body looks even more desirable, legs dangling from Madonna's black garter belt. If she'd only have fewer opinions they'd get along fine, Frank thinks. "What did your mother want this time?"

"To tell me that Dad's going to be here in two hours. He's been doing business in San Francisco and thought he'd come by and say hello."

"Is this the same dad you and your mother constantly bash?"

"We don't bash him unjustly. I just sympathize with her on the issue of their divorce. Dad's bringing Kathy, by the way."

"His new wife?"

"How many times do I have to tell you? Jessica is his new wife. Kathy is his stepchild."

An elderly man is standing at the far end of the pool. He carefully places his towel over a beach chair, his watch on top of the towel, his glasses next to the watch, and his thongs under the chair. Then he makes an imperfect dive into the pool and sidestrokes its length. He stands in the water near Della and Frank.

"I read somewhere that Stephen Sondheim likes to tie people up," Frank says, smiling. "Maybe we could listen to some of his music." If they were getting along, a story like this would cause any tension to melt. Frank would swear on a witness stand that Della has a sense of humor when she wants to.

"What's your source?" Della asks.

The man in the pool appears to be listening. Frank cups his hand over his mouth and whispers something to Della.

"He did not tie you up!" Della says loud enough for the man to hear. "Maybe you wish he would."

Frank rolls his eyes lasciviously.

Della spreads more suntan lotion over her shoulders and onto her thighs.

"You're beautiful when you're angry," Frank says. He reaches to put his hand on her calf. She slaps it away like she's swatting flies.

"Then I must be beautiful all the time since I met you." She closes her eyes. A few minutes later, she says in a different tone of voice, "We should be dressed when they arrive."

"Won't the kid—"

"Kathy is her name."

"Won't Kathy want to swim? When I was a child, that's all I did on vacations. Swim, swim, swim."

Della finishes her glass of mineral water and closes her eyes. After making herself completely comfortable, she says, "Kathy can swim if she wants. We don't have to all join her. We can sit in chairs like adults and talk to my father. I haven't seen Roland in almost a year."

"What shall we talk about?"

Della doesn't answer. She's decided to take a nap. "Cover your legs if you're going to sleep, Frank. They're red as lobsters already."

"Okay, Mom," Frank says. He jumps into the pool and swims twelve laps without stopping.

"I have nothing to wear," Della says, pouting into the mirror.

Frank has put on a long white T-shirt and new jeans with the creases still in them. He's tied back his long hair in a neat ponytail.

"You look like an ad for the Gap."

"At least I'm ready," Frank says. "He'll be here in twenty minutes."

"How about this?" Della asks and holds up a flowered jersey dress.

"It would show off your tan."

Frank has walked over to where Della is standing. He sits in front of her on the bed wincing up at her face because his legs are so burned.

"I'm not trying to display my tan. I merely want to look presentable." She's put on the flowered dress and is hooking a necklace made of small irregular turquoise and coral beads and tiny bells. It makes a slight tinkling sound as she brushes her hair, applies lipstick and mascara.

"I read there's a new mascara for men that defines your eyelashes without adding color."

"First you want to be tied up and now you covet my makeup. Try to hide your perversity in front of my dad, please."

They're sitting in the nearly empty dining room. It's three o'clock, an off-hour at the lodge, and though they serve "High Tea" from three to five, no one's very interested with the temperature over one hundred degrees.

Her father's dressed in a beige poplin suit. He's wearing a light-blue shirt and a pink, yellow, and cream-striped tie. He has Della's thick eyebrows, but his hair is much curlier and mixed with gray. He appears to be amused in advance of anything being said. Della imagines a stranger would call his face sympathetic. Kathy looks like she was manufactured in a different country from her stepfather. Her eyes are light blue and her complexion is pale. Her hair is blonde and thin, worn in a blunt cut that ends abruptly at her chin. She's eleven. Kathy's angularity clashes with the table they've chosen. She tries sitting with her elbows on the table. Then she crosses her legs and folds her arms over them on her lap. Then she adjusts her tank top, fiddles with the drawstring of her shorts, cups her chin in one hand and tells the waitress she'll just have 7 UP. The rest of them have ordered "High Tea." The waitress has brought over a silver and glass pastry tray. Roland makes up a small plate for Kathy and suggests she'll want it later. Della watches her father.

"Dad," Kathy says in an exasperated tone familiar to Della. It strikes Della as odd that Kathy also calls this man Dad.

"Your mom tells me you're up here for a week," Roland says. "Any special reason, or just a little break?"

"We thought we'd get away before I start graduate school and Della begins her job," Frank offers.

"You'll be working in the art department?"

"Right, I'll be answering arty phone calls and Xeroxing arty supply orders."

"You never know how you can make use of diverse training later in life. Jessica has a degree in classics, but she's lobbying now. She writes speeches for environmental lobbies and goes up to Sacramento all the time."

There is a long pause. Della doesn't think that she wants to hear more about Kathy's mom. "What is it you do?" she asks Kathy.

"Not much."

"Kathy's going into sixth grade. She's very good in science and plays the cornet."

"I'm not sure I know what a cornet is," Della says.

"It's a small trumpet," Kathy explains. She holds her fingers in the air and pretends to be playing.

"Frank's in a band," Della offers.

"I play the saxophone." Frank holds an imaginary sax in the air and strains to reach a note. "I started in the Santa Rosa marching band in high school."

"What color was your uniform?" Kathy asks.

"Yeah, what color was it?" says Della.

"Pink with green stripes."

Kathy laughs.

"Really, it was fire-engine red. When I was in the band, I used to pretend that I was playing solos like Sonny Rollins. Probably that's why I wasn't in the band for very long."

"I want to be in a marching band someday."

"A noble ambition," Frank smiles.

"I also like games," says Kathy.

"What kind of games?" Della asks.

"Games my dad and I make up."

"Like what?" Della asks.

"There's one we play called Death Swap."

"Sounds spooky," Frank says.

"How does it go?" Della asks. She thinks she's not feeling very well. The light from the windows near the pool looks too bright. The dish of pastries in front of her appears to be swimming in a cloud. Maybe she has to throw up.

"You think of who's dead and who you want back. Like John Lennon."

"Have you read the latest about John Lennon?" Frank asks anyone who's listening. "Seems he liked to pee in people's—"

Della gives Frank a smiting look.

"So who would you take?" Kathy asks Della.

"I don't understand," Della says.

"I offer you someone in exchange for John Lennon. If you accept him, I can have John Lennon."

"How can I give you John Lennon?"

"This is just a game, Della," her father explains. "Kathy doesn't expect you to give her John Lennon."

"So I tell you who I'd accept in exchange for John Lennon."

"Right. Like maybe a movie star, or it could be a politician or a sports figure. He has to be just as valuable as John Lennon, though."

"How about Michael Jackson?" Frank says.

"You're not playing, I am," Della says. There is a funny light coming off the silverware. She closes her eyes and blinks twice quickly. She sees that everyone is waiting for her to answer. "My mind is blank," she says. "Besides, how do you make points?"

"You don't. Isn't having John Lennon or John F. Kennedy or Marilyn Monroe back enough?"

"Okay, you give me Dad for John Lennon," Della says.

"You can't use people you know. It gets too personal then."

Della is watching her father's face. A smile is covering it like asphalt. "That's my final offer, Kathy."

"Della's a real card," Frank is saying. "Why don't we try it again? Let's you and me play, Kathy. I know how to negotiate."

"Okay, who would you give me for the Big Bopper?" Kathy asks.

"How about Dolly Parton?" Frank replies.

"Excuse me," Della says. She thinks she'll go stand by the pool and get some fresh air. The carpeting is swirling at her feet. Her lips are dry and her throat feels closed, as if it'll never swallow again.

The next thing she knows, everyone's standing around her. Frank is putting a cool towel on her forehead. Her father's in a squat, holding her wrist in his hand. Kathy looks like she's trying to hold back tears. "Will she be okay?" Kathy's asking.

"I think she's okay already," Frank explains. "Too much sun can do this to someone."

Della says she'll get up. She staggers over to the nearest table and holds her head in her hands.

"I feel terrible about this," Roland is saying. "I wish I could stay and make it up to you at dinner. I would have liked this visit to have left us all with a better feeling."

Della waves off the comment with her hand. Then her face clears of its misery. "Why don't Frank and I ride back with you?" Della asks. "This vacation isn't working out anyway."

"I don't think that's a good idea, Della. They have a plane to catch in San Francisco."

"Having us in the car won't make them drive any slower, Frank. Besides, I don't feel well. I think it would be better to be in the city if I'm possibly sick."

"Della, it was just the sun. We overdid it outside."

"I'll be happy to drive you back," Roland offers.

Since it's Sunday night, they're caught in an endless line of traffic returning from Wine Country. Kathy and Roland sit in the front seat of the rented Taurus. Frank and Della share the back seat. Della is closing her eyes and leaning her head on Frank's shoulder. Her father is talking to Frank.

"There's lots of room in arts management. You might consider getting a law degree too. Lots of legalese in every field today. Think of how baseball has changed. Someone couldn't have an agent who isn't a lawyer anymore." He waits for Frank's reply.

"He's asleep," Della explains. "Whenever people talk to him about his career, he always falls asleep. He's going to grad school, but he hopes his band will still make it big."

"What do you think was wrong with you, Della? I never saw anyone faint before," Kathy says.

"Probably just the sun, or too much excitement."

"Playing Death Swap isn't that exciting," Roland laughs.

"What's Frank's band's name?" Kathy asks. She unbuckles her seat belt and sits on her knees with her chin perching on top of the headrest so she can see Della better.

"Pardon me, Kathy, but they're called Cock."

Kathy turns around and fastens her seat belt again.

Roland smiles apologetically at Kathy, who has taken a Mad Libs game out of her duffel bag.

"Give me an adjective."

"Straining," Della says.

"This traffic is endless." Roland hums quietly for a minute in the same way Della does when she's nervous. "We should have been back by now, I didn't think it possible that we'd be cutting it close."

"You can drop us anywhere, Dad, as soon as you're back in the city."

At nine-thirty they pull up in front of Frank and Della's apartment, the second floor of a Victorian near Golden Gate Park.

"I wish you could come up," Della tells her dad.

"My next trip," Roland assures. He's unloaded their luggage onto the sidewalk. Standing at the curb, he gives Della a light hug. "Watch that sunburn," he advises.

Della peers into the back window of the car. "I'll wake up Sleeping Beauty."

Kathy smiles broadly.

"Frank!" She opens the door and shakes his arm.

Startled awake, Frank sits up and stretches, pulls at his ponytail, realizes they're home, and bolts out of the car. He stands on the sidewalk rubbing his eyes with the stupefied look of a child.

Frank and Roland shake hands. Roland embraces Della again and tells her to take it easy for a few days.

"Why did you call your band that gross name?" Kathy asks out of her window before they pull away.

"His last girlfriend suggested it," Della explains, waving good-bye. She watches her dad roll up the car's automatic windows and speed away down the long, sloping street.

"A memorable day," Frank says as he takes a suitcase in either arm up the stairs.

"Who would you give me for Lou Reed?" Della asks when they've reached their landing.

"Lou Reed's not dead yet," Frank says.

"It's good to plan for the future," Della says, hesitating at their door.

Heathcliff

AMY IS CRYING for the third time this afternoon. She's sitting on the bay-shaped window seat and looking out at her yard, where Vincent is raking leaves into neat circular piles. Because they've been fighting on and off all day, he's ignoring her. She watches his back, his buttocks, the crease up the back of his pants leg as he leans over to stuff the damp leaves into bags. She glances away when he turns toward the window to look at her. Letting her tears perch on the rims of her eyes before blinking them away, she watches them land on her belly. She calls it a belly now, which is exactly what it is, something convex, something swollen. It's a luxury to cry so much. Talking to the baby inside her, she says, *Daddy is raking leaves.* She has made a promise not to say anything mean about Vincent to the baby.

Vincent's hands smell of soap. He holds her chin in his palm and rubs it absentmindedly. "Perk up," he says.

"How can I feel cheery when you said what you did?"

"It was supposed to be a joke." Vincent picks up a tiny clod of dirt that has fallen off his loafers onto the hall runner and kneads it between his fingers as he sits beside her on the window bench.

She narrows her eyes and asks, "What kind of husband says, 'I feel as much sympathy for you as I do for any pregnant mammal'?"

"Bambi's mother's husband?" Vincent begins to laugh, a flat, crackly laugh, but when he sees that she hasn't appreciated it, he looks out at the yard and is silent.

The locust tree shakes off a few more miniature leaves. Amy can see that Vincent feels annoyed at the tree. It's making more work for him. He looks like Gregory Peck when he thinks, but she won't tell him that now. She won't please him.

"I'm just saying that we don't have to get sentimental every hour because we're going to be parents. I wouldn't even sit with my parents at the movies. For about fifteen years I would have chosen anyone on earth but them." Vincent tries to take her hand, but Amy withdraws it quickly.

She stares at his familiar knuckles. "That's very sad," she says, shaking her head slowly from side to side and patting her belly. *Isn't that sad?* she asks the baby inside her.

"Or imagine sitting at the park when a smarter, cuter, better-behaved and generally more likeable child than your own climbs up the slide. Don't you think that kids can be as disappointing as parents? Let's drop it though, Amy. I have to go out before the stores close."

"Doing some shopping before your eugenics meeting? Tell them we want our Übermensch to sleep nights from the start."

"I just need a haircut. I've been waiting all week."

"Can't I go along?"

"Amy," Vincent moans, "it's a haircut."

"Okay. Can you just drop me off on the way?"

"Any old place or a particular destination?"

"I'll go to a movie."

"What movie?"

"Who cares? I want to get out of the house."

Amy blows her nose hard. Vincent takes the Kleenex box from her lap, and before placing it on the counter, hugs her in the exchange.

She goes to the hall closet and, parting ski parkas and folded beach chairs, finds her metallic silver rain slicker, which won't close anymore. Amy lets Vincent pat her belly, then follows him out the door watching his neck, how the childishly fine hair curls up as it grows over his collar. She doesn't understand why they're not angry at each other anymore.

"I think it's depressing to have a baby in December," she says. "Everything will be dead outside." She looks at the geraniums and marigolds trimming her walk. She wonders why the most resilient flowers are so mundane. "Bambi was born in the spring," she continues, but Vincent is already at the car, whisking leaves off the hood, too distant to hear her conciliatory joke.

Whatever movie is playing, she'll see it. She'll buy a large Coke without ice and sit so close that the screen will look as big as an ocean. She'll cry her stupid eyes out again. A few weeks ago when they saw *Passage to India*, the baby's movements accelerated to the martial music. Amy had taken Vincent's hand and had him feel the baby's strident kicks and lunges. She knows that babies belong to you before they are born. She talks to hers in a soft adult voice.

�֍

"You're in luck. It's a three-hankie special," Vincent says. The marquee reads *Wuthering Heights*. "Call me when it's over and I'll pick you up."

Vincent waves good-bye. He wants a good haircut, close to his ears but long enough in front so that the thinning won't show. Most important, he wants an understanding attitude on the part of the barber. Ten weeks ago when his fellowship started, Amy sent him to her hair designer, Dawn, who didn't understand the concept at all.

"You mean you're not working," she said. "I bet Amy's worried, with the baby coming and all."

"They want me to sit at home and be creative," he was about to say when the blow-dryer started, and Dawn's thin sharp face showed no sign of interest in his intellectual growth.

Now he wants to find a barber who'll appreciate his efforts. Not that he needs the approval of strangers, but he likes people cutting his hair to show a little respect.

"I don't know why you go to Dawn," he'd told Amy later.

His vehemence made her lip curl up in amusement. "Because Dawn can cut my hair in ten minutes. Because she's not interested in Bedouin eating habits."

"Non sequitur."

"Don't you remember that electrician who wouldn't leave me alone once he discovered that I'd lived in Africa?"

"No," he had said just to be peevish. Amy had been in the Peace Corps right after college. She'd introduced soybeans to an area of the Sudan where they were unsuited to grow. Whenever Vincent wants to feel tender about Amy, he thinks of the shriveling vines she lovingly tended for a year.

Now he is in front of a regulation-looking barbershop. An elderly man is sleeping in a marbled red barber's chair. He wears the high-collared medicinal-blue shirt of a dentist or a pharmacist. The sign outside says "Lucky's."

When Vincent opens the door, an old-fashioned bell rings. Vincent remembers that same ringing from his childhood. He connects it with the acrid smell of a dry cleaner's store that also sold candy, kite string, and eyeglass chains.

Lucky slouches to his feet. He appears to be surprised at the heaviness of his own body. "Hi," he says.

Vincent feels relieved that this is going to be easy. "I need a haircut." He smiles the gratuitous smile of a potential victim.

"Sit down." Lucky fixes a rough terry towel around Vincent's neck with a barber clip. Vincent wonders how a one-man barbershop can keep Lucky in clean towels.

"Busy today?"

"Oh, sure."

He's no talker. Vincent can see himself looking straight ahead in the curved mirror. Behind him are three empty red armchairs, where customers can wait.

"I get the regulars," Lucky adds.

"Steady customers?"

"Right. A man down the street comes in. He's nearly blind, but once a week I trim his hair and do a lot for his ears. Lots of hair in them. He wants to be sure they're working. He's in on Tuesdays."

Vincent wonders if that's Lucky's only regular customer. "Well, I'm in the neighborhood, but I usually get my hair cut at the university." He tries not to look at himself as he lies. When Lucky doesn't respond, Vincent continues, "I'm off this semester researching a book on economics. My wife is off too because she'll be having a baby soon."

"I don't cut children's hair. They won't sit still, not for a minute. I tell their mothers or fathers, 'These are dangerous tools I use.'" He snips the air for emphasis. "But they don't care."

"Been in business long?"

"Thirty-seven years. Right out of the army I started working for Lucky. His heart got bad, so he moved to New Mexico about six years ago. I still think he'd have done better in Florida. He's died since. You know how it is."

"So your name's not Lucky?"

"I'm Dennis."

"Why not call it Dennis's?"

"Why change now?"

In the long silence that follows, Dennis finishes the haircut, shaves Vincent's neck, dusts his collar line from an ancient yellowed container of talc, and holds a head-shaped mirror up to his head.

"Looks fine."

At six he picks Amy up at the movie. She is waiting outside studying the marquee when he pulls up. Her rain slicker looks like a child's. Her profile is more poignant than he wants to acknowledge. "Hey, pregnant lady, want a ride?"

She climbs in slowly and crosses her legs. Her arms encircle her belly. "Who cut your hair?"

"Not Lucky."

"If not Lucky, then who?"

"Dennis, but he won't cut children's hair, so don't ask."

"All right."

"How was the movie?"

"We liked it," Amy says. "Laurence Olivier was a beautiful man." She's quiet for a minute. "How about naming the baby Heathcliff?"

"Wasn't Heathcliff an orphan?"

"That's my point," Amy says. "You don't want to have a child, do you?"

Vincent feels overcome by sadness. He remembers a summer in Greece when he and his parents had three hours on Mykonos before their tour boat was going to leave. Walking in the late-afternoon heat down a typical lane with its white houses and blue-washed doorways, they saw a parlor in which an elderly mother, father, and a son about Vincent's age were watching television. A calico cat was perched on the set, on which Cuba was playing the United States in Olympic basketball. Sometimes its tail swished over the screen, and their view was obscured. Vincent saw that his father looked moved, and asked him if something was wrong. His father had said, "Look at how small the world's become, son." Vincent knew he'd meant more: that they could have been this family, discovered by chance in the middle of an ocean; that soon, since Vincent was graduating college, he would never live with his parents again.

Vincent pulls over two blocks before their house and turns off the car engine.

"What are you doing?" Amy asks.

"I'm too sad to drive," he says, pressing his body toward Amy and nuzzling her neck.

"What are you sad about?"

"Families."

"I know," Amy says. "But our family will be different. No one will ever get old. Our children will always love us. We'll send those silly letters at Christmas that report on Jimmy's art project and Nora's braces."

They both laugh uneasily.

Amy looks into the picture window of the red Georgian across the lawn. The front room is lit by the blue iridescence of a television screen. Amy can see an older woman standing in front of the window facing several others seated on a couch. The woman is waving her hands up and down, her fingers moving in graceful sweeps in and out of the light.

"Look!" she whispers to Vincent. "She's leading them all in a song."

"That's what I mean," Vincent says. "Look at that old woman. She thinks that what she's doing is private, but we're watching her, Amy. People will watch us be parents, and they'll judge. And how will we know if we're right or they're right?"

"Why are you assuming we'll be at odds?"

"Because no one ever understands, Amy. You don't have to lock your children up or abuse them. You just have to be their parents to do something wrong. You're bound to slip up. My parents were kind, but they slipped up constantly in so many ways. It can't be helped."

"Listen," Amy says, putting Vincent's hands on her heaving belly. "The baby is talking to you. What is he saying?"

"I don't know, Amy. Is this a séance?"

"He's saying that he understands. That he forgives you already. He's saying he's glad to know you."

Vincent starts the car. He opens his mouth but doesn't say anything.

Amy wonders whether he has accepted her benediction. Later, when she bathes in the lion's-claw tub that she's grown nearly too large to fit, she'll apologize to the baby for telling this necessary lie.

The Stockholm Syndrome

I T ISN'T RIGHT for a woman with one breast, a woman anyone would call matronly, to go on vacation, meet a man, and never come home. That's what Clarice did last summer, and all I have is a postcard to hint at a reason. I blame Buddy, who made her life difficult at home. She once told us why the book club could never meet at her house. "Buddy doesn't want his privacy invaded," she apologized, jokingly. Maybe he would have to throw on a clean shirt for us or help Clarice serve the refreshments. Maybe he would have to say more than hello. Not that he was a bad kid, but he was a kid for too long.

Clarice would come to our book club meetings prepared, ready as anyone to discuss whatever it was we were reading. One week, long before it became a movie with that sad sack William Hurt, it was *The Accidental Tourist*. Clarice was the presenter, which is how we work it. We take turns. One month Shirley does it, one month Irene, one month it's me, and then Clarice. It's no little thing to be a presenter. Irene, for one, gets a new dress when it's her turn. I remember one Tuesday last March when she looked radiant. It was her turn to lead us in *The Life of Patty Hearst*. I for one wouldn't trade Patty Hearst's millions for her rotten life. But that's another story. Irene was wearing a black rayon suit with little white dots by Nina Piccalino. But what I remember most is how passionate Clarice got defending the girl. She said she might do anything for a lover, like Patty Hearst did. We asked if he'd have to lock her in a closet, and she said no. There's just a time in your life when things are right to do, and I guess when Clarice went to California was one of them.

She was sixty-seven, which means that Buddy's thirty-seven. Now I believe in strong family ties, but Buddy's not a regular kid. He's been known to take advantage. I've known Clarice so long that I remember Buddy as a child. Kids can get clingy when a father dies, but even before Abe passed, it was Buddy needs this and Buddy needs that and Buddy can't do this or that for himself.

That's why that particular book-club meeting on *The Accidental Tourist* is so memorable. Clarice is in the middle of making an important point about one of Macon's brothers. Shirley's in the middle of disagreeing, and the phone rings. It's Buddy. He's locked himself out of the house, and Clarice is supposed to leave the book club to let him in. We can tell she's embarrassed. The discussion isn't half over, and she has to excuse herself because a grown man can't hold on to his keys or hang out in a bar until she's expected home. She says it won't take more than twenty minutes and she's right. At two-twenty she's back, and I really must commend the way she picked up the discussion right where she left off. The sad part was that we were about four chapters ahead, but nobody had the heart to tell her.

One of Clarice's arms is always swollen from the operation she had some years ago. She's a thin woman with a pretty face and clear blue eyes. We call her Einstein, not because she's a genius but because of her hair. I bet when she was little, someone was always telling her to fix her crazy hair. It's the kind of short hair that looks long and wild. She has a nice figure and dresses well. You can't tell except for her arm that she's had the breast removed. I can see how a man would be interested in her face. She'd usually wear full sleeves, but sometimes she would see a nice suit or dress and just buy it. If she can live with her arm, anyone should be able to. I wonder if the man she met noticed the arm or not. I think about it because Clarice is shy, and I worry about their first time in bed if he didn't know.

She sent me a postcard of Chinatown after she decided to stay in San Francisco. Now years ago, I was in that same Chinatown with my family. We were in a restaurant that serves dim sum, those little dumplings with different fillings, and damned if a little Chinese girl doesn't pass us with a cartful of cooked duck's feet. They are as yellow as the sun, and one of my little ones, Andrea, screams. She was a real sensitive kid. If she saw a bug smashed on a windshield, she'd cry. Having three brothers didn't make it any easier for her. One of them was always hurting something by accident, of course. If there was a cat around, its tail might get slammed in a door, or if there were goldfish, maybe one of the boys would leave the bowl in the sun on an early

September afternoon. Their water would get so hot they'd be cooked by the end of school, and poor little Andrea would come in and discover them. So it was really too bad that even on our vacation she couldn't get away from it all.

Clarice never sent photos of duck's feet. She sent a bright-red pagoda, and the message was short: "I'm so happy with Keith that I've decided to stay." Well, if she's happy, I'm happy too, but getting that message made me wonder. You'd think she might have called, but sweethearts like their privacy.

When the postcard came, I phoned Irene. I wondered if we should visit Buddy and inquire after his health. Here's a boy, a grown man, really, but every creature comfort has always been given him. He gets three square meals a day and a warm place to sleep. Putting it that way makes it sound like he's living in a kennel, but you know what I mean. He doesn't have to struggle like the rest of us. Clarice has some money, Buddy has a good man managing his dad's old business, and things are fine. Maybe he meets a girl now and then, but it's never serious enough to replace Clarice.

First Irene says we shouldn't meddle. If Buddy's unhappy, Clarice is sure to know. But I say it's the kind thing to do. Suppose Clarice died. Wouldn't we look after Buddy for her? From Buddy's point of view, Clarice's moving away might not be much different from her dying. So Irene agrees. If I call Buddy and he wants to see us, she'll come along.

I try reaching Buddy for about four nights without much luck. It's a Friday night when I finally get him on the line.

"Buddy," I say. "It's Mrs. Riess." Not that I'd mind him calling me Margaret, but he's always called me Mrs. Riess.

I hear him turning down the television in the background and saying hello at the same time. He doen't sound all that glad to hear from me.

"Irene and I were hoping you're fine. We wanted to say hello." He doesn't say a word, so I'm going on like this. I even tell him the story about the duck's feet before he says much of anything.

He asks me how my kids are. I give him the summary, though I spare some details about Andrea's divorce. That's a topic I try to avoid. It's better for my health. I ask him if he needs anything, and he says he would like to talk to us, meaning me and Irene, and says why not come by tomorrow about four.

When I tell Irene that he wants to see us, I'm surprised at how she reacts. She has no curiosity or confidence, I'm not sure which. She says in her twitchy little voice that Saturday's really a bad day for her, and she already has plans, and about a hundred other things that don't make sense. She uses up every alibi she's ever contrived for this one meeting with a boy of no consequence. I tell her I'll go alone, and she says she promised to go and will try to live up to it.

I've known Irene forever. Even when we were kids, things used to intimidate her. There was a teacher who was crazy. You could have had Miss Nichols certified. It terrified her to be touched. She'd shout things at children like, "Look what you've done! You've made a run in my stockings!" when someone stepped on her toe. We'd intentionally jostle her just to see her face turn red and her eyes get small with anger. But not Irene. Irene spent fifth grade watching extra carefully where she stepped. Once, as a prank, Bobby Roeder pushed Irene into Mrs. Nichols. "We should watch where we land!" Miss Nichols screeched, knowing full well as a teacher that objects crashing through space don't have a will of their own.

Irene honks for me at three forty-five. I'm already out on the porch waiting. I've bought some bakery cookies to take to Buddy, and Irene, the one who doesn't want to go, has baked a marble pound cake. It's sitting between us on the front seat of her Ford. Irene's a slow driver, so we arrive about twenty minutes later, when it should take ten.

We wait a long time at the door before Buddy answers. I expect to find a mess in the house, but the front room is immaculate, and Buddy has laid out some fancy pastries and nice mugs for coffee. He's ground the coffee in a special machine, and it smells much better than the instant I've come to use. Buddy seems to have a house guest too, a nice younger man named Dave. Dave is in the kitchen when we come in, and his sleeves are pulled up to his elbows, and his hands are in the sink. He's washing dishes. It's not remarkable because men are different these days. They take care of things if they have to.

We sit in the front room. Buddy and I are on the couch. Irene's in a light-blue easy chair, and when Dave finishes in the kitchen and we're still making small talk, he joins us too.

"Nice of you to come," Dave says, like we're here to see him, and I begin to wonder if Dave is more than a friend.

"Do you hear from your mom?" I ask Buddy.

"They talk all the time," Dave says. "You should see our phone bill."

The way he says "our phone bill" clears a few things up for me. "I bet you're glad to have Dave around now that your mom's away," I tell Buddy.

I look at Irene, and she's digging a hole in her coffee cup with her spoon. She won't look at me no matter what I do.

"Dave lived here before Mom left," Buddy tells me. "She's happy out there, and I'm happy here."

"So everybody's happy," I add. I look around the walls of the room. There's a lot of Indian art and some is frankly erotic. I wonder if Dave's an anthropologist. "So what do you do for a living?" I ask him.

"I'm a dog groomer," he says. "We met when Buddy still had Bridget." Bridget, their poodle, has been dead for almost a decade. I know that because Bridget died before Rudy, my little collie.

"And you've lived here all these years?" I ask.

"Only seven months," Dave explains. And he shoots this little smile that's only meant for Buddy through the room.

"Have you met Keith?" I ask Buddy.

"The mysterious Keith? No, but he sounds very nice on the phone. He's a retired math teacher. Do you know how they met? Mom went to a Scrabble club, and they played each other in a semifinal round."

"Who won?" I ask, and Buddy says he doesn't know. I think it's strange that he doesn't know the outcome of a story he must tell again and again, but some people are just naturally curious and some are not.

Now Irene, who's been as quiet as can be, pipes up. She doesn't say she likes their furniture or anything normal. "I think it's the Stockholm Syndrome," Irene says.

Plunk, the words just lie there. She's back to stirring her coffee and choosing another pastry. I know what she's talking about, but does she expect me to do all the explaining?

Finally Dave says politely, "Excuse me, but what's that?" It figures he doesn't know about the Stockholm Syndrome, being a dog groomer. It's not like a dog groomer can't listen to the news, but he probably doesn't go in for the big issues like me and Irene and the rest of us in the club.

Of course Irene doesn't answer. There's a moment of silence that makes everyone flinch, and then I say, "It's when captives fall in love with their captors. Like Patty Hearst having a love affair with that man who raped her."

The men exchange glances. I bet they don't expect old women, friends of Buddy's mother, to talk that way. I wasn't trying to be shocking. I was just trying to explain what they asked.

"So you think my mother's being held against her will?"

"Pardon me," I say, "but I was just elaborating for Irene."

That puts Irene on the spot, so she pipes up for once. "This man beats your mother, a very good Scrabble player, and then they fall in love. It doesn't have to be physical, how people overpower you. Keith subdued your mother, and now she thinks she loves him." Her mouth snaps shut like an electronic door.

Two things come to my mind. Dave and Buddy haven't asked why it's named after Stockholm. If either of them were really thinking, he'd have asked. And why is it that Irene thinks Clarice lost at Scrabble? No one said a thing about her losing. "Buddy, did Clarice lose?" I ask.

"She didn't say." Then he's quiet for a second. "But if she didn't say, I'd guess she did lose." Buddy and Dave share a big laugh because they've thought of the same thing at the same time. I remember laughing like that with Norman before the kids were born. I try to smile at Irene about Buddy's conclusion, but it's not the same.

I see that it's getting late outside and these two men are probably busy, so I tell Irene we'd better go.

"Why do they call it the Stockholm Syndrome?" Dave asks before we're out the door. Hoping Irene will do some of the work, I'm quiet. We stand there still as statues until I say that Stockholm's the place that hostages go to get deprogrammed. Buddy makes some joke about a clinic that breaks hearts, and we all laugh at that. I don't know if Stockholm's a romantic place, I'm thinking, but there are all kinds of love, that's for sure.

Dave shakes my hand and then takes Irene's hand in his to say goodbye. Watching Irene's tentative smile, I think of crazy old Miss Nichols.

As soon as we're in the car, Irene sighs. I'm used to her making that same sigh after sixty years, but it says so little that I'm wondering why she's satisfied with it anymore.

Saving the Australian Elephant

BARRY AND JOAN made a perfect olfactory pair. He smelled nothing, she everything. She told him how the logs smelled on the fire. On the morning that he decided to leave, she didn't tell him that their dinner of mussels the night before had left an unpleasant odor in the kitchen. I have this information on the testimony of Joan. Few times are we privy to turning points in people's lives. Mostly we hear about them later and sometimes unintentionally.

Although I hardly knew Joan, her story has become the unifying theme of my week in Australia. If someone other than my boss asks me what I accomplished there, I'll say, "I learned about Joan."

Let's start at the beginning, though. I heard many conversations during my week in Sydney. I'd get on the bus, pay my fare, gauged by the distance I was to travel, and knowing no one and having little to do, listen to people around me.

One morning an elderly couple said this:

He: Frank's a good man.

She: So is she.

He: They have one child?

She: They have five!

I decided that many couples, me and my ex-wife included, were like the bus passengers, unable to agree on the simplest details of living.

Another thing the elderly couple said was that the African elephant was in danger. The husband wondered whether that was the elephant with the larger or smaller ears. The wife said she didn't know. Moreover, she added, as long as the elephants in Australia were fine, she didn't much care what happened to them in Africa.

I had recently visited the Taronga Zoo, where, along with German honeymooners, I'd taken a monorail to the top of the path leading down to the giant panda exhibit from China. From what I know of

German, it seems the couple was having a spirited argument about structuralism. As the husband tried to direct her attention to the lush pathways below, where ibises strolled like Sunday tourists, the woman made her final point. "Barthes," she said, kohl-lined eyes squinting in fervor, "ist sehr alt." The husband laughed and mussed her hair in affection, but I detected the tension. In any case, their knees seemed to point aggressively at me, and I was glad when our ride ended.

The pandas were sleeping when my turn came to view them. Maybe if I could have stayed longer, one would have lumbered to its feet and at least munched perfunctorily on some bamboo. Because the animals were so inactive, I spent most of my time observing the working-class Australian couple who'd taken their children, all wearing ornate cowboy boots, to see the exhibit. They were in an ill humor and frequently slapped their youngest son for disobeying, which included bumping into me. I didn't mind that the little boy was unaware of where his family ended and I began. I thought of telling the parents so, but I'm careful not to interfere in the order of things when I travel. This is a conscious decision based on the time when I removed a sleeping tortoise from a median strip in West Virginia and set it safely in the grass by the roadside. After I'd driven away, I was haunted by misgivings. Had I placed him on the wrong side of the road, ruining his life forever?

I had noticed that the elephants in the Taronga Zoo looked very healthy. The trainer put them through their paces, and the female elephant, who was especially obliging, stood on a barrel and balanced on one foot. She was very calm about it. From what I could gather, the woman on the bus was right in assuming that her own elephants were content. They had nothing to fear from society encroaching or poachers killing off the large males to obtain their tusks.

At day's end, I'd take the long bus ride to Stanmore and recount my adventures to Joan. When I told her what I had heard on the bus and in the monorail, she chose not to reply. Later that night, when I was sitting at her kitchen table planning my next day's activities, she told me what she really thought about zoos. She herself wouldn't visit one, considering how the animals were imprisoned and exploited. She wondered if zoos weren't built so that Americans, the spoiled children of the globe, could feel at home wherever they traveled.

I told her I hadn't had a particularly good time at the zoo myself, what with the sleeping pandas and cruel parents, but that my own experience couldn't serve as proof of a definitive attitude on the part of all Americans. She went on to recount what an American family viewing koala bears had once said: "Look at how tame they are. They look stuffed." What they had said was ordinary enough. It was the manner in which she imitated them that was remarkable. Joan prided herself on reproducing American accents. The previous night I had stayed with her, she'd done an impression of Edward Kennedy talking to Jimmy Stewart, but her Boston dialect left much to be desired. I watched as it pulled her face askew and left her quite exhausted.

I finally began wondering what the real story was behind Barry's leaving Joan, not that I knew Barry or even took much interest in Joan. Just for the sake of truth, I began questioning if what drove them apart had anything to do with her false estimation of her abilities. Maybe she as well as Barry had a poor sense of smell, and several times a day people had to tell them embarrassing facts about themselves. Maybe they sat side by side on a bus discussing magnolias or marinara sauce, and a tourist such as I found himself interrupting their conversation to tell them that the calamari they were carrying home for dinner was causing more than a little unpleasantness for the other passengers. If this had happened too often, I'd imagine it could have placed quite a strain on even the best relationship.

The next morning, before I began the negotiations for which my firm had sent me to Sydney, I told Joan I wanted to take a walk in the Royal Botanical Gardens. My guidebook said they crest several hills facing the harbor.

"I'll draw you a map," Joan offered, "since the gardens are quite large." She sat down at her desk and quickly produced a detailed document. She used a calligraphy pen. The arrow she drew to indicate north seemed capable of flight.

From the map Joan had drawn me, I should have been able to see the art museum after approximately ten minutes of brisk walking from where the cab left me. After nearly half an hour of roaming through large uncultivated tracts and wondering whether I was even in the gardens proper anymore, I crossed paths with a tall middle-aged man and his three sons. All I wanted was to be directed toward the main gate, where I'd get a cab to go to my noon meeting. The man was wearing shorts, a good indication of his Australian origins. He was down from Brisbane for the day, and confessed that he, too, was lost. We marched on like a flock of geese, he leading, until we found a young bearded gardener who showed us on Joan's map where the main gates were.

"And the art museum?" I asked out of curiosity.

He pointed to a place off the map near my elbow.

"So my map is inaccurate?" I added, feeling as if I were already involved in the negotiating process.

"It's a travesty," the gardener said and laughed robustly, displaying handsome teeth.

As I'd expected, the contract was easy to negotiate. Both parties had lots of money to make from the deal, so I was less a lawyer than a courier of goodwill. The firm always anticipated problems that never arose, so I had two more days to spend in Sydney.

That night I greeted Joan and said nothing about my troubles in the garden. I hate hotels and was grateful for my lodgings with this woman, who was a college friend of my ex-wife's new husband. When Joan asked me how I had liked the aboriginal exhibit, I couldn't lie, of course.

"I never got there," I told her, thinking I'd drop it at that.

She exhaled air through her mouth, enough to blow a smoke ring if she had been smoking a cigarette. This was her expression of disgust, meaning I was a damned nuisance for not going to the exhibit after she'd gone to the trouble of drawing the map for me.

I suggested that I take her to dinner at that point, hoping the discussion would end. She was rather pretty in a plain sort of way. She looked like a drawing of simple beauty, one that a fourteen-year-old girl might make. There was nothing complicated about her looks, but her imprecision, which might lead ships to icebergs, was unfathomable to me.

She wouldn't let it drop at that. "I don't know why I bother," she said.

"If you mean the map, it was way out of proportion. Not only could I not find the museum, but I couldn't find a damned Australian who lived in Sydney to direct me out of the gardens." I stopped there, short of telling her about the gardener who'd called her map a travesty.

I heard her drawing a bath in the next room. She stayed in there for a long time and came out dripping wet in a blue terry robe and

Swedish clogs whose scuffing anticipated her arrival into the room. I could see that she'd been crying.

"I'm sorry," she said.

"No, I owe you an apology."

"I used to get things right all the time before Barry left," she said. "Do you know what I do for a living?"

I knew she was an engineer of some sort, but I didn't want to sound like a wise guy. "No, what?" I asked.

"I design fucking highways," she said, pronouncing it like "eye-ways." Then she made some tea. She used milk in hers, so I decided to have mine the same way.

"To highways," I toasted, raising my teacup.

We took the ferry to Mosman Bay and back to the harbor. From the boat you could see the botanical gardens, and beyond that, the museum I hadn't been able to locate.

"Do you still have my instructions?" she asked.

Without thinking, I said yes, and unfolded them from my pocket.

She laughed. It was a preface to anything that might follow. In the waning light of the evening, she studied the sheet with great purpose, eyes squinting. She shook her head in dismay.

"You might just throw it overboard," I said.

"I spoke to Barry today. He says he's interested in trying it again."

"That's wonderful," I said, thinking that my presence in her house had incited her to call and ask him back. Had I caused chasms to fill with regret for lost chances? I pictured the Grand Canyon overflowing with silt as I stood grinning at its rim. To make conversation, I said, "I'm sure Brian will be happy to hear that."

"Who's Brian?" she asked, puzzled.

"My ex-wife's new husband. Your friend from NYU, remember?"

"Brian never met Barry. He won't care in the least." Then she looked up at the sky so different in this hemisphere that I could-n't chart the stars at all. "How could your wife have preferred Brian to you?"

That surprised me enough that I decided to kiss her. When I opened my eyes again, I saw a Greek couple staring at us. I wondered if they knew any English. "Why do you say that about Brian?" I asked.

"He was such a thug in college. He'd batter down everyone's defenses with his smug intelligence, and just when we all wearied of listening, he'd dare to be utterly mundane. I guess that's American, huh?"

"Am I like that?" I asked.

"No, you seem more reticent, almost British. You turn a map upside down and think it leads you nowhere. I find that more British."

She was holding the map now, and before I could grab it from her, she tossed it into the harbor.

"You know what my son used to call our galaxy?" I asked. "Australia's in the same galaxy as we are, is it not?"

"What?" she asked, still flushed with the thrill of destroying evidence.

"He used to say we live in the Easy Way. Instead of the Milky Way," I added in case she hadn't understood.

She took my hand and pointed it toward the sky. "That's the Southern Cross," she said, tracing four lights above us. Then she smiled at me. It was crazy, but for a second I thought that she'd done a perfect imitation of my voice.

Element 109

MY GOOD OLD FRIEND Kenneth just turned forty-one, yet he insists on dating women who are twenty. That means they were born after Sonny and Cher fell from prominence. My brother and I, twelve and ten, respectively, used to dress in Neanderthal fur vests and join forces for a stirring rendition of "I Got You, Babe." Look where it got us. Two divorces later, he's a survivalist pamphleteer with a few essential credit cards. I'm still single and fairly normal, and waiting, I guess, for something. Meanwhile, I observe Kenneth, whose latest lover is Blair. For a period before Blair, they were all named Lonnie. I'd meet Kenneth and a Lonnie for lunch. They all looked as if their eyes were permanently focused on a distant shore. In two or three months it would be over.

Blair, unlike any of the others, has moved in with him. She is adjusting well to life with a man twice her age. It's probably not much different than living with Mom and Dad, but there's no Mom to tell Blair to turn down the CD. Blair seems at ease with her life at Kenneth's. They go for drives in the country and buy antique blue bottles. They try new cuisines at home. This week it was a Madras spinach cheese stew.

"Did the fabric bleed when you washed it?" I couldn't help but ask.

The only thing she doesn't understand, she confides to me, is why Kenneth named his dog Sam Dash.

"Watergate," I explain. "You know, dirty tricks."

"I haven't heard of them. I like the Talking Heads."

"Funny," I say. She looks bored and doesn't answer, brushing the longer side of her hair with an unconsciously alluring gesture. She does have a way. In another life I might kiss her. She displays her left shoulder with the flair of a waiter exhibiting the catch of the day. Then she looks past me, out to sea, but the sea is a window filled with shellacked loaves of bread in autumnal colors.

I try again. "Sam Dash was the Democratic counsel." Perhaps she'll take the initiative to look it up in her *Child Craft Encyclopedia*.

"I thought he chose Dash to make a pun on Spot."

"Maybe he's feeling nostalgic for Morse Code. Kenneth did serve in the army."

"He never told me," she says, listening like a good student.

"He was a medic in Vietnam until he got caught smoking grass by the wrong captain."

"Kenneth? He won't even take an aspirin."

"He was young once too."

"I think he's still very youthful."

Youthful, I think, picturing a graying couple on a pink beach. *Sylvia and Leonard keep their youthful good looks with regular doses of murderous thoughts.*

"I have to go, Blair," I say. "I have an appointment with my chiropractor at eleven. My lumbago's acting up."

"Oh," she says, serious, concerned. Maybe Kenneth loves her because she's so easy to fool. Was I that gullible when Kenneth and I were lovers? Probably, because we almost married before we decided that we canceled each other out. I laughed at all of his jokes before he got to the punch lines, and sometimes I finished his sentences. We agreed on what wasn't funny as well, like the time at the Christmas party when Dr. Keegan, the knee man, sang "Oh, Danny Boy," and wept onto Dr. Lui's lab coat. We became too secure in our perspectives, bitter after a while at having our worst suspicions confirmed daily. Then bored. By the time our relationship ended, our conversations went something like this:

Kenneth: Did you see that Dan looked so—
Marcy: I thought so too. Wasn't it because—
Kenneth: Yes. And did you know—
Marcy: Sure I know. Janie—
Kenneth: Has it all wrong. It was the—
Marcy: For sixteen thousand dollars how can he be so—
Kenneth: Simple. All he had to do—
Marcy: Besides, Dan isn't one to—
Kenneth: I know he likes to—

Marcy: Suffer. He likes to—
Kenneth: Suffer.

In a few years we might have abandoned speech altogether. Public television might have made a documentary on us, along with the man who opens cans by the force of concentration. With Blair there are long hours of briefings, nicely shaped sentences, whole skeins of connections to be unraveled. That is, until Kenneth discovered that Blair understood the Sam Dash allusion.

I received a call at work. I had a deadline to meet. My fourteen inches of type about the best Italian beef on Halsted Street were due in at 3 P.M.

"I have a problem," he sighed. Preceding his sigh was the first full sentence that Kenneth had spoken to me in years. "Blair is growing up."

"She's already six feet tall."

"Intellectually, Marcy. She wanted to discuss Watergate at dinner. She's reading *Blind Ambition* and *All the President's Men*. She disagrees with Woodward and Bernstein about the identity of Deep Throat."

"No!"

"And she's reading my scientific journals. She told me all about Element 109." His voice expressed the outrage of a Bluestocking at a brewer's convention.

"Heavy."

"Right. It's the heaviest element on the periodic chart."

"Don't lug any home. Have it delivered."

"She's turned industrious on me. May I see you tonight?"

"I have pudding class. Tonight it's plum pudding."

"Remember what we used to do at ten o'clock?"

Kenneth means the news. Soon he'll be singing tenor with Dr. Keegan, and he's not even Irish. I don't want to encourage his sentimentality, so I say, "No, what?"

"The news," he whispers.

"That's when news was news. Remember Barbara Jordan? She was a baritone." There's a pause, so I say, "Tell me more about Element 109."

"You'll need a new periodic table."

I have one over my breakfast nook. I love the elements with their evocative names like Xenon. Not even a sunset over Mount Fuji can top Xenon for beauty. When I need a lift, I string the names together for an instant mantra: *Promethium, Europium, Californium, Thulium, Erbium.* It's better than prayer.

"I can't see you, Kenneth."

He sighs. I used to mistake his resignation for pathology, the brave doctor concealing his condition from the woman he loves. Now I'm able to relax when Kenneth gets sad.

"Kenneth, it just wouldn't be . . . "

"I know."

How does he know when I can't imagine how I might have finished my sentence? "I told Blair about Sam Dash. That is, I gave her a clue. I thought of it as a test. Would Blair change her image? I wanted to imagine her at a big oak library table looking studious, if only to feel better myself."

The next morning I go to Warner's Science Outlet, Inc. The warehouse contains three floors of dried ferns, gyroscopes, monkey skulls, and stalagmite kits, all in dimly lit rooms bathed in formaldehyde.

"I want a periodic table with Element 109," I tell the clerk. He's wearing a scientist's smock and has a demented look about him, as if he's inhaled too much ammonia. He's about Blair's age but more solid than she is. Perhaps it's because his legs are short. Does having short legs make one practical and unassuming?

After looking through a black-and-white catalog, he says, "I'm sorry, ma'am. Our periodic tables don't show an Element 109."

Maybe he thinks I made the whole thing up. "It's new. It's the heaviest element." He looks as if he wished I'd go away. "If I come back in a few days, can I pick up a new chart?"

"I'll call the supplier, but sometimes these changes are slow. There are planets beyond Pluto that were discovered years ago, but on the Styrofoam models routinely sold to schools, the planets stop at Pluto."

Duly sobered, I thank him and leave the store.

Tonight I'm supposed to meet Blair for dinner. Her voice was on my answering machine when I came home from pudding class last night. So was Kenneth's. His messages are dots and dashes:

"Call me if . . . oh"—sigh—"forget it." He leaves no name.

I return Blair's call when I think Kenneth will be at his office.

What I've forgotten is that Kenneth is a doctor who takes Fridays off.

"Why are you home?"

"Because I don't golf."

"Is Blair home?"

"No, she does ceramics today. Want to come over?"

"Thanks, but I'm at work. Tell Blair I'll meet her at six. She knows where."

When she meets me at Tosca's, Blair resembles the Clay People who lived in caves on the *Flash Gordon* show. Her overalls are covered with gray dust. Her hair is slicked back and her face is ashen. We order a carafe of wine but decide to forgo dinner.

I wish there were more women in the movies who drank with style. Whenever I drink seriously, I feel like Humphrey Bogart. I know it would be healthier for me to identify with Olivia de Havilland.

"It's Kenneth, Marcy."

"What do you mean?"

"I'm not in love with him. I can't really talk to him, and I don't know what to do."

"Tell him," I suggest.

"I can't, Marcy. He's so . . . "

"Earnest? I guess it's a habit. Do you want *me* to tell him?" I think I said it with some irony in my voice.

"Would you, Marcy? Oh, thank you. All he does is lecture me. He'll listen to you. Do you think that you can tell him tonight? I have to go back to the studio and fire a piece before the kiln is turned off."

"Okay, Blair," I say, eyes meeting the carafe. I don't want to look at her. I have a feeling that her dusty getup is a ploy, that a twenty-year-old humanities major is waiting outside, holding her change of clothes and a crisp copy of *Anna Karenina*. I wish them well.

"I'll see Kenneth tonight," I tell her, half wondering if I'm crazy. Blair stands up, begins to offer me a handshake, withdraws it, and plants a dusty kiss on my cheek. Then she's out the door.

After I've finished my wine, I walk to the corner and wave casually at a cab, which blurs past me. Now my wave becomes an eccentric gesture that combines window-washing with pointing. It works. Johnny Star Cab number 109 pulls over. Turquoise and white, it resembles a police-car illustration from a child's picture dictionary. My cab driver is elderly and has a shiny head with red fringe speckled white, like orange juice dashed with rock salt.

We drive in silence. My driver is slow and thoughtful. We are always the last to leave the stoplight. Finally, he turns down Fifty-seventh and stops in front of Kenneth's. My stomach clenches when I see his lights are on.

Kenneth is watching the news. I've had twelve glasses of Chianti and notice that I'm speaking in the hurried clip of 1930s movies.

"It's over, Kenneth."

"I know. It's been over for years, Marcy."

"Not us. You and Blair. She wanted me to tell you it's over. That's why she saw me tonight."

Harry Reasoner, America's most trusted newsman, beams at us. Kenneth's big sigh fills the room. Slinking over, Sam Dash rests his bullet head in Kenneth's lap.

"She'll be fine. Will you?"

"Marcy, let's get married."

"Right, Kenneth."

We both laugh.

"They don't have periodic tables with Element 109," I tell him. Kenneth says nothing.

The River Shannon

ANCY, MY NEWEST EX, said, "Vacationing alone's like going to see a Velcro bullfight."

"What do you mean?"

"In a Mexican neighborhood last summer, they wanted to have a bullfight, but they didn't want to kill the bull, so they used swords tipped with Velcro."

I didn't understand how they could get Velcro to stick on a bull, but her main point was why should someone pay for a ruse?

"Nancy," I said, "vacationing alone is the trend of my future. It's a talent I have to cultivate, and I've chosen the most obvious place to do so."

I thought about what she'd said on the plane ride home. I had gone away for a week and everything had happened. The first boy who kissed my daughter won a Nobel Prize in genetics, the mayor died, and I met Fiona.

The man behind me was spanking his son.

"Take off your seat belt," he said to the boy. "You need to learn a thing or two."

I admit it's hard to travel with children, but it's not easy to travel alone either. While I had stood at Niagara Falls taking the usual snapshots, the ground had been shifting below me and a fine mist containing all the events of my past and future had hit me in the face.

I stayed on the Canadian side of the Falls at a place called the River Shannon. Don't ask me why they call it that. There wasn't one shamrock in sight. It was a modernist creation done in black, gray, aluminum, and mirrors, somber and streamlined as a funeral home in the twenty-second century. The rooms were colorful, though, and I was happy to see no ice machines near my door. I spent a little time watching Canadian television, mostly American reruns, and a lot of time sleeping.

Two afternoons I went down to the swimming pool. "Swim at your own risk," the sign said, as if a circular bath could harbor danger. That's as big as it was. No one else came to swim. I wondered if there was something wrong with the water or whether you simply don't swim at Niagara Falls. Maybe the Falls itself makes the idea of water superfluous.

I had covered myself with a big bath towel and was picturing a cartoon child playing in a sandbox in the desert when a man in a uniform said, "Mr. Price, you're wanted on the phone." The third day of my vacation and someone couldn't live without me.

I stood at the front desk watching my arms grow goose bumps while the nice gray carpet soaked up the moisture from my bare feet. It was my daughter on the phone. She sounded as if someone had been chasing her when she told me that Ronald Girtz had won the Nobel Prize.

"Who?"

"Ronald, the boy I used to see in ninth grade. He had a serious overbite? You once, um, saw us kissing in the rec room?"

How could I forget that? My daughter's on her second marriage and from what she tells me about Chuck, it's not going well either. She was a whiz kid in school and now she's a bank teller. I noticed my feet, which were bluish. The hair stopped right at the ankles, as if my skin were a flesh-colored sock. I said, "That's great, Felice. Tell him congratulations."

"I haven't talked to him in twenty years, Dad. I just thought you'd want to know."

"Well, thanks for calling," I told her. I handed the man the phone and he smiled at me. It was an obsequious smile. I wondered if he'd been listening. I wondered if Canadians like Americans.

On my last night at the Falls, I decided to have dinner at Van's. The hotel and restaurant directory had given it three stars. The worst part of being alone is eating, though I've found that if I take along a book or magazine and order lots of wine, I can usually turn it into a pleasant experience. Yesterday at lunch I'd read the third chapter of *Exodus* three times while finishing some Romanian merlot.

When I asked at the desk how to get to Van's, the clerk said I'd need a cab. I told him I'd prefer to walk, and he pointed me in the direction.

I started out on a narrow sidewalk that bordered a highway. Soon it dwindled to some fine gravel and dirt, then ended, so I found myself walking on the shoulder of the road. I could see the big neon v of the sign for Van's flashing green in the distance on the other side of the highway. While I was wondering how I might cross the divider and the median strip, I heard a sound like a wet firecracker behind me. Something exploded and sizzled. There was a squeal of brakes, followed by a powerful shove, and I was thrown forward but not as far as I'd expect a car to toss me.

In one sense it was as simple as that, but in a more immediate way the moment was prolonged so that getting up was a series of fragile connections, like building a model airplane with old glue. Muscle by muscle, I lifted myself into a crawling position. Then I squatted and held myself at the ankles for a long time. I was looking down in my lap and rocking back and forth. I was thinking about random things—Felice and Chuck's Christmas card of a snowman doing a backbend, the taxi meter from the airport registering my fare like a photo negative, kitchen wallpaper radishes in the first house I ever owned—and I was shivering all over even though I was trying to keep still.

"Are you okay?" a woman asked. Her forehead was extremely light, but the rest of her face was blotchy. It was so red that I couldn't stop staring at her cheeks.

"I think I am," I said and stood up slowly, more airplane glue and cautious fitting together of parts. Did my head sit on my neck, my spine on my legs? I looked myself over and saw that both knees of my slacks were ripped out, I could feel that the skin was scraped, but that's about all that was wrong.

"Thank God," the woman shouted, waving long fingers into the darkening sky. She looked so grateful that I thought she might kiss me. "I was thinking about a flowchart in my briefcase when I heard a huge pop. I guess I had a blowout and I veered up onto the shoulder. I never expected someone to be walking there. When I heard you hit the fender, I thought I might have a heart attack. Then the car somehow stopped, and I saw you sitting there."

I heard sirens and thought I should save my impressions of the accident for the police. The woman hovered over me. I noticed that she'd been wearing earrings shaped like big white telephones but had lost one in the excitement.

The policeman was very young. He came charging out of his squad car like a safety about to intercept a pass. "Are you all right, sir?" he asked.

"I believe I am. Just a little scraped on the knees."

"We'll need to file an accident report. Did your vehicle sustain any damage?"

"I don't have a car."

"Why are you on the highway, sir?"

"I was walking to Van's for dinner. I'm staying at the River Shannon and didn't want to take a taxi."

"May I see an ID?"

I showed him my driver's license and my American Express card. He walked back to his squad car studying each in turn.

An ambulance pulled up. The paramedic who got out was a thick-waisted young woman who looked Swedish. She told me she'd like to take my pulse and blood pressure and look at my knees. She had me sit on the cot in the ambulance. After she checked my vital signs, clucking her tongue and taking notes with a little pencil, she took tincture of iodine and swabbed some on each knee through the holes in my pants.

"Too bad you don't have a sewing kit," I joked.

"I hope they're not too hard on you."

"For what?"

"Walking on the highway. We have laws against hitchhiking."

"I was trying to get to Van's for dinner. I'm on vacation."

"Where are you from?"

"Chicago." From the way her face filled with import and her brows strained to meet above her nose, I thought she'd heard about Felice and Ronald Girtz.

"Did you hear that your mayor died?"

"You're kidding. That's too bad."

"He had a heart attack right in his office." The gesture she made with her hand pantomimed life and death.

"It seems like celebrities die whenever I'm out of town."

She was laughing at that when the policeman handed back my ID and read the account of the accident in a flat voice. He made the whole event sound so mundane that I felt offended, but I wasn't going to argue with his tone. I shook my head in assent, and he told me I was free to go.

"Can I take you somewhere?" the paramedic asked.

"How about my motel?"

Her name was Fiona but she wasn't Irish. Her parents just wanted to be different. She was twenty-four and had been a paramedic for two years. I told her it must be exciting.

"Only if you like to see people die," she said. "Why don't you change clothes, and I'll come by after work?" she asked. She was holding the back of my wrist and stroking it as if I were her patient and she was looking for a good vein.

Fiona had beautiful eyes. When I picture us sitting in my motel room, that's what I see, eyes like black olives. I was telling Fiona that it's unusual to see someone with light hair and such dark eyes when suddenly she was crying.

"What's wrong?" I asked. She was fiddling with my digital travel alarm. Her upper lip quivered, and her eyes searched the ceiling, for what I don't know.

"My dad," she said.

I wondered if Felice ever cried about me at intimate moments. "What happened?" I asked, placing a commiserating arm around her shoulder.

"I think about him all the time. He lives in South Africa."

"Is he sick?"

"He's as healthy as a horse."

"Well, what's wrong, then?"

"He's so unaware of politics. He writes me letters and tells jokes about the place. Last week some Russian officials visited for the first time since 1956 and the headlines said, 'Reds in Our Beds.'"

"So?"

"How can he live there and be well-adjusted?"

"Maybe he has to be. Why are you thinking about him now anyway?"

When she didn't answer, I put on my reading glasses and opened my book. I thought I'd do something useful.

"Why are you reading?" She closed *Exodus* on chapter four, and slammed it down on the nightstand. She unhooked my glasses and placed them beside the book. Taking my chin in her hand, she kissed me.

"Do you know how to do CPR?" I asked her.

"Sure thing," she said, turning off the lamp. She rubbed her palms together. They made a papery sound. Then she flexed her muscles and started to massage my chest. I closed my eyes and thought about Felice. I wondered if Chuck knows how to make her happy in the right way.

Six-Oh

"Marry a monkey later in life," Lillian read out loud, "Avoid the dog."

"I hope we're avoiding the dog right now." Carl pretended to hold his egg roll up to a magnifying glass.

"I'm reading my place mat, Carl, not commenting on lunch."

"I was thinking of going on the Oprah Winfrey diet," Carl said, pinching his midriff.

"I tried the Richard Simmons diet years ago. I can't say I was too impressed. You had to suffer. Besides, Oprah's diet's for people who need to lose half of themselves. You know that chef in New Orleans?"

"Paul Prudhomme?"

"Right. He could use her diet." Lillian smoothed her hair and patted the bodice of her dress, a gesture she always used when she had finished speaking.

Carl guessed that Lillian had once been shy and still checked to see if speaking had disheveled her. He watched her arms ripple in her short-sleeved dress and her silver bracelet depicting the Hawaiian Islands clank against a teacup. He didn't understand why he found her so entertaining at lunch. At the accounting office, she was a terror.

Lillian reapplied her lipstick in the blade of her butter knife. She saw Carl watching her. "Before I worked for Mr. Dickey, I was a waitress. I learned to do this years ago." She smiled, revealing lipstick over the lipline. "Before I was born, Clara Bow's mouth became the standard. Sweetheart lips." She tossed Carl a demure kiss.

He pretended to catch it. "Isn't it your birthday soon?"

"The big six-oh."

"You don't look a day over fifty-nine."

"I keep worrying that they'll find me dead and use one of those captions under my corpse on TV, 'sixty-year-old bookkeeper.' Doesn't sound too appetizing."

"It could be worse. It could say 'sixty-year-old virgin.'"

"I don't have to impress you with my exploits, dear. I'm old enough to be your grandmother. Show some respect."

"I do, Lillian," Carl said, taking the check from her hand.

"You must be drunk if you're offering to pay. You know what they call you at work? Carl McScrooge."

Carl feigned amazement.

"Why do you think they don't ask you to contribute to the special-occasions committee of the real estate division anymore?"

"Because there's nothing too special about a bunch of ladies having their gallbladders out."

"I had my gallbladder out."

"That's different. I'd have gladly contributed to you. It's just that I object to blanket charity. One's participation should be discretionary."

"You can't speak for ten seconds without showing off your vocabulary. No wonder you don't get along with people your age."

"People my age don't understand me." Carl took the napkin from the empty place setting and pretended to weep.

"There, there," Lillian said, patting his wrist. "Let's get back to the office before the rumor mill starts churning."

✻

Carl stood in the front room. He hoped the man across from him, the one he'd seen doing amazing shadow aerobics, was watching. That was the charm of old courtyard buildings. They brought out the best in shy people. Every night at eleven he stood in the same triangle of light and undressed. Even if the man wasn't interested, he'd eventually have to notice Carl. If not that man, there were six other windows from which someone could observe him.

Before he went to bed, he read another chapter of the book on savants that Lillian had given him. He propped it up on his stomach and read one word at a time. He liked reading slowly before bed, becoming aware of the sounds of letters as sleep overtook him, and he dropped off. He read a fact that amazed him, that savants don't so much have good memories as they aren't able to forget. He recalled a term from college English, "negative capability," and wondered if it had anything to do with the sentence he'd read.

What would it be like to remember every sensation he'd experienced? It might lead to premature aging to be responsible for so much of one's past. He did wish he could remember a few things more accurately. Gavin's face, for instance, was receding from him. His brown eyes were simply gone. Why could he remember every crack and crag of Lillian's chin and not be able to see Gavin's nose anymore? He had a photo somewhere, but that was beside the point, and he was too tired to look for it. He closed his eyes and saw the house in the country where he'd met Gavin. The stairs were made of red brick. The sun was low in the sky. A carpet of bugs hovered over the pond near the barn where his uncle stored tools and a snowmobile.

On Lillian's sixtieth birthday, Carl promised to obey her wish for a quiet evening. That meant seizing the plans for the celebration from the hands of Sheila Vincent, who was in charge of the special-occasions committee. That morning on the way to work, Carl had been thinking of changing his name. It was so guttural, so old-fashioned. What were his parents thinking he'd amount to with a name like his? People spit it out of their mouths like phlegm. "Carl, Carl, Carl," he said out loud as the el train roared through the tunnel.

He should have been less abrupt, but it just came out in a flurry when he saw Sheila Vincent in line for a doughnut downstairs. "Whatever you're planning for Lillian's birthday, she won't like it."

"And who are you," Sheila asked, opening her eyes wide and articulating each word like she was making a political speech, "her lady-in-waiting?"

"Lillian told me to tell you people that she wants no party. She thinks that sixty should be a solemn occasion."

"If I didn't know you'd run and tell Lillian, I'd express my true feelings. As it is, let me speak in my official capacity. I wish to inform you and the Sea Hag that we're merely planning to have cake, coffee, and a gift at work. I couldn't find enough employees to attend a social function for Lillian, unless, of course, it were a wake."

Carl turned on his heels and took the elevator to eighteen. It was better this way. They'd go to dinner somewhere special and maybe see a play or hear music. He'd buy her a corsage.

"It was hard, but I convinced them, Lillian. They agreed to have cake and coffee at the office and leave us alone to our fantasies on the night in question."

"Who did you talk to, Sheila?"

"None other than Ms. Sheet Cake of 1987."

"I hope she wasn't too disappointed."

"She took it like a woman."

After dinner on Lillian's birthday, Carl planned to take her to My Brother's Keeper to hear a gay folksinger named Earl Shilott. Although they had never spoken about it, he was sure that Lillian knew he was gay, especially if Sheila Vincent, with her limited capacity, could guess. Lillian never asked him if he was seeing girls, as his mother still did when he called her in Cleveland Heights.

"Met any good-looking girls in Chicago?"

"Ouch! That's one right now, tearing out strands of my hair. Excuse me for a minute, Mom. 'Judy, put my shoe back where you found it! Get your hands off my shaving mug! I'll give you a souvenir at the door.'"

"Can't you be serious for a minute, Carl?" his mother asked, but he could hear her amusement in the way she said his name.

He'd hardly spoken to his father since the summer before last. They had been riding in a golf cart at his father's country club when Carl had simply said, "You know about me, Dad, right?"

His father had pretended not to hear, and then they were at the next green. Carl had felt the adrenaline drain out of his fingers and had never mentioned it again. Surely Uncle Dan knew, from the way Carl and Gavin had carried on that weekend in the country. Looking back, though, Carl realized that he had been more discreet than he'd planned. He was less so with his mother on the phone or with Lillian at lunch, but he was only truly outrageous at home.

Just last night standing in the window, he had taken his penis in his hand. He knew he could get arrested, but it was his own apartment, after all, and nobody had to look. Let them draw their damn draperies rather than see him double over with pleasure and effort.

Carl didn't know Earl Shilott, but he'd seen him perform a few times and had made important eye contact with him the last time he was at the bar. Shilott was a lot older than Carl, perhaps fifty, and not as handsome as impressive. He was heavyset and barrel-chested, which made him look shorter standing up than he appeared to be sitting down. He had wavy hair that he combed straight back and small features for such a big man. Carl imagined he would look better dressed than naked. Shilott had recorded a few albums but was a well-kept secret from the general public. Carl wondered if he minded how limited his audience was. If he did mind, he could have changed a few pronouns and ended up with entirely different songs. Carl had read on a record jacket that Earl had been a forest ranger and a merchant marine. It was a definite liability for Carl to work in accounting. He'd change his profession to something more exotic. Maybe Greenpeace needed a good internal auditor. Then when someone at a bar asked what he did, he could say he saved whales, instead of changing the subject.

An hour before he was supposed to pick up Lillian, the phone rang. He was taking her orchid corsage out of the refrigerator and putting it with his coat so he wouldn't forget it when he left.

"It's me, Carl," Lillian said. "If you don't think it's all right, I want you to tell me. Okay?"

"How can I say okay before I know what it is?"

"Well, listen then. Vance just dropped in. He used to be the doorman at our building. He wanted to drop over and give me a surprise for my birthday. I suggested that he join us for the evening, but if you don't think so, he'll understand."

Carl was outraged, but he put on his most pleasant voice. "Whatever will make you happy, Lillian. It's your six-oh."

"So you'll pick us up at the same time?"

"Seven. Did you tell Vance about the music later?"

"He thinks that'll be fine."

"Okay then. See you in an hour."

No wonder nobody likes her, Carl thought when he got off the phone. Making a commotion about her quiet birthday until someone better knocks on her door. What was this, an Ivan Albright honeymoon for Lillian and her doorman, with Carl as porter, maître d', and the sucker who'd pick up their check?

He took the corsage out of the box and shredded it into the garbage disposal. Then he turned it on for a minute and listened to it ingest the orchids. The bow would get caught in the mechanism and he'd have to dig it out later. Meanwhile, he felt better. He looked at himself in the mirror on the way out, pulled his hand through the hair he kept longer on top and short on the sides, put on his black overcoat, and waved good-bye to himself.

The car was parked a block away on Kenmore. He began walking and heard footsteps behind him. Two young women made a wide u onto the grass to avoid him as they passed. They were convulsed in laughter.

"That's him for sure!" the shorter one gasped to her companion.

Carl blanched to think they'd been his audience all those evenings. Overcome with embarrassment, he collapsed into his car. Maybe he'd have to move out. He could always go back to Cleveland, where he had better friends than Lillian, or to New York, where no one knew him. Uncle Dan would have him for the summer. Dan liked it when Carl was around, if only because he was afraid to be alone in the country now that Aunt Lottie was dead. Carl and Dan could take long drives through the Connecticut mountains and go into town for little things like nails and drill bits. Carl loved hardware stores, with their metallic hum and impersonal smell. And Uncle Dan was at least interesting to talk to. He'd had a life, unlike most people he knew. Dan could show him the photos he'd taken in Kenya and the Philippines and Liberia. Dan understood him better than Lillian did, that was for sure.

He had ten minutes before he was supposed to pick up Lillian and Vance, but he needed to buy a new corsage. The little Korean flower store on Broadway was just closing. He ran in and asked for a corsage.

"All out," the owner said, looking at the clock.

"Can you make one?"

"Ten dollars."

"Fine."

He thought he'd fall asleep on his feet before the man twirled the last bow around the bent metal stem. When the man began to wrap it as a gift, Carl looked at his watch. He was already five minutes late.

"No bow, no bow!" He placed his money on the counter.

"Ten fifty-seven," the owner shouted before Carl reached the door.

He pulled a dollar out of his wallet, crumpled it into a ball, and threw it toward the man.

"That was lovely," Lillian said, wiping some whipped cream off her cheek. "Flowers and champagne and strawberry shortcake."

"Don't slight the main course," Vance said.

Vance wasn't that bad. He was a little older than Carl would have liked and not exactly suave, but there was some innate charm about him. He was very kind to Lillian and interested in what Carl had to say. He was impressed that Carl was an accountant and asked the kind of questions about Carl's work that meant he was listening closely. He followed Carl with serious eyes and tried to include Lillian as well. When Carl asked Vance what he did, he wasn't embarrassed to say he cleaned apartments so that he could set his own hours and make a good salary working half-days.

"A good salary!" Lillian said. "His apartment looks like a raja's. Leather this and leather that, and you should see his coffee table."

When Vance didn't offer to describe his coffee table, Carl said, "Well, what about it, Vance!"

"Black marble. It's very unusual. I bought it in Milan."

"See, he travels too. Carl thinks you have to go to college in the East to lead a refined life."

"I'm not a snob, Lillian." Turning to Vance, he said, "How can someone from Cleveland be a snob?"

"That's where they're usually from," Lillian said.

"Because it's your birthday, Carl will allow that one to pass," Vance said and grinned at them both.

It occurred to Carl that Vance resembled a younger Lawrence Welk if Lawrence Welk were a redhead with black glasses.

"So Lillian tells me we're going to see Earl Shilott."

"Have you seen him?"

"I know Earl. You get to meet a lot of people in the doorman trade. Earl had a friend who lived in Lillian's building a while back. He'd come to see his friend now and then."

"Did you know him socially?"

"No, we just talked when he'd visit this man. You remember Mark Penney, don't you, Lillian?"

"Didn't he move away?"

"Yes," Vance said.

"And then?" Carl asked. He was becoming annoyed at Vance's reticence.

"There is no *and then*. After he moved away, I didn't see him or Earl anymore."

They rode in silence to My Brother's Keeper. By the time they had arrived, Earl Shilott had finished his first set, and there were no seats at the side tables near the stage.

"Looks like we'll have to stand for now," Carl said.

"Carl, I'm exhausted. Standing doesn't sound like much fun for an old lady like me. Why don't I get a cab and you two stay on?"

Carl was perfectly happy to accept Lillian's offer but Vance said, "We can't desert the birthday girl. Why not come back to my place for some brandy? I'll play Earl's album, and Carl won't miss a thing."

"If it's fine with Carl, it's fine with me," Lillian shrugged.

"Okay," Carl said. He saw the back of Earl's head but couldn't see the rest of him from where they were standing. He'd sound ungracious if he insisted on staying, but he lingered behind long enough to emphasize to Vance and Lillian that it hadn't been his idea to leave.

When they reached Vance's building, just two doors away from Lillian's, Lillian said, "You know, I'm going to sound like a party pooper, but the champagne has gone straight to my head and I need to lie down. You two can get along without me, no?"

"Just one drink?" Vance asked.

"I won't be responsible for the damage at this point," Lillian said and pretended to pass out.

Carl dropped her in front of her building. Vance walked her in and spent a few minutes talking to the current doorman, an elderly Jamaican.

Back in the car, Vance occupied the front seat Lillian had vacated. "To my place, then?"

"Whatever." Carl felt warm and nervous. "Did Lillian set this up?"

"What do you mean?"

"Did you just happen to stop by around six?"

"No, she invited me for dinner. We're old friends, you know."

"Are all of Lillian's friends like us?"

"What do you mean?"

"I mean does she have any women friends?"

"Not that I know of."

"Does she have many gay friends?"

"Not that I know of."

"We're her only two friends?"

"Quite possibly. Plus a sister she sees on holidays."

"You were her only friend before I began working at her office?"

"Exactly, but we can't sit here all night, you know."

Carl started driving toward Vance's, but he had no enthusiasm for finishing the evening as Lillian had ordained. He guessed it was nice of her to think of him, but he couldn't go through with it.

"Can we get together some other time?" Carl asked Vance.

"That would be fine, Carl, if you want to make this an early evening." Vance gave Carl one of his cards. It said, "Mr. Clean. Vance Erdray. 555-2241."

"How was Lillian's birthday bash? Did you two have a cozy time?" Sheila asked.

"It was very nice." Carl pushed past her off the elevator.

Lillian's desk was behind a special partition toward the back of the office. He imagined that she had sat there for forty years in the same position, balancing the books that Mr. Dickey kept on his two smaller enterprises. Lillian was the only employee without a computer. Her part of the office was like an accounting museum.

"Top of the morning," Lillian said, looking up from her adding machine. She patted her forehead and winced. "How did it go last night?"

"How did what go?"

"You and Vance. He's a nice boy, isn't he?"

"He's not a boy any more than you're a girl. He's a man, and for your information, it didn't go."

"Was something wrong?"

"You were wrong, Lillian. Why did you think I'd appreciate meeting Vance?"

"You're new in the city. I thought he might introduce you to some people, you know, show you around."

"I'll thank you to stay out of it, Lillian."

She imitated his annoyed voice. He walked away.

"Ready for lunch?" she said at 11:30. "All I want is some toast."

"I have too much to do." Computer printouts were unfurled all over his desk. "Maybe tomorrow, Lillian," he said, guessing that she wouldn't ask again if he refused.

That night Carl pulled down his shades and undressed in the bathroom. He was thinking of calling Uncle Dan and asking him about the prospects for summer when the phone rang.

"It's Vance. I was wondering if I might drop by. I have something I thought you'd be interested in seeing."

"It's kind of late," Carl said.

"It doesn't have to be right now. It can be tomorrow or the next day."

"Well, I'm awake. You might as well bring it over now."

Twenty minutes later Vance was standing in Carl's front room with a bag in his hand. Carl hadn't asked him to sit down or taken his coat. Carl had gotten dressed again and thrown his dirty clothes, unfolded laundry, and dishes behind the door that separated his front room from the efficiency kitchen.

"Nice place you have."

"Sure," Carl said. "It's temporary."

"I have an old album that Earl Shilott made. Want to hear it?"

Carl pointed to the stereo and stared at the jacket cover. It must have been from the sixties. Earl Shilott was young and much thinner. He wore a Nehru jacket. He had been a member of a rock group called Abacus.

Vance sat on Carl's one chair while Carl took up most of the couch.

"Most of it is instrumental, but Earl's voice is unmistakable." When Earl began singing, Vance pointed his finger in the air. "Hear him?"

Carl listened as Earl sang about missing a girl who rode a horse over a cliff. "I can't believe he'd sing that."

"But his voice. How do you like his voice?"

"I don't much care for it. I like his songs now. His voice was never great. That's why he's stuck at that bar forever."

"Sorry," Vance said. "I thought you'd like it."

"I do. Thanks. I guess I'm just too opinionated."

Vance took off the record and sat next to Carl on the couch. His hand was near Carl's shoulder. "Would you like me to introduce you to Earl?"

"Not really."

Carl wished Vance would go away. He closed his eyes and tried to think of Gavin's face. He saw his Uncle Dan and the Korean florist. He saw his father and their old neighbors, the Igoes. Then he saw Gavin clearly. He opened his eyes and smiled in appreciation.

Vance's face was over his. Taking off his glasses, Vance kissed him. Carl didn't fight it, but he didn't kiss back either. As soon as Vance was through with him, he'd call Uncle Dan and make summer plans. Maybe if he got all the details right, Gavin would sit with him on the red stairs and watch the sun disappear behind the hills.

"Want to go to bed?" Vance was asking.

"I have to make a phone call." Carl thought it was the most stupid piece of truth he could have whispered.

California

C AL WEATHERS LIKED Oleg Lum because of his name. Nothing else recommended the earnest Russian who shucked oysters next to Cal at The Shell. Since Oleg's arrival, no one joked about Cal's name being California or asked him about the weather on the coast. Instead, they said, "Oh, Leg!" when the worst kitchen jobs had to be performed. Just seeing Oleg display his incompetence boldly as a badge made Cal smile.

"What is funny?" Oleg would ask.

"You, man," Cal would answer, shaking his head and letting another gritty oyster slither onto the shaved ice.

When they had finished their early-morning shifts as salad preparers, Cal and Oleg would wash their hands with Boraxo and take their lunches to the card table covered with red oilcloth where the help ate, that is, if Mr. Perke wasn't around. Sometimes the table would be cluttered with week-old guest checks that Mr. Perke totaled on an ancient adding machine, which trailed a pink column of numbers onto the floor.

"They're giving the place away!" he'd wail mostly to himself and then add, "Damn bitches!" to include any employee who had the potential to tote up a check incorrectly.

"Is good food," Oleg commented over his plate of perch and grayish peas.

"Is beginning to stink," Cal mimicked.

At first Oleg hadn't been sure he liked Cal. Cal looked menacing to Oleg, who'd seen so few black people before he left Russia. He remembered Tesfaye, an Ethiopian student he'd known in Moscow. How fascinated he'd been to observe the cold Russian air circulating through Tesfaye's lungs and out of his thin, fine nose. There was nothing about Cal that Oleg would call refined. His jaw had been broken and was jerry-rigged to the rest of his face. Oleg wondered what held it there. Cal's hands also frightened him, seeming too large to connect at his thin wrists. The wrists led to bulging forearms. His arms seemed wasted at the restaurant. Oleg imagined them better serving an iron worker.

Sometimes their lunch hours were taken up by Cal's political tirades. He always talked low so that Mr. Perke could only imagine what he was telling Oleg. Oleg would lean across the table to catch Cal's words.

"See President Peckerwood last night on TV?"

"You mean U.S. President?"

"President Peckerwood. Lives in the Bird House."

"I saw news of President's trip to Rome."

"Peckerwood's always smiling like he's smelling sweet shit. His wife's real hot. He divorced his first wife because she got fat. Republicans don't like that."

"Is true?"

"I read all about it. Don't you read books, Oleg? How do you imagine you're going to make your way in Peckerland?"

Oleg reached for more tartar sauce and stared at his plate. He was afraid when Cal spoke this way.

"Is wonderful country where you can call President bad language."

"Ain't it great? We elect rat brains like him so we can exercise our right to complain. Have you read up on it? I was just going to use mine to tell Perke that I want Saturday off. My grandma died again."

"I am sorry to hear. She was ill?"

"She was dead. Been dead since last time I wanted Saturday off. If Perke had a memory, waitresses wouldn't steal him blind. You watch. I'll ask, and he'll say fine."

Each day when Oleg left work he called Claire, the beautiful American he'd met in the summer. If he were seeing Claire in Moscow, he'd know it was serious. But here in America he didn't know what it meant that a divorced woman and her ten-year-old daughter had taken a liking to him. By the way they cooed and smirked in his presence, it might mean that he was entertaining, like a talking parrot with an accent.

"Today it's weaving," Carrie explained to Oleg. "My mom's on a real self-improvement kick. She's taking a class in making Christmas cookies, and we're Jewish! I'll tell her you called again, Oleg."

"She is unhappy that I call?"

"No, she wants you to come to dinner, Oleg. She thinks you're interesting."

"Let's get ripped," Cal said to Oleg after they finished Thursday's shift.

"I do not understand."

"What do you Russkies understand? Do you understand vodka?"

"Is great painkiller," Oleg said quietly. He was afraid that Mr. Perke planted spies among the kitchen help and that he was in imminent danger of losing his job for talking about sordid topics.

"Get ripped. Drink vodka." Cal raised an imaginary shot glass to his lips. When he thought Oleg didn't understand, he became monosyllabic.

"Drinking is sometimes good," Oleg continued, "but today I am busy. I must talk to Claire, who looks like beautiful Indian princess. She is my friend."

"Good for you."

"And I am worried about story I read in paper." Oleg pulled a folded scrap of newsprint from his pocket and buried his eyes in it. "Baby is left on train downtown. He is not owned by parents but in foster home. What is foster home, Cal?"

"It's like a parking lot for kids."

"I would own this baby, or Claire, who can have no more babies."

"What are you talking about, man? C'mon, Oleg. We can have drinks and then we'll talk about babies. My old lady moved out on me with my three babies. Lamont's the oldest. He looks like me before I got my new chin. Fred's in the middle. He's mean like his momma. Baby Cal's just like me. He's only three. It's not true you love yours all the same."

"You must be proud father, Cal. I was married to getting out of Russia, idea that owned me like wife. I work very hard, and now I am here."

"C'mon, I'll buy you a few drinks next door. We'll watch a little TV."

"Is okay, Cal. I drink with you, and then maybe we find baby even today."

"It can happen that fast, Oleg. A baby can be lost or found in no time. Once this dude I know named Harold was staying at his old lady's. She had to go to work, so Harold says he'll watch the kid. Baby's no older than two. So Harold's been up all night. He's watching the baby. Then he hears, 'Wake up. You're under arrest!' Seems he fell asleep and the baby walked right out the front door. Two cops found him standing in front of Comiskey Park."

"It happened for this baby on el train where maybe drug-taking parents leave him. 'Please help lost baby' I will tell Claire."

After toasting the recent improvement of American and Russian relations, President Peckerwood and his wife, Claire, Carrie, Lamont, and Baby Cal, they started on toasts for improvement. Oleg wished that Cal's middle son would prove acceptable. Cal wished that Oleg would procure his baby.

"People think that guys wanting babies are a little funny, Oleg. You know, there was a guy who dressed like a clown and killed boys."

Oleg looked indignant. "Is not my hope to be killing clown."

"People think the worst. For instance, the first day I saw you, I thought you'd be a real loser. People are prejudiced."

"I go to police and explain. I say baby is like bicycle. If found and no owner, I can buy."

"I'd just say you'd like to know the whereabouts of the baby."

"Okay, we say that."

"We?"

"Cal and Oleg say that to officers."

"What good will I do? 'Who's he?' they'll ask. 'Your good thing?' No, you go alone and act real serious, like you're in a white people's church."

"Okay, I say, 'Police, do not give baby to bad parents, who leave it behind, or to false parents.'"

"I'd be cool, Oleg. If you say things like false, they'll get all riled up, and you won't get a thing."

"Maybe I should wait for Claire?"

"Sure, we'll have more drinks. Then Claire can go with you. Police can't resist mothers. Once when I was incarcerated, my mother came. Ten minutes later I was walking."

"You are then criminal?"

"Everyone's a criminal, Oleg. You just need a little time and less money, and you'll be one too."

Oleg had seen the ring in a pawnshop on Devon Avenue. Pawnshops were sadder to him than anything else about America. No one could convince Oleg that possessions weren't loved. He remembered the transistor radio he'd bought on the black market in Moscow. It was shaped like a Coke bottle. For many years it had been his skyline. It wasn't the object itself but the owner's feelings for it. The sillier the object, the better. The more ostentatious, the better. The more one needed to sacrifice for it, the better. The more degraded its surroundings, the better it looked in contrast.

The ring was the perfect embodiment of useless pleasure. The thought of wearing it while shucking oysters in the smoky restaurant delighted him. He'd waited a month for the owner to repossess it, but it was still in the window on the day he'd set for the purchase.

He hoped the ring would purge his current mood, the darkest he'd felt since he'd left Russia. The desolation of September with the beaches closing, Carrie back in school, Claire busy with her life, and his new job at The Shell left him wondering if he'd left Russia at all, or if Russia was a malady one had for a lifetime, a chill from the tundra producing visions of imminent doom. Even the letters he wrote to the newspaper's "Personal View" column were colored by his new bitterness, a word he thought he'd left behind. Sometimes Carrie's ten-year-old nonchalance annoyed him. The world had no time for ambivalence, he wanted to tell her. Lots of people needed to be warned to change their lives.

Nothing was worse than official thugs, not even the thugs that remove cars from parking lots after disconnecting the finely tuned alarm systems. Thieves were in business for themselves. They were committed personally to Free Enterprise. They risked their lives for shiny fenders, leather seats, and metallic-blue paint. The police risked their lives for a paycheck. They interfered with the individual's religious urge toward ownership. It was hard to understand how a free country could tolerate such purveyors of injustice.

When Oleg first shopped in American markets, he wondered why his fellow émigrés always bought the brashest colors of toilet paper.

Then he remembered the toilet paper lines in Russia. If there were orange toilet paper in America or red with sequins, all the better. It was beautiful to waste beauty. He began winking at old women, so spare in the rest of their shopping. Their carts contained generic cans, cream cheese, and the beautiful toilet paper, usually in shocking pink. Oleg made a mental note to write a new "Personal View" column. Toilet paper might well be the subject.

Upon entering the pawnshop, he took an immediate dislike to the clerk. He was perhaps twenty-five and had thinning hair. His face looked refined, and his eyes were small and alert when he glanced up from his newspaper. Why didn't Americans, charged with the most awesome responsibilities, show any enthusiasm for their jobs? He'd give anything to buy back loved items from desperate people and sell them to ardent new owners. People didn't understand the drama or pathos of their own lives. Once he'd seen a man sitting on a gray couch on the sidewalk amid his belongings. When a neighbor explained to Oleg that the man had been evicted, Oleg was amazed by the man's calm reserve. Why didn't people beat their breasts in indignation?

"May I help you?" the young man was repeating.

"I am interested, please, in the diamond for the hand."

"The Mason's ring? It's a good one, a real one." The young man theatrically displayed a jewel-inspecting device that reminded Oleg of a periscope.

"Please, I can use?" Oleg put the instrument to his eye and enjoyed the prismatic effect of the stone.

"I'll give it to you for four-fifty. You can pay it all at once or put down a hundred."

"Please, I can try it on?"

"Sorry, sir. I can let you try on another ring in the same size, but our diamond jewelry isn't available for wearing before purchase. It's part of our new loss-prevention plan."

Maybe all the cameras in the window were burglary devices, and the mindless television screens contained video-recording equipment. Maybe the man behind the barred window had a gun trained on him. Oleg's left temple throbbed.

The man handed Oleg a discolored silver circle the same size as the ring. It fit him snugly. "Now I am married to loss prevention."

"You can put a hundred dollars down and sign a contract to pay the rest on time. We offer twenty-one percent financing, which is very good these days, and we have a thirty-day return policy. If you decide to return the ring within that period of time, you can have your money back minus a twenty-dollar handling fee. Here are the papers explaining this method of payment."

"And if the ring is wanted by old owner?"

"Once the ring is sold, it's yours. Previous ownership is invalidated. You know, no *backsies,* as we used to say in marbles."

"Is this u.s. law?"

"I don't imagine that I represent the views of the whole government. Pawnshop law is different."

"I will pay hundred dollars and sign mortgage document."

Oleg signed the papers in triplicate, bought an old Brownie camera for Carrie and a digital alarm for Claire. As he carried the items out of the store, he couldn't take his eyes off his hand.

In the few hours that remained before dinner, he'd work on a "Personal View" article for the paper.

Dear Personal View:

Pawnshop law is very good American practice according to Oleg Lum, who purchased diamond from tragic Mason who cannot keep what he loves. I think too that Pawnshop law would be valuable justice tool in missing child cases. Parents get certain time to claim lost child. If child is unclaimed, then any person who has $450, the price of beautiful Mason ring, can own child. There is no need for police in Pawnshop Adoption Plan. It can be business deal involving no backsies. One could sign contract from listless pawnshop man and baby would benefit from new owner who loves his possession.

Thank you,
Oleg Lum

At nine o'clock they decided to begin dinner, even though Cal hadn't arrived.

"Cal is casual man," Oleg assured Carrie and Claire, who were more hungry than interested in the personality of Oleg's new friend. "He is sometimes late for work and sometimes leaves early. He is sometimes sober and sometimes not. Maybe today is not sober day, or one of his three handsome sons has trouble and Cal must play parole officer."

"Are his kids in prison?" Carrie asked.

"No, is little joke I make about school for you, Carrie."

"Oleg, I bought some tickets for a flute concert. Would you like to join us on Sunday?"

"I am delighted to go to concert and to wear my new ring from beautiful land of dreams, pawnshop."

"You got our things at a pawnshop? Aren't things at pawnshops stolen?"

"Is not stolen but sacrificed. The new owners buy and love more than old ones. Like baby I see on news. He is left on el train. He needs new owner, Claire."

"It's a sad story, Oleg. So many unwanted children."

"Maybe you or I could help him?"

"How could we, Oleg?"

"We could say that he is our baby."

"But he isn't our baby."

Carrie dug her fork into her mashed potatoes. "You want my mom to keep this baby, Oleg?"

"Is lost baby. Is lost without us."

"They'll find him a good home, Oleg. You shouldn't worry about so many things." Claire grasped his knuckle and looked puzzled, then amused. "Maybe you need a pet," she said quietly.

"A dog or cat?" Carrie asked.

"Cal says police can get child. That we go to police together. Once when Cal needed release, his mother came and won his freedom."

"This guy's a criminal?" Carrie shrieked joyously. "What did he do?"

"Little Carrie, everyone in America is criminal if he has less money and little time. I have much money to spend on gaining baby."

"You'd need a lawyer, not the police, Oleg."

"There are many babies needing homes and I am good shopper."

The buzzer rang.

Oleg had never seen Cal so dressed up. He wore a mustard-colored leisure suit, black patent leather shoes, and a white shirt with a mustard-orange-and-brown brocade collar. Upon entering the apartment, he smiled broadly at Oleg and said to Claire, "For the lady of the house." He handed her a closed aluminum can that Oleg recognized as from the restaurant.

"Oysters!" Claire exclaimed.

"Oysters look like dead brains," Carrie said.

"Carrie, oysters are high in protein and considered very fancy," smiled Claire.

"Oysters are love food," Cal added, smiling at Oleg, Carrie, and Claire. "Sorry I'm late, by the way."

"There's still plenty to eat."

Oleg was busy serving his friend the leftover food.

"Oleg tells me you're a good cook." Every time Cal spoke, he shared a peripheral nod with Oleg, a habit of conspiracy learned in Mr. Perke's kitchen.

"This is the first time we've had a black person to dinner," Carrie added. "I've read a lot about black people like Harriet Tubman."

"Carrie, what's the point? We know all kinds of people. Oleg's spoken of you so often that we feel as if we know you."

Oleg and Cal stood in front of Claire's building. Dinner had been a limited success. Most of the topics of conversation had been Carrie's and included river rats, Frederick Douglass, men who kill women with electric drills, and why adults lie to children. Outside, the night was dark and the moon seemed unremarkable.

"See the ring, Oleg?"

Oleg held his hand up to Cal's face. His eyes were filled with light. "Is it not lovely?"

"Beautiful, Oleg. You know, I'm going to one big card game tonight. I could really make a killing. I have on my new duds. You like my suit? What I need are some accessories. And you know what would make a fine accessory?"

When Oleg didn't answer, Cal continued. "Your ring, Oleg. I'd give it back tomorrow."

"Is too valuable to me."

"I know, Oleg. I'll take care of it. Don't sweat."

"I cannot give away my property. Sorry, Cal, but ring is mine."

"I know it's yours, Oleg. I just want to flash it around for you. What good is it on your hand when you're fast asleep in bed?"

"Is my dream."

"Is just what my luck needs."

"I can say maybe okay but just for one night. You will write a note saying I can have backsies."

"Where do you get your English?"

"Man at pawnshop says 'backsies.'"

"You'll have the ring tomorrow. I'll give you a bonus if I do fine tonight."

"I can go to card game, Cal? You can wear my ring, but American card game is great event to me like World Series."

"You play stud?"

"No."

"Well, there's no spectating in this game. It's pretty rough."

Oleg handed Cal the ring and folded the note into his wallet. He waved good-bye.

The first day that Cal was out of work Oleg assumed he'd had a late night playing cards. He told Mr. Perke he was certain that Cal would be back the next day. Mr. Perke didn't seem to believe him, but then again, Mr. Perke didn't believe anyone. Oleg didn't think that Cal had a phone, but he got his address from the employee punch-in card.

"Hey, Leg, stop with the oysters and get the soup crock ready," Perke called.

"Yes, I do."

"I don't care if you do or don't. Get the lousy soup in the crock."

Oleg had heard that the West Side once had great mansions. He remembered reading the descriptions in *Sister Carrie*. Here he was riding down the same street that Dreiser had described, West Jackson Boulevard. He saw a great many television repair stores and some large, mysterious warehouses. He wondered if nothing else happened on the West Side but TVs breaking down and needing treatment. He was happy that his own black-and-white set still worked. The antenna needed occasional adjusting, and he'd added a few pieces of tin foil for better reception, but that was to be expected.

Number 2121 West Jackson was a red three-flat with gray trim. When he rang the bell, a dog began barking. He wondered if it was Cal's dog. Cal had never mentioned owning a pet, not even when Carrie had asked him directly at dinner.

"What do you want?" a woman was saying.

"Is Mr. Weathers home, please. I am friend from work."

"Mr. Weathers is never home. Not now. Not later. He doesn't work either. You sure you got the right person?"

"Cal Weathers. Father of three boys. Card player. Once incarcerated."

"Once plus about four. Cal will take whatever's not his no matter whose it is. See my wedding ring?"

Oleg looked down at her empty hand.

"That's right. Used to be there, but Cal needed it back. Let's just say I wasn't too willing to give it to him. Did he take something from you too? If he did, you understand I'm not responsible. I don't know why people go around trusting that man. He seems so friendly."

A little boy came up to the door and looked peevishly at Oleg.

"You are Baby Cal?"

The boy wrapped himself around his mother's legs. "I call him Calvin. It means something to name a child. Bad luck to call him Cal."

"Please, but Cal is never here?"

"Oh, he tries sometimes, but it's always the same. Too much of everything but sense."

"I am sorry to be bothering you. I loan Cal a ring, a diamond, that I buy at pawnshop. Then I don't see Cal anymore."

Oleg thought of looking behind him to see what was amusing her so.

"Would you loan a dog a steak?"

"Foolish use of good meat."

"Right," she smiled. "By the way, my name's Freddy. Short for Fredericka."

"Is nice name."

"You wanna come in?"

"Thank you, but I must go."

"Where are you from, anyway? Germany or somewhere?"

"No, I am Russian. Oleg Lum."

"Stop hanging on me, Calvin. Go watch TV. Well, if I see Cal I'll tell him you're looking. I'd call the police if I was you. No two ways about it."

Oleg took two buses directly to the Adler Planetarium, where they presented something that Carrie called a Sky Show. He sat back in his plush blue seat and looked up as a projector first showed him the sky above the Equator at Christmas and then the North Pole at Easter. Names of constellations clicked in his head like train stops. Oleg watched an eclipse of the moon darken the false sky. He wondered why writers call stars diamonds when diamonds are real.

Oleg was sleeping when the doorbell rang. He'd dozed off reading the Yellow Pages ads for adoption lawyers. Several had mentioned handling difficult cases. One ad that attracted him contained a crude line drawing of a stick figure pushing a baby carriage into which a stork was dropping a parcel. He'd call that lawyer in the morning.

He looked at the Mickey Mouse alarm clock he kept on his bedside stand. It said 3 A.M. He wandered to the buzzer in his underwear. Keeping his door chained, he cautiously looked down the hall. Soon he saw Cal walking up the stairwell wearing the same clothes he'd had on when Oleg and he had parted last. He could see the red veins in Cal's eyes and the stubble of beard decorating his prominent, poorly hinged chin.

"Where you were?" he asked Cal.

"I were playing cards, man," Cal mumbled. In his fatigue, he could hardly get his words out. Oleg had the impression that he was speaking from inside a locked room. "Ain't you gonna invite me in?"

Oleg unchained the door and directed Cal to sit at the end of his hide-a-bed. Oleg took the chair opposite. Feeling exposed in his underwear, he found himself crossing his legs and folding his arms in front of him.

"Practicing yoga?" Cal laughed.

"It is middle of night and I am cold."

"Sure, you was sleeping. Plus, you've given up on me already. You probably called the police."

"I do not call police but I visit Mrs. Weathers on West Jackson Boulevard."

"You visited my mother?"

"I visit a young woman named Freddy."

"Why did you want to see her?"

"I am thinking you live there. I want to see you."

"You're probably looking for this."

Oleg looked in Cal's extended hand. He was holding a ring, but it didn't appear to be Oleg's ring.

"You are magician?"

"What do you mean?"

"You change my lovely Mason ring into this!" Oleg switched on another light and rotated the ring above the bulb. "This ring is maybe glass or even worse." He returned it to Cal's palm.

"Sorry, my man, I got confused with my new wealth." Cal opened another big palm and held up Oleg's ring.

Oleg placed it on his finger. "Thank you, Cal."

"You can have the other one too. The gang banger I got it from says it's real. Take it to your friend at the pawnshop and see. I have to go now."

"See you at work."

"No way. My winnings will last me a month if I'm careful. Perke can shove his oysters you know where." Cal reached around and telegraphed a kiss to his ass.

Oleg spent the next few minutes practicing Cal's obscene gesture. He smiled into the mirror as the ring caught the light of his movements.

Somewhere Near Tucson

THERE ARE PICTURES of Barbara's grandfather looking French: beret and cane, straw hat, awning-striped blazer. No lowly Morris from the provinces of Hungary: an American Frenchman who couldn't speak French, barely English; who drank Jack Daniels and smoked Havana cigars; who cheated on his wife; who was a hairdresser to the stars. Barbara would have liked to have asked him what it was like to cut Clark Gable's hair, but before she knew him very well, he'd disappeared. There were a few postcards from Greece, but they were thrown away. You weren't supposed to leave a wife of forty-two years and take the entire savings account.

Barbara's first plane trip was to Los Angeles. Her mother wore a beige linen suit and the kind of pillbox hat that Jackie Kennedy had made popular. Her legs were thin, long, and shapeless like folded draperies. A cigarette hung out of her mouth. As soon as the plane got off the ground, her mother lit up. Barbara charted their place in the sky by the number of cigarettes she smoked. Three got them from Illinois to Iowa; Nebraska took six. Before she dozed off, she calculated that fourteen more would get them to Los Angeles.

For a week Barbara watched her mother console her grandmother. They took walks along Venice Beach and held hands like sweethearts. Sometimes Barbara and Martha followed them along, walking in their shadows, kicking sand at each other, occasionally resting on benches to give the two women privacy. When late afternoon came, mothers and daughters would sit on folding lawn chairs outside the basement apartment their grandmother had taken to economize. Martha would braid Barbara's long hair and make oaths: that she'd kill her grandfather if she ever saw him again, that she'd never marry a man. Barbara would drift, picturing the beach in Greece where water from the Aegean lapped over his hairy legs. She wondered if he'd brought his straw hat along and whether the new unsmiling lady, whose photo her grandmother kept stacked with the bills on the kitchen table, would like such a hat.

After the apartment cooled off in the evening, Barbara's mother and grandmother would cook dinner in unison, feed the girls silently, and tell them to go to bed. Barbara and Martha took turns on a scratchy embossed couch the color of dirty heather. Mother and Grandmother shared a blonde double bed that Morris had once snored in. They'd whisper for longer than Barbara could strain to stay awake. Sometimes she heard long sobs and words like "bastard." She imagined them twisting her grandmother's benign face. Just before Barbara would fall asleep, she'd picture a photo she'd seen in *Life* magazine. Picasso was smiling, at peace with the world. Many women like her grandmother were crying for him even as he posed for the camera.

Barbara's parents had twin beds, and they certainly didn't make love. They fought once a month when her mother balanced the checkbook. Every two weeks she'd see her father stroke her mother's passing breast, usually in the kitchen after dinner. Helen would say, "Oh-Dan!" as if they were connected syllables. Helen's response was definite enough, but Barbara never understood what it indicated. The needle hovered between gratitude and disgust, giving Barbara too much room for interpretation. She couldn't understand how both feelings could coexist in one mother.

In the top drawer of her father's dresser, along with his monogrammed handkerchiefs and silver cuff links, were his Navy-issue before-and-after photos of Nagasaki. Before the bombing there had been trees and houses. After it, there was rubble heaped on rubble. Strangely, both photos were devoid of people. Because the photos smelled like her father, there was a troubling intimacy about them. She would have tossed them out, but then he'd have known she'd been snooping. Underneath the photos she found the pack of Trojans. As she read the instructions and realized what they were, her heart bumped along like a dump truck. Why would he have hidden them there? He must have meant to keep them a secret from Helen.

Based on her discovery, Barbara concocted a wild sex life for her father, evenings at the Alibi Inn on Lincoln Avenue with his graying secretary Astrid, whose name Barbara remembered by picturing the six-pointed star over the 8-key on her typewriter. It was thrilling to imagine that her father loved Astrid, who wore a hearing aid. Maybe the hearing aid was a ploy. Who would be suspicious of a nearly deaf secretary? Not Helen, whose interests ran more to crossword puzzles and medical lexicons, which she read for entertainment. "Read this," she'd say to Barbara, handing her the definition of "petit mal." Would Helen have cared that Dan and Astrid were on the blue carpet of his office, her little pearl eyeglass string tangled near her pursed waiting lips, Dan vibrating above her like a helicopter? Astrid had short legs and too little chin, but Dan was soft and round and couldn't have complained.

On the day that Barbara married Roger, she thought of asking her mother about Astrid. Now that they were equals, women, they could share the devastating knowledge. They were standing in the fluorescent aqua-and-pink washroom of the Palmer House Hotel. The light made Helen's fern-and-orchid corsage already look limp. Barbara felt like a potted palm in her wedding gown. Weren't brides supposed to look radiant? She was giving off humidity like a rain forest. Beads of sweat collected on her forehead underneath the sequined veil.

"Whatever happened to Astrid?" Barbara asked.

"I think she died in retirement somewhere near Tucson," Helen answered, smacking her lips at the mirror to blot the lipstick.

"Was she deaf?"

"I don't remember."

"Didn't she wear a hearing aid?"

"Maybe."

"Then she must have been deaf."

By then the thick opening strains of Bach had leaked through the air shafts, and it was time for Barbara to walk down the aisle. In a teary pre-marital confession, she had already told Roger of her suspicions about Astrid and Dan. Roger blamed the entire incident on nerves and didn't seem very interested except in Astrid's pearl eyeglass chain. He'd smiled at that detail, recalling a music teacher in grade school who'd worn the same model.

Thinking of Astrid dead in retirement, Barbara repeated her vows listlessly. She watched her parents sitting together in the first row of chairs, small and wrinkled, constrained by their formal clothes, abject in their joy.

Martha was eighteen the summer she and Marc went into her bedroom and closed the door. They didn't lock it. So blatant an exclusion would have provoked Barbara's anger and tears. With the door unlocked, Barbara could theoretically join them, but she never dared to turn the knob. Instead, she spent most of her Saturday evenings alone watching *Hootenanny*. Sometimes she wondered if Jack Linkletter really liked women, or if Paul Stookey ever slept with Mary Travers, whose mouth was so wide and intelligent. And why was it that Barbara didn't know Peter's last name? Surely he had one. And who did he sleep with when Paul and Mary were together?

When the Christy Minstrels were introduced, Barbara took a flying leap off the pastel-green plastic-covered love seat and headed for Martha's door. She heard giggling and saw them in her mind, Martha seductively unhooking her padded bra and Marc caressing every spit curl on her forehead. Barbara pretended that her momentum couldn't be checked and hurled her body into the room. She landed on the center of the leopard jigsaw puzzle that Martha and Marc were demurely piecing together on the linoleum, greeting their questioning faces with an exaggerated smile.

About the same time Barbara and her friend Rhoda practiced making out. Usually Barbara would be the boy. That meant lying atop Rhoda (young missionaries) and planting kisses on her thin twelve-year-old lips. Later Rhoda became a nutritionist, and her brother Cary, who had sometimes watched, drowned while on downers the summer he was twenty. At the funeral Barbara stood to the side, feeling responsible for Rhoda's destiny. Rhoda had grown up thin and wary. Men were probably afraid to touch her. Even in Geneva, Switzerland, where she worked for the World Health Organization, there were military attachés who made wide circles around Rhoda.

One night while Marc was on vacation with his parents at Niagara Falls, Martha showed Barbara how to French kiss. She demonstrated it on the back of Barbara's wrist, where the skin was softest. Martha also performed the swooping kiss, which she said was very European, by draping Barbara over her bent elbow. Twelve years later, when

Barbara was a graduate assistant and a history professor from Amsterdam caressed her in an empty lecture hall, it was the swooping kiss she superimposed on the scene.

"It was so stupid," Barbara later told Roger when summing up the experience. "Imagine kissing me where a student might have seen."

Knowing that Barbara's stories had to be met with polite interest bordering on wonder, Roger leered with feigned lust. "Good thing you weren't horses," he added.

"What do you mean?"

Roger, having grown up on a farm, held the upper hand in nature lore. "Horses scream like people when they're having sex. He'd never have gotten away with it if you'd been horses."

Barbara's favorite story was about Eric, her eighth-grade boyfriend, though boyfriend wasn't precisely right, since Barbara shared Eric with Peggy, her best friend. It was Peggy who wore his portrait inside her heart-shaped locket, and who, they agreed, would marry him one day. Meanwhile, since Peggy would be at an Irish folk-dancing convention, Barbara could ask Eric to the eighth-grade graduation party, a boat ride on the Wendella along Chicago's lakefront. What were the parents thinking kids would do on a dark boat late in June, lights from shore bobbing like needles in the water? It would be the last time that many of them would see each other. Some were moving away. Others, like Eric, were off to private high schools on their way to careers in military intelligence. Of course, they'd feel compelled to say good-bye in bold cinematic gestures, passionately as Tony and Maria or Lieutenant Cable and Bloody Mary's daughter.

Barbara was wearing a seersucker shirt with an enlarged zipper that opened to her navel, so popular that summer of Mod clothing. One hundred feet from shore, Eric kissed her. He touched her breasts through cloth and bra as Barbara mentally rehearsed, "Oh-Eric!" then spoke it without ambiguity.

"We were never really friends," she whispered.

"I'm sorry," he said and bowed his head.

The rest of the evening was an apology that made for Barbara a natural pairing of love and regret. One bounced into her feelings with the other in tow, like a speedboat and a water-skier.

Eric became a high school swimming champ. Barbara and Peggy drifted apart, though Barbara missed Peggy's sauna and her parents' exotic Long Island accents.

Twice a week Barbara and Roger go to a restaurant ostensibly to eat, but their real purpose is to thrash out a point of argument. All week the tension wells up until it spills over into the gyros or mulligatawny or masala dosa.

"You're impersonal," she says.

"What?" Roger asks, wondering how many arguments a week the patient Guatemalan waiter hears.

"Nothing."

"Did you say I'm impersonal?"

"Let's not discuss it." Barbara focuses her eyes on a light equidistant between the ceiling fan and a slate announcing the catch of the day.

"Okay, we won't discuss it."

"Well, you are," Barbara prods.

"Are what?"

"Discussing it."

Barbara is distracted by a woman at the next table telling her companion, "You always bring me gifts that are dead!"

She surveys their table for evidence but sees only margarita glasses, guacamole, and chips with salsa. Barbara pictures the man in a pet store, aquariums swarming with skeletal fish. Then she hears the woman say, "Stop giving me your sick plants!"

Barbara shares an amused look with Roger. She wonders who will spread this story first among their friends.

The next day Barbara is waiting for Roger to pick her up at school. She has signs of a head cold and hopes that the Joseph Cornell show at the Art Institute will rev up her depleted curiosity.

Standing near her is a dignified Indian man, who might be a fellow faculty member. He is wearing a camel-hair coat, a white crewneck sweater, and gray-and-black houndstooth slacks. The slacks are slightly long so that they spill over the toes of his shoes, looking salt-stained and defeated.

The man is speaking. At first Barbara doesn't understand that he's speaking to her. She sees him pointing, but before she connects his voice with his gestures, he has removed a man's shoe, cut out to resemble a woman's sandal, and is pointing at his toes.

"Aren't they beautiful?"

"Beautiful?" Barbara asks dreamily.

"My toes. I think that they are beautiful." He is wiggling pink polished toenails under a nylon stocking.

"They're very nice," Barbara replies and looks down, down, down.

At the Cornell show she feels bored and distant. She can't concentrate on the boxed owls and children's blocks or naive collages suggesting false age. She remembers an exhibit she saw in Paris of the little dolls and chess pieces of the murdered Dauphin. She can see them as clearly as the boxes in front of her.

On the way back to the car, Barbara tells Roger about the Indian man and his toes.

"You have radar for those types," Roger smiles. "They must know how interested you are in theories of love."

Later that evening Barbara is shaving her legs in the bathtub and thinking about a dinner party when her grandparents were still together. At the same time that her grandfather seemed to be giving her grandmother an admiring glance, Barbara noticed a large white brooch perched asymmetrically on the black bodice of her grandmother's dress. She watched it moving slowly down the slope of her grandmother's breasts as she breathed. She realized it wasn't a piece of jewelry. It was a fish bone making its way to her lap.

Where Events May Lead

FREDERICK USES HIS summer vacations in the way that other people use alcohol, cocaine, religious retreats, class reunions, warrior weekends. Fifty weeks of the year, he is the husband of Elizabeth, who's kept her maiden name, Griffon, and the father of Amy Griffon-Tandy and little Jonah Griffon-Tandy. But two weeks every summer, while Elizabeth goes to a resort with an innovative camp program for the children, Frederick goes off alone to see what he is like. Some summers he agrees with the world's assessment of him that he is dull, the summer he took the tour of Vermont's covered bridges, for instance. Another summer he shot the rapids of more than one petulant river and came back to try his cases with a new deep register in his voice. Frederick likes the way the world, clear as a glass window, ignores him this morning while he sits at the harbor near the ferry landing, one of many tourists in colorful cotton shirts who've just invaded Vinalhaven, Maine. To escape the feeling of being part of the mob, he's lagged behind while the other passengers are reclaiming their cars or taking to foot. In the distance, he can see a row of white frame buildings that must be his eventual destination.

"The harbor's crowded today." Frederick looks up and sees a girl whose face is simple and shiny. "Lots of tourists."

"I'm a tourist," he says, slightly embarrassed, admitting that he's sought out a place the locals may think ordinary. It's like discovering that your wife, viewed at a distance at a noisy office party, isn't as pretty or assured as you had once believed.

"Where ya from!"

"New York."

"You live right in the city?"

"Across from Central Park." Should he tell her that he is a district attorney, or won't she care? He notices that the girl always breaks eye contact when she speaks. She has a good profile, though her nose is a little short, making her what one would call cute rather than pretty. She wears a blue-striped tank suit and cutoffs. Her bones are delicate and her breasts small. She is barefoot, but around her right ankle is a bracelet, as was the fashion when Frederick was her age twenty years ago. If he squints down, he can almost read the name, Lois or Louise. Restrained by a black ribbon, her hair is luxurious. The color of apricots, it flares in a pool at her meager, thin neck.

"I'm a district attorney," he adds. What harm can it do?

"You mean you arrest people?"

"No, I just convict them when I'm lucky. My name is Fred."

"Like Flintstone?"

"Like Frederick," he blushes.

"I'm Dolores."

He feels confused. Why is she wearing an ankle bracelet saying Lois? Has he read the name wrong? He'd put on his glasses, but they make him self-conscious. He takes a longing look at the bay, where lobster boats filled with weather-beaten traps are bobbing out of focus in the high water. Maybe the inscription says Louis. Maybe she's going steady.

"Are you here for the summer?" Frederick asks.

"We're natives. My mother's a schoolteacher, and my father runs the business at Shears." Dolores points to an adjacent concrete-slab building, whose yellow-and-blue sign displays the profile of two Neanderthals in need of grooming. "Heard of Carver's?"

"I haven't heard of anything here."

"The granite for your sidewalks came from this island, but the quarries are only used for swimming now. Carver's the nude quarry."

Frederick sits down on the stone wall of the harbor. Her news doesn't strike him as momentous but the innuendo does. "A nude quarry wasn't on the list of sights I remember," he says almost coyly. He regards his pale body, its sparse hair. Maybe if he doesn't wear his glasses to the quarry, he will be able to forget himself. If he can't see the world, will the world see him?

"I go there sometimes. It's kinda fun."

"I can't imagine people here going in for such things. One thinks of New England as a conservative region."

"Know the sixties?"

He thinks of his street, its monolithic gray apartment houses, Jonah's foldable stroller propped against a struggling, fenced-in tree.

"The nineteen sixties," Dolores smiles. "Nude swimming became popular. We get lots of tourists who still like it, mostly the Europeans, and a few locals. I don't see anything wrong. Nudity is quite natural, you know."

He guesses that her mother teaches biology. "One can't disagree with that." He holds up his hands in surrender.

In the long silence, he watches a mother calling to her small tow-headed son, who's climbing on a pile of sinister ex-quarry rocks near the pier, "Come closer," she shouts. "You gone deaf?"

Frederick thinks that he doesn't have an accent of any kind, prep school dulling it, Northwestern smoothing its edges. The islanders' speech sounds so raw and exaggerated to him. He wonders if people can affect group eccentricities.

"We could go there," Dolores offers, her voice taut with promise.

"I'm not sure."

"Well, the other quarry's fine too. Only there are lots of rocks in it and too many people, but I could tell you where it's safe to dive. Why don't I meet you here tomorrow at noon, and we can decide on which one."

"Okay," Frederick says tentatively. He needs film for his camera. Maybe Dolores can take his picture at the pier with its expanse of ocean. Most of his vacation shots are vacant of people. Tonight when he calls Elizabeth at the dude ranch, he'll tell her that he's going swimming and that the locals are friendly.

He stretches out in the lackluster sun, pulls his knees up toward his stomach for balance, and closes his eyes. He can feel Dolores watching him.

"I like your shoes," she says.

"They're deck shoes."

"I know. But they're blue. I like 'em."

Frederick brushes Dolores's hand, which she has placed over his eyes like a blindfold. "I'll see you tomorrow," she says, moving backward away from him.

When he sits up to wave good-bye, she's halfway inside the door to Shears.

"It's not so bad that Amy wants to be a nurse," he is assuring Elizabeth on the phone. Elizabeth has this thing about nurses, who are emblems to her of everything wrong in men's treatment of women. "Besides, men are also nurses, and Amy is six. When I was six, I probably wanted to be a fireman."

"More sexist bullshit," Elizabeth shoots back. Not only do vacations make her virulent, but she has recently decided that swearing is all right, and she indulges the habit like the new follower of a creed. "And Jonah calls everything horses. 'It's a bull,' I tell him. 'Mama, horse,' he says."

"Maybe the kid needs glasses."

"I'll have his eyes checked as soon as we get back. Or do you think I should drive him into Jackson Hole?"

Elizabeth treats their children as adults with infirmities. Frederick pictures Jonah wearing a monocle along with his orthopedic oxfords, which are his punishment for running awkwardly, in Elizabeth's view.

"I'm going swimming tomorrow at a quarry." He won't fill in the details.

"I'm reading a lot."

He pictures her curled in a lounge chair, a book propped on her long, freckled thighs, her tongue wetting her lips in a gesture of concentration.

"Did you know that foot-binding actually damaged the woman so much that she was unable to walk? Slaves or servants had to cart her around. She was a slave of her slaves."

"Horrible," Frederick manages, thinking about the quarry. "This is costing a fortune. Give the kids a kiss. I'll call you in two days."

He is afraid to undress because he doesn't want to look at his body before he meets Dolores. He can steam up the room and take a shower in which everything, including himself, will become invisible. But steam can't erase the image of his sprawling self, his heavy legs that can't get tan all at once. He wishes he had a small, compact body, the kind that Frenchmen have, one that could absorb light as evenly as a flat stone. He pulls on his swimming trunks and watches them hang over his thighs. He wonders what one wears to a nude quarry.

Today the children will put on their Western show even though Elizabeth has a drumming headache and is on a crucial chapter of her reading. She has fashioned Amy a cowgirl outfit out of a checkered plastic tablecloth. Jonah will wear his overalls and a cowboy hat she bought him at Jackson Hole. All week Amy has been telling Elizabeth about Hadley: "Hadley knows a neat song. He let us ride our ponies out of the circle. Hadley's a real cowboy."

Elizabeth doubts that real cowboys are counselors for the two-to-six-year-old group. In the New West, many of the cowboys sport designer shirts, chinos, and athletic shoes, as if an ocean and sailboats were tucked behind the austere gray mountains they face at breakfast. She has noticed one authentic-looking cowboy sitting among the college boys in the mess hall. While the Teton Trio played "High Noon" at supper, he appeared to be smiling at her. She felt her lips tug back in acknowledgment. Later she classified it as one of those sympathetic looks that men give to women traveling alone with children. It says, "I'm glad I'm not you." Besides, she doesn't want to make eye contact on her vacation, just read and get away from the kids for six to eight hours a day. She is relieved to be sharing a dining table with a couple from Germany who don't know much English. "Der Cowboy ist auch Singer," the tall gangly wife tells her perpetually amused husband. He spends every meal videotaping the cowboys serving them beef tacos, barbecued chicken breasts, and macaroni salad.

It is rumored that a real former astronaut sits at table number one next to Mr. Dennison, the owner, who is fondly referred to as "Big D." Meanwhile, his wife, Little D, runs the kitchen, appearing briefly after the Apple Brown Betty to beam randomly at the checkered tables.

Elizabeth's headache throbs above her left eye, making her think of Frederick, the locus of her pain. Her vacation exiled from him, children in tow like a brave little tugboat, is not her idea. Maybe she should fight for two weeks together, away from the children, instead of traveling two thousand miles in order to pout and read angry feminist tracts. Of course, he'll remind her that they vacation together without the children every January, and that while she doesn't work, he is a pressured attorney who needs time away to relax.

Amy is singing a song about tumbleweed, and a cool breeze is making the cheerful gold corduroy curtains of their cabin puff with air. The place is almost tolerable with its old-fashioned heavy maple furniture, cast-iron washbasins, and sleek handheld shower and cable TV. It has "authenticity without forsaking comfort." She can't dispute the colorful brochure's claims. Of course, she could stay in New York, but it just doesn't seem fair. Maybe she could send the kids to her mother's in Albany, but they've never been invited. This thought causes a new ray of pain to radiate from her eye. Jonah is pounding his fist on a little drum that the Warriors, his group of two-to-three-year-olds, fashioned out of oatmeal boxes. Elizabeth is braiding Amy's hair, which is too fine, and slips between her fingers. Besides, she is unable to see on the side of her headache. "Forget it, kid. Maybe you can wear a bonnet."

"Hadley says we have to wear—"

"I don't care. Your hair won't go. Tell Hadley that your hair is the last frontier."

"It's not fair! Hadley says!" Amy screams, knocking Jonah over for good measure. He falls on his oatmeal drum, crushing it, and begins to sob, his little shoulders hunching in and out for emphasis.

"Hadley—"

"I don't care. Tell him to leave us alone," Elizabeth is saying when a voice interrupts with, "Anybody home?"

"Hi!" Amy shouts to Hadley Incarnate. Running to the door, she hugs his waist. "Mom, this is Hadley."

If she stands up too fast, she might vomit. "Pleased to meet you," she says, twisting her neck forty-five degrees toward him.

She's noticed Hadley at dinner. He has an open face, handsome without being showy. He is delicate, and all his features seem minia-ture; small green eyes, a careful nose, thin lips. Nothing has grown to the point that Hadley will have to excuse himself for possessing it. It is a face one can admire without being effusive. She wouldn't even have noticed it in the Guggenheim or Bloomingdale's. But on vacation, encouraged by the novels she'd read as a stalky, unpopular teenager, in which girls have summer romances with stevedores, carnies, and cow-boys, and by Frederick's ostentatious absence, Hadley's face can lead her anywhere.

She forces herself to rise for introductions, preserving a distance from him so that perspective can work in her favor. Clearly, she may be taller than him by half a foot, but across the room, it is hard to judge. Assuming her best maternal pose, she slouches over Jonah, who is still moaning, and beams at Amy. "I'm Elizabeth."

"Aren't you feeling well?"

"I have a terrible headache. I think it's allergies."

"That's odd. I come here summers because my allergies improve so much. I live in Los Angeles. The pollen count goes off the scale there."

So they have a bond of rashes, running noses, drumming sinuses, and watery eyes, "We're from New York." Elizabeth manages a smile that divides her face into the well and the unwell.

"I can tell by your accent," he laughs. "Can I get you anything? I have some allergy pills. They're prescription, but I don't suppose they'd hurt!"

"Would you mind?"

"No problem. I'll take Amy along. She's always wanted to see where the cowboys live."

Has he used the word cowboys ironically? Is he propositioning her six-year-old daughter? She guesses not. She guesses that none of his words have any meaning beyond their registered intent.

The evening sun has a way of setting on the island that reminds Frederick of cardboard scenery. One minute it will flood the bay with colors; the next minute it is gone, as if a prop man went home early with the essential scenery. He has noticed this summer how things bump along, having little flow. Even the moon, which he's observed nightly while still in New York, adds its portion in childish increments. He hardly ever considers landscape, but tonight it concerns him. Lying naked in his motel room at the Tides, he imagines how he might have looked if he had been bold enough to go with Dolores to Carver's. Instead, he'd offered to buy her a crab roll at Ronnie's. They'd sat in a booth where initials had been carved over initials, a palimpsest of mundane meals.

"My dad might be going to Carver's today anyway. Wednesday's his day off."

"Does your mom know your dad goes there?"

Dolores laughs pleasantly. "It's hard to hide a full body tan."

She'd smiled at him a lot and promised to meet him for lunch Thursday, but lying in the motel room, listening to the waves catch under the bridge at the Mill Race Inn next door, Frederick knows he won't see her again. He takes a huge blue sleeping pill, and before falling into his black dreamless hole, resolves to leave the island tomorrow. It is too confining here. The geography conspires to make him feel inadequate. The only large impersonal place is the ocean, which is too cold for swimming, and over-fished; and Dolores is sixteen. Tomorrow he'll call Elizabeth and take a flight out from Portland. She'll probably welcome his company. Maybe these summers apart are a little self-indulgent. Will he remember his resolution in the morning? he wonders, as he covers his head and lets out several soothing, sleep-inducing sighs.

The children's program is an unqualified success. Even people without children are here to see the Wild West in Song and Skit. Amy, without braids, is Annie Oakley. Hadley settled on pigtails out of sympathy for Elizabeth, not because he'd lowered his standards. He is a demanding director. Do people realize the difficulty of getting children to speak loudly and clearly? Hadley has succeeded. Elizabeth sees his uncomplicated eyes shining toward hers as even Jonah, whose part is to sing the last Indian in "Ten Little Indians," makes a gallant effort to pronounce his r's. "No maw Indian boyers," he shouts at the German's video camera, and Hadley beams.

The two allergy pills haven't worked on her headache, but they have made Elizabeth too punchy to care. She can concentrate on events only through great effort, which, she notices, is a way of fine-tuning the essentials. With unexpected power, she orders Amy and Jonah to take a nap before the chuck wagon cookout.

She leaves the cabin to find Hadley. The bunkhouse where he stays is actually a series of small bedrooms with washrooms and a shared, gloomy lounge. His bunk is number 7, he had told her after the program. The rooms smell of paint, and she sees two buckets outside of room number 4. The color is champagne semi-gloss. She imagines a college boy spending his off-hours painting the walls of his temporary quarters a more appealing color. She wonders why people take such enormous efforts with their surroundings when there is so little energy in one's supply.

"Hi!" Hadley smiles.

"I thought I'd see where the real cowboys live," Elizabeth says tentatively.

Hadley laughs. "Your kids were super, especially Amy. She can really sing." He takes a Coors out of a cooler near the door and hands it to Elizabeth. "Come in."

"Thanks," she says, taking the opened can. "You work so well with children. You must love them."

"Well, it's part of my philosophy."

The word makes Elizabeth flinch. There's nothing worse than a college junior with a philosophy. When Elizabeth doesn't ask what his philosophy might be after the expected interval, Hadley continues.

"I think that if you show people you think the most of them, they'll give the most to you."

Instead of agreeing, Elizabeth asks if he's a business major.

"Management engineering. I hope to work for a big firm, but human service also interests me. You can't take the human element out of business." He glows at her, a Buddha of the Private Sector.

"So this is where the cowboys live," Elizabeth repeats almost to herself and laughs.

"Yeah," Hadley says, smiling quizzically. Then he lunges at her mouth, kissing her precisely. Hadley's small hands massage her back and slip down her behind, which he cups in his hands.

"I have a bed," he says.

"I suppose you do." He moves to kiss her again, and before she can decide what her next act will be, he's helping her remove her shirt and bra in several efficient strokes. She throws her skirt and underpants onto his speckled linoleum floor.

"Hadley, I can't find my mom," Amy is saying. She has Jonah in tow, still barefoot and sucking sleepily on his two middle fingers.

Hadley points to his wall, which Elizabeth faces, asleep. His cow-boy-motif bedspread covers her shoulders. Hadley hopes that he's blocking Amy's view of her mother's clothing. Holding his finger to his mouth, he whispers, "The allergy pill made your mom drowsy. I told her to take a little nap."

Though the story might end here, readers often worry about the after-math. It's especially perilous to leave two adults asleep, estranged by temperament, habit, and geography, so here is the epilogue: If Frederick holds to his resolve to join his family almost a continent away, Amy will tell him that he shouldn't have missed her starring role as Annie Oakley. While Elizabeth pales, Frederick, never good at discerning her moods, hugs Amy and plays with her fine mousy hair. He feels his heart strain with regret and vows to repay his children with his animated presence in the future. Amy adds that Hadley ("their counselor," Elizabeth breathlessly explains) treated her to a banana split. "Me too," Jonah states with such animation that he tumbles off a step and bumps his head. In the comforting of the child and the getting of the ice that ensues, Amy loses the thread of her story. She will not recount that the ice cream outing occurred while her mother slept naked under Hadley's bedspread.

But, since memory has an odd way of reinsinuating itself like a vengeful distant relative, Amy may recall those details later, causing Elizabeth to anticipate a vigorously entertaining digression. In fact, the whole incident improves Elizabeth's imaginative capacity. Waiting constantly to be exposed by some trivial circumstance of Amy's recollection, she perfects anecdotes for every social occasion and a melting way of looking at Frederick that says, "You'll never want to go away without me again."

Around Christmas, she is is observed telling stories at Frederick's business gatherings and regaling the party-goers, even those in the remotest corner. People remark to Frederick that they never knew Elizabeth to be so entertaining, and Frederick thinks that his wife has grown into a mature and charming woman. Remembering Dolores now and then, he'll decide that a sixteen-year-old with a vulnerably thin neck can't match up to this formidable, confident wife with long freckled thighs under her tasteful crepe suit, this source of growing pride and desire.

If, however, Frederick's untormented sleep weakens his resolve to join Elizabeth at the Big D Family Resort just outside of Jackson Hole, I can't be held responsible for where events may lead.

Something to Admire

HE TALL VIETNAMESE woman held her son's hand as he circumnavigated the ice-skating rink. She half-ran, half-walked to keep up with him. Lawrence imagined that she was wearing sandals on bare feet, but he saw stylish boots, ones that a weekend hiker might order from a Lands' End catalog. His own rented skates were laced tightly, but he hesitated at the gate of the rink. Not that he didn't want to skate. It was the best way to get away from the heat of this particular summer. Even Rinny panting on the tile kitchen floor reminded him that he'd owed his dependents a better life. Rinny was the only one who'd stuck it out. Gwen and Brian were probably in Boston by now, visiting her parents and looking for a suitable apartment in Cambridge. Then she'd settle in with her usual care, choosing just the right off-white paint and subtle accessories for her new life teaching art history. He'd kept Rinny, his teaching job at the junior college, and a sadness that instructed his ankles to tremble onto the ice.

In the middle of the rink, several girls, lanky and blonde like Brian but probably a little bit older, were figure skating. Occasionally the Vietnamese mother and her son would pause to observe them as they skated backward. She'd say something that would cause the boy's face to contort in thrilled laughter. Maybe she was promising him that come next summer, he'd skate as well as those American girls. Lawrence doubted it. The girls were able to keep their balance on one leg as they flipped over in midair. It was a natural act for them, like lighting a cigarette used to be for Lawrence. His hand gripped the rail. So far he'd done little skating, but just being in a new environment made him feel more hopeful. He hadn't skated in perhaps fifteen years, though it was one of the activities he'd promised to share with Brian when he finished his dissertation, when he had more time for fun.

"Fun's pretty low on Daddy's list of priorities," Gwen had explained. She had said it kindly to Brian, but as Lawrence wobbled across the ice, he wondered if his son would want to visit him at holiday times and in future summers. Lawrence would work at being entertaining. He'd make lists of plans, the way he used to as a child, but keep them with adult resolution. He was thinking this when the back of his left skate blade hooked the right, and he tumbled forward onto the ice with a low hiss, like air escaping a balloon. He wasn't hurt, but he wasn't sure he could get up either. There was something perilous about moving, as if it would prove him incompetent in yet another area where many people are naturals.

The woman was tireless. Her son, no more than five years old, hung on to her from time to time, but she sustained him, his ballast, his will. Lawrence imagined himself in England, trying to turn Brian into a cricket player. He wouldn't know the first thing about the sport, nor would he try to learn. He began wishing ill upon the woman. Maybe she'd trip, or the little boy, worn out with motion and effort, would cry in frustration. When the black-and-white-shirted rink guard approached to ask Lawrence if he was all right, he decided to leave. The woman and her son were racing in competent circles.

Everything annoyed him in summer-school class the next morning. His new khaki shorts rode up his crotch. His handwriting on the board seemed childish. The air conditioner rattled. Morton next door was doing oral drills on the past participle, and his voice filled Lawrence's classroom, deflecting off the plastic chairs, metal desks, the overlarge wall clock, and the Russian women in their housedresses, gossiping as usual, while Lawrence tried to explain the homework. He wished he could drop his own class, leave the instructor's desk vacant and never return. At the same time he was sorry that he felt this way. His students had to notice his peevishness. Maybe the lack of language between them made his emotions more available to them. Maybe they could see every inflamed nerve ending in his brain as they went over infinitives, as he asked Chanh to see him after class.

Chanh was his best writing student, an older, dignified man who'd been an art teacher in Vietnam. His writing contained the details that the others' work lacked. Chanh could describe the rice crop failing and make it sound beautiful.

"Not another boat beset by pirates," Lawrence told Chanh after class. "Was everyone's boat attacked? Didn't anyone escape without incident?" Then he began quoting from the paper, how they had run out of water, how the sea had rocked them mercilessly.

"That is what happened, Professor," Chanh explained politely. He was perhaps fifty. In America he worked in an auto-parts store and wore cheap polyester shirts, the kind Lawrence's father would wear on Memorial Day to be sporty.

"Your experience has become a cliché. Didn't anything else unusual happen to you? Or did something ordinary happen?"

"So many things, Teacher, unusual and not."

"Did your wife ever leave you?"

"I was not married."

"Did you ever take a damn vacation?"

"To Disney World with my sister."

"Well then, tell me about it. Don't forget to say it was your happiest experience. That it was worth risking your life to see this phenomenal amusement park," he added, with so much malice that he immediately felt embarrassed.

"I will tell a different story, Teacher. I will tell you about my photos. I would also like for you to see my hobby."

"Bring them to my office. I'm somewhat of a photographer myself."

"They are large. They do not transport easily. Come to my apartment some evening. My sister will cook us dinner."

Desperate for company, Lawrence agreed to visit Chanh on Friday. "I'll bring some beer," he offered in a voice that he heard straining to be jolly.

He thought he'd clean something up. He settled on the refrigerator, which was almost bare. Removing the Spicy V-8, the wilted celery, and a half-eaten tube of liver sausage, he sponged down the shelves. When he opened the freezer, which he hadn't done since Gwen and Brian left a week ago Friday, he saw the frozen slabs of meat. Maybe he'd be a vegetarian in his new life, his cleaner, simpler one. He got a green plastic garbage bag and began loading it with bricks of rump roast, pork shoulder, and frozen sirloin, "Good for B-B-Q," the label exclaimed. He'd make life as easy as possible. Maybe he'd pack up the dishes, leaving only three or four to eat from.

He didn't understand the whole year, why Gwen was gone and he was alone. He didn't understand why their dish towels were plaid. He hated plaid. Gwen hated plaid. Who had commandeered their marriage and steered it in so many false directions? Who had laid claim to their kitchen and filled it with the ugliness that finally caused Gwen to flee? He'd ignored most things. It was her own design she was leaving behind, the drab gray paint, the beige nondescript wood.

Rinny nuzzled the bag of frozen meat. Lawrence slipped on his shoes to take out the garbage. Rinny followed him to the door, where he whimpered to be let out.

"Go," Lawrence said. Rinny, who wanted to be walked, continued to whine. "I'm not in the mood," Lawrence said, shutting him outside. He heard Rinny howling on the porch.

Lawrence decided to fix something else. He'd change the oil in his Toyota. He'd put on his old cutoffs, his navy-blue Cubs shirt, and wear some stupid hat. He'd take along a can of beer and his transistor radio. He'd jack up the car, lie on a beach towel, and drain the oil. He'd think of all the men he'd observed doing this over the years, discussing it later when the moment arose or not. "Changed the oil today," he'd tell someone or other later. Maybe the clerk at the Redi-Gas. "Yup," the clerk would say. "Take care of a car and it'll take care of you." Maybe he'd wax the car by hand after washing it. No ride through the automatic car wash, radio blaring something classical, *Adagio for Strings*, that would make him ache for Gwen. He'd take care of things. He'd function. He'd call friends and ask them to supper. He wouldn't discard the dishes after all. He'd be needing them soon.

When he got outside, he noticed how cloudy it was. Wash a car and it rains, he thought. There was Mrs. Renchler reading on her porch. She'd probably ask about Gwen and Brian. She'd look at him with her tired, too-wet eyes. He'd remember that she'd had major surgery for something serious, and act too polite. If he looked very purposeful, she'd see that he didn't want to be disturbed.

"How's it going?" she asked as soon as he slammed the townhouse door behind him.

"Can't complain." He wondered why he called her Mrs. Renchler and not Donna. She was no more than seven years his senior. She seemed older, though. His generation had fought or protested the Vietnam War and refrained from joining in family life until it was too late to master it properly. Her generation, already married when he began college, knew game-show hosts by their first names and traded up for better properties whenever their husbands got raises at work. He knew Mrs. Renchler worked at something, but she didn't have a career in the sense Gwen had. He'd seen Mr. Renchler carrying cardboard boxes of what he sold. Apparently his firm wasn't among the Fortune 500. Here the Renchlers were, married perhaps twenty-five years, in a modest town house like his own.

"I bet the dog misses them," Mrs. Renchler said. "I hear him whining."

"He whined before. He has arthritis."

"Poor thing. I see you're working on the car. It must be nice to be handy."

It was so humid that Lawrence could feel sweat dripping into his eyes, making them sting. "I just thought I'd change the oil."

"Planning a trip? I know Jim always does that before vacation. We're flying this year to Ireland. Jim has family that we'll visit in Cork. Imagine that. Then we'll tour Wales, where Richard Burton was born."

Lawrence turned away and thought he'd begin. He propped the hood open. A fine rain began to fall and the trees shook. The Renchler's mulberry tree had left a purple stain on the sidewalk between their town houses. He watched the stain thin out and spread like a watercolor sunset as the rain got heavier. He sat on his front stoop while the rain blew over his street. He wondered if it was raining in Boston or if this rain would travel east overnight.

Mrs. Renchler was shouting to him. "Aren't you going to close the hood?"

Lawrence ran to the car and slammed down the hood with explosive force.

Once inside, he realized that Rinny was still in the yard. He took off his squeaking wet shoes and opened the back door. The dog darted in before he could stop him. Rinny began shaking himself in the bedroom on a stack of linguistic texts and toward the French lace curtains. Lawrence took a beach towel and rubbed Rinny dry. "Some rain," he told Rinny, who jumped up on Gwen's side of the bed and closed his eyes.

He bought a six-pack of Corona, his newly favorite beer, and drove to Chanh's address, a low-rent high-rise in Uptown near the college. The air had been cooled by the storm and a foreboding chill filled it, as if summer had prematurely surrendered to fall. In fall Brian would begin second grade at a new school, and Lawrence would be free to be anywhere he wanted. Usually he made Brian a cheese sandwich and turned on a cable station that showed Japanese monster cartoons. They'd sit silently watching purple dragons devour whole cities until Brian's cheerful, pointy face would say good-bye and Lawrence would go back to his writing. Maybe he'd teach days now. Then he'd have his evenings free to entertain or barhop if the mood struck him.

In front of Chanh's building on Lakeside, some children were playing in the sprinkler. Every child had black hair. They were from any country where strife had torn families apart. Haitian children were spraying Cambodian children with Chicago's purified water. Many were barefoot and small. The language spoken even in shouting was English. One little boy, an Ethiopian child of tremendous beauty, was shooting the others with a toy laser gun. "G.I. Joe," he sang out into the night.

Chanh's sister Ha had made an American dinner in honor of their guest. Tenderloin steaks nearly as big as the plates were surrounded by cottage-fried potatoes. The salad dressing came from a bottle that said "Rancher Roy," and everything was ready the moment he arrived. They sat around a card table covered with a plastic tablecloth depicting rowboats repeated on a white background. Here and there a duck could be seen in tall grass. The rowboats were empty.

Ha was younger than Chanh and less good-looking. She was perhaps thirty-five, but she was so thin that in profile she looked older. When Lawrence looked at her head-on, she resembled a studious child. When they were introduced, she offered him a very tough little hand and held on until he stopped shaking it. He gave Ha the beer, which she took to the efficiency kitchen. She returned with an aqua tumbler for each, beer filling it to the brim.

"Do you go to school?" Lawrence asked her.

"DeVry Institute. I specialize in electronics. I work in factory too, making transformer parts."

Chanh, who was dressed in a Hawaiian shirt covered with surfers, said, "She is the breadwinner. I am the student."

"You work too," Lawrence added.

"She makes more money." Both Ha and Chanh laughed broadly at this. American economics obviously puzzled them.

Lawrence surveyed the tiny apartment for ethnic touches. Mostly he saw used furniture—a grayish-gold velveteen couch, walnut veneer end tables, and a braided blue circular rug. There was no evidence of a bedroom. Lawrence wondered where they slept. They were small enough to sleep almost anywhere. There was no evidence of Chanh's photos.

They ate quickly, without much conversation. Now and then Chanh and Ha would share a joke: that supermarkets sell fortune cookies, about the name of a street. Both found School Street, where no school existed, outrageously funny. It began to bother Lawrence that they probably carried on like this at every dinner. Of course, they'd speak Vietnamese and have their bowls of rice and cups of tea. Other than the change in menu, it mattered little that he was there. As quickly as he finished the beer, Ha silently took his plastic tumbler and refilled it. He must have finished four of the six beers before dinner had ended.

After Ha had cleared the table and they had shared dessert, lychees and Rocky Road ice cream, Ha excused herself and Chanh invited Lawrence to sit on the couch.

"I will get the photos," Chanh said and walked down a dark hallway to the closet.

He came back holding a wide envelope half his height. It wasn't the fancy kind that Lawrence had seen ad execs carry on the Michigan Avenue bus. It must have been made in Vietnam of colored rice paper.

Chanh positioned himself on the floor at Lawrence's feet. He would sit there, he explained, and hold up his photos for Lawrence.

"Sometimes in America people think differently of beauty."

Then he searched through the envelope and extracted a surprisingly small photo, an 8-by-11. It was of a naked Vietnamese woman. She was not voluptuous, nor did she seem particularly interested in the camera. She appeared to be angry at something outside the camera's range. The second photo was of a girl, maybe fourteen years old, who was naked from the torso up. She was holding a piece of fruit and pretending that she was going to bite into it. Lawrence couldn't identify the fruit hidden in her hand. There was little play in her pretending.

Lawrence began to wonder whether it was Chanh's inability to relax the subjects that made for such detached and almost vicious attitudes, or whether it was life itself during the war that made the women unable to open up to the camera. Of course, they weren't professional models. No one had trained them to ponder beauty or coyness or money, or whatever would have properly composed their faces. Chanh showed him a series of perhaps ten more women. The last one had very pointy breasts like triangles and hid her face in her hands.

"Lovely," Lawrence said, feeling at a loss.

"Thank you," Chanh replied, apparently satisfied. "I took those in my country. The next photos are different."

Chanh removed a series of snapshots, obviously shot with a camera of poorer quality.

"Here is water. Here is sky. That was my escape."

Lawrence took the photos in his hands. He wasn't sure that he could distinguish water from sky. Both swirled. Both were gray.

"Were you alone on the boat?"

"There were many people, but it was not a time to photograph them. We had too much trouble." He lit a cigarette and offered one to Lawrence.

"No, thanks."

"I have other photos," Chanh said, "but I did not take them. Many are of people I no longer know." He smoked silently. Lawrence felt paralyzed with drunkenness.

"Do you like the photos of women? I would sell them to you if you like them. I used to sell my photos in Vietnam."

Lawrence couldn't imagine what he'd do with one of Chanh's photos. Chanh looked eager for him to reply. "How much do they cost?"

"For you, Teacher, twenty-five dollars. In Vietnam I make many hundreds with my photos."

Lawrence guessed that Chanh was lying. No one would have wanted Chanh's nervous nudes, except perhaps a few American G.I.s with no sense.

Lawrence remembered an ugly scene he'd witnessed a few years ago on his way home from work. A middle-aged man in a green Oldsmobile, the car was the clearest image that remained of the man, had propositioned a Vietnamese student waiting for a bus at the corner of Broadway and Wilson. "How much for a suck?" the man had shouted. The girl had pretended not to hear him, but when the car circled the block again, the girl had run away. Lawrence had watched it all from a distance. It occurred to him now that he should have stood close to her.

"I'll buy one, Chanh," he said. He thought of offering to buy the entire sea-and-sky series. What a pretentious gesture it would have been to buy art that showed abstract suffering, art that was so personal. "I'll buy the first woman you showed me."

He'd keep the photo in his bedroom closet. Now and then an angry woman, angry at what the camera had never captured, would fall off the shelf when he reached in to get a shirt.

November

D RUMMOND NATTINGLY had charted in musical notation the sound that rabid dogs made roaming France in the nineteenth century. The top note registered well above high c. He had also measured the hatbands of twentieth-century dictators for a symposium on brain size held in Montreal. Though Gail could have filled a calendar with Saturdays spent in tense limbo over the whereabouts of garden tools that Drummond had mislaid, she found his preoccupation with knowledge endearing. Anyone observing Drummond and Gail at parties hunched together, whispering like mutinous sailors on an ill-fated voyage, would have called their marriage a success.

Discovering the article on rabies that Drummond had contributed to a French magazine, Evan asked, "Dad, do you get paid for this?" Without reading it, Evan placed it on top of the stack of journals his father kept on the bedside table. His parents' bed was currently littered with Drummond's charts and graphs about Bangladesh. As if to verify his theory of the region as a laboratory for catastrophe, just three days ago a ferry boat loaded with 182 people had sunk in a monsoon. Two weeks prior to that, an entire village had vanished in a mud slide. Shortly before the mud slide, fire had swept through one of the few indoor markets, crowded with shoppers before a Muslim holiday. That one country could be beset by so much tragedy had to have meaning. Because he wasn't a religious man, Drummond consigned its significance to the sphere of metaphysics, his statistical domain.

Drummond spent his afternoons in the reference section of the university library using microfilm to chronicle the country's calamities. Randomly choosing three years, he calculated that 1.3 times a month, a natural disaster involving the loss of more than one hundred lives occurred. Sundays, followed by Tuesdays, were the most common times, even days rather than odd, and November was the most pernicious month. These facts once ascertained, he wrote letters to UNESCO, the Ford Foundation, The National Science Foundation, and three international organizations of lesser status, requesting funds to travel and complete his research.

For the second time in sixteen years, Gail was pregnant. Even as she wondered how it could have happened again so belatedly, she spent her time marveling at how spring was transfiguring Chicago. Though the air was still cold, she drove with her car window down, sniffing the breeze off the lake. The perennials coming up in her yard had a poignancy she'd never noticed. Stray cats in alleys sang to her, and when she undressed at night, she caught herself patting her taut abdomen as she imagined it swelling.

Drummond was agreeable to having the baby, remembering how Evan's infant presence in the house had provided a startling solidity to objects. Walking Evan in his stroller, Drummond hadn't strayed once from the moment he inhabited. It seemed dangerous to travel even mentally from his baby's side. Still, he wouldn't prevail upon Gail to give birth if it weren't her choice. He was too old for naive romanticism. Besides, Gail's work was vital to her. What would happen to her study of shark cartilage as an immunological resource if she interrupted it to raise a child?

Drummond accompanied Gail to her first obstetrics appointment and stroked her hand as the doctor, almost young enough to be their son, explained the risks of pregnancy at forty-four. He furrowed his brow upon discovering a certain slackness of her cervix and advised her to rest in bed if she began to spot. After their appointment, they toasted their second child at the Fondue Stube, where they used to eat on special occasions as graduate students.

"To my last glass of wine," Gail said, raising her goblet.

"To November," Drummond said, clanking his wineglass into hers.

While Gail rested, she thought that the best time to have a baby would have been April. Animals had their babies in spring. She had watched a show where little lynx cubs were born in a den in the North Woods. Her daughter, for she hoped it would be a girl, would be delivered in late November at a birthing center, a concept invented after Evan's arrival. Drummond would coach her and Evan could be present too. She closed her eyes and thought of names. Maybe Carolina, as in

"Carolina dove" and "Carolina pink," phrases she'd discovered in the dictionary the night before. Evan Grant Nattingly. Carolina Dove Nattingly. Maybe just Caroline.

The phone rang three times. It was Jamie wondering where Evan was. He was supposed to meet her in front of the school. The next time it rang, Gail answered on the first ring. A woman whose accent intersected several continental boundaries said she had important news for Dr. Nattingly.

Evan Nattingly sat in Louis's car wondering how he could be friends with such a nerd. Louis's science fair experiment with hydroponic lettuce was far more annoying to Evan than anything his father had investigated. Evan spent half his life out of school in Louis's passenger seat watching him disappear into libraries and bookstores.

"Hurry up! I'm supposed to meet Jamie at three!"

Louis took a mechanical pencil from behind his ear and jotted notes on a miniature legal pad. Once Evan had his own car, he'd avoid Louis totally and stay away from home as much as possible. His parents were becoming stranger by the minute. Just last week Drummond had insisted that Evan show his band teacher the score of rabid-dog sounds. Drummond had pressed so hard that Evan finally put the damn magazine in his Eddie Bauer book bag and promised to show Mr. Dieter. Of course he hadn't, and of course his father had forgotten about his fleeting insistence that Evan betray his family's foolishness to the world.

Evan and Jamie had kissed each other repeatedly while working on a Spanish project, a list of items to pack for a trip to the Amazon. Jamie had taken care of the food and clothes. Evan had figured out the camping gear and contingencies. He was glad he went to a progressive school. The assignments were so unusual that they hardly seemed to be homework.

"You might try being on time now and then," Jamie snapped as she climbed into the backseat of Louis's car. She said nothing to Louis.

"Sorry," Evan said. "Louis had all this junk to buy for his science experiment, and then it looked like he was writing a letter at the steering wheel."

"I think your mom's home."

"Why do you think that?"

"I called looking for you and she answered."

"She won't mind if we stop in. She likes to know how humans live. She used to be one herself."

They sat on Evan's bed for a long time and listened to an old Moody Blues album that had been his mother's.

"Nights in white satin . . ."

"Never reaching the end . . ."

They took turns singing the lines in falsetto. When the song ended, Evan kissed Jamie's neck. She kissed him on the ear and began unbuttoning her blouse.

"My mom's here," Evan whispered, though he hadn't heard a sound from her bedroom in an hour.

Then they heard feet padding around upstairs and a shower running. She usually showered before making dinner, which made sense to Evan considering that she touched shark tissue all day.

"She takes twenty minutes," Evan said.

Jamie took off her blouse, revealing small breasts with light brown nipples. Tiny nipples, Evan thought.

They lay down on his bed. He touched her breasts and tried putting one in his mouth. It felt too strange to him, though Jamie seemed to like it all right. She lay still under him. Then they rocked back and forth on his bed until they heard footsteps on the landing and then Gail's voice downstairs.

"Evan, are you home?"

He grabbed his T-shirt and pulled it over his head.

His mom was sitting at the kitchen table looking pale. Even her eyes looked somehow lighter.

"Hi! Doing homework?"

"Jamie's over. We're doing homework together."

"A lady with a strange accent called. Dad must have gotten one of the grants he's requested."

She appeared to be gripping the table. "Something wrong?"

"Just a stomachache," Gail said and flashed a smile that swallowed itself in self-consciousness.

Before he could leave for the three weeks in Bangladesh that the U.S.I.A. had arranged for him, Drummond needed shots for hepatitis, yellow fever, dengue, smallpox, and cholera. The doctor wasn't sure which one he was reacting to when he got feverish at the library and had to go to bed for the rest of the week.

"More tea, honey?" Gail asked on her way out the door to work. She was still fatigued and spotting a little, but she couldn't take a leave of absence at this important juncture in her research.

The week passed with Drummond succumbing to various fevers and making complicated travel arrangements between them. Gail worried about him as they kissed good-bye at O'Hare. After his plane took off, Gail would take Evan to a coffee bar and tell him about her pregnancy, news that had gotten lost in the shuffle of events the weeks before.

"Want to get some hot chocolate?"

"I'd like to, Mom, but I have to meet Jamie."

"You two see a lot of each other lately."

"I guess we do." Could his mother tell by his reticent speech what they'd done in his bedroom on the days she'd been working?

"Will you be home for dinner?"

"I think Jamie's mom wants me to stay."

"Is Jamie's mom home when you go there?"

"Sometimes she isn't, but her older sister always is."

"Are you two serious?"

"Kind of," Evan said and stared out the window.

Gail hated being alone in her kitchen. She looked around for signs of family and found a half-eaten bran muffin on the counter. She spread butter on it and ate it standing up. She stared at the full briefcase of work she had taken home for the weekend, but it was hard to concentrate on anything but imagining her baby's features. The face would be round like hers, with her small nose and lips. She hoped the baby would have Drummond's intelligent gray eyes. Her own eyes were somehow less important in the world. She decided to take a bath and get to sleep. When Evan came home at 2 A.M., she didn't hear him open the door.

Saturday morning she planned to have breakfast with Evan and tell him about the baby. Why was Drummond leaving it all to her? So far, only he and the doctor knew. Her mother, her son, friends, colleagues, and the rest of the world had no idea. She remembered telling everyone the minute she and Drummond knew about Evan.

"Evan, we need to talk," she said, knocking at his door.

"What time is it?"

"Ten."

"Damn. I have a field trip to Argonne National Lab. The bus leaves in thirty minutes. Can you drive me?"

"We'll have to hurry."

Her gray cotton jogging pants barely fit over her stomach anymore. Bending over to lace her shoes, Gail felt a twinge of pain in her abdomen, followed by a wave of nausea that left her weak. She sat on the bathroom floor observing the shining wavy lines that floated over the real lines of the tile. She wished that Drummond were home. Standing up, another sharp pain gripped her. She wet a washcloth, scrubbed her face, and splashed water onto her eyes.

"What time will you be home?" she asked Evan in the car. "Kind of late. I think I'll be at Jamie's for dinner again," Another pain shot through her. She concentrated on keeping her foot on the gas.

"I want you home for dinner tonight. That's final."

Jamie was waiting in front of the bus. When she saw Evan, her face lit up.

Evan waved to her and bounded up the stairs without looking back at Gail.

Gail was planning on driving straight home and calling the doctor when the pains suddenly stopped. Maybe she'd sit in the park before she went home to rest. She chose a bench close to the playground. At her distance the scene was an abstract of color and good cheer. She angled her head up to the sun, closed her eyes and allowed the light to bathe her forehead, cheeks, and chin.

"Excuse me" were the next words she heard.

A father and son had taken possession of a nearby bench. The pardon was meant for the son, whose ball had landed at Gail's feet.

She formed a smile that was supposed to denote understanding but meant much more to the father. He told her his name was John, that he had joint custody of Justin, worked in a Shaker furniture store, missed being married, thought Reagan was destroying civil liberties, liked to try meatless recipes, and had had disk surgery two years ago. To this banquet of information, John added another fact—that he found Gail attractive.

Just as she was thinking of escaping, Justin asked her to watch him play catch with his father. For twenty minutes, she followed the ball as it passed between them. Now and then Justin looked to her for approval and she nodded in recognition. Then the pains began again, first perceived as a quickening of her heartbeat and a chill beginning at her scalp. Grimacing, she doubled over. After the pain ungripped, Gail sat up straight and looked at her watch. When the sequence repeated itself three minutes later, she knew something was terribly wrong.

"John," she shouted, and waved him toward the bench.

"I'm sorry," she began, "but I think I'm having a miscarriage. Can you get me to a hospital?"

Despite John's whispers of reassurance in the car and the doctor's lack of commitment to the worst possible scenario, she had miscarried by 4 P.M. The miscarriage itself hadn't been as bad as the cramps that preceded it. Three more sharp pains led to a gush of blood, a feeling of general weakness, and a semi-faint in which she imagined that Drummond was at her side and that Evan was being born.

Then she lay in a hospital bed with a clear tube in her arm. The doctor said that a D & C might be necessary but that she could rest for now. Assuming that John was her husband, one nurse asked if she'd like to see him. Thinking she'd thank him for getting her to the hospital, Gail said yes. When the nurse returned, she told Gail that it seemed he couldn't be found.

She drifted to sleep and dreamed she was in her house having dinner in an empty room when she heard a sound like "Kuk! Kuk!" In flew a hummingbird, which fluttered over her plate, and then disappeared upstairs.

Waking in a panic, Gail dialed Evan. "Mom, you sound terrible."

"I'm at St. Francis Hospital. I'm all right, honey, but you need to come here so we can talk."

"What happened?" Evan asked, his voice shivering.

"I'll tell you later, Evan, but I'm really okay."

Locating Drummond would be nearly impossible. She had the number of two hotels he'd be using but couldn't remember which one was first or what time it would be in Dacca. Waiting for Evan was unbearable. Before he knew he was going to have a brother or sister, she would have to tell him he'd lost one.

"C'mon, it's fine to feel terrible," the nurse said, observing her miserable expression. Gail acknowledged the nurse by pushing some tears into her eyes. She knew she'd cry later, when the parks were full of women who had names for their babies, small insignificant names.

When she opened her eyes again, Evan was standing over her.

"Have you been here long?"

"Just a minute. Why are you here, Mom?"

She motioned for Evan to sit. He slumped into a chair and kneaded his face with his fingers.

"Evan, I was pregnant, but then I had a miscarriage."

He looked down at the floor. "Mom, I didn't even know."

"I'm sorry, honey."

"Does Dad know?"

"He knows I'm pregnant. He doesn't know I'm here."

"Are you going to tell him?"

"Of course. When we find him."

"Can I call Jamie?"

"Why?"

"I just need to tell her."

Gail watched Evan's back as he dialed the phone. She remembered how she had loved to kiss him between his perfect little shoulder blades when he was little. As she listened to Evan telling Jamie about her miscarriage, Gail felt surprised at the news.

"Jamie says she's sorry."

"We're all sorry," Gail said and reached to hug Evan.

She found Drummond the next morning at the second hotel on the list. Since she'd come in unexpectedly, Evan had brought clothes for her to wear home. She hadn't thought of telling him what she would need. When the call from Drummond got through, she'd just discovered that Evan hadn't packed any underwear.

"Gail, I'm sorry," the scratchy voice said. For a minute they both breathed together in sympathy. Then Gail sighed. It was hard to believe in Drummond at this distance.

"Me too," she finally said.

"Shall I come home?"

"No need," she said wearily.

The cab dropped her in front of the house. She gave the driver, who'd been playing loud gospel music, her last ten dollars and went inside. She was lying on the sofa when she heard noises in Evan's room. She dragged her leaden self up the stairs and stood outside his closed door listening to the headboard banging against the wall and bicycle wheels humming. Then a girl screamed, and Gail opened the door.

"Evan!" she shouted as he dived under the covers.

"Mom!"

"How are you feeling?" Jamie asked in a voice full of composure. She had smoothed her hair and arranged Evan's Marimekko car and truck sheets so that they covered all but her neck and face.

"You'll have to leave," Gail said without looking at her. "Evan, get dressed and come downstairs."

Evan and Gail sat at the kitchen table. They were drinking canned mushroom soup and looking at a map of Bangladesh. Evan found Dacca on the map. Drummond's unpronounceable hotel was named after the local river. They took turns practicing its impossible name. Gail began laughing at how Evan struggled with the word. Evan was so glad to hear her laugh that he tried to hold the sound in his ears. Pressing his hands over his eyes, he thought of Jamie's hard little nipples and wondered why he suddenly hated her forever.

Keys

HEN ELLEN'S MOTHER was dying three winters ago, she won the first prize of her life, a stuffed elephant toy, in a holiday-bazaar raffle. When she phoned me to ask if I'd pick up the gift for her, I asked why she hadn't called Ellen.

"Ellen has her own problems," Grace told me. "I hate to hear about them. And I figure that I've known you almost as long as my own daughter." She reminded me of the time she had taken me on the parachute ride, the most terrifying ride at Riverview, three times in the summer of 1960. Ellen, who was afraid of anything but the merry-go-round and a spinning pink teacup ride, had laughed from the sidelines.

I didn't know if Grace knew that Ellen had told me about her illness. If I wasn't supposed to know, why would I be so eager to help? If I was to know, what should I say to the woman when I dropped off the toy?

I decided to call Ellen and ask her what her mother knew about my knowing her situation. Ellen's son Adam answered. He'd be an excellent solution to the elephant problem, I thought at the time. "Adam," I asked. "Did you hear that your grandmother won a toy elephant?"

"So?"

The word stretched out in front of me. It opened caverns of pity I never thought a word capable of holding, "So your grandma is sick and she won an elephant," I told the little brat. "And I assume you don't want the thing because she's asked me instead of your mom to bring it to her. Is this situation familiar to you or not?"

"My mom's not talking to Grandma, at least not really."

"What does 'really' mean?" I asked him. Was he suggesting they talk officially but that a call about a gift would be construed as unofficial?

"Sometimes Mom talks to Grandma's doctor, but she never talks to Grandma. I think it has something to do with Rex."

I still thought of a dog when I heard Rex's name, but instead of a dog I forced myself to picture the stooped paleontologist for whom Ellen had left a perfectly capable husband, now known in conversation as "Adam's father."

"How's Adam's father?" I'd ask Ellen, wanting some news of John.

Misunderstanding my question, Ellen would tell me that he more than willingly paid child support and that he'd never canceled a Sunday visit. It seemed there was no way to access the file labeled "John Cantos," at least not without Ellen's editing it so severely that its contents would be suspect anyway.

"He felt disdain for what he'd made me," was the line I remembered best. I thought of the lesson in perspective from my high school math book. A man in a fedora receded down a seemingly endless railroad track. Though he appeared to be standing in front of me, I knew I'd never shake his hand or arrive close to the point in space where I might touch his imagined lapel.

After speaking to Adam, I realized I was alone with the prize. I'd deliver the stuffed elephant without further reflection on John, Ellen, Adam, or the nature of memory.

Dinner that night was at Celeste's apartment. I couldn't help conjuring up Babar's wife posed with her back to the audience and dressed as a bride on the last page of my childhood book. This Celeste, however, was a bench-pressing lesbian, our former neighbor, who only invited us over after a lover had jilted her or a job lead had fizzled. Her indifference to cuisine bordered on fanaticism. In fact, we had met when she had knocked on our condo door, asking to borrow salt and a can opener.

"I wanted to cook an Iranian dish, but I couldn't get the kind of yogurt I needed," Celeste said as she placed a tureen of grayish soup in front of us.

I tried not to look at Charles, who takes dining seriously. When the pressure of shared speechlessness pressed too heavily, I finally asked him, "Why do you took so abject?" His response was a kick under the table, which meant that he didn't like dinner, and a question to Celeste about Salman Rushdie and the Ayatollah. I remembered one evening when Charles had sulked over his bouillabaisse, while Ellen and I sucked the meat out of our crab legs. "Let's share," I finally told him, to preserve our marriage and our credibility in Ellen's eyes.

"I'm just thinking about sadness," Charles said.

"As a cause or an effect?" Celeste questioned.

When Charles said, "An effect," they both exhaled together. It was a strange moment of misunderstood empathy. While Charles was picturing rack of lamb and new potatoes, I'm sure Celeste was seeing the face of Renata, a bookstore manager who'd been her lover until late last Thursday. I felt a strange tingling in my face. The trouble with red hair is how easily you blush. I plunged my spoon into the concoction with new vigor, hoping the moment would pass.

When we had finished the still-frozen cheesecake, Celeste started crying softly. "I look like a bear," she managed.

"What do you mean?" Charles asked.

"Look at me. I'm all muscled and hairy. Weight lifting is supposed to make me sleek."

What could we say? Charles told Celeste that we're all getting older. He forced her to pinch his midriff. "Go ahead," he said, pushing his chest in her direction. "See what I mean?"

I told her not to worry, that potential lovers are everywhere. Furthermore, we all resemble animals.

We turned the rest of the evening into a parlor game involving our animal identities. Gerald Ford, political affiliations aside, was an elephant. Sammy Davis, Jr., was a ferret. We all agreed that Johnny Carson was a definite prairie dog.

Celeste noticed that animal characterization seemed easier with men. I suggested that Meryl Streep resembled a lizard.

"No more than William Buckley," Charles added to be difficult.

The evening finally ended with kisses at the door and promises that we'd send any women resembling baby harp seals Celeste's way.

"Where do you think she got a name like that!" I asked Charles.

"That was another problem all evening. The food aside, I couldn't remember her goddamn name."

"Babar's wife."

"Huh?"

"Celeste."

The building where Grace's prize awaited me resembled an asphalt-siding rendition of an Argyle sock. I entered the unmarked door and went to a reception desk, where a woman sat stamping invoices. I wondered if I needed a coupon to redeem Grace's elephant or whether it would be surrendered without complaint.

"I've come to pick up a stuffed elephant that a Mrs. Pankrot won in a raffle."

"Frankie, look in the prize box," the clerk said without looking up. Did I need to explain that it wasn't for me? I stood there quite a long time trying to guess exactly where I was. Obviously it was a business, but what kind of business? Did they make stuffed elephants here, or was that ancillary to something more serious, say, the manufacturing of mold remover or paper clips?

After several minutes a man presented me with a yellowed plastic bag the size of a piece of carry-on luggage. Inside was an unadorned elephant doll. No hat, coat, tie, or shoes. No tail that I could see. I wondered if Mrs. Pankrot would notice the missing tail as I tossed the toy into my back seat.

Mrs. Pankrot lived in the third geriatric high-rise on the block. The building was called "The Breakers," as I read on a large billboard when I parked my car. I pictured two tough guys, movers with rolled-up sleeves, ready to help little old women grocery shop or move their furniture to dust under a difficult corner. I considered leaving the prize with the doorman, but that would have disappointed Grace, who must be lonely for conversation to have called me in the first place.

She had prepared a little snack for us. On a card table in the living room directly in front of the console television was a loaf of banana bread, sugar and cream in matching crystal bowls, and a pot of tea warmed inside a paisley tea cozy. I was to sit on the "good chair," as Grace called the matching card-table chair. She seated herself slowly on the couch that hugged the longest wall in the apartment. Above it was a Winslow Homer print. Apparently I was to eat alone.

She didn't have much to say to me while I used my fingers to break off pieces of banana bread and sloshed them down with tea. When she talked at all, her comments were on my eating habits. She didn't think it was healthy that I took my tea black. Two lumps was how she always drank hers. She thought that maybe she should have provided butter for the bread, but with what we know about butter, it's like helping a guest kill herself.

I began to feel self-conscious eating alone, but I assumed that her not partaking had something to do with her illness and was hesitant to ask.

After I pushed away from the table, which proved to be the signal she was waiting for, she began. "The year that Ellen left John, she changed her keychain four times. For nine years they are married, and she has the same chain all the time. Then comes year ten and every time I see Ellen, it's something new. First she has one that looks like a fist. Then it's a big ribbon made out of metal. Then she has one that looks like a little shoe. Before then, you always knew it would be a plain silver ring. I know she has to be up to monkey business to change her keys so many times."

She cleared her throat, waiting for me to answer. Putting a pillow behind her neck, she closed her eyes for a moment, scratched her head vigorously and looked at me with disappointment.

"When you're fiddling with keys, you break things. It's that simple."

She opened her arms wide in a satisfied pose and smiled, mostly with her eyes.

"I brought the elephant. It's on the bed with my coat."

"You want it?" she asked.

"Thank you, Grace, but after all, you won it," I said rather tentatively. Was it sadder to picture her keeping the thing, or me driving away with it in my back seat?

"Maybe you know a child," she added.

"How about Adam?" I asked.

She closed her eyes for a long time, as if the curtain had come down, ending the first act of an opera. When she opened them again, she had changed subjects.

"Do you and Charles still travel so much?"

"Less now," I told her. "Charles used to have to go to England almost every month. Now we get away maybe twice a year."

"Where did you go recently?" she asked.

"Let's see. We spent two nights in Salt Lake City, but you mean something different, right?"

"Once, when Ellen was just a baby, Jordan and I went to Cape Cod to see the sights. There was a flag or placard at one point, I can't remember which, that said, 'This is the spot in the United States closest to Europe.'"

"Did you get to Europe?" I asked.

"The funny thing was," she continued, "that I didn't even consider that the sign had anything to do with me. I was Ellen's mother. That was a sign about geography." She folded her hands and sighed. "Knowing what I know now, I should have started swimming."

She laughed at her joke for a long time. I sat there wishing that Grace had won a better prize. I thought about what I had in my purse to give her, but nothing came to mind.

"So you must be a busy girl," she said, "I won't keep you much longer." She got up slowly, marched into the bedroom, and came back holding the elephant still wrapped in plastic. She unwrapped it with great energy and sat it next to her on the couch. It was the cheap kind of stuffed animal that would lose an eye in maybe a week.

"Does Ellen know I won a prize?"

"I called but Adam answered."

She shifted on the pillows and stroked her hair, troubled by the news.

"That boy is like his mother."

"He does favor her," I agreed, knowing she meant something completely different.

"Give it to him when you see him," she said, handing me the toy. "How do you say what it would mean if I kept it? That it would be too ironic?"

"I guess that's the word."

"Funny that there's a word for an old woman who would want to keep an elephant."

From

Bop

The Spirit of Giving

Y SISTER COLLECTS primitive art, so on her birthday I sent her an Eskimo calendar. Each month shows a different block print of Eskimos hunting, sitting around a fire, or stretching seal skins on frames. The prints are done in rich primary colors. They are striking in their simplicity. After the year is over, the prints are suitable for framing.

My sister and I are close. Although she lives in San Francisco, we talk several times a month. When I didn't hear from her for three weeks after I'd sent the gift, I decided to call her.

"I hate it," she said on the phone in a nervous voice. "I know it's unkind of me to tell you, but I'm used to speaking the truth. The prints are finely executed, but I hate what's omitted. All the blood spilled, all the flesh rendered."

"I should have sent you photos of bok choy," I suggested. "Or of a tribe that only eats dead bumblebees they find in the grass. It's life, Martha."

"I know," she answered. "Who's the anthropologist?"

She is. We talked about other things—Andy, the kids, nuclear war. Then she told me she had to go to her stained-glass workshop. Seemed she was in hot pursuit of a hummingbird.

After the call I went back to my desk to write her a letter. I asked her how it felt to be such a sentimentalist. I questioned her own studies of primitive art, if much of it isn't sacrifice and blood, even human blood spilled to assure favor. I never sent the letter.

Two months later I was looking through those shopping catalogs I get in the mail, the ones from famous Texas gift houses. Last year I could have bought a ticket to ride on the first space shuttle to carry passengers or an oil painting by Richard Nixon called "Boats Escaping, Retirement Years." I opted for a new bathrobe of green velour. I bought Ted some sheepskin earmuffs he never wore. In fact, when I gave them to him, he said, "You have to be kidding, Jane. I'm a translator!"

"Maybe you wanted a plastic replica of the Rosetta stone?" I asked. Our relationship has gone downhill since. Sometimes we meet for pasta and Chianti, but our conversations are strained.

This Christmas I'm determined to choose gifts with more care. Martha still hasn't forgiven me, though her hummingbird was a success. She sold it at a small art fair for a hundred twenty-six dollars and fifty cents. The fifty cents might have discouraged customers, but she's uncompromising.

First I consider gift certificates, but they're safe as white bread. Then I call a friend and ask her what she buys for her sister. "House slippers. My sister loves house slippers. This year I bought her a pair monogrammed MM. I found them in an art-deco shop."

"Are those her initials?"

"Marilyn Monroe. They're *her* initials. I thought my sister would get a kick out of wearing Marilyn Monroe's slippers."

My friend is no help. My sister would call me uncaring. "That poor woman died in her bed. Some people even say she was murdered. How sad to own the slippers in which she thought her last thoughts," my sister would say.

A few nights later I'm reading a journal of aging. As we all know, the Eskimos used to leave their elderly to die on ice floes. The old took it in good spirits, but even so. Now it's more popular to have the elderly move in with unmarried daughters, who not only care for them in their final illness but if they have no teeth, chew the tough and gristly seal meat for them.

That night I dream I'm a young Eskimo woman with very strong teeth. My job is to chew seal meat not only for my parents but for my sister's in-laws, my great-aunt Ida, who has red hair in my dream, and her pet retriever, Yuk-Yuk. When I wake up, my jaws ache, and I remember it's December seventeenth. If I don't send Martha a present soon, I'll have to send her an apology.

When I get home that night from dinner with Ted, this time moo-shu pork in a crowded basement in Chinatown, I call Martha.

"Did you ever eat moo-shu pork?" I ask.

"It looks like chewed food. I don't like it," she says.

How is it that my sister always knows my thoughts and has a ready critique?

"Did you know that Eskimos no longer let their parents die on ice floes? Rather, they chew the food for their toothless elders and care for them the rest of their lives."

"The job usually falls to the unmarried daughter," she adds, meaning me.

"That's right! I'd be the one chewing the food."

Martha chortles. I can hear Andy in the background telling the kids not to paint on the white rug.

"How are you and Ted?" she asks.

"He didn't like the earmuffs I gave him."

"Speaking of presents," she says, "I sent you a purse I got at an ethnic fair. It's from China. It shows a duck hiding in some rushes while a feast is taking place in the palace to the left. I thought it wonderfully humorous."

"Did you ever think," I ask her, "how nothing is funny except predation? Think of cartoons, the roadrunner eluding the coyote, Bugs Bunny hiding from Elmer Fudd. The punch line is 'You can't eat me.'"

"You're deep, Jane." We say good-bye soon after.

The next day I'm in a little gourmet shop that specializes in French cheeses and dessert items. Still thinking of those Eskimo women chewing for their parents, I'm having trouble doing any worthwhile shopping. Finally, I buy Ted two pounds of brandied cherries. As long as he can't wear them on his ears, I feel certain he'll like them. Now for Martha. I look up at a shining mountain of white food processors, able to grind, purée, stir, aerate, and liquefy, among other verbs. I ask the clerk to wrap one and enclose this card: "When Mother needs an ice floe, remember who owns the food processor. Love, Jane."

Bop

HE MACHINE WOULD not cooperate. It photographed his original, but when Oleg looked in the metal pan, the duplicate was zebra-striped and wordless. Three more times he inserted the grocery ad. He got back stripes leaning toward each other and crossing in the middle like insane skate blades.

"Please, if you will."

It was obvious that the woman wasn't interested in her job. You could tell by the way she handled the paper. Her nails tore the pleasant green wrapping that reminded him of larger American money. Her eyes never met the machine that perhaps needed ink, fluid, straightening, or encouragement. Her behavior wouldn't be tolerated if he ran the place.

"Can I ask you something?" she asked.

"It is free country. One may ask what one wishes."

"You come here every day with something different. I know I'm not supposed to look, but here you are again xeroxing garbage and your machine is acting up. Why do you make me so busy?"

"Please, I will tell you. The duplication of materials is of great interest to me. Since I came to this country, for three years now, I make copies of everything. If I could, I would copy my hair, my clothing, my food, and my bowels."

She had walked away. He left the office carrying the perfect finished copies of the grocery ads. These went into the large books stamped *Souvenirs* purchased from Woolworth's. He had filled fourteen already.

Now he was back in his small apartment, whose attitude toward America was one of total acceptance. Plastic-molded coral and gold-flecked seats blended with torn leather. A portrait of a sailboat edged up to a Degas dancer. A Cubs schedule followed. Family photos marched along in the parade. A wall clock resembling an owl's face kept the beat. And leading the line was a caricature that a street artist had done at a fair. Since he already thought he resembled a red-haired Pinocchio, the artist didn't need to use much imagination. His eyes were blue points, his mouth a slit, his ears question marks, and his nose pointed aggressively, like a blind man's white cane. His hair was unruly. He was never going to win a beauty pageant, but maybe his odd array of features would not be discouraged on the quiz shows he loved to watch.

"Please," he'd say to the checkout girl, "what city has the highest ratio of pets to people?" If she didn't know it was Los Angeles, he'd tell her right out. But he wouldn't embarrass her. He'd say it gently, as if he were providing her with a blessing. One checkout woman, whose badge read *Marta*, seemed especially eager to see him on market days. "There's Mr. Know-It-All," she remarked to her bag boy. They both laughed. Americans were very pleasant.

Upstairs the jesters were at it again. That's not what they were called, but he could never remember the name for what they were. How could two men practicing the art of silence make so much noise? Was it the rope pull or the human washing machine they were doing? Were they sizzling down to the floor like angry bacon, or were they sentimental clowns on an invisible tightrope? He hated what they did. It reminded him of loneliness, of which he already had enough evidence. He had taken to tapping the ceiling with a broom lately. The jesters had taken to giving him free tickets to their performances.

He went to the kitchen, poured lukewarm tea into a *Star Wars* glass, and went back to the letter he'd left that morning. "I am sorry to say," he continued, "that there is proliferation of bad ideas here. It reminds one, if you please, of the duplication industry. For a nickel, which is very small, a man can copy anything, including his ears. However, who is it that needs four ears? The same with ideas. Everyone in America has the opinions. I read a paper and there is opinion on where dogs should leave their excrement, there is opinion on homosexuals adopting infants, there is opinion on facial hair and robins. There is opinion on cooking cabbage without odor. A child even has opinions. He thinks the governor is fat. Here is large black cat in ad choosing one cat food. If you please, why is every goddamned thing discussed in America?"

He would leave the "goddamned" out when he sent it to the "Personal View" column of the paper. If it was printed, which it wouldn't be with cursing, he'd receive five hundred dollars. But for now it exhilarated him to curse. He pounded the table for emphasis. The red Formica was unresponsive.

He worked every night from nine until five in the morning. His job was to sit at a switchboard that was hooked into store alarms. If an alarm rang, his switchboard would wail, and he would call the police, giving them a code, and call the store owner with the news. In his eleven months of employment, there'd been only twenty-seven alarms, and most of those were due to faulty wiring. He was able to spend most of his time sleeping, just as Mr. Kaplan had suggested upon hiring him. Mr. Kaplan had been insanely happy to give him a job. Just sixty years ago, Mr. Kaplan's own father had come over here, untrained, illiterate, and if it weren't for a *landsman,* he would have perished. Mr. Kaplan got very emotional then and swiped at his eyes with a big hankie and hugged Oleg Lum stiffly and told him, "Welcome, brother." Oleg thought Kaplan might burst into song, an American spiritual. Although his job paid minimum wage, he had his days free to do as he wished. Usually he wished to go to the library.

The influx of Russian immigrants to the Rogers Park area had altered its environment. Russian shoemakers hung shingles on every block. Several Russian delicatessens displayed gleaming samovars next to pickled fish in windows, and the library had begun to carry a good amount of Russian language books but mostly the classics. He had already read those books in Russian, which he had once taught. Now he wanted to read American books rich in history: Sacco and Vanzetti, Sally Rand, Nat Turner, and Howard Hughes. And when he flashed his neat green library card at the girl, who even in summer required a sweater, she always smiled at him. Maybe she, like Mr. Kaplan, assumed he was uneducated, a pretender to the American shelves. She never spoke, but once when he'd asked for a book on the process of photocopying, she had looked worried, as if her patron might be a spy.

He liked sitting at the blonde wooden tables with the other patrons. Though protocol barred speech, there was good spirit to share in silent reading. He liked watching the old men who moved their lips as they read. Maybe their false teeth read words differently, trying to trick them. And children, he noticed, read in the same way. For the last week he'd observed a girl about eleven years old who had been sitting across from him. She always used encyclopedias and took notes. She was plump and had hair that wouldn't cooperate. It deserted its braids and bristled in front like a cactus. Maybe even American plants had opinions, he suddenly thought.

"Have a pen? Mine's outta ink."

"Please, for you to keep." He handed a ballpoint to the girl. Americans were generous, and so he wished to practice in small ways. He kept pens and paper clips and rubber bands and note paper in his pockets for such occasions.

"Thanks," she said and began copying again.

He was rereading the part in *The Grapes of Wrath* in which the turtle slowly, slowly crosses the road. The passage is marked by adversity, he'd have told a classroom of students. At one point the turtle is intentionally hit by a sadistic driver, yet it survives. In fact, the driver speeds the turtle across the road with the force of his cruelty. Oleg had arrived in America in the same way: the crueler his government had become, the more reason he had to leave. He would write an article entitled "The Cruel Kick," as soon as he had a chance.

"What's your name?" she was asking.

"I am Oleg Lum."

"Nice to meet you, Mr. Glum. I'm Carrie Remm. Where're you from?"

The other people at the table were eyeing them. He suggested with a nod that they move outside. Taking her spiral, she followed.

"I am from Moscow," he said, once outside. "And you?"

"Chicago. I'm ten years old, and my parents are divorced. My mother always looks sad because she had an operation. Now she can't have children, but since she's divorced, I'm not sure it matters that she can't have children. I just think the operation was the last straw. Anyway, I like to get out of the house. She makes me nervous."

"Please, what means *last straw?*"

"It means *curtains, cut, that's it, I've had it.*"

"And your mother is alone then all the time?"

"Oh, she calls her friends. But she never goes out. When my dad comes to pick me up on Sundays, she looks a little better."

Cars whizzed by, as Lum smoked a cigarette. He liked the bold bull's-eye of Lucky Strikes.

"You would like a cigarette?" He kept an extra pack at all times for his generosity training.

"No thanks. Kids don't smoke here."

"You would like maybe ice cream?"

They walked silently to the Thirty-One Flavors, took a corner booth, and talked all afternoon. They decided on dinner for Saturday night, his night off. On Saturday night Mr. Kaplan's son Denny answered the phones for time and a half. Once when Denny had had a tooth extracted, Oleg had taken his place.

Oleg was worried about Mrs. Remm's grief. Losing one's reproductive ability, he imagined, was tragic for a thirty-four-year-old woman. He might buy her a get-well card, but he didn't know that she was really ill. Maybe a sympathy card was in order, and flowers, but they'd have to wait for Saturday.

"Please, if you may help," he asked a small wizened woman who looked like a lemur he'd seen at the Brookfield Zoo. When one got old, hair and face turned gray together, and fine down started growing everywhere. The woman's cheeks, chin, and ears were furry. She looked as if someone had spun a web over her.

"Yes?"

"If you please, a dozen flowers."

"We have roses, carnations, combos, mixed in-season, zinnias, peonies, Hawaiian, birds-of-paradise, honeymoon bouquets, orchids, the woodsy spray, and dried. Can you be more specific?"

"The woman has lost her reproductive abilities. I wish to supply her with flowers."

"How about roses?"

They cost him fourteen dollars and ninety-five cents, and accompanying them was a card with etched blue hands folded in prayer. Inside, the card read, "With *extreme* sympathy upon your loss." He signed it Oleg, hoping for the intimacy of first names. No one called him Oleg anymore, except an old friend from Moscow he saw now and then at The Washing Well. Sometimes it was hard to remember that Oleg was his name. "In *extreme* sympathy," he repeated, liking especially how the word *extreme* looked in italics. They were a marvelous invention. He hoped for an entire evening of wavy italic emotion. When he caught his reflection in shop windows, his nose appeared optimistically upturned, and the bouquet he held, wrapped in paper depicting a trellis of ivy and roses, waved like a banner.

"Get the door," he heard through the wood after he'd been buzzed into Claire Remm's apartment-building hallway. Claire was a lovely name. It reminded him of water.

When Carrie opened the door, she appeared cross. "You're on time. I thought you were the pizza. I was hoping it'd come first."

"I am not pizza. However, it is good to be here." He hoped she wouldn't assume the flowers were for her. He hid them behind his back. Since she didn't ask what he was holding, he knew she understood.

"Mom, it's Mr. Glum."

"Who?" She sounded confused, but her voice was melodic, a song, a tribute.

"My friend, Mr. Glum."

Never, he thought, had so much natural beauty been wasted on such a negligent caretaker. Not on the American side of Niagara Falls, not in those Tennessee caves where stalagmites and stalactites are overwhelmed by tepees and imitation Indian blankets. Claire Remm had blue eyes, shiny black hair one usually saw on Japanese women, and a complexion somewhere in the range of infant pink. She wore furry slippers, blue jeans, a sweatshirt that said SPEEDWAGON, and no makeup. Her hair wasn't combed but stuck over one ear as if it had been glued there. Her eyes looked dried up, like African drinking holes.

"For you, Mrs. Remm, with thanks." Oleg extended the flowers in a shaky hand.

"Who are you?" she asked, peering over the flowers. She had the look of someone who doesn't care she's being observed, a look he'd seen on sleepers and drunks.

"I am Oleg Lum, friend of Carrie."

"I thought . . . Well, I'm sorry, Mr. Lum. I thought Carrie had invited a child."

"It is no problem. I eat very little. Like a child." He smiled so hard he thought his face might crumble.

"You don't understand, Mr. Lum. I've ordered a pizza. I assumed you two would eat and watch TV while I read a book." Her thin neck wobbled.

"The plans can exist. And may I ask, what book is engaging you?"

"*Pride and Prejudice.* I haven't read it since college."

"Is tale of civil rights or of women's movement?"

Claire laughed and called Carrie. "Why didn't you explain, Care?" Carrie shrugged her shoulders and left the room again.

He pointed the flowers in Claire's direction, and she finally took them. "Please," he said, "if problem, I can exit."

"No, Mr. Lum. The pizza should arrive soon. Would you like a beer?" She had put the flowers on a silver radiator.

"May we plant the flowers?" Oleg asked.

"Oh," she said and told Carrie to get a vase and water. Lum wasn't certain, but he thought maybe she was smiling ever so slightly like someone who is trying not to laugh at a joke.

While Carrie and Claire sat on the couch, Lum sat in an oversized tan corduroy chair that made him feel fat. He assumed that the chair was Mr. Remm's and that Mr. Remm was a large man with bristly hair like Carrie's. He wondered if it made Carrie sad that he was sitting in her father's chair. He would have asked, but Claire and Carrie were watching *Dance Fever.* They concentrated on it like scholars at the Moscow Institute of Technology.

"Is good for fashion education."

"You bet," Carrie assured him. Claire watched the television and absentmindedly dissected the pizza, which sat in the middle of the floor. Carrie had placed the roses next to the pizza in a green vase that hid their stems. He wondered whether Claire might reach for pizza and come up with a rose. The room appeared freshly painted, meaning that everything had been taken down and the walls whitewashed. No decorations had been rehung where picture hooks and curtain rods waited. It looked as if a civilization had perished there. The place made him feel foolish. It was not the first American home he'd visited. Mrs. Kaplan's was, with its plastic-covered everything and miniature dog statues and candelabra. But hers could have been the aberration.

Suppose Americans were more like Danes in character than he'd imagined: melancholic, spare, and joyless.

During a commercial he spoke. "Mrs. Remm, your daughter is very clever girl and hard worker at library. She tells me about you. She is sorry for you."

"She is?" The voice was shrill, a verbal grimace.

"She is sad that you are not able, may I say, to reproduce."

"Carrie, why did you tell him *that?*" The entire room vibrated with new energy. He imagined lamps crashing to the floor. Carrie shrugged her nonchalant shoulders.

"I am sorry, Mrs. Remm, to cause this trouble. She is loving you and wanting to be of help."

Now Claire was smiling and Carrie exhaling. It couldn't have been his explanation. Some signals, he imagined, like those baseball coaches use to coax on their runners, must have been exchanged in the blink of an eye. The blink must have been invented for such a purpose. What had happened in the invisible moment was a détente. Finally Carrie spoke.

"Mom, he's okay to tell things to. Who do you think he knows?"

Lum smiled. He knew he'd been insulted, but the insult was harmless. Besides, it had made Claire smile again.

"Mr. Lum," she began, "I expected a little Russian boy. You know. Pointy ears. Fat cheeks. Shorts. Sandals. Instead, you walk in knowing everything about me, bringing me flowers. I guess I must be very glum!"

They all laughed. It was a moment of joy, one he'd recall along with his first erection and leaving Russia. A triptych of pleasure. Claire kept laughing even after he and Carrie had finished. Quacking and quacking like a beautiful blue-eyed duck until she said, "I haven't read the card. Let's read the card." She opened it with high drama and stared at Oleg's hopeful smile. More signals were exchanged with Carrie, who, after reading the card aloud, stared at him too. Mother and daughter then slapped hands palm to palm, and Claire suggested that they all take a walk.

"Better yet," Oleg said, "a trick is up the sleeve. I have procured tickets for an event of pantomime to begin in twenty minutes. We should begin our arrival now."

Claire excused herself. He and Carrie stood in the doorway at nervous attention. He could look beyond Carrie and see down the hallway to the roses opening in the vase next to the pizza cardboard. "Let's go," Claire was saying as she joined them, "or we'll be late." She was dressed as an Indian princess.

Dear Readers of Chicago:

It strikes me as new American that much is made of largeness in your country. Examine, if you please, the Mount Rushmore. Here are the great stone faces of the profound leaders of men. But here is a man also. He is cleaning the stone faces. Up the nostril of Abraham Lincoln, freer of slaves, the cleaner climbs, as a fly, without notice. Or, let us say, a family on vacation takes his photo. There is the great stone Lincoln. There is the tiny man with huge brush for nostril cleaning. Thus is humor because the size of man is made small by large design of beauty.

In America I hear many jokes. Some are about women whose husbands cannot meet their desires, which are too large. In others, several members of Polish nation are trying to accomplish small goal, the removing of light bulb. Their effort is too large for smallness of task.

On a certain Sunday I was driving with American acquaintance down the Madison Street. My American said, "You'll never believe what we waste our money on here," and it is true that in Soviet Union largeness is always minor premise of grandeur. There are large monuments to workers, huge squares to fill with people cheering for politics, heads of Lenin the size of cathedrals, and many women with large breasts, who are called stately by Russian men. Now on American Sunday I look to right, and there stands a huge bat of metal. It stands, perhaps, fifty feet tall like apartment building. I say to my friend, "The baseball is grand American entertainment. The baseball is your Lenin."

"No," says American friend, "the bat is joke about wasting money. It has nothing to do with baseball."

The bat is then humorous. I believe words of my friend, who is businessman. In poor or undemocratic countries there is no humorous public art. History is the only public art. The huge stone pyramids are not meant as joke. In America the bat of abundance is cynic's joke. Same cynic points at huge genitals of corpse. He makes public monument to frozen bat. The lover of art points to the living genitals or makes the beautiful statue like Michelangelo's *David*.

As the huge Gulliver was tied down by the little citizens for possible harm done, so the public shows the disdain for size, even with its power. Thus is opposite, humor from largeness. The bully is, yes, strong, but he is also fool. He is laborer digging in dirt. His brain is mushroom producing no truths. Largeness is victory and also defeat. To largeness we prostrate ourselves and then up our sleeves die laughing.

Thank you,
Oleg Lum

Since it was Sunday and Carrie would be away, he thought of calling Claire and arranging a private visit. The evening before had been a success, the pantomimists having done a version of *Antony and Cleopatra* in which the larger, bearded Cleopatra swooned into the compact Antony's arms. Carrie quacked like her mother. Claire cried when she was happy. Both mother and daughter had walked him home, kissed him good night, and said they'd treat him to lunch on Monday.

If he called her now, the spell might be broken. She'd infer the obscene length of his nose in his altered phone voice. She'd laugh at his misuse of articles. He'd not flirt with ruin. The beach beckoned with its Sunday collage of summer bodies.

"What is your name, little boy?" Lum asked the child who sat next to his towel squeezing sand between his toes. He wore a seersucker sunsuit and a bulging diaper. His cheeks were fat, but he was not tan. In fact, he was pale and resembled Nikita Khrushchev with his spikes of just emerging white-blonde hair. He was no older than a year and a half, though Lum might be wrong, having had no experience with babies.

"Do you know your name?" Lum asked again. The sun was behind them, and he felt his skin radiating heat. He'd fallen asleep in the afternoon, and, judging by the sun's angle, he'd slept two or three hours. It was evening. People were beginning to pack up for the day.

The lifeguard, who had made a white triangle of cream on his nose, looked bored. Not enough people were swimming, Lum observed, much less drowning, to give his life definition.

Lum offered the child a piece of banana, which he greedily accepted. He mashed it in his hand and pressed pieces slowly into his mouth.

"Bop," said the boy.

"Pleased to meet you. I am Oleg Lum." The child looked at Oleg's extended hand.

"Of course, babies do not understand the handshake," he explained. "Tell me, little Bop, is your mama here?"

Bop stood on tiptoe in the sand, wobbled, and tumbled to Lum's towel. A cascade of sand followed him.

Lum pointed at a young couple loading cans of Coke into a cooler. "Do you know these people, little Bop?"

Bop ignored all questions, sharing Lum's blanket, kicking his feet in the air, and humming, "Gee-dah, Gee-dah."

After an hour of Bop's company, Oleg thought of asking the lifeguard about a lost-and-found service. He was afraid, though, that the lifeguard would call the police and scare the boy, who looked at Lum with such peaceful eyes, who joyously accepted crackers, and who laughed at the seagulls' w-shaped assaults, at bugs he found in the sand, and at Oleg cooing, "little Bop, little Bop."

Bop had fallen asleep at the edge of Oleg's towel, sucking the corner he held in his fist. Oleg folded another triangle over his back to protect it from the waning sun.

When the lifeguard was tying up his boat and the sun had changed to a forgiving twilight, in which couples twisted together on blankets or faced each other with their legs folded Indian-style to share a joint, Oleg realized there were no families left to step forward and claim Bop. It was clear in this instant that he would either have to call the authorities, men whose hands shot lead at robbers, who poked sticks into kidneys, or keep the child with him. The law would not recommend that decision, he was sure, but parents who'd forgotten a child at the beach, in the way he might leave an umbrella on a bench, weren't worthy of a search.

He'd carry the child home with him. In the morning he'd read the paper, hoping for news. And if news didn't materialize, there was

Claire waiting, arms open, bereft of the ability to reproduce. She had said the night before, admiring Carrie's impressions of the mimes, that she'd have liked to have had one more child, a son. Then she'd wrinkled her nose, frowned, smiled, looked away, asked for a cigarette, and shrugged. Every emotion could be observed as it changed direction like a sailboat wobbling to shore in crosswinds. She'd thank him for the child. It was clear the police weren't needed.

The lifeguard had left the beach, surrendering the safety of its inhabitants to Oleg. He'd not disappoint the lifeguard.

He put his book and wallet and keys in his back pockets, slid into his sandals, gathered the child up in his towel, and began walking, Bop snoring soundly in his arms.

He'd never thought of having a child himself. He had spent his years getting out of Russia, while other men searched for lovers or wives. Now, diapering the boy with the clean supplies he had bought at midnight last night when the need presented itself, it seemed he had never done anything more natural. Oleg soothed Bop's rash with Vaseline, powdered his plump half-moons, and watched in awe as Bop cooed and pulled his pink penis, doubling over it, snail-like, and curling around his softer part. At least the parents had fed the poor child and not in any way hurt him. He was mottled pink, plump, and clean in all places but the creases, which were easy to overlook even if one was diligent.

The seersucker sunsuit was drying in the washroom. The child had eaten crackers, cheese, a peach, and milk already. Bop pronounced "milk," "shoe," "dog," and "bird."

Oleg pronounced, "Little Bop is very clever." Bop pointed at Oleg, wordless. The morning passed quickly.

Walking to Claire's, he hoped that Bop would not soil himself on Oleg's new shirt. He had even given Bop a bath for the occasion and combed his sparse hair so it stood in neat little rows, like toy farm crops. He wanted to meet Claire upstairs with the child rather than on the street, where her reaction might be too private for display. Suppose she thanked him with tears or fell into his arms, a crest of emotion filling her chest. Suppose she suggested marriage on the spot, Oleg Lum the father of little Bop, she the mother, Carrie the big sister, a home on a quiet street, maybe a dog, lots of American television to cool his rapid-fire brain. He carried Bop, who mostly smiled. Oleg smiled too. It might be his wedding day.

"Just a minute," he heard through the door. As he'd hoped, Claire answered. But she didn't meet him with sobs or whispers of praise.

"What, Oleg!"

"Is boy I found at beach. Is he not handsome?"

"You found him at the beach? Didn't he have parents?"

"Parents could not be located. I wait until beach closes and only drug takers remain. Then I take him home."

"He spent the night with you? You didn't call the police?"

"I do not want government thug with stick in belt to take child and frighten him. I want you to take him."

"Me, Oleg?"

Lum looked hopeful. Bop offered Claire a sucked-on cracker.

"Oleg, let's sit down." They walked into the front room. Carrie was not home. Bop sat on the floor and busied himself by dismembering a magazine. "I know you mean well, Oleg, but laws are strict. If a child is lost, he must be given to the authorities. They'll find his parents."

"Parents dump child on beach like trash. They leave him there. Why should such parents have themselves found?"

"It's true, Oleg, but there are laws. I wouldn't be surprised if his damned Easter picture weren't being flashed on every newscast."

"Is no damned flashing. I watch last night and news today."

"Oleg," Claire continued, "you could be considered a criminal."

"Is no crime to help little Bop and to hope that you will also help."

"How do you know his name?"

"I ask him, 'Baby, what is your name?' He says, 'Bop.'"

"Oleg, Bop isn't an American name. Bop isn't any kind of name. Babies make sounds."

"Bop is not name. Parents are not caring. Police are not called. What should I do? Take baby back to beach? Leave him in rowboat like Moses?"

"No, Oleg. I'll call the police. They'll come for him and find his parents or relatives. You were very kind to care for him. Bop is lucky to have found you, Oleg." She kissed the crown of his head.

"Please, before police, let us sit together and watch Bop."

Claire sat down next to him and took his hand. Bop was pretending to water some violets with an empty watering can. Then he sat down opposite Oleg and insisted, plainly, on milk. Claire got a small glass and offered it to Bop.

"He is needing help," Oleg suggested and held the glass for him.

They sat hand in hand for an hour, Oleg enjoying the most mundane fantasy. They were at an American pediatrician's, taking their child for a checkup. She was the bride he'd met in college, and she still wore her modest wedding ring, though he'd have liked to have been more extravagant. She didn't have to talk, his wife of many years, just sit and admire their little son.

"Police are not needing to be called."

"I'll call them now, Oleg. I'll explain. You go home, and I'll phone you after they've left."

Oleg felt large tears forming under his lids. He watched Bop shredding the interior-design magazine. The blurry room lost its sofa, its draperies, its rug. Everything was in pieces. This was not to be his wedding day.

Dear Personal View:

Everything in America gets lost, sometimes stolen. I lose my umbrella on el train. It is never returned. Meanwhile, baby is left on beach to weather, danger, criminals, drug takers, God knows. Parents come to police. Say they are sorry, so baby is returned. Why in America is easier to find lost baby than umbrella costing nine dollars? But I worry most for sandy American baby who is found on beach like walking rubbish heap called Bop. He is dirty, hungry little immigrant. I give him new life visa, which police revoke.

The switchboard was howling. An alarm had gone off at Cusper Motors, but Oleg closed his eyes and listened as the howling continued. He was not going to call the police. Let the thieves do as they wished to Cusper's Fords. The police were worse than criminals. They were blind men, liars, fools. He disconnected the phone, and in the sudden silence, he willed his eyes closed and tried to fall asleep. He would sleep until his shift ended, until all Mr. Cusper's Fords were taken, until the police were running over the whole city in search of car thieves and drug takers and lost babies.

Infinks

IN THE SHARK-GRAY Lincoln limousine that Ben had rented for three hundred dollars, Sam and Gilsa laughed from too many joints and shared a private awe as fog plunged into the Sonoma Valley. John poured drinks for all except Sarah, who was trying to get pregnant and thought that drinking might discourage the healthy sperm from spawning with the egg upstream. Rita sat backward on a folding leather stool, watching hills and vineyards announce themselves to her after they had disappeared to the others. Sitting in this way was appropriate for her fortieth birthday, a time to look back at the fifteen years she and Ben had shared.

"Such fun," Gilsa slurred.

It wasn't her French-Swiss accent that put Rita off as much as her expertise in everything. Her accent seemed like another skill she had developed for Sam to score. Usually Rita would have signaled her annoyance to Ben, but Ben, admiring the view, the chauffeur's driving, the achievement of such surprise, was hardly a partner tonight. What Ben would do when she turned fifty had been Rita's other thought. Really, she couldn't imagine. He could already be planning something, Ben, who told her so little, who worked so hard at his obstetrics practice and barely seemed to notice it was anyone's birthday until a limousine gave proof of his involvement.

When Rita later told him that the birthday had made her uncomfortable, Ben's eyelids puckered in indignation. He blamed it on Gilsa and Sam: "There's nothing worse than stoned Republicans."

But it wasn't the evening that should have been different. It was Ben. Something had to be done about him, yet Rita wasn't sure what. She was forty, and they were childless, though Ben had wanted children for many years of their marriage. Their lives had always been going too well to risk changing them. Maybe it was turning forty itself that had created the need for action. Maybe it was the limousine ride that reminded her of funerals. Maybe it was driving backward through fifteen years of acceptable marriage and questioning her standard. Maybe it was Ben with his smug good plans.

Whatever it was caused Rita to swing into action, tying her hair back, chain-smoking, and making phone calls. She had threatened Ben with the project since the wildlife center down the road to Muir Beach had opened. Its purpose was to rehabilitate animals that had been injured by man or environment. Ben called it the broken zoo. Now Rita phoned Mrs. Bryan and said she was willing to become part of the research team. She would take the next goose that hatched and adopt it for the imprinting study.

Driving to the center, Rita felt slightly insane. Her eyes were glazed. Her temples throbbed. She drove too quickly, worrying that the goose would arrive before she did. But, of course, there were other geese. And even yesterday she hadn't considered being part of the project. Why was it that suddenly she had to participate? If the goose were a male, she'd call it Stanley after Stanley Mosker, whom she had loved in first grade. He had a great mole on an earlobe and grass-colored feline eyes. If it were a girl, she'd call it Charlotte, which is what she had always wanted to call a daughter in the days when she had wanted children.

It was a gentle evening, the sun dipping behind trees, an almost passive breeze, very warm for May. In ten years we could all be dead, she thought, and cried big tears that hit the steering wheel.

"Get Charlotte off the table," Ben said as Rita drank her morning coffee. Charlotte was three months old now, and her downy feathers were turning stiff. Still, she seemed to Rita like an infant needing protection, even from Ben's criticisms.

"Imagine what it's like when a teacher criticizes your child," Rita said.

"You obviously don't understand that Charlotte's a genius even though she is a goose," Ben said. "I'll have the school board look into your record on equal opportunity. I bet it's not the first time a goose has been made an example in your classroom."

Charlotte sat patiently at Rita's feet. Every now and then she made a noise that was close to a honk but always a decibel too high so that it sounded more like a complaint.

"We'll have to start saving for her education," Ben said.

"You know, Ben," Rita felt obliged to say, "I didn't get this goose to replace a child. I could still bear a child if I wanted. Ellie Lawson had a perfectly healthy son last year, and she's forty-three."

"I was at the big event."

"And remember what I did before I married you?"

"You slept with your professors."

"Funny."

"You were a biologist and a Woodrow Wilson Fellow. Did you know that, Charlotte?"

Charlotte was cocking her head toward Ben. Rita was sure she knew her name, though it's always too easy to assume what an animal knows.

Sarah was five months pregnant and starting to show. Rita asked her to lunch so they could talk, which they hadn't done in several months. Rita wondered whether Sarah's being pregnant made her nervous around Rita. Everyone thinks I want to get pregnant, Rita thought. Charlotte had followed into the bathroom, where Rita was lining her eyes. She didn't understand why she felt it necessary to line her eyes for Sarah's visit, but having an almost grown goose with her in the bathroom didn't help to steady her hand. "Get out of here, Charlotte," Rita told the goose.

Today Charlotte seemed to have amnesia. She wouldn't respond to her name at all. She sat on the edge of the sink pecking at the mirror. "Get the hell out," Rita told Charlotte and pushed her to the floor. It was her first instance of goose abuse.

Sarah looked radiant as pregnant women allegedly look. Her complexion glowed, her stomach made a delicate slope under her denim jumper, and she was eager to describe every movement that her baby made in the womb.

"I've quickened, Rita. I can actually feel her move. Why did I wait this long?"

Rita supposed she wasn't expected to answer. Anyway, she didn't know. The coffee was ready, so she poured each of them a cup.

"Oh, no," Sarah protested. "It changes the fetal heart rate. It gives the baby tachycardia."

"Bump bump bump bump bump bump bump," Rita said to illustrate.

"What?" Sarah asked.

"Nothing. Want some megavitamins or some juice?"

"No thanks. Rita, I brought some pictures."

"Did John fashion a periscope?"

"No, there's a book from Sweden. Here's a photo of a five month fetus. Can you imagine that it already looks like us?"

"This one looks like a loaf of bread with hair. Yours looks better, I'm sure."

Charlotte was sitting at Rita's feet. Sarah kept eyeing Charlotte suspiciously.

"Mrs. Bryan at the Center tells me that Charlotte is very intelligent. If my data is correct, she knows her name, my name, Ben's name, how to get into the bathroom when the sliding door is closed, and how to show Ben that she wants the water turned on."

Sarah didn't acknowledge her. She was looking outside Rita's window at a layer of fog covering Mt. Tamalpais. "You know, I think I got pregnant on your birthday, Rita. The fog was the same that night."

Charlotte was standing in the middle of the kitchen flapping her wings. Outside two Scrub Jays were contesting territory, circling around and around a redwood tree.

"Want some tea or a sandwich?"

"I have to go, Rita. I'm learning to crochet this afternoon at The Knittery. The class is at one. Want to join me?"

"Thanks anyway, Sarah. Charlotte has a checkup this afternoon."

Rita knew that she was avoiding friends since her birthday and that Charlotte was a convenience. It was even a way of avoiding Ben, feigning deep involvement in her project that would end in four weeks when Charlotte would be six months old.

Now that she could fly, she was destructive around the house, and Ben decided she'd have to stay in the yard. Of course, Charlotte, with her keen sense of humor, took it out on Ben. All week she had been following him to work, trailing after his car as it headed toward San Rafael until he had to return home and lock the goose in the garage. "Imagine," Ben said, "telling your patients you're late because a goose was following you!"

In laughing, Rita burned her tongue on her coffee. She felt a little peeved that Charlotte chose to follow Ben, who hadn't even fed her or paid her any mind. And when Charlotte wasn't following Ben, her new habit was to sit in the carport waiting for him to return. Rita noted in her log that Charlotte's behavior seemed a bit neurotic since she'd been banished to the yard. Then she crossed it out. It didn't seem fair or scientifically objective to call Charlotte's interest in Rita bonding and her interest in Ben an obsession.

Rita decided to go for a ride. She needed some vegetables for dinner and a birthday gift for Gilsa.

To her disappointment, Charlotte didn't follow Rita's car into Mill Valley. She looked overhead several times but saw no hopeful vee in the sky. Ben had said it was odd recognizing the bird following you as you might spot an old acquaintance at an airport. Rita looked in her rearview mirror at the warm blue sky filled with nothing.

Now that the bird was gone, Rita asked Ben if he'd like to spend a weekend with her in the country. The question sounded too formal. Besides, she didn't want to spend time with Ben at all. She just wanted to get away. Thinking of herself asking in the first place, Rita felt twelve years old and dishonest, as if she were bargaining with her parents about when to leave for Four Leaf Clover Camp. She'd always make alternative plans when it was time to go. Trips to museums, libraries, visits to elderly relatives—anything to postpone her inevitable departure. Once she got there, with riding and swimming and cookouts and only a few mean girls who'd pinch her in the dressing room, she never really hated it. Rather, she dulled her personality, toned down her laugh, and peered up instead of looking directly at people. Maybe the same strategy would get her through the weekend with Ben.

On the way to Little River Inn, they didn't say much. They gossiped about Gilsa and decided that the problem with Sam and Gilsa—most problems were with couples, it seemed—was that they lacked a sense of humor. When a sense of humor surfaced, as it had the night of Rita's birthday, it was so private their friends felt they were watching a Masonic ritual. Even when Ben had suggested something very funny to add to Gilsa's achievements, Sam and Gilsa had eyed Ben like a man with food on his mustache.

"What was it you asked Gilsa?"

"I asked her if she wasn't the first woman to have scaled Mount Everest in high heels."

They laughed again at his joke. Gilsa had liked the *Cooking Hungarian* book they'd given her for her birthday. "Sicilian Grecian Vegetarian Hungarian," Sam had sung, his new mantra.

Though the inn's choice rooms away from the kitchen had been taken, their room was pretty with tiny cinnamon flowers dotting everything, like chiggers, Ben said. All Rita could picture were Charlotte's tracks in the mud of their yard. In thousands of years, when their own civilization had gone to defeat, an archeologist might find the fossil tracks and conclude that domestic geese had been part of Northern California culture. Rita was sorry to mislead the woman, whom she pictured as a female Albert Einstein, but it was reassuring to know that Charlotte's feet might get them into history. Nothing else she could imagine would remain of them.

At dinner the couples opposite them were elderly and freckled. The women had snowy hair that bristled around their heads. One man had a full head of palomino-colored hair that swirled on his forehead like the curve of a conch shell. Their dinner conversation centered on flagstone versus concrete for walkways. At the end of the dinner the couples' voices rose to an uncomfortable pitch, and Rita, who had been focusing on her stuffed trout as a means of avoiding Ben, was relieved to have a new point of concentration, the argument that ensued over the bill.

"Me and Helen aren't poor, goddamn it," the one with the lovely hair was saying, "but don't you know, before I can eat my pie, you always grab the bill."

The other man, bald, smaller in frame and more reserved in tone, was saying, "Calm down, Whitney." But Whitney and Helen in unison, as if on cue, had stormed out, a wind of indignation trailing them through the dining room filled with crystal, daffodil wallpaper, hanging plants, and cut wildflowers.

"That's what I like about vacations," Ben said. "They bring out the best in people. I've noticed, Rita, that this vacation has made you particularly talkative."

"I guess I haven't much to say."

"Empty-nest syndrome."

"No, it's turning forty."

"You seem to have forgotten that we're the same age, that you, in fact, followed me over the hill by more than six months."

"What's it like for you?" She'd never considered that he might be feeling as bad as she felt. Looking at him now, sanely for the first time in months, she did seem to detect signs of wear. His hair was longer than he usually let it go, his forehead wrinkle appeared ironed in, and his eyes looked pink and sad. She wanted to say something like "Poor Ben," but he hadn't answered or confirmed her diagnosis yet.

"Not so bad for me," he sighed. "Thirty was bad. Remember? I kept thinking I was an adult, but I kept feeling like an adolescent with a receding hairline. Forty seems what I should be."

She felt Ben's leg touch hers under the table. "When I was thirty-five," Rita began, dropping her fork for emphasis, "I used to think, 'My life is half over.' Marking the middle seemed so neat. Now all I think is that my life is more than half over, and what have I done?"

Of course, there was nothing to say. Both knew what they had and hadn't done.

"We're still kids," Ben smiled. "Infinks." Now both his legs were touching hers.

"I was thinking," Rita said. "Maybe it isn't too late to really change things. Maybe we could start again. I remember when I used to start again every year. School was about to begin, and I'd go buy my new supplies. I'd buy folders of every color and pencils to match and pens and new chewy erasers and wide-lined notebook paper and then, last, the best of all, I'd get new shoes. The soles were always beige and cleanly stitched in white. And do you know what I'd do with those shoes the first night?"

"Don't tell me," Ben teased.

"I'd sleep with them in my bed. Then school would begin, and the shoes would give me blisters. I'd have to rest them for a few days. That was my new start. Guaranteed every year. Then the day when it became fall—not the date but the weather. The air felt different, and I felt definitely older."

"That's when older was older."

"So, I was thinking," Rita continued, "we might make a new start."

"Buy some new, ill-fitting shoes?"

"No," Rita said and waited for Ben to speak. It was like waiting for the wheel of fortune to spin. If Ben suggested a baby or divorce, she'd say yes. Becoming religious, marriage counseling, and hang gliding were definite nos. She couldn't imagine what would rate a maybe. She was too old for maybes.

Whitney and Helen returned to the dining room without their perpetual hosts. They sat across from each other and ordered second, legitimate desserts to replace the contested ones.

Ben smiled at them. It was obvious he had no suggestions for a new start.

Back in Mill Valley, Rita called Sarah. She didn't want Sarah to think that Rita wasn't interested in her pregnancy, though she wasn't. Sarah said she was big as a Winnebago and had developed varicosities. Rita offered her sympathies, which Sarah accepted, and wondered why her meager little sympathies were suitable for so many occasions. Was she ever really more sorry sometimes than others?

Then she called Mrs. Bryan to ask for a new goose to imprint.

"The imprinting project is over, honey," Mrs. Bryan said. "Besides, I've found that second geese just don't measure up."

That Summer

T HAT SUMMER ALL Amy could picture were drowning men, men drowning. On postcards they appeared, small and hopeless on the horizon. In museum catalogs the hulls of ships filled with them, and, God, all the awful poems she noticed about drowning men compared to withering plants, to fingers, to paper. No, there couldn't be so much drowning. It must be something else, maybe bad art, maybe the end of civilization. Amy wasn't sure.

That summer there was Raymond, who prided himself on living through the darkest hours in his own history. Raymond of private schools for disturbed adolescents, of washroom wastebasket fires. Raymond of the insect eyes that never closed, who loved to dance and call celebrities by their first names. On a *Saturday Night Live* rerun, John Belushi imitated Joe Cocker, rocking spastically like a fat windup child, self-indulgent, sneering as beer poured out of his mouth, wetting his shoulder. "You fucked up, John," Raymond said. Of course, John didn't answer. When Amy said, "Turn it off. I don't want to see a dead man imitating a living man," Raymond thought it too funny, laughed until his knees seemed to buckle and his eyes finally closed. Famous among his friends for never blinking, Raymond washed out to sea, Amy explained on her better days.

The Sunday afternoon Raymond drowned, Amy had a cold. They were supposed to go to the lake for a beginning-of-the-summer picnic. Amy was an art major, fond of small, busy prints on luxurious fabrics. She would design bedspreads and sheets someday, she told her father's friends, corporate lawyers, who thought Amy so lovely that they really cared what she said about raw silk. Amy's mother was usually away, a career woman before the fashion, radio-advertising troubleshooter, jetting between Omaha and Akron, charting slumps and trends in bold red marker. When Amy was little, she'd take the marker and draw intricate maps of imaginary neighborhoods, naming them Red Rod Village and Triangle Square. Humor appeared in Amy's colorful designs, and Amy was sure it was humor that attracted her to Raymond. Tall, sweaty, uncompromising, Raymond was considered by others a pain and a tease and a bully. Still, he was brilliant, a fellowship student, the son of a Nobel Prize winner. So what if his father had lobbied for the prize, calling Stockholm as often as others call the weather. Still, Dr. Ricks had found a cure for a rare enzyme deficiency with four names.

Amy remembered a night at an art opening. The show contained erotic ceramic mugs, molded into breasts and penises and testicles and vaginas. Raymond spent the evening pretending to appreciate the works by holding them in a subtly suggestive manner. That was the charm of Raymond, Amy thought. Though he was most certainly caressing the breasts of a mug, one couldn't be certain. Raymond was the lewdest man she'd ever dated, but half the time she imagined he couldn't be doing what he plainly was. Raymond became Amy's own worst idea of men, blended with the suspicion of his innocence. "You're irony embodied," Amy told him at another picnic in front of his English-major friends, who could appreciate the comment. Raymond quickly mimed a scene from *Oedipus Rex,* of course the one in which Oedipus puts out his eyes. The picnic dissolved into hoots and laughter, since Raymond's prominent eyes would not cooperate. Even closed, playing the blinded king, they animated his face.

Amy had all the symptoms of a classic summer cold, plus a terrible taste in her mouth, as if she'd eaten some green acrylic paint, she told her mother, who smiled without looking at her. She called Raymond to tell him that she couldn't go to the picnic but to wish all of his fellow Joyce scholars well. She liked her role in the group as the nonverbal artist. It kept the pressure off. Once Lois, a stalky Ph.D. candidate, finishing her dissertation on point-of-view in Hardy, remarked that Amy's eyes looked subterranean, opaque, absent. Lois was a master of the triple entendre, and Amy hadn't known what to reply. "Thank you" had been her decision, and so the subject was dropped.

"I'm sick, Ray," Amy told him on the phone.

"Shit," Ray said. "And I had a surprise for you."

"Can it wait?" Amy asked.

"Not really. It's a demonstration. Remember last summer when I couldn't swim?"

The picnic last summer had been a disaster. Not only did Raymond not know how to swim, but the others, by force of Raymond's neurotic, childlike pleas not to leave him on the shore rotting like a piece of driftwood, were constrained from swimming. By the end of the afternoon everyone was sick of Raymond, vowing to forget his phone number. Only Amy had felt sorry for him. She remembered times when she was little and her mother was away. She had interesting plans made for her in advance and money to spend on movies or ice cream. Listless, she'd sit on her bed, counting the spots on the butterflies' wings of her wallpaper or half-sleeping day and night. How can you move when you're all alone with no one to notice that you're moving? Amy loved Raymond because he couldn't bear to be alone either, would never leave her, was perfectly needy, and understood the threat of total, endless separation. Amy would lie in her bed as a child imagining the most terrible deaths for her mother. "Because you hate her for leaving you so often," a therapist once told her. "Because people die and children are left motherless," she countered in her clear, eight-year-old mind.

Raymond could swim, but no one would really care. Amy wished she felt better. "Ray?" she asked. "Why don't you come over instead? We can watch TV or sit in the yard or see my father's slides of Tahiti." It didn't sound like much fun to her either.

"Gee, uh, thanks anyway," he teased. "I'll see you this evening then."

"Okay," Amy said meekly. "I have some letters to write," though she knew they wouldn't get written. "See you tonight, and remember," she added, "to close your eyes when you swim." She pictured Raymond torpedoing through the water, open-eyed, not having the sense to know that water is dirty. Amy sometimes exaggerated his lack of sense. She realized that she mothered him in contrast to her own mother's lack of involvement, and usually Raymond didn't object. Only once he had angrily said, "Until I met you, I never remembered to zip my pants. Thanks for keeping me out of the halfway house."

"Iron lungs," Amy thought. She was lying on her floor listening to the Plantagenets. The record cover showed four men dressed like royalty from the neck up with ruffles, pointy beards, and crowns. From the shoulders down they were punk. "Death," Amy thought and pictured Ann Boleyn's wardrobe, an exhibit she had admired once in England. She had seen the silk, four centuries old, and the intricate, woven fastenings. Amy hated zippers as much as she hated Raymond teasing her. Raymond had told her of a fourth-grade teacher who loved to embarrass him. Once she'd screamed, "You ran my nylon!" when he approached to show her a drawing. Another time, when he had stomach flu and needed permission to use the washroom, Miss Burch had shrieked, "You could have thrown up on me!" She was probably frigid, Amy had explained in bed with Raymond. Amy loved long summers home from college when her parents were away and she had the luxury of making love in her own, comfortable bed in her room with the worn, irrelevant wallpaper. She could live without food, she thought, but summers in her parents' house were necessary. Sometimes she hoped that she, an only child, would inherit the house, where she'd never change anything and use her room for decades of love. The Plantagenets were singing, "I'm slip-slip-slipping into the abyss-byss-byss." Downstairs she could hear the insect throb of a lawn mower. Her mother was asleep in another bedroom, resting on a stopover from travel. Tomorrow she was to "problem-solve" for a Latino rock station in San Antonio.

Once when Amy was eight, she'd gone with her mother on a business trip to New York. Her father had the mumps, caught from Amy, a situation that her mother had found incredibly funny. While her mother made her rounds of stations, Amy spent her time with a droll babysitter provided by the hotel, a premed student named Gretta, who left her textbooks on a table with lion-claw legs. First the claws interested Amy, but as the week wore on, the medical texts became her entertainment. Amy read about iron lungs and saw skin diseases in such vibrant colors that they burst before her eyes like Disney fireworks. When her mother got her home, there were long weeks of seeing Dr. Pimm, a cherubic British psychiatrist trained in treating children. No one seemed to believe that Amy's vivid nightmares were inspired by the medical texts. It had to be more, and her mother, good businesswoman that she was, was determined to find the real cause. Twice a week Amy spoke to Dr. Pimm, cautiously accepted a cup of tea with cream, and staged listless dramas with his nondescript puppets. Finally, bored by Amy's lack of progress, her mother terminated the relationship. Then her mother cut down on her amount of traveling, her father finally taught her how to ride her bike, and a new era of family harmony was launched with a trip to Disneyland. Amy remembered sitting in a little car shaped like a teacup that suddenly spun into a tunnel, cracking her front tooth. The broken tooth ended the era. School began again, and Amy went dully back, while her mother reactivated her full schedule and her father spent most of his time at the office. As Amy circled the block on her red Super-Tube bicycle, she felt vaguely grateful to Dr. Pimm.

Amy thought of Raymond's naked body, his muscular legs. She always pictured him standing. To imagine him horizontal, suspended in water, was impossible. Raymond was so quick and energized. He snapped through rooms and changed the air behind him. He danced like a dynamo. He was Amy's way of releasing herself, being real, she thought. The record was still playing, "x is not y, no, y is not x." True, Amy thought, but not very interesting. She closed her eyes but found that she couldn't breathe with one pillow. She rearranged the bed, propped herself four pillows high, and tried to sleep.

This fall would be her last semester in college. She was to spend the summer testing prints that she would transfer onto cloth in the cold art studio smelling of sawdust. She pictured swirling colors, holiday reds and greens, cool blues melting into gray, swimming colors, some dangerous, others light as a glance. She traveled down long corridors of designs so intricate that she'd never be able to print them. Once she'd seen a movie in which a dying woman meets all her friends down a deep, tunneling hallway. When Amy died, she wouldn't see people, though Raymond might be there, a voice, a laugh, an amorphous good mood. Mainly there'd be colors and designs so intricate she'd never get them right, never fuse them: y is not y, but purple can dissolve into blue and red or lose its shyness and burst into fire. Amy felt herself falling asleep through the colors and the lawn mower and her mother's rousing Beethoven, always the *Eroica*.

It was about three o'clock when Raymond entered the water. He'd had half a bottle of Chianti and smoked some really good grass. "Eye-closing dope," he had called it. It felt good to be in the water. It felt endless.

He closed his eyes and relaxed. He surfaced and reopened them. Why had he waited until he was twenty-three to learn to swim? Why hadn't someone told him how cold water felt, how much distance he could cover? His father wanted him to be well-rounded, a swimmer, a man. After all, hadn't he, a first-generation American, won a Nobel Prize? Couldn't he, jaw jutting, shoot a round of golf in the eighties? Raymond felt the sun pour on his head. Swimming was like an amusement park ride. You wanted to shout. You wanted people to know you loved it. You never wanted to get out. Raymond thought of Amy, how she'd have waved to him from her Indian blanket or curled over his back like Esther Williams as he propelled them through the water. He thought of her parents, so deadly proper and aching for something. Amy's dad had actually said to him, "We think you're very liberating for Amy." He had smiled like a Boy Scout with a badge in psychology.

Now the afternoon was dimming, the wind had changed, and the skyline was dropping. The Hancock building was shrouded in clouds or smoke or fog, and cinematic blue people were gesturing from shore, past him, he thought. He had swum out too far, could never get back, he realized, and the water was feeling cold, like the air in a tent he once shared with his brother in the North Woods. His father hated camping but felt it was good for his sons. *Nature,* his father had said with too much emotion, is our *source.* His father must know about nature, Raymond conceded. So far out it was easier to feel objective, forgiving. It was like being in a plane so distant from earth that you feel compassion for people, so small, so diminished, whole cities the size of auditoriums, invisible houses, the idea of dinner tables, of couples in bed, of books open on nightstands. Now he was shaking, his legs had disappeared, his head was filling with sounds, with nothing really helpful. "Swim" or "kick" or "dummy," he kept saying but couldn't obey, and all he could see was water, and it really didn't matter. It didn't feel so bad. His arms were missing now, and all that was left was a heart, a heart in the water beating so abstractly that it wasn't Raymond.

At five the phone rang. Amy stirred, sat straight up, blew her nose and felt her forehead, probably a fever. "Mom?" Amy called. "Mom?" But instead of her mother, her father came in the room looking grave and distracted, like a bad boy sent to the principal's office. He was still wearing his mowing clothes, old shiny pants, a pink golf shirt, and the work boots that were usually banished to the downstairs utility room. So Mother was softening in her old age, abandoning rules. Amy thought it odd that a woman who logged hundreds of thousands of air miles a year could care so much about seven hundred square feet of berber carpet.

Her father was saying, "Amy, Amy." And instantly Amy knew something was wrong. Once she'd heard that tone when Aunt Emily had her first stroke, mild Aunt Emily, who'd brought Amy miniature cuckoo clocks from Switzerland and the sweetest, darkest chocolate on earth. Amy noticed her mother standing in her bedroom doorway, looking small and crumpled, like Mrs. Robinson in *The Graduate* after Benjamin takes up with Elaine. "Amy," her father said again, and Amy felt a chunk of wood in her mouth so real she could chew it. And her mother was crying and urging her father on: "Tell her, Frank. Please, Frank." And Amy seemed to miss all the connections but heard "Raymond" and "swimming" and "sorry" and "tragic." She saw her wallpaper raining and streaking. And her own hands were beige, and her fingers were gray, and maybe, she thought, she was dying, though her parents told her she had just fainted, a normal reaction to grief.

At the funeral, which Amy was too upset to attend, friends said that Raymond's father delivered a eulogy. "Raymond loved nature," he said sincerely, and people had wept. And Lois, the Hardy scholar, read something about the maiden voyage of the *Titanic*, very gripping and gray and inappropriate, Amy's father reported. Amy received polite calls from many of Raymond's friends. No one knew what to say, and Amy was unable to connect much of what was spoken.

That fall, designing the pattern for her senior project, a design so subtle it depended on texture, not color—so different, her professor remarked, from her less mature work—words came back to her. In the uncertain light of early November afternoons while Amy worked alone in the studio, words spoken to her came back, unencumbered by feeling, trees in a forest falling and only Amy to hear them.

Degan Dying

SINCE THE FIRE that burned down Degan's Discount Warehouse in 1968, Arthur Degan had worked at Chairs Unlimited, where plexiglass light fixtures highlighted matching plexiglass chairs designed with contortionists in mind. In the next room were the director's chairs, waiting to be matched with Hollywood magnates or widows who needed some color for their high-rise balconies. Finally there was Loungeland, Degan's favorite room, where loungers promised to twist, swirl, rock, massage, bump, and grind, he liked telling potbellied buyers' wives. And to the newlyweds starting to furnish their thin-walled apartments, Arthur Degan always asked the same question: "What do lovers need with chairs?"

He sat in the living room in his own lounge chair, inherited in 1947 when Fanny's mother died, leaving them the Valencia flatware, now owned by Lill, and a reproduction of *Song of the Lark*, lost in a moving van somewhere. Chairs Unlimited didn't sell leather. That was its one limit. Doing his best Henny Youngman, Degan said, "Please, take my life," to Lill, who refused on principle to laugh.

"Enough, Dad."

"Enough Dad to go around!"

"Really, if you can't feel your arm, you need to see a doctor."

It was true that he couldn't feel his arm. He had awakened that way, showered, hoping it would come back, called Lill, still waiting for the pins and needles of new blood, and then called work. "Watch, as soon as I hang up, I'll be like new," he told Morry Grassler. "Lill," he said, "if I can't feel my arm, how will the doctor feel it?"

"Dad, listen. You may have had a little stroke." Her hairdo made her face look asymmetrical, and Degan wondered if she might have had a stroke instead.

"Lill, what will the doctors do? Tell me I'm dying? When you're dead, you can't feel a thing. I can feel everything but my arm." He saw the sun coming through the window and landing on an end table stacked with dishes. He really should dust. He lived like a pig.

"An arm is enough not to feel, Dad." She made a loud sucking sound as if she needed to reinflate to continue. "You must want to die."

"Nuts, Lill. Besides, if I wanted to die, why would I have waited this long? You've given me plenty of opportunities over the years. Like—"

"Don't start on Franklin again. I don't want to hear." She looked down at her jogging shoes and then flashed Degan the same violated look he had seen on her face for forty-seven years. "Don't remind me of that lousy two-timer."

"Should I remind you about Teddy?" Teddy, her son, had dropped out of college and become a cocaine smuggler and a charter member of Omnivores for a Healthy Planet.

"I'm not responsible for him. Dr. Ripon says it's not my fault. If Lou hadn't died—"

"He'd be sitting here nagging me too. Lou saw a doctor, didn't he? And as for Teddy, where is he? Flying into O'Hare with a balloon of white powder stuffed up his ass? Or running around the country defending meat and potatoes against their detractors? You know what we used to call kids like him in the old neighborhood? Icemen."

"Why?"

"Because they'd end up cold and dead before too long." She squinted and popped her lower lip in and out of her mouth like a piece of soft candy. He was sorry that he had hurt her.

"Dad, you need to see a doctor. Will you come with me in the car, or do I have to call you an ambulance?"

"I've been called worse." Again she didn't laugh. "I use my best material on you, but do I even get a smile? Smiles cost so much?"

"Dad!" He knew her business voice. She'd take no more.

"Okay, I'll see a doctor, but first let's go out to breakfast. The crap they give you at hospitals could choke a goat."

He dropped his fork three times, spilled orange juice in a sticky circle on the tablecloth, and took twenty-five minutes to cut up his omelet and butter his toast. All the while, he flirted with the waitress, whom he called "sugar," though *Janice* was plainly monogrammed on her frilly pink apron. Finally annoyed at him, she said, "My name is Janice."

"Sorry, but I don't hear so well anymore, Sugar. What did you say?" He winked.

After finishing his eggs, with Lill on her fourth cup of coffee, he said, "Let's go. My leg is feeling strange now too. Maybe I'm turning into one of those new chairs. Have you seen them? There's no back. It's just a seat and a bar for resting your knees. It looks like you're always praying or practicing a position in one of those love books."

It was a humid early-fall day, a day that could also have been at the end of spring. Seasons were interchangeable with him, as were funerals. Most seemed to take place in the winter, though perhaps it was the cold that made him remember those better. Lou had died on Groundhog Day. Teddy had been in a play at school that morning.

A wind blew off the lake, and the air had the pungent, salty odor of a body after love. Why did Lake Michigan smell salty? Oceans he could understand. And why were there so many cars on the Outer Drive heading in their direction? Degan saw Lill sweat with the concentration this driving required. She overtook cars going the speed limit, flashed her finger at an old woman whose Cadillac lurched toward their lane. "Where's the fire?" he asked.

"Can you walk, Dad?" They had pulled up opposite the emergency-room doors, two portholed aluminum reflectors that twisted Lill's blue Vega in the middle.

"Is the Pope Catholic?" he asked, opening the car door with fumbling and curses. He plunged onto the driveway.

Three days later, as abruptly as he had collapsed, Degan woke up. His chest was attached to a machine, his mouth was taped to a tube. One eye was taped shut, and even his armpits felt wired. He was sure his toes were in sockets, and his sad old prick plugged in somewhere too. His leg and arm weren't with him. Maybe he'd left them in Lill's car. He'd ask her as soon as he could.

"Mr. Degan?" a voice in the right corner of his room said. He could hear only in that corner, and he could see only that half of the room. "How are you today, Mr. Degan?" Degan pulled off every wire and pipe he could reach with his good right arm and said, "Eat-shit-stupid-stinking-ignorant-pissbag!"

At Degan's right some daisies were propped on a table next to a kidney-shaped bowl and a plastic water pitcher. On his left could have been a nightclub with strippers, for all he knew. He couldn't move his neck or see to the left. Fanny had died in a room like this with a crazy roommate, who, as Fanny was dying, kept crying, "Lord! Lord!" He'd have Lill take him home today. Degan saw another white uniform step into his field of vision. The man was dark and had a mustache that grew over his lip.

"I hear we've arisen," the mustache said. "My name is Dr. Ravishani. I have been tending you. You have had a vascular incident, but you'll soon be propped up, and we'll make sure you find solace if you just yield and do not remonstrate."

"Eat-shit-you-stupid-catgut-pissbag!" Degan shouted, but Ravishani continued undaunted.

"I know you are hindered, Mr. Degan. It's natural to feel unused. Furthermore, I assure you we will retract your demonstratives, if you note."

In walked Lill and behind her, sheepishly plodding like a large dog on a short leash, Teddy. "Dad," she said and bent closer to kiss his good side. "They just called and said you were awake. And look who's here to see you."

"The iceman cometh."

"We're so glad you can speak, Dad. There was some worry about your speech."

"Oh?" It sounded to him as if Lill were talking to a person on the left side of the room. He wanted to be interested in what she said, but he really didn't care. And Teddy looked lost to him, like a man in a lingerie store. "Speech is fine." He made sense, but his voice sounded bumpy to him, as if someone were pounding him on the back as he spoke. "My doctor, though. Did he fall on his head?"

Teddy laughed, and Lill elbowed him. "He's Indian, Grandpa."

"Apache?"

"From India, Dad. He speaks British English."

"He speaks Venus English."

Teddy laughed. "You know, Grandpa, it's a shame that you're sick, but it'll be really nice getting to know you better."

Degan closed his good eye and decided not to open it again until they left.

Dr. Quincy, medical examiner, was shouting out of the television about honesty. "How can you be so blind?" he was screaming at the top of his lungs. The woman he was screaming at looked menacing. Her eyebrows were angular, her eyes mean slits.

"She did it. Whatever it was, she did it," Degan said to Teddy, who dozed at his bedside. Teddy's whole body lurched forward.

"Morning, Grandpa. How are you feeling?"

"Where's Lill?"

"Oh, she had to show a house, and then she's going bowling. You know, she's the third-best bowler in her league. She averages a hundred and fifty-two."

"Splendid."

"That doctor was in before, Grandpa. He said, 'The man is soundless for strength renovation.' He's really strange."

"You know how many times I've been sick?" He held three fingers right in front of Teddy's nose, as if it were a vision test.

"Three?"

"That's right. One with appendix, one with gallbladder, now this. Seventy-seven years. Three times."

"Weren't you hurt in the war too, Grandpa?"

"Balls blown off." Teddy gasped. "Just kidding. A broken wrist. I tripped over a helmet on a beach in Italy. Ever been to Italy?"

"No."

"Been anywhere?"

"To Central America a few times."

"Your business. That's right. Most of the stuff comes from Colombia, I hear. I saw a whole report about how smugglers swallow balloons of the stuff to get into the country. They're called human suitcases. Only, if the balloon breaks—" and Degan gestured a cutting motion toward Teddy's neck.

"It's just like Prohibition, Grandpa. As soon as the government legalizes the stuff, there'll be no problem. And don't worry about the human-suitcase stuff. All I do is carry money back and forth. It's like I'm a banker."

"If Quincy is so smart all the time, why is he going off the air?" Degan said.

"Ratings, I guess."

"I guess." Degan closed his eye and hoped Teddy would go away. Teddy annoyed him with his goodwill. "I'm feeling tired," Degan said. "Don't you have some drugs to deal?"

"Mom wants me to stay with you. I told her I would till she comes back."

"Bring me two things when she comes back: the green photo album on my kitchen table and some of that stuff you sell to children."

"I don't think I should bring it here, Grandpa. It wouldn't be good for you. It has a tendency of raising the blood pressure."

"I don't want to use it. I want to call the police and turn you in, you lousy dope peddler."

A nurse brought Degan a dish of gray pudding.

"What's that? Horse brains?"

"A healthy mix of meat and vegetables."

"Feed it to my grandson. He's an omnivore." He pointed toward the door where Lill and Teddy stood. Degan could play tricks with his good eye. He could wink them in and out of view. It was the only way he could make them disappear. "I don't eat horse," he said to the nurse. She left it on the stand and said something to Lill.

Lill bent down and kissed him. "Teddy has the album, Dad. Do you want to look at it? Watch some TV? Listen to the radio?" Degan sighed, wondering if Fanny hated him all the months she was in the hospital. The disease was eating her alive, but she was always polite and cheerful. Even lapsing into a coma, she had excused herself. She must have been lying through her teeth.

"Do me a favor, Lill."

"What, Dad?"

"Come back tomorrow."

That night he removed the tape over his left eye. It let in more dark though he'd turned on the light. Then he decided he'd kill himself before morning. Hedda Vincent down the block had done it with blue pills. The problem was that he couldn't imagine what he could use. If he ate the flowers, Lill would just laugh, and he couldn't locate anything else that had potential. Maybe he could smother himself under the pillow, but he knew for a fact, from reading somewhere, probably *Reader's Digest*, that it was impossible to make yourself stop breathing. He was no swami. "Shitting son of a bitch!" he moaned into his pillow and turned on the radio. Someone had kindly left it on a Muzak station, thinking it an old man's obvious listening pleasure. The rendition of "Misty" sounded like raindrops beating a xylophone to death. He tried turning the dial, but he found he couldn't move his body well enough to reach the selector. He batted at the radio with his fist until it hung on its cord, swinging near the floor. The album was on his bed within reach. There was little Degan, propped against a piece of fur, dressed in a bonnet and those little potato-sack dresses that boys wore in 1917. There was his mother, corseted, standing near a huge fern. Her eyes were kind. Degan cried out of his one good eye.

In the morning he noticed a terrible smell in the room. "I stink," he told the nurse. "I smell like I'm dead," he told Ravishani.

"We have altered the events so that you may have a liquid cleansing this forenoon."

Three nurses dragged him out of bed and into a wheelchair. They washed him with a sponge.

"I don't stink anymore," he told Lill and Teddy that afternoon.

"Good, Grandpa." Degan saw Lill flash Teddy a menacing look. "Not that you stunk before, but you must be feeling . . . clean."

"They dress up corpses too. What are you going to wear when you die, Teddy? Jailhouse stripes? Lill, I bet you'll wear your bowling shirt. Mr. Karnikowski—under me, you know—he got buried in his gas-meter reader's uniform. His wife wanted it that way. Maybe I can be buried in my sentimental favorite, my bathrobe. And you know how they stuff your cheeks so you look robust? Remember how robust Fanny looked even though she weighed seventy-two pounds? Well, I was thinking they could stuff my pecker so that it sticks out of the coffin. Maybe it could be waving the flag of Israel."

"I'm going to get coffee," Lill said.

Degan winked at Teddy. "You know what, Teddy? Last night I tried to kill myself, but I couldn't because hospitals don't leave things around for you." Teddy cocked his head, listening. "They make you not die until you die. Then they say it's best you're dead because you suffered so. Makes sense, huh? So I was thinking, Ted, that I want you to do me a favor."

"Sure, Grandpa."

"I want you to bring something. Enough to kill me. If I get worse, that is."

"Grandpa, I can't. You'd die. I'd get arrested. It'd kill Mom."

"No one would know. Ravishani won't want an autopsy. Don't Indians believe we need our bodies to come back as flies?"

"I think so, but Grandpa . . ."

"Man to man, Ted. Please."

Degan thought he felt something on his left side. His heart pounded. Then he realized that it was his right side that was on fire. His toes burned and were gone. The fire consumed his leg and rose to his chest and arm. "I'm dying," he said, but no one was in the room.

When Degan regained consciousness, Dr. Ravishani was standing over him. "I am sorry, Mr. Degan, that you are again the victim. The blood lacks consideration. You are stationary, moreover."

"I want Teddy," Degan whispered, this time with huge effort. Teddy's name came out as "I ask."

Lill and Teddy came into the room. Degan could see that Lill had been crying. "Yawn," he said to Teddy, meaning *now*. "I'm slurp," Degan said and closed his eyes.

He heard a noise in the room. Then David Letterman said good night. It must be midnight. Teddy's face floated above his. He could see the longish jaw that was also his, but Teddy's face lacked the meanness that gave his focus.

"I brought some stuff," Teddy whispered close to his ear, "and a needle. It won't take long, but you have to promise that this is what you want. You have to say it, Grandpa. And mean it."

"Yes, please, Teddy. I can't see the sense. It's time," was what he wanted to say. Teddy heard "peas" and "factory" and "yes."

"I'm giving you morphine, Grandpa. A friend gave it to me. It's pure and won't hurt." Teddy squeezed above his grandfather's elbow, and a vein popped out. The needle went in easily in a recent needle mark, and Degan felt all the warmth and pleasure he had ever known, swimming yellow pleasure, like peeing in bed. "Thank you" came out "can't."

Don't Send Poems, Send Money

I AM TALKING TO MY FRIEND LORI. We go back to high school, though our relations have sometimes been strained by small acts. When she changed the spelling of her name at fifteen to the then fashionable *i* ending, when I decided not to be a scientist, when my child Sari was born (Oh, how time changes one's attitude toward spelling!), there was a wedge between us. "Do you think we'll ever get along?" I once asked her. "Why should we?" she replied, and I am sure she wasn't teasing. Lori hadn't understood the problem suggested by the question. That's the way she is.

Today Lori is on speed that an old doctor friend "lent" her. He lends her drugs. Sometimes on Sundays Lori lends his girlfriend her roller skates. It's all very congenial, considering that Lori and the doctor were lovers for seven years. At the end of their affair, he said, "Sorry, I found someone I really like."

Lori is upset. She bites her lower lip and sucks in her cheeks and stirs her coffee so that it slaps against the rim. She still isn't married, which isn't a problem, I assure her. I am married. Am I always happy? Has marriage changed me? Lori is sure that the man intended for her died somewhere in Little League. "He probably played second base, and one day a stinging liner got him in the Adam's apple." That's something else about Lori. She likes using baseball as a metaphor for life. When she had an abortion, it was "like sliding home without kneepads." When my father died, she kept repeating, "How can a Cubs fan die?" I'm not kidding.

Well, what should she do, she's asking, be a widow all her life?

"How can you be a widow when you've never been married?"

She ignores me. "Go out and face the sea? Always wear black? Light a candle every year? Never sleep with another man? Act damn decorous?"

She's biting her lip furiously. I want her to stop. "Did I ever tell you about my mother?" I ask. My mother is a real widow, but that's beside the point. "Whenever she gets the notice from the funeral home that my father's Yahrzeit is coming up, she goes out and buys a commemorative candle the same day. The notice is sent a month ahead, but the day it arrives, she burns the candle. She doesn't want to connect the candle with his death. She just wants to get the thing over with."

Lori is looking past me. She avoids me with her pale green eyes, the color of the candy-coated almonds one eats only at movies. "So?" she says and smarts. "You're married. Your mom was married. My mother is married. I'm thirty-four. Your daughter is growing breasts, and I'm not married."

"Sari is precocious," I try to console her.

That strikes her. I'm reminded of those old horror movies in which the mere act of brushing one's shoulder against a wall sets it spinning, revealing a secret room filled with horrible skulls.

Lori explodes. "Is that supposed to be funny?" We're sitting at the Desiree Coffee Shop, and suddenly Anne the waitress and Spirow the cashier are wondering too. "Is it funny to you, Elaine, that my life is half over, that I'll never have children, and that someone who's been married two hundred years is telling me that marriage isn't important?"

I should be quiet and reverent at a time like this. I should eat my doughnut or look at the clock's cartoon hands or tap out "Que Sera Sera" on the silver laminated counter, but I don't understand keeping a low profile. I've always been able to cheer Lori, until today, and I can't stop trying now.

"Twelve years, Lori, and it's just a training bra."

"What are they in training for?" Lori scowls at her age-old joke. She's trying to be brave.

"Look, Lori," I begin. "I know you'd like to get married, but don't be like my mother. Wait until the act has meaning for you. Hell, if you just want to marry anyone, it can be accomplished in three months. It's quality you want."

"I'm not so sure," Lori says and stares at the geometric display of Winstons behind the counter. We're both getting older. Lori's mouth has begun to turn down, and her cheeks seem puffy. My own hair is streaked with gray. Though Sari says it makes her worry I'll die soon, I like it, and Peter likes it. Besides, I connect dyed hair with Richard Nixon sweating through his TV pancake makeup. I picture myself at a concert—Berlioz, open air, late July. A leaf falls from a tree. I go to brush it off and come up with a handful of hair color. It's one of those nagging worries, like sitting on a bench marked WET PAINT, remote but statistically possible. I trace the fear back to the time I saw a homely, well-dressed woman chasing her French-rolled wig down State Street. Her own hair was thin and apricot-colored. It was pinned to her head with scores of black bobby pins, her skull resembling the aftermath of a forest fire. Graceful aging will be my forte, I decided long ago.

I hug Lori and go home, walking down side streets for seventeen blocks instead of taking the el. Spring is just starting to decorate the trees, and the air smells ionized. On one corner three boys are chasing each other around and around in an ever smaller circle. If I watch them long enough, they might become one boy, occupying the same space at the same time, though Sari's natural-science book assures us it's an impossibility. That's one consolation of having children: you learn new things, or you learn the things you've forgotten. One summer I worked as a waitress. An older colleague told me about her mother in a nursing home. She had forgotten she had a daughter, so every time Donna visited, she had to reintroduce herself. And her mother always seemed pleased to meet her.

That night I tell Peter how depressed Lori seems. "Does she still see the roller-skating doctor?" he asks.

"Only to get pills now and then."

"Too bad," he mutters from the direction of the shower. He takes a shower before dinner. "Maybe she should advertise," he says.

"Are you serious?" I shout through three off-white rooms.

"Why not?" he asks. Then I hear water hissing, a stock-market report on the radio, and Sari knocking on the front door: three, the magic number.

At dinner Peter says, "She can say SWFRNRS desires A for marriage."

"What are all those initials, Dad?"

"Single white female registered nurse roller skater," Peter smiles.

Sari explodes in histrionic laughter. She rolls her eyes toward the ceiling. She covers her mouth. She ignores dinner.

"What's A?" I venture.

"Anyone," Peter says.

"Isn't it numb?" Sari asks.

"What?" I say.

"To be as old as Lori and not be married."

"Not really, if you can't find the right person, or if you're happier single." It bothers me that I'm raising a child with pronounced monogamous tendencies. I remember once that Sari told me she wanted to have five children, three boys and two girls and the girls last. I flew into a rage. I shouted out permutations on the figure that included twins, quintuplets, all boys, no boys, four girls, one boy. I ranted while Sari looked cool, waiting for me to subside. I hate that she's decided matters that are better left to chance.

Later the phone rings. It's Lori at the hospital, where she's a pre-emie intensive-care nurse. "It's slow tonight," she says. "All the babies either died or went home." I wonder if she says things like that when she meets men. I can see her sitting around the whirlpool at her expensive health club with its all-night salad bar featuring truffles. She pays two hundred dollars a month to belong. "What do you do?" asks a red-bearded guy with a racquetball bruise on his left forearm. "I wire small babies for sound." Oh, the odd looks, the hasty retreats!

"Lori," I ask, "how would you like to come to dinner Saturday? There's a new lawyer at Peter's office, just in from the coast. He wants to meet people, and Peter says he's very bright." I hold my breath, half-hoping she'll refuse, because Peter hardly knows the fellow, thinks he's superficial, and had an argument with him at the watercooler about a certain olive-green plastic tumbler.

"Fine," Lori says. "I'm off Saturday. Formal?"

"No, roller skates. I'll probably wear a dress."

"Red or white?"

"I hate red. It makes me look like a cow, and white is out before Memorial Day."

"I mean wine."

I hadn't thought. "Why not white?" I ask without considering, and instantly I'm committed to fish or fowl. The whole world of red meat is out of the question: no beef, pork, lamb, giraffe, or buffalo. Life is simpler now. That's how I like doing things, on impulse. Sari was one. So was Peter.

Maybe Lori's problem is that she considers too much. I can see her training her eye to watch the life signs of the preemies, this one cyanotic, that one born without a gullet. "If they live, it's hard. If they die, it's worse." The many nuances she has to be aware of. This one's respiration is one beat slower. That one spit up a microgram of blood. I'm glad I never became a nurse. I owe my marriage to it.

"Peter," I say, "since Christmas is over, it'll be seen as sheer kindness."

"What will?"

"Asking over the Larson fellow. I want him to meet Lori."

"He's a creep," Peter states, wiping his hair dry after running. Sweat is racing down his face. He looks as if he's crying. "Why do you want Lori to meet a creep?"

"Maybe your friends think I'm a creep."

"Probably," Peter whispers theatrically.

"Maybe she'll love him."

"When?"

"Next Saturday. It's her day off. She's bringing white wine."

"Good. I'll tell him to bring the main dish and dessert, and we'll go out."

"Funny," I say. "I can make that bouillabaisse."

"No," Peter says. "Larson has a beard."

"So?"

"Bouillabaisse is too messy to eat. I don't want Lori to indict him on table manners."

"Well, I can make a crabmeat quiche and cook it very well. I can make a salad and chop the spinach leaves very small. I can make a chocolate mousse but leave off the whipped cream. Then Larson can have no embarrassments."

"Mike."

"Mike. Is he really a creep?"

"Nothing he's done at work indicates otherwise."

"I hope I'm doing the right thing," I say and go make Sari's lunch for school. Sari is in a rut. Every day she orders the same things: cream cheese and sprouts on whole wheat, a tangelo, and a granola bar. If we were in a fallout shelter, that's all Sari would accept for lunch. I hear Peter making a call in the other room. He sounds jovial. Larson, Mike, must be accepting.

I can remember the first time Lori met Peter. He and I had practically been living together for a month. I kept all my clothes in two neat shopping bags in a corner of his bedroom. He was beginning law school. I had all my credits in science but wasn't interested. "But my dad is a chemist," I'd whisper in bed. "You don't have to be your dad" he'd tell me. Peter has serious eyes. I believed him.

Lori met us after dinner that night. Nixon had just invaded Cambodia. We went to a sit-in and then spent the night together being processed in an ultramodern urban jail with track lighting, where the policemen looked younger than we did and just as nervous.

"Larson says okay. I told him seven o'clock. He didn't ask what color wine."

"Inconsiderate," I say and stuff Sari's "Annie" lunch box into the refrigerator. A piece of wilted lettuce rests on Sandy the dog's ear.

The week goes quickly. I'm working on a story for a woman's magazine about battered husbands. Today I'm scheduled to interview yet another, a man whose wife once broke his arm.

I wonder why I always feel nervous before these meetings. After all, I didn't do anything to any of these poor fellows. I've never so much as pinched Peter under the dinner table for revealing that I was pregnant with Sari when we got married. I'm to meet the man at a local restaurant specializing in ribs. Thinking of the difficulty of interviewing and eating ribs at the same time, I've already decided on a salad. He told me that he has brown hair and a lighter mustache. I realize, as I'm surveying the room, that I'm looking for someone wounded. For some reason I always picture a Revolutionary War Minuteman with a fife and a bloodied headband. I've told him I'll be wearing a gray trench coat, though the day is unseasonably warm and I'm sweating. Anxiously I wait, doing my duty. A tall man approaches.

"Hello. You must be Elaine."

"Nice meeting you," I say and extend my hand, pressing his ever so gently.

We sit down and order. The waitress acts very polite and consoling, as if she knows this is no ordinary lunch. My salad arrives, his ribs, my lite beer, his bourbon on the rocks, and we begin. It all happened eight years ago when he was a law student.

"My husband was a law student too," I tell him.

"Oh yeah? Where?"

"Chicago. Class of seventy-four."

"Me too," he says.

"That is strange," I say. "When did your wife begin her actions?" I smile nervously. I sound too indirect, tentative. It's more like a class reunion.

"What's your husband's name?" he asks.

"Peter Rediger."

"I know him," Mr. X says. I never ask their names, to assure confidentiality. "We used to go out for a beer now and then. He was seeing this weird woman. She had a degree in physics, but she didn't want to do anything with it. So she got pregnant."

"Really?" I say and call for another beer.

"So they got married and he was in law school and she was having a career crisis, and meanwhile Peter had to support a family and go to school. Then she decided that she wanted to be an artist, knit rugs or something. So she got a little part-time job for pin money, but it was all on Peter. I'm surprised he was able to do so well in school."

I realize three things. First, I'm writing down everything he's saying about me. Second, I'm some shade of burnt mauve. And third, I might abuse him, given the chance.

"So you're Peter's second wife."

I brace myself and dig in. "No, I'm the first."

"Oh," he says and coughs quietly. "I have this memory that won't quit."

"Your best quality, I'm sure." I try to begin again. "How was it that your wife began to *abuse* you?" I even stress the word.

"We had no money. She wanted things. I couldn't give them to her."

"What was she doing at the time?"

"She was in school too. Getting an M.A. in art history. She was studying Giacometti."

"I always loved Giacometti."

"Shadows," he says bitterly. "Little spidery shadows. I'd want dinner when I came home. She never had it ready because she was reading some new work on Giacometti. We'd fight. Once I threatened to take her books and burn them, and she went wild. She pulled my hair and slapped me and kicked me on my knee."

"Did you try to defend yourself?" I ask. He is a tall, well-proportioned man.

"Sure I did, but not really. I didn't want to go and deck my wife. So she's kicking and screaming *she* never liked me, her parents liked me, and I pick up her book and throw it out the window."

"The window?"

"We lived on the fourteenth floor of student housing. Then she goes insane. Our little studio becomes a carnival booth. She's throwing dishes and tearing at place mats and spilling talcum all over the place, and I can't stop her. So I slapped her."

"You slapped her?"

"Yeah. She was like the Hulk. She's overturning chairs. She's small, maybe a hundred pounds, but she's doing something funny to the hide-a-bed, and it's not even ours. I thought slapping her would help. All of a sudden she takes my arm and twists it behind my back, and I'm on the carpet seeing the Milky Way. Then she gets all concerned and takes me to Billings Hospital, and they set it."

"Did they ask you how it happened?"

"Yeah, but I just said it was an accident."

"Then what happened?"

"I went home, took a pain pill, went to sleep, and in the morning she was gone. She'd moved back in with her parents."

"Did you reconcile?"

"No. That was it." Now he chews furiously on a rib and seems finished.

"Would you say the pressure of being in college and being married got to both of you?"

"We all do things differently. Some people throw books out windows. Others get pregnant and don't become physicists."

"Chemists. And it was writing."

"Yeah. We all do it differently."

I start thinking of Lori. No wonder she's so selective. I politely thank him, offer to pay for his lunch, leave eight dollars to cover my share when he refuses, and go home. It's already four o'clock, and I should go shopping for groceries, but I feel wiped out. Chances are I'd forget half the items. So I go home and lie on my bed. Sari is in her room playing her "Annie" record. "The sun'll come up to-mo-ro-o-ow" repeats itself over and over. Apparently she's fallen asleep before taking it off her kid's record player.

A while later I hear water running and know that Peter's home. He bends down and kisses me. I notice that he still wears his wedding ring, and suddenly I feel better. I really can't blame him for Mr. X. Nevertheless, I feel curious.

Peter is peeling off a tie raining umbrellas, a pink button-down, a sweaty T-shirt, then gray flannel slacks, beige socks. He's down to his shorts when I say, "I ran into an old friend of yours."

"Really?" he asks. "Where?"

"He was one of my abused husbands."

"Hard to believe. What's his name?"

"You know I don't know their names," I say too sharply, "though he seemed to know a lot about me. He said he used to drink with you and he admired you for doing so well in school despite your unfortunate marriage to a woman who was going to be a physicist but turned out a mother."

Peter sits next to me on the bed. He looks embarrassed. "The creep said that?"

"Yep."

"It's all surmise and misinterpretation, Elaine."

"I believe you, Peter," I say. "Besides, it's too long ago to matter. You can't be responsible for every jerk you've known."

Peter seems relieved. He kisses me lavishly and does a little naked pirouette on the way to the shower.

I get up and go into Sari's room. She's fallen asleep in my old negligee and Grandma's satin slippers. She's wearing rouge, lipstick, and a fan barrette from the fifties. Her little record player wobbles on and on at the foot of her bed. I turn it off, and she continues to sleep.

The next morning I go shopping for our dinner party that night. Despite Lori's promised white wine, there's a sale on rolled rib roasts, so I buy one and Idaho potatoes to bake and chives for the sour cream and fresh wax beans and ingredients for a lemon meringue pie. My interview with Mr. X has made me nostalgic for what I used to cook, my Sunday best, a roast.

When I get home, Sari is manipulating her Rubik's cube without even looking. She is watching one of those reassuring kids-are-likewise-human Saturday morning shows. They're interviewing the youthful editor of a magazine that prints writing "of children, by children, and for children." "And how should kids in our TV audience send to your magazine?" the cheeky emcee asks.

"Don't send poems, send money," the twelve-year-old with the Frankenstein forehead and shiny glasses says. "We need to establish a broader base." Do children have to be shaken down so soon, I wonder.

Peter is reading some office work. They're involved in a big case against a paper manufacturer that's polluting Lake Michigan, the kind of case that he rarely wins but that makes him feel good about himself for weeks. I kiss him and say, "Tonight it's Sunday Dinner Revisited, Old Cuisine, Return to University Place."

"Huh?" he says. When Peter's concentrating on a case, he hears one-eighth of what I'm saying. Of those words he might have caught "Sunday."

"I'm making a roast."

"Fine," he says and looks back at the documents.

At seven o'clock Mike Larson is scheduled to arrive. I've hardly thought about him or Lori all week, which is the problem with dinner parties. By the time they take place, their original impulse is lost. It's like sending a Christmas card into space and hoping an alien finds it on the right date. That's why they send chemical equations and geometric shapes.

At 6:30 Peter is scheduled to take Sari to Julia's for the night. There they'll make popcorn, read each other's diaries, and whisper about Julia's mom's new live-in boyfriend. Sari told me he imports something, but she didn't remember the word. "It must be foreign," she said. Then one night she said, "Lookahs."

"Hookahs?" I asked. Julia's mom has a Ph.D. in histology, and she's dating a pusher. Oh well. Sari assures me they're very polite to her and make the girls go to bed by ten.

Before Peter gets back, the doorbell rings. If I'm lucky, it'll be Lori a little early. I'm not lucky. A tall bearded man is standing at our front door. The porch light is broken, and in the dimness all I'm able to see is his beard, only I imagine it covered with food, decorated as a Christmas tree.

"Won't you come in?" I ask.

"Thanks. I'm Mike."

"Larson," I add to show expertise.

"And you must be . . . "

"Elaine. Elaine Rediger." It's a reflex to say both, though I know he knows my last name.

"Come in and have a drink. What would you like?"

"Vodka on the rocks. Where's Peter?"

"Driving our daughter to a friend's. He'll be back any minute."

The doorbell rings again. Certainly it's Peter. I ask Mike to get the door while I make the drinks. I'm in the kitchen for a long time before I hear voices, one male and one female. It is Lori. She looks as if she's been routed from her apartment by fire before she could finish dressing. Her hair is wet. She's wearing a pretty maroon dress that looks like silk but with penny loafers and no makeup.

"I thought I'd be late," she says apologetically. "May I use your washroom?"

"Be my guest," I say. "Oh, Lori, have you . . . ?"

"Yes, we met."

Larson and I sit down to share a drink. He tells me Peter is a fine lawyer and an enthusiastic worker. I feel as if I'm meeting his civics teacher or the commandant of his prison camp. I'm stirring some vermouth and waiting for Larson to speak when he chokes. His face turns scarlet, his cheeks puff out, his eyes water. He looks like a fearsome fish from Sari's animal encyclopedia. "Are you all right?" I ask, knowing he can't answer. Then the phone rings.

I go to the phone, half-thinking Larson's going to die on us, but even as I leave the room, it gets quiet, and I hear him draw a deep breath. I pick up the phone.

"It's me," Peter says. He sounds as if he has a mask on.

"Where are you?" I ask.

"At the hospital."

"Why?" I ask. I can feel my heart accelerate.

"After I dropped off Sari, a guy rear-ended me at a stoplight. I'm really okay, but I hit my lip and the cut seemed deep, so I went to the hospital and they're going to sew it up."

My stomach turns. I see an ocean of Peter's blood.

"Do you want me to come there?" I ask, thin-voiced.

"I'm really okay, Elaine. It just needs four or five stitches and I'll be home. It's a busman's holiday for me."

"What do you mean?"

"I get to chase my own ambulance."

"Did they take you in an ambulance?" I ask, heart daredeviling.

"Just a joke, honey. Have a drink. I'm fine. I'll be home as soon as I can."

When I get to the front room, Lori has poured herself some tonic and looks finished. She has switched to gray sandals, and her hair is perfectly dry.

"That was Peter," I say. "He had a little accident, but he's okay. His lip needs a few stitches. It's nothing to be alarmed about." Neither guest seems alarmed, so I decide to minimize it. "Speaking of stitches," I say, "Lori is a nurse."

Lori shrugs and nods the way Sari does when I announce that she can play Chopin.

"I think Peter told me," Larson says. He has stopped choking and has returned to his normal hue, a faintly tanned, rosy one.

"Do you jog?" Lori asks him.

"I never took it up," Larson says. And then a few seconds later he remembers he should ask her. "Do you?"

"I used to, but then I joined the Mid-Center Health Club, and I've taken up swimming. I swim seventy laps four days a week."

Larson says nothing, concentrating on his drink. I wonder if he's recovered from his accident.

"Lori and I met in high school," I say. "She was always a good athlete."

She nods politely. "And Elaine was always a brain. She was going to be an astronomer."

"Chemist," I correct.

Larson smiles. "I once wanted to be a pilot."

"Me too," says Lori, "only I wanted to be a stewardess."

I look at the two, Ken and Barbie, only Barbie is a little jowly and Ken is subject to fits of choking. I excuse myself and go into the kitchen to work on the dinner. Lori's forgotten the wine she promised, so there'll be no problems with the red-meat issue.

"I hope you both like roast," I shout from the kitchen, thinking how odd it is to hope such a thing. I'm reminded of those signs that say EAT HERE or give other obvious advice. This is America, and though we may not eat as much, we all like roast.

Larson walks into the kitchen. He is very thin and has deep brown eyes. "There's a problem," he says. "I'm sorry that Peter didn't mention to you"—and here I imagine him confessing that he's an ex-abused husband—"that I'm somewhat of a vegetarian." I look him over, try to check his belt to see if it's made of animal hide, look for signs of falseness about his hair. If he's a Hare Krishna, I'll throw him out on his ear. A few years ago they were everywhere, at airports, tollbooths, the gynecologist, but I can't imagine that one would turn up in my house. "I eat fish," Larson says, "but not roast."

"That's okay," I say. "I have some tofu in the refrigerator or cream cheese with sprouts."

"Please don't make any extra effort," he says, hand resting on some of Sari's refrigerator art.

"Are you sure?" I ask, picturing his nearly empty plate.

"Sure," he says. "May I have another drink?" I hear a car door slam and a key tumbling in the lock. Peter is home, mended. He walks in. I hear him saying a muffled hello to our guests. Then he enters the kitchen. His upper lip is swollen to twice its size and stitched together with what resembles shoelace.

"Can you eat?" I ask him.

"I don't think so," he slurs. "It's full of novocaine."

"Are you hungry?" I ask Lori.

"Not really," she says, eyes focused on Peter's prominent lip. "A good job," she says.

"Lori used to be a surgical nurse," I add. Lori gives me a smiting glance. I'm supposed to stop doing her press releases. "Well, since I'm the only one who's eating, why don't we do something else? The food will keep. It's no problem."

"How about a movie?" Lori asks.

"Fine with me," Larson says.

"Okay," Peter says, "as long as someone else drives."

We walk out to Larson's car. Lori and Larson get into the front seat, Lori sitting as close to her door as she can. Peter and I sit in back, close to each other and silent. I watch Lori watching Larson. He's telling her about the funny man who sold him the car. "He looked like his ears were on backward." Lori tilts her head back, thinking maybe she should smile. I sit next to Peter, his hand in mine. We don't know what movie to see. I feel as if I'm on a date with the guy who scored the winning touchdown for our team, only where is his letter sweater, my Angora-covered class ring? I plant a kiss on Peter's stitches, and he winces.

As Larson pulls away from the curb, Lori begins, "Did I ever tell you about the time Elaine and I were robbed at gunpoint?" Larson laughs too loud. It really isn't funny at all. "Of course I didn't," Lori answers. She looks glum. "I haven't told you anything."

Heroes

THE SUN, HAVING nothing to do, leaned in the window. Having still less to do, Harvey Brilligbusch watched it with perverse concentration. As usual, he was translating his name into English. Brightbush, he thought, lengthening the syllables, accenting the first, then the second, rhyming it with other words that came to mind: *light push, nightstick, tight lush.* He liked that better: Harvey Tightlush. And the fact that Rachel's last name translated to Black Sky should have been an omen.

The sun snapped into place on the crossword puzzle's forty-seven down, which was *salamander.* Why did the *Times* always use the same tired words? Harvey wrote *eft* in pen in the three spaces. He was never wrong about words. Downstairs, Belinda, a sturdy child with stout legs and crooked teeth, whom the divorce lawyer had given him for eight more summers, was twirling on the sidewalk. He hoped she wouldn't fall and bump her face or lacerate her lip or scrape her nose or chip her tooth or dislocate her jaw or die. The list of perils was endless if events went predictably. Rachel's daily calls, made in the high-pitched clip of a commentator at the Hindenburg disaster, were justified considering Belinda's post-divorce pattern. First it was a broken arm and then a stitched forehead. Rachel must have given her subliminal accident plans when she sent Belinda packing for the summer: Sustain injuries. Old Frightwish deserves it. Now Belinda ran down the sidewalk toward Caroline's house. The trouble with summers was that Harvey felt he spent most of his time leaning, waiting for something bad to happen, afraid to take his eyes off the window.

Now he felt hungry. That was his other summer problem. Since his divorce, summers provoked in him a terrible hunger, a monstrous hunger, a hunger beyond human possibility. He thought of the vegetable slime that carpeted the gorilla cage at Lincoln Park Zoo. His hunger was larger. And his wish for sex. During the academic year, he comported himself properly. Summers he wanted to prowl. He wanted to go to the beach, which he usually hated, which burned his forehead and back and legs. There he wanted to mount every woman under forty. No. That was unfair. He wanted to mount grandmothers, invalids being wheeled by their nurses, children too small to consider without a lurid shiver. Even men appealed to him in summer. *Brightwish.* It was love that he felt. He wanted to consume the world.

He tried to remember how he had felt in the summers before he and Rachel divorced. Whenever he tried to remember, he was a victim of partial amnesia. He was sure he had had a life then, but memories of it were as hazy as the photos of Nassau that Merle Dusback showed him at the faculty party. Upstairs, Dr. Christman had been so noisily humping Sandy Olesker, a pretty graduate student, that someone turned on a tape of German drinking songs to cover the groans. He knew he had never done crossword puzzles before or hungered so or lusted so. He had never watched where the sun decided to lean or cared if Belinda twirled on the sidewalk. "Stop it!" he shouted down to Belinda and Caroline, as they balanced on a low stone fence surrounding the front yard of his three-flat.

"What?" Belinda called up without looking, in her new manner of cautious independence.

"Get off the goddamned fence!" Both girls giggled up at him from the sidewalk.

It was already hot, and Harvey felt the sweat dripping down his temples, slithering down his chest, and beading under his beard. Maybe he should shave his beard, but it was part of the Brightbush image. Summer had just started, and he had already sweated more than he remembered ever sweating when he was married. Even when he and Rachel used to make love in the summer, he didn't remember sweating like this.

Belinda had been under his care for only three days, and already his temper was short with her. His study was in the back of the apartment, a place he seemed to haunt only at night with Belinda safely in bed. He couldn't consider going there now with Belinda so close to ruin. Now she and Caroline were tossing a Frisbee that might land on the street or under a moving truck. Chasing after it, Belinda resembled a cleaning lady going after a cobweb. Her friend Caroline was lovely, small-boned with boyish hips. Harvey blinked her away, then watched the sun sidle to another location on the table. It landed on the ashtray.

So he smoked now, a new peccadillo Rachel would certainly remark on when she next visited. Did everything Harvey do have to mean something? Was it charged with significance that Rachel's new haircut resembled shredded lettuce, that she was in therapy, that she worked as a flight controller though her training was in philosophy? She would survey his life like a reconnaissance pilot. "A new ashtray?" "So it's bourbon?" "Since when do you buy *TV Guide?*" If she could line up all his new possessions and shoot them, she'd annihilate his existence since Rachel. And if he showed her something wonderful, his new article, for instance, she'd smile her "Merely clever." But Rachel had never been effusive. Why should she change now, especially after her declarations of hatred for him?

Belinda and Caroline disappeared around the corner shouting something about "park" and "lunch" and "later." As soon as she was out of sight, he could relax. Could he be responsible for her off of the block, renting bodyguards or stationing police at every intersection that a plain ten-year-old might cross? He could go back to his study and open the letter that Reitle had sent from Berlin. But he was too sweaty and wrung out to follow Reitle's German, even if it was news he wanted to hear, that the "new" Kafka work had been verified. No, he'd go ring Holly Noble's bell and see if she was eating lunch or wanting company.

Before he walked down the fourteen green shagged steps to Holly's, he would freshen up. He went to the bathroom and sprayed deodorant under his T-shirt. Then he saw the full moons of sweat staining the shirt and took it off. He looked swollen in the mirror. His eyes were smaller because his face was larger, and even his beard couldn't hide the new fullness of his cheeks. He looked like a round loaf of bread. God, he *was* repulsive. Rachel was right. He looked away quickly and went into the bedroom, thinking about Holly's cool and streamlined arms.

Once they'd made love after they'd both had too much retsina, but he couldn't remember much about it, only that in his excitement he had delivered too fast. She had seemed amused about it. In fact, Holly seemed amused about everything. Harvey tried not to think about her amusement. Sometimes it frightened him because he associated it with a lack of intelligence. He pictured her laughing through cathedrals and art museums, in hospitals, and at great works of literature, which he guessed she had never read. He heard her giggling through *Heart of Darkness* and *Oedipus Rex*. Stop thinking that way, Tight Ass, he told himself. She's good for you, Tight Ass. Now he buttoned a blue Oxford-cloth shirt and put on a newly laundered pair of jeans and a belt with a jaunty red stripe and his tennis shoes and sprayed himself liberally with Adam, "the cologne that tempted Eve before the apple."

He took a bottle of Chardonnay from his refrigerator and jumped the stairs two at a time. Maybe he should have appeared at her door wearing a suit. She'd have giggled and said he was all suited up. Once she told him to see a nutritionist because he'd said he felt Byronic.

He knocked on the door. Inside he could hear a computer keyboard being slammed. That meant she was transcribing and probably had on her earphones. He wondered how she could work in a room hung with the quilts she had designed, none of which matched each other. The walls had the look of a Byzantine bazaar or of a bad acid trip. He knocked again. He heard her work stop. Holly was dressed in cutoffs and a white T-shirt. Her hair hadn't been combed, and her feet were bare and dirty.

"What's this?" she smiled good-naturedly, pointing at the wine.

"I thought you might come up for lunch. I brought down a sample." He didn't know what he'd give her if she accepted, but he couldn't risk being downstairs too long with Belinda away. Tomorrow he'd give Belinda a key and tell her to let herself in and out. Maybe he could start spending lots of time at Holly's. And what would stop him from sleeping there? After all, he'd be closer to Belinda vertically than they'd be horizontally in the same apartment.

"But I have so much to do, Harve."

She called him Harve, which reminded him of *starve*. That depressed him, but, after all, his name did mean *bitter*. Holly, on the other hand, didn't remind him of Christmas but of *collie*. She was thin and fine-boned and sad-eyed as pets in children's books. When she smiled, which she did often, her teeth were even pointed like a dog's. Her hair was the honey color of a golden retriever's, and the few times she had been in his apartment, she had followed him from room to room as dogs do. If he

were a man prone to using endearments, he might have called her "pet."
Once he had called Rachel "little bird," mainly because her features were
sharp and drawn, and she had said, "Drop dead."

"Tell you what. I'll come up in an hour after I finish this report.
I'll bring some fruit." She laughed. He wondered why fruit was funny.
"I just bought some huge strawberries. Oh, and by the way, I'd love to
meet your daughter." That was funny to her too.

"She's somewhere," he said.

"Okay. I'll be up at two. Now don't eat without me." Then her
quick canine smile. Why would he eat without her? Could she sense
his hunger? Then she waved three times and said "Bye!" twice and
closed the door. He stood there listening to her fingers moving on the
keys, not wishing to go back alone to his apartment. Maybe he'd open
the wine and drink it on the stairs. No, he'd save the wine for her.
Comportment. Discipline. Instead, he'd go up and have a beer or three
and try to concentrate on Reitle's letter.

The apartment was sweltering. Harvey tried sitting at the kitchen
table to catch the cross breeze between the two open windows. The
curtains swayed as curtains do. He had bought curtains not because he
liked them but because he hated how depressing divorced men's apartments look. He didn't want to be part of the generic description of ex-
husbands. Reitle's letter looked very thin. He balanced it in his hand,
weighing what it might contain. Some kids were shouting in the alley.
They reminded him of Belinda, who had been gone a full half-hour.
Suppose she had been killed by a stray bullet or impaled on the monkey bars by a worker's flying fence spike?

"Come on, faggot, throw the ball!" one boy shouted.

"Your mother's a dyke," the other answered. "Fuck yourself blind."

A noble aspiration, Harvey thought.

The bell rang, probably Belinda home just in time to ruin lunch
with Holly. Harvey buzzed her in, thinking of ways to get even with
Rachel for the next eight summers. Maybe he could have sex manu-
als sent to her address or a continuous stream of unordered pizzas.
The feet on the stairs were too heavy to be Belinda's, and the voice
was Alf Lester's, which obviously rhymed with *pester*. Harvey missed
his ex-colleague, who had been denied tenure on the basis of his "creative" dissertation, *The Leap-Second, Beckett, and Me.* Now he was a

part-time instructor at a local Cambodian Refugee Center and a novelist, though he'd never finished any of his novels. When Harvey had questioned Alf about what he taught to the Cambodians, Alf had answered, "What's the difference? They need to learn everything." Harvey pictured the preliterate Hmong tribesmen debating poststructuralism. "I'm glad you're home, Harvey. I have a great idea for a novel. It's very Marquezian."

"Want a beer?"

"No, I have to teach in an hour." Harvey was relieved that Alf would be gone when Holly arrived. Harvey was sweating again. His shirt was darkening. He could feel little rivulets under his beard. He thought of Holly and imagined he could hear her tapping downstairs.

"The idea is that an Eastern European explorer in the sixteenth century sets out to discover a new spice route. I'm calling him Balto. *The Adventures of Balto Prisbic.* Anyway, Balto ends up in South America, where he's turned on to hallucinogens by a tribe of Indians, and the rest of the novel deals with Balto's cultural hallucinations."

"The unreliable narrator."

"Right. He thinks their culture is highly complex and advanced over his own, but we can never be sure whether he's hallucinating the ceremonies that take place or not. It'll be a study in the ritual of the imagination. Of course, before he gets there, his boat will be beset by pirates, people will die of cholera. You see, only Balto will get off that ship alive. I can't risk other characters complicating the narrative."

"Aren't most of the Eastern European countries landlocked?"

"Well, he can sign on under a British or Spanish flag. Probably Spanish in homage to Cervantes."

"Of course."

"I can go into his adventures along the way. You know, the whole picaresque thing. Inns. Coaches. Villains. Knights. The part that really interests me, though, is what kind of hallucinations a sixteenth-century mind might have. They'd have to deal with God, of course, but maybe Balto could be ahead of his times. Maybe his voyage could be a discovery of ideas to, say, existentialism."

"It sounds promising, Alf, but the more you discuss ideas with me, the less you ever get written. I'm telling you that as a friend. You know what Rachel used to say about you?"

"No worse than what she said about you."

"That you're potential energy divided by chattiness."

"She said that?"

"Why do you sound so awestruck?"

"Maybe Balto can say that in the book."

"He'd better not. Rachel would sue."

Alf appeared more serious now, which made him sink into himself, his clothes growing larger and the lines coming out on his face. Over the years Alf, Harvey noticed, had gotten sparer, while Harvey had grown robust, making him feel guilty in front of his friend. "Tell me, Alf, did I used to sweat like this in the old days?"

"I can't remember, Harvey."

Harvey was feeling insanely hungry. "Want a nice bologna sandwich, Alf?" He liked feeding Alf, whose salary barely kept him in rice and beans.

"Sure."

Now Harvey wouldn't have to wait for Holly to eat. His hunger was a deep, twisting ache that cut him from navel to groin. If Alf hadn't been there, he would have eaten the meat right from the package and gulped down the bread afterward to save time. "Why does meat have to be inside bread for it to be a sandwich? Why aren't two pieces of bread on one plate and two pieces of meat on another called a sandwich?"

"A problem of conjunction," Alf smiled.

"Alf, what would you take to a deserted island?"

Alf smiled, acknowledging the historical allusion. It was a topic both of them had used as graduate students teaching composition to the supposedly bright group. The ones who'd wanted A's had answered "great books." The really clever ones said "drugs." The future lawyers all said, "I wouldn't consent to go to a deserted island" and stated their rights.

"I'd take my bed," Alf said. "I can't sleep anywhere else."

"Know what I'd take?" Harvey smiled. "You."

"What's that in your hair?" Harvey asked Holly. She laughed and glanced up from the sink where she was slicing strawberries, peaches, and grapes into a fruit salad. Holly had changed into a red-and-white-flowered sundress under which she wore no bra. Standing to the side, he could see her breasts through the silk-screen pattern. "No, I mean it. I don't understand what holds back your hair."

"I think it's so nice," she said, "that your daughter is able to stay for summers. It's so important not to lose touch." She smiled at him.

Could teeth be sexy? Could hair fasteners be sexy? Could fingers daubed in strawberry juice be sexy? "Listen, Holly. Let's go to the bedroom. It's cooler in there, and I'm kind of full. My friend Alf was over. He looked so hungry I offered him a sandwich."

"And you ate too. Harve, you shouldn't have."

It was a lie that he wasn't hungry anymore. He didn't want to frighten her by shoveling in all the fruit and then going on to the powdered sugar until it landscaped his beard.

"How old is she?"

"Who?" Harvey asked, walking backward down the hallway toward the bedroom.

"Your daughter."

"Ten, but she's at the park."

"You're very lucky."

"I know. We can be alone now."

He heard her talking from the kitchen in the serious voice a teacher uses to address an audience full of high-school seniors. "I didn't get to see my father at all after my parents divorced. My father moved to Palm Springs. Did you ever visit Palm Springs? It's one big desert with some hotels stuck in it. My father owns a restaurant there. I always picture him in the same coffee shop, with pink and white counters and a beige cash register. Don't ask me why it's always those colors."

He hadn't intended to ask. He could hardly hear her for all her effort through the asthmatic humming of the air conditioner. "It's cool in here," he called from the bedroom.

Holly came toward him, balancing the fruit salad, two forks, powdered sugar, and the bottle of wine on a tray. "Look! A movable feast!"

"I'm really not hungry."

"Of course," Holly said, irritation in her voice for the first time. A thin line of sweat marched across her upper lip. She placed the tray on the floor.

"Is it always this hot in summer?"

"I think so."

"I don't remember it being this damn hot, except in New Orleans once. As soon as you got into the car, the windows would sweat."

"That's humidity," Holly offered.

"Right, humidity." She was still standing over him. He touched her lightly on her waist.

"Did you travel much with your wife?"

"To Europe once, and we planned a trip to China."

"I'd love to visit China. I hear it's very interesting."

He took her hand and pulled her toward him on the bed. Smiling so that her face shifted sideways, she said, "No, Harve." He let her go.

"China is very interesting. But then again, so is Ohio."

"Do you think that if I went to Palm Springs I could find him? You know, no heartfelt scene, just tell him who I am, have a cup of coffee, and chat."

"Sure you could. Remember, it's women who change their names, not men."

"Isn't that strange? I've always liked my name." She sucked on the insides of her cheeks and looked over him toward the door, as if someone were standing there. To the door phantom she said, "You know, Harvey, I'd like to see more of you, but it has to be different than this."

"This?"

"You know."

"Well, we could go to interesting places. Have you ever been to Montreal? They speak French there."

"I took French in college. You speak several languages, don't you?"

"French, German, Old English, Latin—but not too many Romans to address these days." Shut up, he told himself.

"I was an art major in college," she said. "Sculpture. I began with pottery but found wood a more expressive medium."

"Wood's really solid."

"You know, Harve, I should be working. I'm losing money by not working this afternoon."

Sweat was starting again. It slid down his back in long discrete trails. He turned off the light and closed his eyes. "I'm tired, Holly, and you're losing money, and besides, this afternoon isn't really very interesting."

As soon as she was gone, he knew. Everything was too thin: the air in the room, his patience, Reitle's unopened letter. It had to be bad news. A letter confirming the Kafka stories and proposing his American editorship would contain plans, provisions, multiple copies. He opened his eyes, thought of reading the letter but decided to wait. Closing them again, his body took him deeper into his misery.

The doorbell rang and Harvey jumped up, head drumming. He always awoke with alarm, as though without his attention the world had fallen into ruin, war breaking out on the next block. When Rachel taught nights in the early years of their marriage, he'd had a phobia about falling asleep before she came home. Suppose he woke up and she still wasn't there? It wasn't her loss that he feared suffering. It was the pain of being so horribly surprised. He collected himself. Where was Belinda? He guessed he'd been sleeping for nearly an hour because the room had grown chilly and he felt the mottled bumpy flesh on his arms. Leaning long on the buzzer, he wondered what her excuse would be. Maybe he could return her to Rachel a little early, saying some scholarly business in Germany required his immediate attention.

He heard two voices on the stairs, Belinda's saying, "Home, Daddy?" and another voice saying something to Belinda. A flight down he could see his daughter slogging up the stairs, muddy and wet, followed by a policeman. Had she been rolled in the park? Was she injured?

His breath whistled. "What's the matter?"

"Nothing to get alarmed about. Can I ask your name?"

"Harvey Brilligbusch."

"That's a strange name. German?"

"Yes."

"I'm German too. Family changed its name, though. We used to be Bleistift."

"Pencil?"

"Officer Pencil. Imagine that! Now we're Schmidt."

"What happened?"

"I just thought you'd want to know that your daughter's a real hero."

Harvey looked at Belinda's tentative smile. "What did she do?"

"Do you want to tell him?"

"No, you," Belinda said. Her face was streaked with mud. Her braids were soaking wet.

"Your daughter and her friend are by the lagoon. You know, where kids sail their boats and dogs swim. I tell kids, 'Stay out of that water. It's not for swimming.' Lots of bacteria."

"Right."

"So your daughter and the other little girl are at the playground going on swings, monkeying around. There's even some teeter-totters in it. You don't see as many as you used to. They're a little dangerous. See, kids don't think. They just do. A little boy wanders off from his day-care group. A little black boy about three. What's his name?"

"Carlos."

"Well, maybe he's Puerto Rican then. Puerto Rican is different."

"Please. What happened?"

"Little Carlos wanders off. No criticism, mind you, of the park personnel. So he's walking toward the lagoon. Then he sees a dog in the lagoon. Now I'm just guessing at this part, but I bet he decides he wants to swim out to that dog. So he wades in. And the water isn't blue. It's brownish. And little Carlos is dark."

Harvey could see Belinda getting nervous. He watched her tapping a soggy shoe.

"These two girls see little Carlos, and then they don't see him anymore. They still see the dog he was swimming to. Of course, three-year-olds can't really swim. Now I hate to think of this part. What do you see? You see a little boy sinking in the dirty water. He's going to drown. But your girl jumps in wearing her pretty pink shorts."

"Lilac," Belinda murmurs.

"She swims out toward the dog. She surface-dives in and out. It's not too deep, so she's able to find him and carry him out of the water. Meanwhile, her friend runs and gets me. I'm in the field house eating my lunch. And when we get back, she's giving him mouth-to-mouth resuscitation. How did you learn that?"

"On TV."

"So I get there and take over. The kid's coughing up water and crying. His teacher is crying. Lots of people are standing around. And can you beat this? Someone has called a minicam."

"I got interviewed, Daddy."

"So she's a hero. It'll be on the news tonight. You can tell the wife you really have one special kid."

Harvey followed Belinda into the apartment, where she went silently into the bathroom and locked the door.

"Clean up!" he shouted to her. He knew she was already doing that, but he had the habit of ordering people to do what they were already doing. "And then come out. I want to talk to you." He walked into the kitchen and opened the letter. As he'd expected, it said that the Kafka stories couldn't be verified. Of course, that didn't mean they weren't Kafka stories, but one couldn't base an entire book on an argument from ignorance. Reitle was "profusely sorry" that they couldn't collaborate on a project whose results would have been "a harvest from the magical orchard." There was still the possibility of doing a study of veracity, the "truth of posthumous works." There'd be Dickinson's poems, "the fertile fields of Joyce," and, of course, a chapter on the alleged Kafka stories. Harvey was to respond in September, when Reitle returned from Rhodes. Meanwhile, he wished "dear Dr. Brilligbusch a sunny summer of endeavor."

Belinda walked into the kitchen wearing a bathrobe. Her face had the shiny wet look of a rubber bath toy.

"Daddy, should we call Mom and tell her? Won't she be proud?"

Sweating again, watching the stupid curtains, he looked at his child and thought she might disappear.

"She'll say I wasn't watching you. She'll have you all year. Why did you have to save him?"

The Hills of Andorra

WHEN MR. EWELL hired us, he spoke of three prohibitions: late arrivals, early departures, and consorting with the clientele. "Consorting" was the word he used, evoking black garters and women spies obscured by fog. Every waitress at the Silver Rooster was suspect. Mariel and I, younger by ten years, college-educated, part of the dwindling counterculture of the mid-seventies, were below suspicion. What would women who wore no makeup, who didn't shave their legs, who probably thought a Tía Maria was a grenade used by Che in the Bolivian jungle, want with paunchy businessmen doused in English Leather? I was twenty-three, finishing my thesis on Beckett. Mariel was twenty-four, trying to finance her journey westward to California, where James, the man she lived with, might pursue his set-designing career. His career was all Mariel's idea. At home James was happy painting detached human forms on their bedroom walls while Mariel supported him. I wanted to tell Mr. Ewell that it was James, not Mariel or I, who needed a rich liaison: his tastes ran toward designer towels, Austrian goose comforters, and brioche for breakfast, served on a rattan tray.

Mariel and I had actually met earlier, in a college German literature class, where the words slipped off her tongue, all honey and smoothness. Though I was expert at understanding, whenever I spoke the language, I felt insulted upon its behalf, as if calling upon me was an error of inclusion. Professor Hambling, raising his pointy chin and narrowing his eyes, would concentrate on an invisible umlaut on the ceiling. If my accent did anything, it betrayed my knowledge of Yiddish, learned from my grandmother. Mariel had been born in Germany after the war, of a displaced Lithuanian father and a mother who'd fled Dresden during the bombings. The family clung to each other as many refugees do, seeing their daily existence somehow in peril despite an ample bank account and roasts on the table. Everyone worked to send money back to relatives who had stayed in Frankfurt, whom Mariel would visit, bringing home lovely souvenirs to decorate her apartment: dishtowels embroidered with aphorisms about Gemütlichkeit, miniature finches tweeting atop a teapot when the water boiled, doilies scented in rosewater, porcelain baby dolls, their curly hair the texture of corn silk.

Even at work Mariel was discriminating. While I fretted behind the waitress station for eating a forbidden muffin, Mariel pilfered whole steaks, etched sherry glasses, wicker wine stands. Maybe in the gray barracks of the D.P. camp where she had been born, her first feeling of deprivation had been an aesthetic one. Whatever the reason for her needs, she tried brazenly to satisfy them, sneaking past hotel security every night. Did her quilted purse contain special compartments for contraband? Happy as a prince, she'd display her daily plunder to me at the bus stop. Alone in my apartment after work, amid my useful possessions, paperback books, an oak writing desk, an aluminum teapot, I admired Mariel's style.

There is a theory that all public servants are frustrated performers. Why else did Anton, our maitre d', add capers to the steak tartare so slowly that tension built? Why did Yvonne, a career waitress whose coif resembled a ruined birthday cake, fix her nylons in a mirror that customers might observe? And why did I practice applying Brandied Raisin lipstick, which I'd never worn before, in the bread knife's blade, as Yvonne had demonstrated that rainy, slow morning when Mariel didn't arrive until noon?

Yes, Mariel was often late, defying rule number one. And sometimes she left early because of terrible menstrual cramps. She blamed them on her Catholic upbringing, the fears and cautions against showing one's legs, wearing silk underwear, and coming of age, as if someone could will otherwise. Having matured young, she felt the twisting ever after. Monthly she was doubled by it, bent sideways. Despite Anton's patience and my efficiency at covering two waitress stations, despite the painkillers Yvonne dispensed from her locker-room apothecary, Mariel would leave work early and creep to a cab to frighten the driver with her paleness, convinced that her womanhood was cursed.

Perhaps she was right. Three months after she was hired, Mariel was fired for breaking rule number three. Over coffee and stale sweet rolls in the employees' cafeteria, a veteran bellhop approached us. He needed a woman that night to act as "secretary" to a visiting manufacturer, to accompany him and a client to dinner and to make herself available afterward. The pay was two hundred dollars, all that Mariel needed to make her escape to California. "After you," we both teased each other, but as we joked, a feeling rose up in my stomach more sour than the warmed-over coffee. Mariel was considering the offer. I could tell by the way we stopped looking at each other.

Mariel never got to the floor that day. Apparently a house detective, one of those comical dog-eared, fray-cuffed, droopy-eyed snoops, caught wind of the deal before it was concluded. Later I imagined old Ewell lying in bed, his arthritic knees flaming, devising the plan to test his new employees. Mariel was hustled out of the hotel, warned never to return under penalty of law. The bellhop-turned-pimp got off free. At least they could have stripped him of his fake epaulets. I spent the rest of the summer explaining Mariel's absence to the customers who missed her who-gives-a-shit way of sliding their drinks onto the table, her style. Mariel's only regret: she still needed two more etched sherry glasses to finish her set.

Even before I opened the letter, I could tell by its scented beeswax seal that it was from Mariel. I was living with David, enjoying the first months of nesting, when even grocery shopping is magnetic. We would stop to buy raspberry-coconut juice or to admire the blatantly sexual squash. Once David met Mariel at a party, but all he remembered was a woman with brown hair. Mariel was plain. Above average height, dark-eyed, there was nothing to distinguish her, except an occasional accessory, like a pearl nose ring. My own dim surroundings had taken a turn for the better. I imagined her approving of our Polish circus posters, our Indian floor mats, and our Wagnerian candelabra— a full-busted, green-winged Valkyrie carved from wood.

Mariel and James, her friend Sharon, and James's friend Russ, moved to San Francisco that fall. Along the way there were failures, mechanical and human. James's jalopy, a '62 Chrysler, broke down in Salt Lake City. Sharon spoke of self-immolation at Lake Tahoe. Settling near the Presidio in an apartment too small for two, the four constantly bickered. While James halfheartedly looked for a job with a theater company, he worked for a Japanese gardener. All day he crawled in the dirt or carried burlap-swathed evergreens from truck to soil. The owner planted everything himself while James tilled the earth. It was very biblical. Mariel was a pastry waitress in a ritzy café on Union Street that catered to young tourists. Though the pay was good, she detested the little dirndl skirts and puff-sleeved blouses. They reminded her of her D.P. photos, only now she was taller than her father was then.

Often Mariel spoke of her father, how during the war he'd hidden in the woods for six months to avoid the Russians, how at night he'd repaired trains to evacuate Lithuanian freedom fighters from the countryside, a candle his only light. He still had pitch-black hair, a droopy mustache, and fiery eyes. James was a poor imitation. Thin and frail, he could have fit inside her father like those wooden dolls containing ever smaller versions. After six months of close quarters, the group split up: Sharon to be healed by a masseur schooled in herbology, Russ to a group of gay-rights street mimes. Sometimes Mariel would see him playing a flute or giving away flowers at Ghiardelli's. On Castro Street, James ran into Michael, a former lover, and decided to move in with him. Mariel showed no resentment, just spoke of cultivating a California tan, watching whales spout off the coast, and planning another trip to Germany. I didn't hear from her the rest of the year.

Men to whom I am attracted are always the physical opposite of my short, bald father. David was a towhead, a foot taller at six feet, four inches. That we were still living together after a year testified to my insight in avoiding fatherly types. By now we'd merged our checking accounts, bought a sofa with joint funds, and shared an electric typewriter. David was working in book design for a university press, and I was substituting at an alternative school for pregnant girls, when we received a postcard with the photo of a glistening herring: "Back from Germany and Scandinavia. I have my hair cut short like a boy's. I am living with a man named Roger. He's a comedian—and F U N N Y." I wrote to tell Mariel that in a few months David and I would be coming west to visit my sister. Hopefully we could arrange a night on the town.

Before our trip was scheduled, I received a few more letters from Mariel, each a messy parcel of grief. Mariel had had an abortion and felt very bad. At the efficient new clinic, all aluminum and white tile, they had hurried through it. There'd been a lot of pain and blood. In the recovery room afterward, Mariel was the oldest, but despite her desire to comfort the other girls, some as young as thirteen, her screams were so loud and persistent that they had to give her a sedative. Sharon had really tried to kill herself (by Seconal rather than fire), and her mother had come all the way from Chicago to take her home. If Roger was funny, I couldn't discern his influence on Mariel's letter, except in the following detail: Sharon's mother was terrified of planes, so she'd taken Greyhound west. By the time she arrived, frantic with visions of Sharon in a locked ward or a zipped morgue bag, Sharon was feeling so much better that she refused to leave. Sharon and her mother spent the next week at Fisherman's Wharf buying all the cheap keepsakes they could load into shopping bags.

About a month later, another letter arrived, misery seeping through like a bathtub overflowing on a rug. Roger was back, working in a sporting-goods store after losing the comic lead in a play. Mariel had had a second abortion, this one a cinch compared to the first. Then Roger's adoptive mother had sent him an urgent letter. She'd received word that Roger's real father had Woody Guthrie's disease and that Roger had a fifty-percent chance of contracting it by age forty. If Mariel stayed with Roger, they could never have children. I imagined that at this rate Mariel would have twenty-four abortions before she reached menopause.

Mariel's boyish razor-cut, her new thinness, and Roger's vivacious hostility were all unanticipated. David didn't recognize Mariel at all, having remembered a different person with a nose ring from the party. Surrounded by blue-haired elders brought by sightseeing bus, stop number three, we spent the evening at Finocchio's, a slick transvestite nightclub. I kept evaluating Roger's movements for symptoms of the disease. Remembering how ravaged Woody Guthrie appeared in *Alice's Restaurant*, I gasped when Roger bumped into another table on the way to our seats. Onstage a beautiful platinum blonde transvestite with real cleavage sang "Moon River" so intensely it made me nervous. The sad transvestites, those with muscles bulging under their slit gowns and fishnet hose, were saved for the chorus line. One was Chinese, petite with a waist-length fall and delicate eyelids. The face was beautiful, but the legs were wrestler's, the feet wide enough to support Rodin's statue of Balzac.

We walked around Broadway and said good-bye at the bus to the Sausalito ferry. Mariel and I had spoken little. She was wholly self-absorbed, turned inward like a clam. It might have been Mariel, rather than Roger, who was dying of something romantic and devastating. Worried for both of them, I clung to David on the ship's top deck. I felt colder than was reasonable, since the wind was still and the night air filled with warm vapor, clouding the lights on the distant hills of the bay.

David and I broke up. He accepted a book-designing job in New York and moved there on his savings, leaving me a couch and a distaste for raspberry-coconut juice. There had been no intrigue, just a gradual wearing down of the mechanism for concern. Still feeling numb and displaced, I found a job teaching English and German at a small parochial school. Grading essays on "Successful Women in Science" and eating canned gazpacho soup, I opened the first letter Mariel had sent in months. Like those colorful seed packets advertised in Sunday magazines that one never orders for fear they won't sprout, Mariel's ornate envelope was full of disappointments. Roger had gone to visit his family in Texas, where he met an old high-school girlfriend. I imagined Cybill Shepherd in *The Last Picture Show*. He had decided to stay with her. Mariel wondered whether he had made up the whole story of Woody Guthrie's disease so that she wouldn't decide to stay pregnant. Mariel was angry. She'd been tricked and didn't trust men. I sent her back a commiserating letter, telling her my own problems with David. "We're going through our petulant mid-twenties. Let's seclude ourselves in the hills of Andorra and wait for wisdom." I never received an answer to the letter. Before she received it, Mariel had left for Frankfurt, where her favorite aunt was dying.

In Germany Mariel learned that her father had been an enemy of the Russians not for his freedom fighting but for his Nazi collaboration. He was still subject to extradition by the u.s. government should they uncover his activities. This secret, which Aunt Lydia had intended to take to her grave, was told to Mariel in her aunt's hospital room eleven days before she died. I imagined theatrical stage whispers, powerful organ music. Mariel promised not to tell anyone. Supposedly her mother had never known and wasn't to know. Only I knew, and the letter should be destroyed. Holding it over my Wagnerian candelabra, I turned it to ash. It seemed an appropriately dramatic gesture.

At the same time I damned her for the knowledge. Kept awake by it at night, I saw her father repairing death trains by candlelight. I pictured rows of sad Jewish faces lined up at a snowy station. In my half-sleep version, Mariel's father confiscated their purses and kept the valuables, tossing the useless or sentimental onto the tracks. No wonder her mother had a boyfriend, I thought, a sad little man from church who designed surgical tools and was called Uncle by the family. No wonder her father's recent layoff from his job as a diesel mechanic was a symbol of doom, causing a two-week collapse and a nervous reunion at his bedside. Still, I assured Mariel I'd visit when I came west that summer.

The afternoon of the visit, I was in charge of my nieces, ages four and six. Lilly, the older, has black wavy hair and aquamarine eyes. Miranda is all chestnut: hair, skin, eyes, warm as a sunspot on a rug. In a pink stucco apartment house we met Mariel's new boyfriend, Carlos, a wealthy Spaniard. He was working as a waiter at the St. Francis until he found the best place in the city to open a grillade. The visit came shortly after Franco's death and Prince Juan Carlos's democratization of the country. Though I knew little of Spanish politics, I had read *For Whom the Bell Tolls* and had seen *Guernica*. I expected that Carlos, whom Mariel had described as passionate and full of ideas, would be basking in his country's good fortune.

Mariel was wearing a purple silk Japanese robe. Her hair was long again and pulled back at her temples with red combs. She had never looked more radiant. The apartment smelled of strong coffee and baking bread, the product, a braided wreath, surrounded by earthenware jars of sweet butter, jam, and honey. The other aroma was musk oil, emanating from Carlos, who, like all of Mariel's boyfriends, was short, slightly built, and handsome. His eyes were the color of Lilly's. In fact, he asked if my nieces were Spanish, for they looked like so many children in Barcelona.

"Russian and Romanian, Jewish," I answered.

In all seriousness Carlos said, "Such nice-looking people are rare here." Puzzled, I wondered if Mariel had ghoulish acquaintances.

"Carlos thinks Americans are ugly because there's so much mixing of nationalities," Mariel explained. Worse yet, I could tell she believed what she was saying. Aside from wanting to look in a mirror, I was unable to respond. I imagined dachshunds welded to Airedales, the union of a fish and a goat. My mind spun with mythological half-breeds.

The children, unaware of the tension in the dining room, munched on huge chunks of bread that Carlos tore off with his hands, tried on Mariel's straw hats, and chirped back at her canary, Liebchen. Lilly cradled a clown doll, twisting its orange straw hair. Miranda pored over the black, thickly inked wood carving in a German fairy-tale book. Afraid to probe further, I drank my coffee. When I could no longer stand my own silence, I asked Carlos how he liked the new government in Spain. "With Franco we had money. Now we have taxes, very bad for families like mine. Money is freedom."

A sour feeling rose in my stomach. I wanted to take the children away. I wanted to cut myself out of the scene with the precision surgical instruments Mariel's "uncle" designed. Instead, I said a polite good-bye to Carlos when he left for work and even let him kiss my hand.

I spent a long afternoon with Mariel, listening to her reminisce about Professor Hambling, Mr. Ewell, James, Sharon, Russ, Roger, David, Aunt Lydia, her father. I watched indistinct shadows lengthen and consume each other. Weighed down, I couldn't have moved if the children needed me. I thought of my own father, short, bald, pale-eyed, honest, dead the same year Mariel had her abortions. For the first time in years I remembered the maple hutch where he kept his war mementos: a saucer-sized piece of shrapnel, a photo of his supply ship, before-and-after Navy-issue postcards of Nagasaki. I hoped my mother hadn't kept the grim souvenirs after he died. I didn't want to see Mariel again. There was too much death between us.

Yet as I listened to her describing our times together, holding each moment up in the dim, webbed light of late afternoon, I understood. A refugee child, Mariel saved things. I was American. I wanted to throw everything away.

Enough

LAURA LIKES TO LIE DOWN and rest in the heat of the afternoon while Matt sleeps in the next room, swathed in crochet like a large, pleasant insect. She closes the shades and turns on the old cool-jazz station and shuts her eyes. She plunges down into her bed, and even when Matt cries through the wall and she knows he is crying, she is able to stay inside, sealed off. "I'm not being a bad mother," she says, shaking her head, wiping sweat from her hairline, wondering whether Duke Ellington, who is playing now, minds that a baby is crying and that she feels serene. Once Billie Holiday sang "God Bless the Child," and Laura found herself weeping into her pillowcase. Glenn Miller strikes up "String of Pearls," and yogurt waits cold and lovely in the humming refrigerator. A kid across the street is shouting, "It's not fair!" but Laura feels light and hazy as a cloud. It's relief, like swimming underwater on a hot day. At three when the news begins, she'll comfort Matt and become a mother again, but nothing is to interrupt her hour off.

A bell rings. She thinks it is part of "Take the A Train," but no music has ever insisted so. If she doesn't answer it, if she doesn't . . . answer . . . She whirls into a sitting position, rubs her eyes, slips a terry duster over her bra and underpants, and runs down the stairs. She thinks about her unpolished toenails as they precede her into the hallway.

Through the screen door that she always locks ("Even with it locked, your life is in peril," her mother has warned. "Where do you think you live, Utopia? Consider the baby."), she sees a bald head and squinting eyes, a pale and scholarly burglar sizing up the booty. And then a voice, familiar but as hard to understand as the voice on the phone the first time she made a call in France.

"Laurie!" Harold always uses the diminutive to remind her that he is Bob's older, more brilliant brother, who was a full professor in history when Bob was still a high-school audio-visual aide with bad skin. "Anybody home?" crackles a voice behind him, invisible but unmistakably Binky's—Harold's wife, Faithful Companion, Sidekick, Comic Relief. Binky is the size of a large child, and though she is a crack archaeologist, she carries on like Andy Devine, following Harold, praising his slightest effort, apologizing for his indiscretions. "Harold is sorry we're just barging in. "We didn't have your phone number, but we remembered your address." Behind them Laura hears kids' voices, high and insistent, something about "onesies" and "backsies."

Upstairs Matt is howling. It isn't fair. It's past three, and Laura is supposed to be on duty again. She unhooks the lock and says, "Excuse me. The baby is crying."

Back in the bedroom, Laura smooths the covers, turns off the radio, and picks up Matt, raging in his crib. His skin is mottled red, and his ears smell of milk. He needs to be nursed, so Laura sits on the bed and holds him. His mouth begins sucking even before she has offered her breast, and his head bobs back and forth like a wind-up toy, blue eyes bulging, mouth furious, trying to feed on air. "Wait, wait," she consoles. "Mommy is getting ready. Here she is." And the crying turns into short tugging grunts, frantic and pitiful. She feels so sorry for Matt and for herself. The boredom of sitting still while he nurses. She wants to be reading or watching some anonymous group of ballplayers make an orderly progress around an artificially green diamond. There is something so anxious and explosive about Matt. He sucks and sucks, and Laura thinks about the yogurt and maybe a walk.

"It's summer outside, Matty. We'll go to the park. You can meet other babies. Then it'll be fall, then winter. Then spring, Matt. Summer, fall, winter. Summer, fall, winter. Soon you'll be all grown, Matt, all grown, no more baby!"

"Anybody home?" Binky asks. Harold has probably sent her up to size up the situation.

"In here," Laura says and tugs Matt away from her breast. He sputters and cries and sucks at her shoulder.

"Here they are," Binky shouts to her family below. "In the bedroom, Clea. Randy, come see your new cousin." She whispers to Laura, as if whispering will help, "He's beautiful, a dream."

Laura notices that Binky has lost a canine tooth and hasn't replaced it. She thinks of Matt's pink gums, so amazingly strong. Two children built upon the same general plan shyly step into the room. Clea is ten and Randy eight, or vice versa. Binky and Harold had their children in the nick of time, Binky likes to say. Clea has a high IQ, Laura remembers from a letter. Nothing much ever gets said about Randy. She looks him up and down. He is watching himself chew gum in the mirror.

"Come up, Harold," Binky shouts. "Laura's been nursing the baby." The last detail is meant to reassure Harold that it's safe. No marauders can seize him. No one can challenge his ascendancy over the Mortons. Laura is disarmed, nursing a baby. Harold looks distracted. He eyes Matt casually and seems to reserve judgment.

"Was I that small?" Clea asks.

"Don't you remember?" Harold answers.

Laura thinks of the foolishness of his reply. Or maybe it is the beginning of their act: Dad asks Clea if she remembers being small and gifted. Clea launches into the minuscule details of her infancy à la Proust. They can play literary conferences and English-department parties from coast to coast.

"No," Clea says. "How could I?"

Laura likes that. A traitor in their midst, willing to challenge Harold.

"Where's Shirlee?" Laura asks about Binky's mother, an aged ex-ballerina.

"She's too old to travel much, honey."

Randy has taken to carving his name in the velour bedspread with his index finger. "Randy Randy Randy Ran," Laura sees from vista to vista. It's clear he can spell.

"Her heart is enlarged," Binky adds.

Laura pictures Matt's demure heart, the size of an unfolded tulip. "Too bad," she says, for of them all Laura likes Shirlee the best, Shirlee of few words, good-natured delegate to the world at large. When Shirlee visited, she never seemed to know anyone's name or care what she was served or want for anything. Soon she'll die, Laura thinks, and assume omniscience. That's reassuring.

Too bad some of Shirlee's generous vagueness hasn't rubbed off on Harold. Laura watches him stare at her and Matt vigorously without self-consciousness. He looks like a quiz-show moderator about to ask a brilliant and difficult question. This is Harold's constant look, but the brilliant remarks are few. He saves them for his books and lectures. In fact, he's in Chicago to address yet another conference, the Society of Humanities Professors Emeritus, the theme, "Your Commitment to History." The title is elusive, another Harold strategy. Only he understands what it means. Given an hour, the audience will too, but only if they are daring enough to climb the steep sharp slopes of Harold's mind, a difficult journey for retired professors. There are no gentle hills or stairs. There is only one path, and if they don't care to follow, then they can stay in the cabin, watching the fire die. That's what Laura decided to do long ago. Laura thinks that Binky has secretly come to the same decision. She remembers asking her mother what Mrs. Santa did while Santa was delivering all the toys. "She stays at home and rests. It's her happiest night of the year."

Randy has taken to searching Laura's closet for entertainment, and Clea looks drowsy. Binky smiles blandly and pulls at Matt's little hand, which clings and tightens and flails and finally rests on Laura's shoulder. If Laura had the energy, she'd tell Binky what an infant's hand can already accomplish, what slow-motion films reveal about the apparently random movements, a strategy, an effort to grasp objects and control its world. But she is too tired.

"So where's Bob?" Harold finally asks. A trick question. As Harold knows, Bob is at the Pioneer Chemical Engineering Building, where he is every day of the year except weekends and major holidays and the three weeks he gets off for good conduct. Poor Bob, the plodding engineer, the practical one.

"Whenever anything broke, Mom took it to Bob," Harold once said. "Whenever there was a *real* problem, Mom came to me." The life summed up. No way to bring back Mrs. Morton, dead twelve years now, to annotate the text. When Laura asks Bob to fix anything, no matter how simple or urgent, his reply is "Later." Then Bob secretly repairs it, but she can't see him do it or know until he is finished. It's a game they both understand. Harold only understands his own games. That's the problem with Harold.

"By the way," Harold is saying, "there's one more guest you haven't met."

Then Randy explodes out of her closet in a flurry of shoes. "Yeah, Dad. Tell her." It is a long nasal whine which inspires fear. Nothing they can spring on her will be worse than the sound itself. Laura feels sweat gluing her robe to her back and wipes more from her forehead. A drop falls in her eye and makes it smart.

Binky begins. "Since our last visit—when was it, a year ago Christmas—we've both added to the family. You have Matt, and we have a dog. The children really love him, but I'm afraid, as busy as we are, that he isn't well-trained."

Clea looks up at the ceiling like a guilty thug, and Randy is bouncing up and down on an invisible string. Harold has left the room to get the dog from the car, where he's already eaten the steering wheel, and bring him upstairs on cue. Before Laura can question, protest, or say no, in walks Harold with something yellow on a leash. It proceeds to jump up on the bed and make itself at home. Laura sees that the dog has the potential to be lovable. She sees the children still looking at her. She looks at Binky, all seersucker and good intentions, and at Harold, whose grim job it is to keep the animal at bay until Laura agrees to its presence. She imagines that at the moment when she says yes, he'll unleash the thing, and it will transform into a whirlwind of milky saliva and doggy stench.

"Okay," Laura says weakly. All she wants to do is to close her eyes, lie down in the forest of Randy's name, turn on her jazz, and sleep. She tries to summon a song, but the best she can imagine is Johnny Mathis and "Chances Are." She looks at the dog, content, panting, dozing off on the bed, and says with too much force, as if she had a position on the subject of dogs, "I don't want it on the furniture."

"Randy, honey," Binky croons, "get him off Aunt Laura's bed. Why don't you take him downstairs or go play with him in the yard? Aunt Laura has a nice yard. Clea, go with him."

Laura wishes Binky would stop calling her Aunt Laura. She doesn't want to think about that connection.

"No," Clea says and slumps back into the rattan chair, where Laura sometimes sits holding Matt. The chair has a worn area on the arm that Laura casually dissected one afternoon when every appliance in the house was broken and Bob was in a petulant mood.

"Clea," Harold says in a voice of command. Clea immediately leaves the room. The dog, leash and all, chases after her, and Randy shoots down the stairs behind. As soon as the kids are out of the room,

Binky says, "Are you all right, Laura? Bob wrote that you haven't been well since the baby was born. Is it fatigue or what?"

How can she explain it? Whatever it is, it has her by the ankles and knees and thighs and stomach and chest. Sometimes her head surfaces but only to breathe in some music. Whatever it is has a firm grip and jaws. Whatever it is makes her sweat, even when it's cold, and fear Matt, even when he is peaceful and unclenched. Laura hears shouting in the backyard, Randy's voice, the dog, laughter. "It's nothing," Laura finally says. "Matt never sleeps. He has allergies."

Harold looks suspicious.

"What else did Bob say?" Laura asks. She wasn't aware that Bob had discussed her "condition" with anyone.

"Oh, nothing," Harold says quickly. Laura will ask Binky later, privately.

Suddenly Clea and Randy are back in the room. Randy is crying, and Clea is shouting, "He's gone." She shoots poison at her brother. "You shouldn't have let Randy go out with Breezer."

"What happened?" Harold booms.

"Randy disobeyed. He went in front with Breezer, and Breezer started running. I chased him for a block, but I couldn't catch up. And you know how Randy helped? He just sat there."

"Randy is in a special school," Binky says consolingly.

Clea falls onto the bed, weeping and kicking. Randy stands like a tree rhythmically swaying. Harold leaves the room. Outside Laura hears a car door slam.

"He's going to look for Breezer," Binky reassures the children. "We're in Laura's way. Let's put our things in the guest room, and then we'll go out and look for Breezer ourselves. He can't be far."

"There is no guest room," Laura says. "Matt lives in it now. You'll have to use the basement."

"Okay," Binky says. "Come on, kids." She reminds Laura of a Girl Scout leader. They follow her out, a deflated little family leaking sweat and disappointment.

After they leave the room, she puts Matt back in his crib in the old guest room and lies down on her bed. Her eyes are heavy and sting. She closes them very gently, thinking of locking a big storage trunk, the kind her grandmother kept old hats in. She'd like to hide in one, grow small in it, and disappear. "And where is Laura?" Harold will say. "She didn't obey," Clea will answer. "She climbed into the trunk, and we can't get her out."

The next voice Laura hears is Bob's. She opens her eyes to see him frowning down on her. He looks tired and wet and has a leaf caught in his hair. He looks so disheveled that Laura wonders if he has swung home from work through the dark shiny cottonwoods that snow on their yard whenever a strong wind blows.

"Why are you asleep?"

"Because I'm tired."

"We have guests," Bob is saying through his teeth.

"Did they find the dog?" Laura asks.

"What dog?"

"The one that ran away."

Bob is irritated that he doesn't understand. "Do you think you can get up?"

Laura closes her eyes. No, there isn't a chance that she can get up. She will stay in bed forever. "I'm very tired," Laura says and closes her eyes. Laura sings to herself "In My Solitude."

When she is finished singing, she counts silently to fifty backward and forward. When she opens her eyes, Bob will be gone.

"What are you doing?" he asks. "Do I have to call your mother?"

"Why would you do that?" Laura asks feebly.

Each word feels as if it can't escape whole, as if it might break, so she whispers, but now she can't stop and Binky is stroking her brow and saying, "Okay, rest, you rest."

But Laura isn't listening. She is falling deeper and deeper into her bed. She is smaller and smaller. She is floating under turquoise water, a shimmering tan shape contracting and relaxing, contracting and relaxing, to the sound of a straining clarinet.

COLOPHON

Some of Her Friends That Year was designed at Coffee House Press
in the Warehouse District of downtown Minneapolis.
The text is set in Caslon with Gill Sans titles.

William Caslon released his first typefaces in 1722. His popular
typefaces were based on seventeenth-century Dutch designs. The
first printings of the American Declaration of Independence and
the Constitution were set in Caslon.

Gill Sans was released by the Monotype Corporation in 1930.
Designed by Eric Gill, the typeface was modeled after the signage
of the London Underground.

THE COFFEE HOUSE of seventeenth-century England was a place of fellowship where ideas could be freely exchanged. The coffee house of 1950s America was a place of refuge and of tremendous literary energy. At the turn of our latest century, coffee house culture abounds at corner shops and on-line. We hope this spirit welcomes our readers into the pages of Coffee House Press books.

MORE STIMULATING SHORT STORY COLLECTIONS FROM COFFEE HOUSE PRESS

Bend This Heart, by Jonis Agee

$9.95 / PAPER / 0-918273-51-X

"These odd, original stories, keenly alive with language, make the heart and mind work." —AMY HEMPEL, THE NEW YORK TIMES BOOK REVIEW

With penetrating sensitivity, these epic short sagas explore the intense entanglements of human love.

Crowning the Queen of Love, by Susan Welch

$13.95 / PAPER / 1-56689-058-6

"An unusual, powerful collection. These are love stories of the highest order."
—TOBIAS WOLFF

Attempting to find acceptance and love, the women in these stories struggle to break through stereotypes, personal barriers, and beliefs. Confronted by life's harshness, they discover unsuspected gifts for transformation.

Garden Primitives, by Danielle Sosin

$14.95 / PAPER / 1-56689-100-0

"[Sosin's] careful descriptions of the natural world and of realistic psychological states mark the book with a distinctive, memorable style." —PUBLISHERS WEEKLY

Sosin's characters are at once base and complex as we see the continuous motion of their inner lives as they mingle and withdraw from the external world.

Prayers of an Accidental Nature, by Debra Di Blasi

$13.95 / PAPER / 1-56689-083-7

"Di Blasi's themes of sexual obsession, physical beauty, and lost love ignite this notable effort to define intimacy." —PUBLISHERS WEEKLY

"Whether urban or rural, rich or poor, young or old, Di Blasi's characters are driven by perpetual yearning: for love, sex, healing, even for death. This virtuoso collection of cutting-edge short stories with a subversive undercurrent is marked by dazzling versatility." —PUBLISHERS WEEKLY

Good books are brewing at coffeehousepress.org